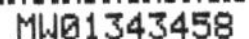

The Seven Miracles of Beatrix Holland

The Seven Miracles of Beatrix Holland

Rachael Herron

GRAND CENTRAL
New York Boston

Cover design by Elizabeth Connor
Cover art from Shutterstock and Getty Images

Grand Central Publishing
Hachette Book Group
1290 Avenue of the Americas, New York, NY 10104
grandcentralpublishing.com
@grandcentralpub

First edition: August 2025

Print book interior design by Marie Mundaca

Library of Congress Cataloging-in-Publication Data

Names: Herron, Rachael, author
Title: The seven miracles of Beatrix Holland / Rachael Herron.
Other titles: 7 miracles of Beatrix Holland
Description: First edition. | New York : Grand Central Publishing, 2025.
Identifiers: LCCN 2025008287 | ISBN 9781538767320 trade paperback | ISBN 9781538767337 ebook
Subjects: LCGFT: Magic realist fiction | Novels
Classification: LCC PS3608.E7765 S48 2025 | DDC 813/.6—dc23/eng/20250321
LC record available at https://lccn.loc.gov/2025008287

ISBNs: 9781538767320 (trade paperback), 9781538767337 (ebook)

Printed in the United States of America

CCR

10 9 8 7 6 5 4 3 2 1

For Aura

The Seven Miracles of Beatrix Holland

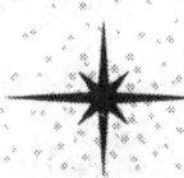

CHAPTER ONE

We are all interconnected at the cellular, molecular level. That's what Spirit gives us. That's what Spirit wants us to know. That, and that email as a form of communication is overrated.

—*Evie Oxby, keynote at Dreamforce*

The first tortilla chip Beatrice Barnard bit into was so stale, it didn't even crunch. Nachos on a ferry should have been a good idea. They sure *seemed* like a good idea—Beatrice imagined gooey, bright orange cheese melted over jalapeño slices, beans, and salty chips—but the reality, when it arrived in its red paper tray, sailed right past disappointing into disgusting. The chip smooshed between Beatrice's teeth like a greasy piece of damp cardboard, and if the ferry hadn't been so crowded, or if there hadn't been a stranger sitting across from her at the small table, Beatrice might have spat the food from her mouth back into the container. But instead, she swallowed the chip, regretting every life choice that had led her to eating this, starting with marrying Grant, the man who was supposed to have been sitting next to her now. Instead of starting his birthday trip and suffering through these chips with her, Grant was probably at this moment having limber, rambunctious sex with Beatrice's ex-friend, Dulcina.

Dulcina had once confided to Beatrice that she was so flexible, she'd modeled for art students as a nude contortionist to pay for law school. No words existed in any human language that could express how very much Beatrice wished she didn't know that fact about Dulcina.

Thank *god* Dulcina and her perfectly dew-kissed face wasn't here right now. Beatrice had wrestled at the break of dawn with a dull eyeliner and dried-out mascara in the musty back bathroom at her father's house. But now, after flying nearly three hours from LAX to Seattle, and a forty-five-minute delay at the ferry landing, she could feel that her eyeliner had melted into the corners of her eyes, and she couldn't bring herself to care whether her wan skin was shine-free.

Beatrice poked again at a suspiciously gooey chip.

Her soon-to-be ex-husband, Grant, was a health freak who didn't believe in chemicals in food. He'd been the whole reason Beatrice had ordered the snack-counter nachos today. How, exactly, did someone not believe in chemicals? Chemicals were life. Literally. That was like not believing in gravity. But somehow, his dedication to "clean eating" had been such a point of pride with him that, out of respect for his preferences, Beatrice had eaten carefully, too.

At some point on this trip, Beatrice would get a McDonald's cheeseburger, by god. Maybe two. And she'd love every minute of eating both of them. With a large fries. And a Coke. No, a chocolate milkshake, extra-large, followed by two apple pies. All of it ordered from the drive-through, eaten in the parking lot, like an actual human being.

The teenage boy Beatrice had bought the nachos from walked

past her table carrying an empty tray. "Hey! How's your food treating you?" He'd been so excited when Beatrice had ordered. *The nachos are my favorite. On shift, I get to eat one order a day!*

"Um..."

"Oh, no, you don't like them?" His eyebrows disappeared up into the shag of his badly cut hair. "I made them myself. Usually the steward does it, but he's out sick, so I tried, but maybe I got them wrong?"

Beatrice shoved a chip in her mouth and spoke around the sogginess of it. "They're the *besht.*"

The guy's smile reset to full wattage. With a happy nod, he shuffled away.

Out the window, a long, blue expanse of water unrolled below the clouds. Kids hurtled through the main cabin to the stairs, which they thumped up and raced back down like raging herds of spooked wildebeests while small clumps of adults chatted and watched the scenery. Some were obvious tourists, like the old man with a camera that looked as vintage as his mustache, while others might have been locals, like the people at window seats who never glanced up from their laptops.

Across the table from her were a woman and her young daughter. Beatrice and the woman had nodded to each other when they'd all sat down, but they hadn't spoken. The child wore a red polka-dot dress and flipped the pages of a picture book, while the woman kept her head lowered, reading a paperback. The backs of the girl's heels drummed against the seat, a steady thumping metronome.

Were they traveling away or toward someone? Who was waiting for this pair? Who loved them?

Beatrice's heart, which had felt stubbornly resilient until that moment, suddenly ached.

Nope, she didn't have time for unnecessary emotion.

Altogether too much of that lately. She shook her head to clear it and clicked the shortcut link on her phone, pulling up the *Birthday Trip* spreadsheet.

Grant's requests for his fiftieth-birthday trip had been simple. He'd wanted to golf in Skerry Cove, an expensive course he'd never played off the coast of Seattle, and he'd wanted to bring his favorite people: Beatrice, his teenage sons, and his two best friends.

It had turned out that Beatrice hadn't been able to book the trip until two weeks after Grant's birthday, but she'd thought that would work perfectly, since they'd end up traveling on her forty-fifth birthday. Two birthday birds, one convenient vacation stone.

So at this point, had things gone according to her plan, there would have been six of them on this ferry. Grant's two sons would have ordered and then scarfed these nachos, no matter the chips' level of squishiness or their father's level of disapproval. Grant and his friend, Emmett, would have been watching golf on their phones, while she and Dulcina, Emmett's wife, would have been happily chattering their way to the island.

But two weeks ago, Grant's law partners had thrown him a surprise party at the office. When it was time for him to blow out the candles, he'd been nowhere to be found. Beatrice had eventually located him in his office, where she'd found Dulcina blowing out Grant's candles in private.

If Beatrice hadn't caught them, she still wouldn't have known that they'd been having an affair.

For seven years, apparently.

Beatrice had only been married to Grant for six.

So now, on her birthday, it was just her on the ferry. No husband, no stepsons, no ex-friends. Just Beatrice and her phone, full of her very well-laid and utterly useless plans. The eyewatering greens fee she'd paid to the golf course was nonrefundable, but as she stared at the decimal amount, she let herself imagine showing up to stroll the fairway tomorrow morning. Would they notice if she didn't rent a cart? If she carried no clubs? Would they care if she just screamed her way from tee to tee? She *had* managed to cancel the dinner reservations, but the fanciest suite in the hotel people loved most on Tripadvisor turned out to be as nonrefundable as the greens fee. She'd decided to be a no-show for the whole thing, sucking up the pain of the cost. But then Grant had asked if he could go on the trip. *With Dulcina.* "I mean, you already paid for it, right?"

It had taken her less than a pained heartbeat to change her mind. "*I'm* going on the trip. Alone."

Now, as the ferry hit a swell, Beatrice sighed.

Truthfully, it would have been so much easier *not* to go on this trip. Staying under the covers of her father's spare-room bed would have been effortless. She could have done it for the next, oh, thirty or forty years. Easily. But Dad had looked so relieved that she'd decided to do something that didn't involve crying or rereading *Pride and Prejudice* for the thousandth time. At some point, she knew she'd have to go "home" to the house she'd shared with Grant, if only to box up the hundreds of books in her towering to-be-read stacks. But she could have put off moving a muscle for quite a while longer.

So here Beatrice was. On the ferry. Alone.

She didn't even know she'd sighed deeply until the woman across from her looked up from her book and said, "You all right, hon?"

"Oh!" Beatrice straightened. "I'm fine."

"Okay." The woman had tired eyes and a kind face. "Let me know if she's bothering you at all." The little girl's heels were still thumping steadily against the seat as she turned the pages.

"Not at all. She's sweet."

The woman stuck her finger into her own book and leaned forward, and there it was—Beatrice could read it on her face. Small talk, incoming. She'd ask something innocuous about where Beatrice was from, what she was doing on the ferry, and Beatrice did *not* want to talk about herself. *Deflect.* "What are you reading there?"

The woman smiled and held up the book. "Evie Oxby's newest book. Have you read her?"

Of *course* it was Evie Oxby's book.

As a Hollywood entertainment lawyer, Grant had his fair share of eccentric clients, but none was higher paid (or more frequently sued) than young Evie Oxby, the Palmist of Palm Springs, who claimed to see and hear the ghosts of strangers. Her latest book, *Come at Me, Boo*, was still on the *New York Times* bestseller list twenty-four weeks after its release, and her first one, *I Ain't Afraid of No Ghosts*, had sold more than a million copies.

"I haven't." That was true, at least.

"She's so *good*. I tell you what, I don't go in for that woo-woo stuff, but she knows what she's talking about."

"Mmmm."

Evie Oxby had been at Grant's fateful birthday party a few weeks back. That night, she'd looked incredibly young and very pale, as if the weight of the ghosts she claimed she could see in the room was stripping the life from her. It had been a good act, yes. People had flocked around her, hoping that one of her *feelings* would come through for them, but Evie had just kept quiet, her lips tight and white.

After Beatrice had discovered Dulcina using Grant's bat to get to third base, she'd bolted straight through the party for the elevator. Her hand had shook as she'd hit the ground-floor button.

"Hi."

Beatrice had jumped—she'd barely noticed that Evie Oxby was already in the elevator car.

"I'm sorry," the young woman said to her. "You've just had a shock."

Fuck, did *everyone* know about Grant and Dulcina? Even his clients? Beatrice hadn't answered.

The doors opened to no one on the eighteenth floor. She stabbed the button again.

"And I have to deliver another shock, I'm afraid," said Evie.

Beatrice's sigh felt like it came from the bottoms of her feet. "Do you *really* have to?"

"You're going to experience seven miracles."

Did she look so terrible that Evie thought that might be a pick-me-up? "Huh. Thanks." She knew her tone said, *I don't care*, and normally, she'd feel bad about that. Not tonight.

But Evie didn't take the hint. She continued, "And you will die. It will happen very quickly."

Beatrice sucked in a sharp breath. "Amazing. Well, my night just keeps getting better. Thanks very much for that."

"I'm sorry." Evie's gaze fell to the carpeted elevator floor.

After the doors had finally opened on the ground floor, Beatrice speed-walked to the parking garage without looking back or saying good-bye.

Evie Oxby was known for her directness and her humor, not for being mean, so it had been a weirdly cruel thing of her to say. But the threat of her "prediction" was empty. Beatrice didn't believe in any psychic kind of magic. What she *had* believed in, up until that night, was that she and Grant had a strong partnership based on mutual respect.

Now, the woman across from her on the ferry said, "I swear to you. Evie Oxby is always right."

Sure she was.

Thank god, a text pinged.

Beatrice held up her phone as if she was getting a phone call. "Oops. I have to take this."

She stood and moved toward the bar area, unlocking her phone with a spark of hope. A birthday greeting? She hadn't gotten one yet, not even from her father, who normally never forgot.

You there yet?

Beatrice typed back to her best friend, Iris. On the ferry now.

Send proof.

You srsly think I'm still holed up at Dad's?

PROVE IT.

Beatrice held up the phone and snapped a picture out the window of the blue skies above the water. Then she turned the phone and took a photo of the interior of the main cabin. She sent both. Satisfied?

Is that a fortune-teller? Can't zoom in enuf.

Beatrice hadn't even noticed until then, but yes, a young woman with white-blond flyaway curls had placed a red scarf over her table on the other side of the boat. A propped-up hand-lettered sign read, "Tarot Read by Winnie."

Yes.

Dude, go do it!

If Iris were here, she'd already be dragging her over. Beatrice typed, Not my style, you know that.

Because Grant wouldn't like it?

Ouch. Sometimes it sucked that, in true bisexual fashion, she'd kept her ex as her best friend. Even if Iris never remembered a birthday (even her own), sometimes she knew too much about Beatrice.

Don't be mean.

His biggest client is Evie Oxby, and he wouldn't even let you get your tea leaves read at her book release party last year!

She hadn't told Iris what Evie had said in the elevator. Because it had just been mean. And ridiculous. He didn't NOT let me. He was right, she's his client, it would have been weird.

Go get your fortune told.

I will not.

K. He still runs your life. Got it.

Grant had never run her life. If anything, it had been the opposite—he was a great lawyer, but not very good at getting other things done. The day-to-day running of their life had been her job, and she'd done it well.

Said with love, shut up. Even though she knew Iris wouldn't spontaneously remember her birthday, she still typed, Anything else you want to say to me?

Iris sent a string of kiss emojis.

Beatrice looked over her shoulder. Her seatmate's gaze had gone back into her book, but what if she wanted to chat some more?

Bathroom it was. She needed to pee, anyway. They were almost to Skerry Island now, the mass of green land drawing closer by the minute, so hopefully she could avoid small talk for the rest of the ride.

Winnie the fortune teller was seated between her and the bathroom. She looked up as Beatrice walked past her table, her gaze bright above the black stars-and-moon T-shirt she wore. "Are you here for your future?"

"No." Beatrice's voice was too curt. "Sorry. Just going to the bathroom."

As she stepped forward, the ferry hit a swell and lurched. Beatrice stumbled, her hip glancing against the table. She grabbed at the back of Winne's seat, touching the woman's shoulder with her forearm.

Winnie turned, her eyes large and ice-blue. Her hand whipped out to grasp Beatrice's. "Beatrix, you're going to die. Soon."

CHAPTER TWO

When the universe speaks, your one job is to listen.

—Evie Oxby, on Mastadon

Beatrice stuffed down her impatience. She'd already been short with the woman—there was no need to be impolite. "Sorry, but that's not my name. With respect, I don't believe in... what you're doing here."

"*Fuck.*" Winnie's entire demeanor changed as she slumped into the booth, her shoulders dropping. She was older than she'd looked from across the cabin, Beatrice realized, maybe late thirties or even mid-forties.

Beatrice felt an unwelcome surge of sympathy. "Really, I don't want to—"

"Lord, I hate this shit." Winnie leaned forward, putting her head in her hands. "I'm moving here, you know that? All my stuff is in boxes somewhere on this ferry. I thought I might get *away* from accidentally touching people if I left the city. Not have it happen on the damn way here."

"I'm, um, sorry?" Beatrice itched to step away, to escape. "But you must have heard someone—the ticket taker?—say my name when we boarded, but you misheard. My name is Beatrice, not Beatrix."

Winnie's head snapped up. "You're the one who touched *me*."

This woman was upset, and Beatrice had only wanted to go to the bathroom, not freak out a stranger. "Again, very sorry. I lost my balance. I didn't mean to bother you while you're doing... this. Telling fortunes or whatever."

Winnie grimaced. "Reading tarot cards is a good money-maker, but that's not my true skill. Look. I have premonitions sometimes when I touch someone. And I got one with you. I get words and numbers and names and predictions."

"That must be hell on a crowded bus." Beatrice kept her voice light, but Winnie's face darkened.

"I don't *go* on crowded buses because of this bullshit, and yes, it's a pain in my ass. But I don't get them for everyone—only when someone needs to hear something. And I don't have any idea how to sugarcoat this message, so I'm just going to tell you what I got, okay? It's like I'm sending you a ZIP file—I'll tell you what I know, and then it's up to you to open it and deal with what's inside."

This woman couldn't be serious, could she? Beatrice opened her mouth to protest one last time before walking away, but Winnie looked tortured.

"Fine. Tell me."

"Your name isn't Beatrice, it's Beatrix. I'm sure of that, even if you aren't. And you're going to die. Soon. I'm getting the number one but I can't tell if that's weeks or months. It feels longer than one day, and shorter than one year."

"Mm." This was idiotic. Literally everyone in the whole world was going to die at some point. It must have been the surest prediction to make for anyone, ever. But even though Beatrice—yes, *Beatrice*—didn't believe a word of it, the hairs rose on the arms. "And?"

"Not an and. It's more like a but. You're going to die soon, but you'll also experience seven miracles."

"Oh, *come* on. Is this a social media trend? Like, is there a YouTube channel where y'all chat about what the hottest predictions will be this season?" *Taupe and black are in, along with fuzzy clutch purses, glitter boots, and predicting seven miracles and sudden death.*

"Someone told you this already." Winnie leaned forward. "They did. I can see it in your eyes."

"No." The lie felt stupid and dry in her mouth.

The boat lurched again as it turned to move toward the dock.

"If you've heard it from two psychics already..." Winnie lifted her hands before letting them drop to the table. "I see numbers in my mind—I can't explain it or prove it, and I won't try. But I've never been wrong."

It was the first thing Beatrice could almost understand. "I'm an accountant. I see numbers in my head all day long."

"You get it, then. I saw the number two floating on the image of a calendar with a red circle around today's date. So you'll experience the first two miracles today. Then five more, and..."

Beatrice was good at counting. "Two miracles today. Then five. Then I kick the bucket. Got it." At least it would make a great dinner party story someday. The ferry thunked as it made contact with its mooring. "Anything else?"

Winnie laced her fingers together and stared at them. "I'm sorry. I am. But maybe, now that you know, you can change some things?"

"Your numbers said I need to change things, too? Like what?"

"Way above my pay grade. Maybe let people know how you feel about them or something?"

Oh, Grant already knew how she felt. "In my brief remaining time? Sounds like I'm going to be busy."

"Ah, fuck it." Winnie looked miserable. "I know you don't believe me. After you receive those two miracles today, maybe you will."

The woman's pained face made Beatrice regret her sarcasm. She pulled out a twenty, the price listed on Winnie's sign. Gently, she slid it across the table. "I'm sorry. I didn't mean to sound like a dick. Please take this. I'd pay more at the movies getting popcorn and candy for myself. And if nothing else, this was more entertaining than any movie I've seen in a while."

CHAPTER THREE

What we fear seldom comes to pass. Of course, what *actually* comes to pass would have scared the heelie-bejeezees out of us had we known it was on its way.

—Evie Oxby, in conversation with Terry Gross on Fresh Air

Once off the ferry, Beatrice took a deep breath and pulled up Google Maps on her phone.

No signal. She held it into the air.

"You won't get cell service most places here," said the woman who'd been reading the Oxby book. "Skerry is Scottish for 'island,' but around here we say it's Scottish for 'stuck in the eighties.' You'll have Wi-Fi at your hotel, though. Are you at Skerry Cove Lodge?"

Beatrice nodded.

"It's that way, two blocks, then right on Third."

"Thanks." She waved as the woman and her daughter trundled off.

Not a big deal. Seriously, not being able to open Google

Maps was *not* a big deal. But Beatrice's heart hammered in her chest.

Of course I'm not dying.

Obviously, Beatrice wasn't about to expire. Real life was run by making good, sturdy plans that were backed up by numbers, and then executing those plans well. Real life was *not* run by hysterical hunches and random pieces of colorful cardstock wielded by a stressed-out blonde on a boat.

Walk. Move your legs.

It was still a bit too early yet to check in at Skerry Cove Lodge, but her carry-on bag was light. A stroll would do her good.

Skerry Cove appeared to be the kind of adorable that TV producers made whole series about, filled with people bustling about like they were in a Richard Scarry book. Over here a baker, carrying a tray of still-steaming muffins, over there a woman leading a parade of toddlers holding hands. Sunlight streamed through the old trees that lined the sidewalks, and the air smelled like brown sugar and salt.

The whole downtown area didn't look to be more than seven blocks long, if that. A hand-lettered sign in the window of a general store proclaimed it was the General Store, and the pharmacy was called Your Pharmacy. Maybe you didn't need a catchy name or a great marketing plan when you were the only game in town? Beatrice passed the Skerry Cove Bookshop, but she wouldn't stop yet—book shopping in a new town was a pleasure she never missed, even though she loved her Kindle, too. She'd want time and energy for a good bookstore plunge, not to mention the mental bandwidth to work out how many new books would fit in her carry-on to go home.

Home. Where was that? Not Dad's. Not the place she'd shared with Grant. Living with him for six years had never made his house her home.

Later. She'd figure it all out soon.

Later, bookstore therapy might help. But she couldn't help slowing down just enough to eye the new releases in the window.

The bookshop's door stood open invitingly. "Hey, there," the bookseller called from the counter just inside. She was maybe a year or two younger than Beatrice, and wearing a red jumpsuit that complemented the scarlet beads at the ends of her dark twists.

"We got it!" the woman said.

Beatrice scrunched her face into a squint. "Pardon?"

"That new knitting memoir you wanted. It's in. I just have to pull it from the box; give me a sec?"

"Sorry, you must have me confused for someone else, I think?"

"Oh, my god, you're a riot. Be right back, don't move." Laughing, the woman turned and walked toward the rear of the store.

Weird. Beatrice didn't *have* to wait, did she? Of course she didn't. A weird hard sell, that's all it was. She strolled another block, passing a violet-scented soap-making shop and a pet-grooming place, which had not one but two short black dogs lazing in front. Both leaped up and wagged their tails when they saw her, as if she was an old friend. Because she wasn't a psychopath, Beatrice complied with their requests to be petted before continuing down the street.

There must be a café nearby—she could smell coffee beans roasting in the air. It was totally going to be called something like Java Jive or Espresso Express. And yep, there it was on the corner, Java Express (she was so close!), and the extra-hot cappuccino she got from the incredibly friendly barista was excellent.

But it was hard to tell him so, because he hadn't really stopped talking to her since she walked in. He was one of those people who assume you know exactly what they're talking about all the time, which Beatrice didn't mind in the slightest. People like him made being an introvert like her easier. He was medium-height with pale skin, and his big bushy eyebrows danced as he put the finishing touches on the story she hadn't followed even a tiny bit of.

As he slid her coffee to her, he said, "So I told her that returning all those shopping bags to the store wasn't going to be an insult, you know? Not like when she mooned the mayor on Christmas Eve, remember? And bonus, she's helping mother earth!" He bent to the mirrored side of the silver espresso machine to peer at his perfectly groomed eighties mustache (it had to be ironic, right?). "You think?"

The name tag on his chest gleamed gold. *Fritz, they/them.*

Beatrice recalibrated her brain and said to them, "Sure. This capp is delicious, by the way. The foam is perfect."

They grinned. "Glad you like it. I thought the doc took you off caffeine, though?"

Ah. She must have a doppelgänger in town—that would explain both the bookseller and this person. Beatrice just gave a half nod and let them interpret it whatever way they wanted. Maybe someone would point out this look-alike to her while she was here, and she'd have an unspoken moment of thinking, *Really? I look like her?* Once, while visiting London, a British couple came up to her in a restaurant, convinced she was their cousin pretending to put on an American accent because they'd forgotten to send her a Christmas card. Even after she'd showed them her passport with amusement, they'd insisted on showing her the picture of their cousin. Yes, they'd shared pasty white skin and brown hair (without the silver stripe she had now) and brown eyes, but that was it. The couple had whirled off, offended by her insistence on maintaining the lie.

She thanked Fritz, and carried her coffee outside, where the air was warm and the sun danced in and out of bright cloud cover. She slung her carry-on onto a chair in front of the café, and sat, trying to resist the urge to pull out her phone.

Wasn't this what people did with coffee, just sat around drinking it, as if that was enough of a Thing to Do? In Los Angeles, people usually got their iced lattes to go, and slugged them down while listening to podcasts at double speed and changing lanes without signaling. But in a small island town on an early summer day, when the breeze was scented with sunshine and line-dried laundry, wasn't there some sort of law that you had to sit down with your coffee and enjoy it leisurely? Sure there was. Even if you were dying.

She snorted and took another sip of the excellent cappuccino. Two miracles coming today? Oh, yeah, she'd be on the lookout for *those*. Maybe she'd learn that Grant and Dulcina had both been carried away by two giant hawks and dropped into the mouth of an erupting volcano. Count 'em: one, two miracles, right there.

I love Dulcina, Grant had said that terrible night after his party. Through tears, he'd admitted he'd *always* loved Dulcina, ever since law school. Ten years ago, before Beatrice had even met him, Grant had missed Dulcina's wedding to Emmett, claiming he'd been unable to get back from a trip to Cabo in time, but apparently, he'd been in the hospital getting his stomach pumped after trying to kill himself.

The reason—the *reason*, he said, like it was something to be proud of—that he'd fallen for Beatrice was that she was so different from Dulcina, so quiet and self-contained. "Dulcy is loud, wears everything right out there, says whatever she's thinking. Not like you. You're strong. Dulcy can't even take care of a houseplant, but you take care of everything—you take care of me and the boys, and you were there for Naya when she was dying, and I've never regretted a minute of being with you."

It was one thing for him to bring up himself and his boys, but bringing up Naya, as if the time Beatrice had spent caring for her was a big deal, was *infuriating*. Of *course* she'd been there for Naya. She'd loved her stepmother more than anyone in the world besides her father. That's what you did for people you loved. You studied the problem, you figured out the best solutions, and you never gave up. Even at the very end, when Naya had been panting in the hospital bed set up in the living room, Beatrice had been searching for a cure. That's what you *did*.

You took care of those you loved.

You didn't break your marriage vows.

You didn't love someone else. Not like that.

Beatrice clutched her coffee cup. No, nope. She wouldn't think of him now. Not in this sunshine-filled village. She forced herself to relax into the peaceful, small-town afternoon. Groups of kids tromped past in various formations, little ones and big ones, visibly high on early summer vacation joy. Two women walked by, hand in hand, both laughing in a way that made Beatrice's jaw ache.

Skerry Cove was so Stars Hollow that she felt almost no surprise as a busker wandered past strumming a guitar, singing about lost love. He walked past the picture-perfect gazebo and leaned against the ladder of a gigantic tree house set high in a maple tree.

She texted Iris. This town is apparently made for the Hallmark Channel, so fucking adorable I can't stand it. Look at this. I swear I'm going to climb into that tree house behind that guy.

She turned on the video—maybe she could capture the voices of the kids laughing in front of the toy store (Ye Olde Toy Shoppe, for real) and the sound of the guy singing—but as she panned the camera, a tooth-rattling whine rose from a wood chipper parked across the street. Two burly woodsman types tossed in branches and logs from a pile behind them.

So instead of the video, she snapped a photo of the busker, his bright hair lit by the sun, and pressed Send. Then she stood, stretching her back with a groan. Forty-five might not be *young* young anymore—perhaps it was at the (very early) edge of middle age—but she could admit her body didn't travel quite the way it did twenty years before. The hotel suite had a hot tub—maybe the front desk's amenities would stretch to a foam roller so she could work out some of the kinks? Or maybe there was a yoga studio in town? Who was she kidding—of course there was, and she'd give her own damn self a high five if it was called Om Sweet Om.

The message she'd sent to Iris made a bonk. Of course, the crappy cell service.

Beatrice stood. She put her purse over her shoulder and tossed her empty cup into the trash can with a satisfying swish.

From behind, someone pushed her *hard*, right between the shoulder blades.

Crashing to the sidewalk, she landed painfully on one knee and one elbow.

And then all hell broke loose.

CHAPTER FOUR

If you let Spirit guide you, you'll find angels in shocking places. The bar? The Dairy Queen? The butt-ass end of Skid Row? Don't forget, angels like a good time (and an Oreo Blizzard) as much as the next celestial being.

—*Evie Oxby,* I Ain't Afraid of No Ghosts

The sound of a slammed *thud* was followed by a shredded scream.

Beatrice sat up, legs splayed, to assess the damage. Who had shoved her? There was no one close. Had she just tripped? But no, she'd felt that strong hand on her back, so what the hell? A quick scan behind her showed no pavement crack, no sudden trip line strung across the sidewalk.

The thud—what had that been?

The scream had come from a woman, and *of course*, it was Winnie, the tarot reader from the ferry. She came at a run, dropping to her knees next to Beatrice almost as hard as she'd fallen herself. "Sweet holy shit, you could have *died*."

Well, it was certainly possible she would die of embarrassment if Winnie screamed like that again.

Beatrice stood. The knee of her jeans was ripped, and not in the on-purpose way. Blood trickled from a gash in her palm, but otherwise, she was okay. "I'm fine."

Wild-eyed, Winnie said, "It's a miracle. *The first one.*"

Still flustered, Beatrice tugged at the suddenly-too-tight neck of her T-shirt. She just needed to get out of here, that was all. But a couple of women hovered behind Winnie, the barista peering around them.

The two men running the woodchipper raced toward them.

"Jesus, lady," one said. "I'm so fucking sorry. I have no idea how that happened."

The other man gasped. "I've never seen anything like this. I can't believe it. How did—Rick, should we call the supervisor?"

Wait, were they teasing her? Why would they do that? "Seriously?"

The guy named Rick said again, "I'm *so* sorry."

They were serious, apparently, which made her fall even more embarrassing. "Okay, yeah, I normally know how gravity works, I swear. I felt a—no, I must have tripped somehow. But I didn't break anything. I don't need a supervisor or an ambulance. Sorry to worry you."

"Oh," said Winnie. "You haven't seen it yet."

Belatedly, Beatrice realized that the gathering crowd wasn't looking at her. Instead, they were staring at the chair she'd been sitting in.

Or rather, at the three-foot-long metal blade that had ripped through the chair's chrome back, sinking deeply into the wooden wall behind it.

"Where did that come from? What... *is* that?"

Rick said, "It's a reversible double-sided blade for that

side-discharge chipper over there." He pointed one thick finger across the street at the chipper. "I've been working this kind of machine for twenty years, and nothin' like this has ever happened."

He reached toward the metal, but the other man stammered, "N-no, leave it there. Let Pete deal with it when he gets here. I'll get photos. Insurance is going to need it."

"But I'm not hurt," Beatrice said weakly.

Rick rubbed a meaty hand over his scalp. "Thank god for that. But we're going to have to pay for this wall. And the chair. But—whew." He literally wiped sweat off his forehead. "I'm just glad we won't have to pay for damage to…you."

Damage.

They sure as hell wouldn't have been paying her medical bills. The blade had sliced through the metal chair as if it were paper, embedding itself at least six inches into the wall.

One more second of sitting in the chair, or one more second of standing where she'd been standing, and she'd have either been decapitated or cut clean through at her belly button. Her hands moved to touch her neck, then the part of her T-shirt that covered her belly button.

"Goddamn miracle," said the man who wasn't Rick, before turning away to talk to his supervisor on the phone.

Beatrice didn't believe in miracles. She believed in science, and math, and facts. Sometimes a full solar eclipse or a warm-from-the-vine tomato could *feel* like a miracle, but otherwise, no. Her hands trembled as she smoothed back her hair. "Well, if you don't need me—"

"Hang on, lady, we might," said Rick.

Winnie stepped forward. "Do you *see* her? She's as pale as the ghost your little machine almost made her."

"For the paperwork…"

"For the paperwork, you find her. Beatrix, you got a card? Give it to him."

"It's Beatrice." She fished a business card out of her bag. After she handed it over, Winnie tugged her into a close hug. For a moment, Beatrice was freaked out enough that it felt good to be held.

Then it just felt weird. She extricated herself. "Thought you couldn't touch me."

"Eh. I've already felt the worst from you. Now, a drink," said Winnie. "Down at the bar. I'm buying."

Beatrice's voice shook. "I need to get a couple of things from the store, and it's time to check in, I think. At my hotel." *I need to lie down.*

"Rain check, then. You've got one more miracle coming today, don't forget. Later, a drink, yeah?"

She nodded, although there wouldn't be a later. Her legs wobbled slightly, but she straightened her back as she walked away from the group. It took another two blocks to realize that she'd passed the general store.

Turning around, she heaved in a breath of the salty air.

Alive. She was alive. Even without believing in miracles, Beatrice was allowed to feel relief, wasn't she? Was it gratitude that fluttered up her throat as she reached the market's door and grabbed a basket?

You are afraid, said a voice deep inside her mind.

Shut up. I am not. Her own voice seemed just a little less sure, which was annoying as fuck, really.

CHAPTER FIVE

> When in doubt, take a few deep breaths in and out. Imagine light filling you from the top down, until you warm from the inside. If that fails, get in the tub with a whole Lush bath bomb and try again later.
>
> —*Evie Oxby, "How I Survive My Own Life,"* Medium

Trying to ignore her jackrabbiting heart, Beatrice found the antacid she suddenly needed, then forced herself to wander the aisles like a tourist would, inspecting the locally made bread and homemade jams. Out of nowhere, she was *ravenous* and wanted some of everything. Isn't that what they said happened when you had a narrow escape from death? Fight, fuck, or feast? She didn't want to fight anyone on her birthday, and fucking was obviously right out.

So feast it would be.

She chose three kinds of marbled cheese, a loaf of still-warm olive bread, and a bottle of red from an island winery. Too impatient to wait, needing to chew something right *now*, she tore off a piece of the bread and shoved it into her mouth. It was so good, she had another bite, then another, as she continued to add treats to her basket: chocolate caramels wrapped in cellophane, green olives packed in oil, one tiny red velvet cupcake.

In line, the woman in front of her chatted with the checker as though they had nothing better to do all day. Beatrice gritted her teeth and took a breath. This was a small town, after all.

Finally, she checked out, only slightly embarrassed that a third of the bread was gone. On her way to the exit, she passed an old-fashioned message board hanging next to the manager's desk. A little box on the desk held the three-by-five cards that the board was covered with. The charming level climbed to eleven.

Perusing the board, Beatrice learned that Mrs. Muggins was selling tomatoes. Someone named Jax wanted to give saxophone lessons, and a drummer was willing to trade grass for gas for a ride up to Vancouver. Were these cards left over from 1987? They were piled two and three deep, push-pinned on top of each other, so she moved some aside to peek underneath.

She uncovered a card that read, *Room for Rent, daily, weekly, monthly*. The handwriting was spidery and the email address had AOL in it, so the owner must be more than a hundred.

"Oh, my freaking god. Who *are* you?" exclaimed a voice at her elbow.

Beatrice jumped.

The voice was attached to a girl who looked like she'd fallen out of a manga book about a haunted candy factory. Thin and very pale, she wore a black dress, pink-and-white-striped stockings, and heavy black shoes decorated with cat faces. Her dyed-black hair was pulled back in two messy side braids, and her winged eyeliner, while professionally applied, was so thick it made her blue eyes look smaller than they were. She was trying to look about eighteen, so she was probably quite a bit younger than that.

"Pardon?"

The girl blinked. "Holy shit. This is—*wow*."

"I'm guessing I have a look-alike in town."

"Wow. Yeah. What do I do here?" She looked at the card Beatrice had just uncovered. "Oh, you don't want to stay at that place."

"No?" Beatrice turned the card over in her fingers. Nothing on the back. "Serial killer?"

"Worse."

"There's a worse?"

"She has birds. Like, seventy of them, all in her living room." The girl picked up a pen attached to the desk below the board and fiddled with the chain. She darted a look up at Beatrice and back down at the pen. She frowned, as if trying to decide something, and then spoke all in a rush. "I mean, I can get behind a myna or a crow. I'd just about die to see a sandhill crane. Or a spoonbill! But people keeping that many birds in a house? Honestly, it doesn't seem sanitary."

Okay, so maybe this girl had been treated badly by the bird lady? Beatrice stuck the card back on the board just where it had been, under a card offering training sessions for prospective midwives. "I'm going to trust your judgment because you're rocking those shoes."

With a satisfied sparkle in her eye, the girl self-consciously touched her nose piercing. Probably new. "Thank you." She clicked the pen rapidly six or seven times. "Thrifted."

"Which makes you stylish *and* clever."

The girl grew at least two inches at that, which warmed Beatrice's cold Los Angeles heart a corresponding number of degrees.

"You should stay at my house."

Beatrice raised an eyebrow.

The girl smiled. "My mom's house, I mean."

"Thank you, but I don't actually need a place to stay. I was just browsing the board. And I'm pretty sure your mom doesn't want you foraging for random people at the grocery store."

She tilted her head, her smile wide. "I've foraged for stranger things."

"Impressive. But truly, I'm fine. Don't need a room."

"You never know. You might find you want to stay with us for a while." The girl stuck out her hand. "Minna."

Her hand was cool and the tiniest bit sweaty.

"I'm Beatrice. It's nice to meet you."

"You, too. And I *mean* it." Minna reached up and scrabbled through the cards. "Ah. Here. She keeps hiding it, and I keep uncovering it. This is us."

The writing on the card was in fine black ink, the letters round and self-consciously old-fashioned. Minna's work, Beatrice would guess. *Private apartment, water view. Good muffins. No pets on premises normally but please feel free to bring yours, especially dogs that like treats.* The listed phone number would probably ring in Minna's pocket.

For a strange moment, she wished she could make this girl's day by accepting the offer. "I'm assuming you're the property manager?"

A wild look of pleasure crossed Minna's face. "Exactly! It's just an extra room, but it has its own entrance and bathroom, and I'm in charge of cleaning it and making the muffins—I swear I'm really good at both things, and I even wear a hair net when I'm baking, just in case, because hair in food is disgusting, and I always bleach the sheets, but then I hang them in the sun because it smells so good. I get to keep any of the money that comes in."

Minna's earnestness was adorable, and Beatrice knew better than to say so. "Very savvy."

The girl pulled her cell out of a rhinestone clutch. Her fingers flew over the screen. "Okay. Just told Mom I've booked the room."

Whoops. "I'm so sorry, I admire your eagerness, but I'm staying at the Skerry Lodge. Can't get out of it, and believe me, I tried. If I could, though, your place would be my first pick."

"Oh, *no*. How long are you staying?"

"Just two nights."

"No, you *have* to stay longer."

This girl needed something Beatrice couldn't give her. She looked at the ground. "Well. Thanks? It's been lovely talking to you."

"Why did you come here? To the island?"

"My husband wanted to play the golf course."

Minna swiveled her head. "Where is he?"

"Not here."

The girl's eyes traced Beatrice's face as she touched her own cheek. "You've always had that dimple?"

"Of course." The dimple was so deep that she knew it was visible even when she wasn't smiling.

"I can't believe you have that. This is em-effing *wild*." Then the words tumbled from Minna's mouth without stopping. "Where are you from? Seriously, you're just here because of *golf*? How long have you been married? Oh, my god, do you have *kids*? Have you ever done the 23andMe thing? Are your fingers double-jointed?"

Only her thumbs were double-jointed. But this strangeness had gone too far, and Beatrice wasn't going to tell this girl about her bendable digits. "Um, I really have to go—"

"I mean, just the thumbs. Are your thumbs double-jointed? You really have zero idea. Will you trust me?"

Hang on. What the hell? Beatrice's thumbs twitched.

What would a teenage girl need a total stranger to trust her about? For that matter, why on earth would Beatrice trust a girl who might be struggling with mental health issues, a girl who had imprinted upon her like a hatchling duck? "How old are you?"

"Sixteen." A pause. "Almost."

While it was pretty unlikely that a fifteen-year-old wanted to take her out back and mug her (Minna would have youth on her side, but Beatrice had decades of accumulated feminist rage on hers), trusting any stranger wasn't a good idea, even on an idyllic little island. Which was why Beatrice was flabbergasted when her mouth said, "Okay."

Minna smiled. "Get ready for a miracle. Follow me."

A miracle.

Gossip traveled fast in this town—Minna might have even seen the blade that could have killed her, what, just thirty minutes before? Minna would probably lead her to another competing psychic. Once you had a sucker on the hook, you had to keep them wriggling.

Even so, Beatrice followed. Or rather, she race-walked to keep up with Minna's speedy gait. Two blocks away from the market, Minna stopped in front of a shop. It was old-fashioned looking, as if at one time it had been a mercantile and sold things like horehound candy and blackstrap molasses, but in the windows were brightly colored sweaters, piles of yarn, and several spinning wheels that looked right out of *Sleeping Beauty*. The hand-lettered sign moved gently in the breeze—*Which Craft*.

"Here we are." Minna spun to face her. "Oh, my god, I forgot to say Happy Birthday to you."

Beatrice almost dropped her grocery bag. How could this girl be the one to give her the first birthday greeting of the day? How did she know?

Pulling open the door, Minna said, "Here we go!"

Inside, a woman with short dark hair and tattoos snaking up and down her arms sat at a long bench, whittling something. As she looked up at them, slices of thin wood curled at her feet. Her voice, when she spoke, sounded rusty, as if out of practice. "Fuck *me*."

"Right? Where is she?" Reaching back, Minna grabbed Beatrice's hand.

And for some reason, Beatrice didn't pull away. Something was happening, or was about to happen, and excitement—no, make that straight-up fear—sluiced through her veins, sharp and electrifying.

The whittling woman jerked a thumb toward the back.

"Thanks, Reno." Tightening her fingers around Beatrice's, Minna pulled her past colorful rows of fabric bolts and tables piled high with skeins of yarn. "Mom! *Mom!*"

Another woman bustled out of a back room, wiping her hands on a canvas cobbler's apron. "Minna, baby, you don't need to—"

Beatrice's whole body froze in place. Her feet stopped moving, and her heart slammed in her chest so hard, it almost hurt.

A mirror.

She had to be looking into a fucking mirror.

There was the same dark hair with the same thick silver stripe on the right side, although this woman's hair was longer than hers. And she was perhaps a touch taller than Beatrice, but maybe she was wearing heels—Beatrice couldn't look at her feet, though, because she was too busy looking into the woman's round brown eyes, and they were *her* eyes, and how was this possible? This was so far past doppelgänger—sure, this could happen, but oh, it felt too bizarre. Too surreal. This was her own *face*, including the dimple. Did she need to sit down? Was it dizziness or just exhaustion that made her feel like she didn't remember how to speak, how to say anything at all?

The woman had frozen, too, her hands paused in midair, as if she'd been about to reach for a hug from Minna but had stopped halfway through the plan.

Her mouth opened once. Then twice. Finally, she gasped, "Beatrix."

Beatrice finally found four words that she remembered, but she couldn't say them louder than a whisper. "That's not my name."

CHAPTER SIX

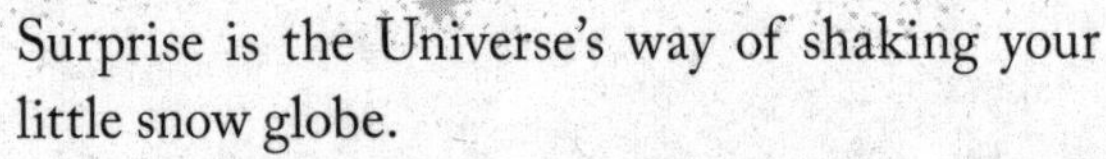

Surprise is the Universe's way of shaking your little snow globe.
—*Evie Oxby,* Palm Springs and Bat Wings, *Netflix*

It didn't make sense—none of it, not one little bit—yet when the woman wrapped her arms around her, Beatrice wanted to cry.

And Beatrice was *not* a crier.

This woman, though—here was a woman who knew where her faucet was located.

"I can't believe it." She wiped tears from her face and laughed, looking at Minna and the woman named Reno. "Oh, my, we have to sit down, Minna, can you bring that chair—yes, Reno, grab that one there."

Without even choosing to bend her knees, Beatrice found herself seated in a wicker chair, her clone sitting opposite. Near them, Minna and Reno both pulled up chairs, but Beatrice couldn't have made herself look away from the woman if she'd wanted to.

Which she didn't.

It was stranger, deeper, than just finding a woman she freakishly resembled. A swell rolled beneath her, as if the entire building had been placed on the ferry, as if she were sailing over something enormous and aqueous. It felt primeval. *Damn*, she was losing it. "I don't understand."

The woman's eyes—that exact shade of clove, the exact shape that Beatrice saw every day in the mirror—darted to Reno. "Where's—"

Reno said, "Went to yoga. Twenty minutes ago. Told me to tell you."

Beatrice sat forward. "Who *are* you?"

The woman pushed her hair over her shoulder and leaned forward. "I'm Cordelia. And you . . . you found me. You found *us*. Finally. You're alive."

"I don't understand."

Cordelia reached forward, her hand moving quickly, her fingers touching Beatrice's face. "You are alive, right? I'm not dreaming this?" She glanced at Minna, who nodded encouragingly.

Beatrice said, "I don't think we're dreaming. Maybe . . . do you have me confused with someone else?" Perhaps her father had a cousin out here or something? But Dad always talked about how tragic it was that their family was so small—after her mother had died of lung cancer, it had just been the two of them until Dad had married Naya. At one point, Beatrice had been such a lonely child, she'd made imaginary friends with her own image in the mirror, chatting to it, swearing that sometimes it answered her back.

Fumbling with a small bag next to her chair, Cordelia drew out some kind of yarn project that involved very small needles. But as if her fingers were having trouble knowing what to do, she made no move to start knitting. "I'm not confused. Not if you're Beatrix."

"My name is Beatrice."

"Beatrice, then. Yes." A small shake of the head, as if to clear it, and then Cordelia said, "But you died. In the accident."

"What accident?"

"The car crash when we were thirteen months old. My mother told me that my father and twin sister died."

This was too much. It simply couldn't be. Beatrice leaned forward. "When's your birthday?"

Cordelia's fingers began to manipulate the yarn around the tiny silver needles. She smiled. "Today, of course. Happy Birthday, Beatrice."

It felt like a punch to the kidneys. "Plimmerton Hospital?"

"In New Jersey. Yes."

Was this really happening? Beatrice said, "Twelve thirty p.m."

"You're older than I am. I was one fifteen p.m."

No.

No.

This didn't happen to normal, regular people who did normal, regular things. Beatrice paid her taxes by the end of February and got her teeth cleaned every six months. She bought everything bagels fresh on the weekend and froze them for the week ahead. Normal people did not find their long-lost *twin* while on a weekend earmarked for golf.

Move. Think. She sucked in a breath and stood, unsure where to move to next. But it helped to stand up. Something rose inside Beatrice's chest—a flame of heat that might sear her lungs forever if she didn't articulate the feeling that was rising inside her. "Is she alive? Our mother?"

Cordelia's fingers never stopped knitting, but she kept her gaze on Beatrice. "Alive and spitting."

Minna muttered, "Emphasis on the latter."

No.

Her mother was dead. Had always been dead. Beatrice had been furious for so long about the cancer that had taken her mother when Beatrice was less than a year and a half old. It hadn't been *fair.* She'd been robbed of something that all her friends had: a mother to soothe their bumps and sing them to sleep at night. She didn't even have a single memory of the woman she'd lost. Sometimes, at Christmas, she'd smell a cranberry candle mixed with the smell of cinnamon, and something would twist inside her, something that felt like the memory of something maternal. Or was it just a manufactured scent meant to evoke that exact sentiment? She'd reach to grasp it, but it would slip away from her, and then Dad would yell from across the office that it was time for their daily chess match, and the warm feeling would evaporate back into a dull resentment at death for stealing something she needed.

But her mother was alive.

Cordelia stayed in her chair, her fingers now clicking the needles, but their motion was smooth, as if she didn't want to frighten Beatrice.

Too late. Beatrice was crashing onto the shores of panic. "Why are you so calm? Why aren't you freaking the fuck out, too?"

Cordelia paused. Then she said, "Mom said you'd died. But she's not always the most... trustworthy."

Minna snorted, and Cordelia shot her a glance before continuing. "I'd have been able to feel it, if you were really gone. I've always felt that we'd find each other someday."

Had Beatrice felt the same thing? Was that where her ribbon of loneliness, the one at her core, came from? "But still—this *could* be the wildest coincidence to ever happen, that we were born close to each other and look so much alike." Okay, that was completely ridiculous. "Do you know your father's name?"

"I don't. She would never tell me."

"My father is Mitchell Barnard. He said my mother's name was Astrid Evanora Holland Barnard." *All of this will be explained in a way that makes sense.* It had to be.

"That's exactly right. Our mother's name is Astrid Evanora Holland." The knitting needles went still in Cordelia's hands. "Mitchell? Mitchell Barnard. Huh. Now I know my father's name."

Beatrice tugged at the neck of her shirt. "Holy fuck. Oh, shit."

"This is a miracle." Cordelia's eyes blazed. "A miracle."

Miracle number two.

Beatrice's breathing was high and tight in her chest, and the more she tried to get one good, full breath, the harder it seemed. Had her heart ever banged so loudly before? Was it too fast? Oh, yeah, it was *way* too fast. It hurt, in fact, bands of heated pain tightening around her chest.

"You okay?" Cordelia's voice sounded far away.

"Fine." Her voice was a wheeze.

"How about sitting down again?"

Reno, who had been silent, stood and reached for her arm, but Beatrice shook her off.

"No." She didn't need to sit. She needed to—what? Figure out why her father had lied to her for *her whole life*? The one person she trusted most in life, her rock—he'd lied, this whole time. Struggling to raise her voice over the pounding of her heart—surely they could all hear it—she said, "So *was* there an accident?"

Cordelia lifted a shoulder and let it drop. "I don't know. I'm inclined to say no. That they just separated us like those half-heart necklaces."

"Dad wouldn't have just let a child—you—*go*. It doesn't make sense." But did any of this make sense? The tightness in her chest clamped again, and she dropped back into the chair she'd vacated. Darkness moved in at the edges of her vision, and her breathing sounded like a fish lying on a dock, the desperate flapping of her gills trying to get oxygen. A high whine started at the back of her head, as if someone had turned on a saw.

She turned her head to find the noise, but instead of ascertaining the source, she saw Cordelia's knitting drop to the floor as Cordelia leaped toward her. "What? What's going—" But her voice wasn't really working, and her lungs cramped...

Hands touched her shoulders then, Reno's low voice saying something in her ear. Beatrice was gently folded in half as her head was urged down between her knees.

"Take a breath. There you go. Just give it a minute."

The whine ceased almost immediately. It took a bit longer for the darkness to recede, but clearheadedness came right on its heels. The stubbornness that flooded through her veins felt like ice-cold water, exactly what she needed.

She sat up. "I'm *not* having a panic attack."

"Of course you aren't," said Cordelia.

Great. She was being patronized. "I've never had one, but I know all about them." Grant got them sometimes, usually after he lost a game of golf. "That wasn't one."

"Probably just light-headedness."

Cordelia was right. That was all it was. No matter that she'd never come close to fainting before. This was a day for new things, apparently. Grateful for the way the air seemed to fill her lungs completely again, she turned to face Cordelia, who had moved her own chair close to hers.

"You're my twin," said Beatrice.

Cordelia nodded.

Now that her brain had been handed back to her, Beatrice took a moment to stare at this woman. After all, this was what

Beatrice was normally good at—clear judgment and rational thought.

Cordelia's nose leaned the slightest bit to the right—there, that was different. Living in a town chock-full of fake noses, Beatrice had always been idiotically proud of her perfectly straight snoot. Cordelia's lips were maybe a touch fuller? "Your freckles."

Nodding, Cordelia said, "They're in different places than yours."

"It's so *weird*." It was like seeing a constellation hung in the wrong part of the sky.

Cordelia rocked herself backward, and Beatrice felt glad for the increased distance. At the same time, she wanted to reach forward to grab her twin's hands. Cordelia's fingers were curling in and out of fists, and somehow Beatrice knew she wanted the same thing. Just to be on the safe side, she stuffed her own hands into the pockets of her jeans.

Cordelia said, "I did 23andMe. And Ancestry.com. Anything that would take my spit and give me a result, I signed up for. I waited."

"It never even crossed my mind." Dad said that the two of them were all each other had. *We're all we need, Button.* His parents had died when he was young—but, Jesus, *had* they? He had no siblings, or was that just what he'd said? An electrical storm flashed at the base of her skull. That anger was going to boil over soon, but right now, she didn't need to stoke the heat. "I thought Dad and I were alone."

"Did you really feel alone? I mean"—Cordelia looked down at her hands, the ones that looked like Beatrice's, but covered with silver rings—"I just kept waiting for you."

I was so lonely. But she'd rather die than say it out loud. "What's our—what's she like?"

"She's incredible."

Minna said, "Incredibly difficult."

Reno gave a snort-huff sound.

Cordelia went on as if she hadn't heard them. "She's powerful, and opinionated, and brilliant. She knows everything. We co-own Which Craft, but she can be a little possessive of it. It's weird that she's not here, honestly, but she'll be back any minute. Are you ready to meet her?"

Absolutely not. No way.

But a door in the back creaked, and a loud voice filled the air. "Ah, so *this* is why my ears were burning! And *you*. I should have known."

CHAPTER SEVEN

Women and gender-fluid people have more power, as a rule. Men can be powerful, too. Sure. But I find they're sometimes less willing to try as hard.

—Evie Oxby, Reddit reply to "Can men do magic?"

Astrid's eyebrows drew together into a magnificent wave that crashed in the middle of her forehead. "I heard two different female owls cry this morning, seven minutes after sunrise. Now I know why."

Beatrice stared, but found Astrid difficult to focus on. Rather, she was made up of so many disparate parts that a singular focus felt impossible. She was tall, wider at the hip than either Beatrice or Cordelia. Her hair was the reverse of theirs, stark white with one dark stripe, and it was piled on her head, speared with something that appeared to be an actual twig. She wore a long red-and-black tunic that was a goth-hippie mash-up with a black mesh bodice, bells dangling from a cord at the neck, and snakeskin print on the sleeves. Below the tunic hung a longer black linen skirt adorned with tulle ruffles. She escaped looking like the village witch with a perfectly applied slash of crimson lipstick.

"Hello," Beatrice managed.

"And where did you come from?"

"Your uterus, apparently. Forty-five years ago today."

The left side of the eyebrow wave crested. "Is your father still alive?"

"Last time I spoke to him, yes."

"Mmmm." She narrowed her eyes. "I knew he'd finally break. Always the weak link, that man."

"Mom—" Cordelia's voice was a warning.

Beatrice didn't need protecting, though. "He never told me. Though he should have."

Minna said brightly, "It's all coincidental, Gran, can you believe it? She's here so her husband can golf."

"Coincidences are for lazy atheists. As I am neither, I reject this outright." Astrid looked like the type who had never believed anything she didn't want to, including the fact that she had two daughters, not one.

"Dad said you were dead. And apparently you told my twin that I was? Seems like you and Dad both intended to keep the fuckery permanent."

The door of the shop opened with a bang, and a man tumbled inside, his eyes huge, his shirt buttoned wrong.

Reno was already moving toward the back room. "I'll get your bag."

Cordelia nodded, moving to a wall of small bottles that Beatrice hadn't noticed before. She took down five or six of the bottles, slipping them into a brown lunch bag.

The man barreled directly at Beatrice. "She—it's all happening so fast, this can't be normal."

Crap. "Sorry, I'm the wrong one. Not me!"

"Tim." Cordelia's voice was calm. "That's my sister. I'm over here."

Tim's gaze traveled from me to Cordelia and back again. All he said was a simple "Oh."

"Who's with her, Tim?"

"Her aunt."

"Good. Why didn't you just call my cell?"

"Shit! I didn't think of it. I just ran."

"Well, we're so close, that makes sense. I'm sure I would have done the same thing." Cordelia threw an unruffled smile over her shoulder as she reached up high for one last small bottle. "It's going to be okay."

"It's *not*," he gasped.

Cordelia was a midwife? What else didn't Beatrice know about her?

Astrid spoke then. "Tim, there's no one better at this than Cordelia. It will happen just right."

Her mother's voice was hypnotic, a slow swirl of smoke that released something tight in Beatrice's chest.

Tim took a deep breath and nodded. "All right. Yes."

Reno came back with a black case that looked like an old doctor's bag. Cordelia put the paper sack into it, her movements swift and easy.

"Okay, Tim, let's go." As they left, Cordelia said, "Minna, darling, will you get Beatrice's number and text it to me?"

"Yeah."

Then Cordelia focused on Beatrice. "Beatrice, you are the best birthday present I've ever received in my whole life. I wish I had time to prove that to you now, but I'll call you tomorrow. And then, we'll *talk*. Oh, my sister, we'll talk."

It actually ached to feel so much warmth, as if Beatrice's body had been ice, and the thaw was agony. She tried not to gasp aloud.

The door closed.

Astrid, Minna, Reno, and Beatrice stood in awkward silence until Minna broke it and asked for Beatrice's number.

She tapped it into her phone. "I'm texting you now, so you'll have my number, too. You can text me anytime. Or call me. I'd love that."

Astrid turned to face Beatrice, the bells at her neck jingling like the bells on a dangerous cat's collar. That cranberry and cinnamon scent Beatrice had always wondered if her mother smelled of—nope, that wasn't possible. This woman probably smelled of sulfur and fury. Not that Beatrice planned to get close enough to find out. "Do you have it?" Astrid hissed.

Beatrice jerked. "Have what?"

That sinuous eyebrow wave again. "Don't be coy. Did you get the Knock? Is that how you got here?"

"I took a ferry."

"Oh, goddess, you're not even *activated*. But I can feel it coming off you. Unused and dusty, perhaps, but it's there."

Beatrice tried to smile. "That's quite a personal attack."

Astrid barely blinked. "She called you Beatrice. But that's not your name." Her voice held none of the comforting tone she'd offered Tim.

"It is."

"You are *Beatrix*."

"No." Beatrice's jaw tightened with stubbornness.

Minna rolled her eyes in an unmissable, almost audible way. "Great. Another name for her to accidentally get wrong on purpose."

Astrid whirled to her. "And you! You must love this! Yet one more name for me to screw up. But I've been getting your pronouns right most of the time and I haven't called you—"

Reno leaned forward, a knife cutting through flesh, placing

her body between Astrid and the girl. "You will not deadname her."

"I won't! I *haven't* called you by your boy name in so long. Have I?"

"Not this week," whispered Minna.

Minna was trans? It felt like a lovely thing to know. But Astrid shouldn't have outed her like that, and something about the girl's abashed response made Beatrice feel feral. She could leap forward—she could bite Astrid on the leg, straight through to the bone—

Astrid, unaware of the danger her limb was in, turned back toward Beatrice. "And your last name is?"

When Beatrice had married Grant, she'd kept her father's name as her last, since their shared company was Barnard Family Finance. Now she was grateful she wouldn't have to change it back. But she owed this woman nothing, not even the privilege of knowing her full name. "Minna, thank you. Astrid..."

The older woman drew herself up very straight and tall. "I'm *not* scared that you're here."

What? Who said she was? In Astrid's gaze was a flash of an emotion Beatrice couldn't parse. It didn't seem to be fear. And it couldn't possibly be love, obviously. It wasn't hate, and it certainly wasn't indifference.

Astrid's scowl grew deeper.

Whew. All of this was way too much, and Beatrice needed to be anywhere but here.

And since she had never known she had a mother who wasn't dead, she had spent exactly zero time in her life working on the perfect parting shot.

So Beatrice just left.

CHAPTER EIGHT

For betrayal: light a black candle. Carefully gather your reserves along with your herbs and crystals. Then cry for a while before you do anything else. This part is very important.

—*Evie Oxby, Instagram post*

Both of Beatrice's legs were asleep. She hadn't noticed them getting tingly, just as she hadn't realized the sunset she'd been watching had turned into dimness and then dark. Night had fallen at some point as she'd sat on the hotel room's balcony, her wine untouched beside her. In the dark, a couple's laughter drifted up to her from the beach below, their forms as invisible as the scent of brine.

All Beatrice could see in front of her eyes were Cordelia and Minna's faces.

She tottered to her feet, zombie-walking back into the hotel room as the feeling returned. At some point, she'd need to connect to the internet. Perhaps that point was now? It was a small task; she knew that. It wasn't insurmountable. Was it?

Don't be an idiot. She took a deep breath and punched the digits into her phone to connect to the hotel's Wi-Fi. It rattled to life, filling with pings and bloops as messages landed, and before she could chicken out, she opened the messages app.

Most of them were from her father. Happy birthday, honey!

Honey, I'm sorry I'm so late texting you, but I was at the store buying every single treat you've ever loved.

Button? You having fun?

When you get home, we're having Frito pie for dinner!

Did you make it all right?

Tell me you're there safe, okay? You know I worry.

Beatrice closed the sliding door but immediately opened the window to let out—something—she wasn't sure what. She just needed more of the cold night air to breathe, to suck into her lungs.

The right thing to do would be to call him. Beatrice knew that.

She dialed Iris instead. "It's my birthday."

"Fuck."

"I forgive you. As usual."

A heavy sigh. "Well, why would this year be any different? Thanks. I'll make you dinner when you get home. How's it going?"

"Hm." Despite the sentences flapping around in her throat, the words got stopped up just behind her teeth.

But Iris knew her well. "You did it. You got your tarot read."

"Um."

"I knew it. Tell me."

Beatrice didn't even want to say it out loud. "So... at Grant's birthday party, I talked to Evie Oxby. She predicted that I would experience seven miracles and then I would die."

"I'm sorry—what? You're just telling me this now?"

Wincing, she said, "Then the tarot reader said the same thing. And that the first two miracles would happen today."

"I—I don't—" There was a long, long pause. Then, "The *hell*?"

"This really is your fault."

"Oh, my god, the two miracles happened?"

Gah. "I almost died. But then I didn't." Beatrice explained the woodchipper blade and the push from someone who wasn't there. Iris's gasps grew louder with every word. "If I hadn't fallen to the ground . . . I mean, it was just luck, right? Very good luck."

"And an invisible push? That sounds pretty miracle-ish to me, but okay. What about the other one?"

"I found . . . a twin sister?" No, it wasn't in question. "I have a twin sister. I found her."

Iris, who'd never run out of words once in her whole life, was silent.

"And a mother. And a niece."

"But—but your mom died when you were little."

"That's what my father always said."

"*No.* Mitchell wouldn't lie like that."

Sudden tears were hot in Beatrice's eyes. "I'm so angry at him, I can barely think about him, even for a second."

"How could this—no, your father is the best man I know. He's the best man *any* of us know."

It was true. Everyone loved Mitchell. Honestly, it was probably why she'd fallen for Grant. Both men's friendliness was flavored with the same exuberant kindness, the attention to detail, the ability to listen wholeheartedly. Beatrice's stepmother had often begged him to just thank a checkout clerk once in a while instead of getting their life story and inviting them over for barbecue. *He exhausts me, Beatrice, he really does.* When Naya died of chronic obstructive pulmonary disorder two years before, it was the first time Beatrice ever saw her father unable to smile.

"Well, it turns out he's a pathological liar."

"There has to be something you don't understand. Maybe he *thought* she died? But no, not if you have a twin—Jesus. Maybe your mother survived the cancer and then stole your twin sister away from him, and he could never admit—no, that would be fucked, too. Holy shit. What's she *like*?"

Beatrice described Cordelia's knitting and Minna's cat shoes and Astrid's crimson lipstick, and all the while, her father's betrayal twisted, knifelike, somewhere in the region of her solar plexus.

"I wish I still smoked. This is a such a cigarette conversation, isn't it?" In the background, Beatrice heard Iris open what would be her seventh or eighth Coke Zero of the day. "Are you scared? Do you want to talk about it?"

Beatrix, you're going to die. Soon.

"I don't believe any of it."

"Except for the two miracles."

"I think they're more like coincidences."

"Mmm. What are you going to do next?"

The words came to her quickly. "Hide in my room until I leave."

"Sure. Okay, yes. And see your sister again? And your niece?"

Holy shit. "Or...I could leave early!"

"Aren't you there for just two nights?"

Somehow, impossibly, it was still only Friday. She had tomorrow and tomorrow night, and then on Sunday morning, she'd leave. She and Dad were courting one of their biggest client prospects ever on Monday morning, which was something she refused to think about now. "Yeah."

"So you see them tomorrow."

"Or I just sleep all day."

"Sleep in if you need to. Then see them."

"I really can't stand you sometimes."

"Irrelevant. Tell me more about how it felt to see your sister."

Beatrice did, and then, exhausted, she did her best to convince Iris that she was okay. Because she was. If okay meant still awake and breathing. And true, she wanted to keep breathing. The awake part, though...

So she got into bed a good two hours before she normally would. Her Kindle held nothing she wanted to read, so after flipping between the pages of four different books, she let it drop from her hand to the lavender-scented sheets.

The dark room filled with the violent sound of crashing waves.

Sleep felt impossible.

In one day, Beatrice had somehow lived through an accident that should have killed her. She'd found blood relatives she'd never known about. Someone had told her she was dying. And she'd learned that the man she had loved most had betrayed her, utterly. (Grant's betrayal could have felt like practice for this. But it didn't.)

In travel bag of daily vitamins was a blister pack of sleeping pills. They were Grant's, left in her bag from their last trip together. He rarely took them, and she never had, not before tonight. She cracked one of the blisters and popped a pill into her mouth, letting its bitter promise dissolve under her tongue.

If she hadn't caught Grant and Dulcina, they would have all come to the island together. Still in blessed ignorance and not wanting Grant to tease her mercilessly, she never would have talked to Winnie on the ferry. She'd have been so busy organizing the trip details, she wouldn't have gone to the general store at the exact right time to meet Minna. She wouldn't have met Cordelia. It was totally possible the men would have golfed while she and Dulcina found somewhere to get a massage, and then they all would have gone home on Sunday. She would have walked the short distance from her house to Dad's. He would have hugged her before making her a cup of tea and telling her about the latest financial scandal he'd picked up from watching *Bloomberg*.

The men in her life would have remained good men, and she would have remained unenlightened.

That would have been really nice.

The sleeping pill worked faster than she thought it would. One moment her heart was pounding with confused rage, and the next, she was being dragged gratefully under, to a sandy floor where the waves far above crashed so loudly she could barely hear herself cry.

CHAPTER NINE

If a spirit comes through that you're not expecting, don't be rude. They're not like the religious zealot knocking at your door. They're not trying to convert you. They just want a connection with a human. With you.

—Evie Oxby, NYT *Style section, "What Not to Do with Ghosts"*

The next morning, Beatrice hung up the Do Not Disturb sign and resolved not to open the door for anything but the coffee she ordered from room service. Thanks to her shopping spree at the market, she was set for bread and cheese and chocolate, and there was always delivery if ice cream became essential for survival.

At seven thirty, she heard a knock. When she opened the door, a coffee carafe was waiting for her on a tray. Good and strong and hot. She drank her first cup on the balcony and tried to concentrate on synchronizing her breaths with the waves rolling into the cove below. Eventually, she'd figure out how to build enough bravery to text Minna, to ask if she could perhaps see her and Cordelia again.

Or maybe she'd stay in the room all day and night. Maybe she'd leave tomorrow and work on building bravery at home. Nowadays, people built whole relationships online. That's what Zoom was for, right? She could do that with Cordelia and Minna from home. She could come back and visit them when she knew them better.

Except—Beatrice didn't have a home. Although technically her name was also on the deed now, Grant's house had always felt like his home, not like hers. Six years ago, when she'd moved in, she'd sold her condo and all her furniture because his house was already so perfect: heated slate floors, wine cellar, skylights and a greenhouse, furniture finer than she'd lived with before. He'd always said that at some point they'd sell and buy a new place that was their own from the bottom up, once both boys were done with college and settled somewhere, when they didn't need a bedroom to come home to when it was his turn to have them.

And she obviously couldn't stay any longer with Dad.

He'd sent a couple of texts already this morning. Loving ones. Is it the vanilla granola you like or the maple kind? Then, I got the Wordle in four but knowing you, you got it in three, am I right?

The tightness in her chest made her lungs ache, as if they were made of thin glass that was starting to crack.

Focus on the waves. Maybe if she got the breathing just right, the knot in her stomach would ease.

At 8:00 a.m. came another gentle knock.

It had to be important if someone was knocking even though the sign was on the door, right?

Beatrice cracked it to find a housekeeper holding up a pile of fluffy towels.

"Just checking to see if you need anything, ma'am."

"Oh." She shook her head. "No, thank you."

After the woman had left, Beatrice double-checked the sign. No, she hadn't accidentally hung up the *Service Please* side of the card. It still read, *Shhh. I'm Counting Sheep.*

At nine came another knock.

What the actual hell?

Maybe Beatrice didn't understand what counting sheep meant. Maybe up here it meant "come say hello to me" or something?

"Yes?" she called through the closed door, trying to keep the impatience out of her voice.

"More coffee, ma'am? Or a crumpet, fresh baked? Or your bed made up?"

"No! I mean, no, thank you!" What kind of hotel was this? Was there something wrong with wanting to be left alone?

At ten came another knock. Beatrice gave a short, tight scream she couldn't hold back. "Jesus! Go away and leave me *alone*!"

Silence was the only response.

She felt terrible for yelling, and at the same time, she was relieved to hear footsteps in the hall recede.

Fifteen minutes later, a text landed. I'm very sorry I knocked I just wanted to see if you wanted to hang out or something. Coffee cup emoji. One tear emoji. Minna

Ah, damn it, what an asshole move. Minna hadn't deserved that. Sorry. Not a good time tho.

She should send something else, explain herself.

But she couldn't.

If only it were tomorrow, so Beatrice could leave this room and this island.

Perched on the edge of the bed, she straightened her spine.

She'd leave today, no matter what. She *could* start a new life. And she *would.* New apartment. Maybe a new part of town. Closer to Iris, maybe? She didn't love Redondo Beach (who did?), but it would be a place to start over.

She tapped her phone, searching for a plane ticket, but no, apparently she'd missed the only ferry that could get her to the airport today in time for the only possible flight. That goddamned sleeping pill. If she hadn't taken it, she would have had these thoughts at three in the morning, and she'd be halfway home now.

Or halfway to somewhere.

Impossible. It was all impossible. Beatrice wanted to kick the walls, to howl into a pillow, to light something precious on fire just to watch the flame devour it.

What a fool she was. What an idiot. She'd always considered herself a strong feminist. She made her own money. She kept a separate bank account and maintained her own savings and retirement accounts. But apparently, trained from birth by a liar, she was also someone who'd believe anything a man told her.

Fine. Beatrice would make a plan, a good, solid, color-coded, spreadsheeted *plan* to come back to this island, after she sorted out her life. Then she and Cordelia could get to know each other like the adults they were. For now, she'd hide in this burrow like a scared, furious mole until it was time to catch the ferry out tomorrow.

At noon, there was another knock. In case it was Minna, Beatrice stayed silent.

The knocking got louder and more insistent. The housekeeper again? Needing desperately to fold a towel into a swan?

The tapping graduated to pounding.

"Holy crap, *what?*"

The voice was low. "It's Reno."

Okay, that one she hadn't seen coming. Beatrice rose and went to the door, but she didn't open it. "Having a pretty horrific day. Can this wait till later?"

"It's about your niece, and no, it can't."

My niece. A tiny glow of warmth rose in Beatrice's chest.

Reluctantly, she tugged open the door. "How did you get my room number?" Minna had known it, too. Wasn't that the kind of thing a hotel kept private?

"Small town." Reno strode in without hesitation. Against the deep olive of her skin, her gaze was icy, the swirl of blue tattoo ink that ran up the right side of her neck just as cold. "I don't care what you decide to do about your sister. That's up to you two. But you don't get to hurt Minna."

"*Hurt* her?"

"I'm warning you. You'll have to go through me first." Reno did look formidable. Her head was shaved on both sides, leaving a thatch of dark curls on top.

"Hang on. I did shout at her through the door, but—"

"If you can't accept her being trans, you can't be in her life. Period."

Beatrice gasped. "Oh, god, *no.* Did she think I didn't accept her?"

The frosted scowl grew deeper. "You run away the second her grandmother outs her, then you shout at her to go away. She's devastated."

"I swear to you, I'm currently furious at everyone *except* her and Cordelia. And you, I guess."

Reno blinked. "Oh."

"I'm not angry at Minna. Not in the slightest."

"Well." Reno rubbed the side of her neck where the swirling tattoos rose to twist behind her ear. "You better clear that up, then."

Beatrice nodded. “Should I text her again?”

Reno raised an eyebrow. “We’ll go to her.”

“Go outside? Now?”

Firmly, Reno said, “Now.”

Fair enough. “I’ll get my bag.”

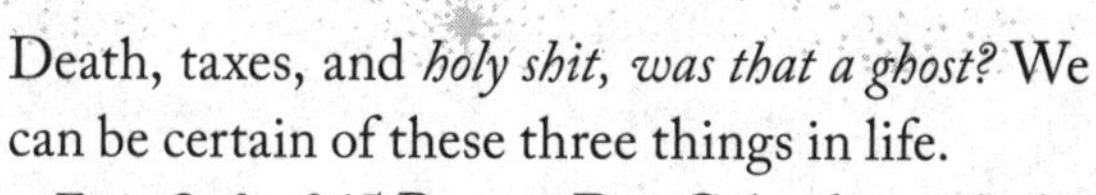

CHAPTER TEN

Death, taxes, and *holy shit, was that a ghost?* We can be certain of these three things in life.
—*Evie Oxby,* 365 Page-a-Day Calendar with the Palmist of Palm Springs

Beatrice followed Reno through the lobby, keeping her eyes on the back of her neck, where the dark hair had been shaved to a vee at the nape, where the blue lines of her tattoos slipped downward under the collar of her red plaid flannel.

The sun was up and shining, but unlike Los Angeles sun, which poured down and into every crevice, here the sun was muted. Subtle, as if it might slip behind a cloud at any moment, even though the pale blue sky held no clouds.

They left the main street, walking a block away from the water, then two. The houses were mostly Victorians, old and multistoried and grand. Scattered between them were a few more modern eyesores, and their steel-and-glass look clashed with the aged, graceful wood of the older homes. Enormous trees arched over the streets, allowing the shy sunlight to dapple through.

Reno's pace was quick, and Beatrice's heart rate matched it. She was going to Minna. She was going to her niece. Would Cordelia be there, too? God forbid, would she have to see Astrid?

Reno slowed, opening a white wooden gate.

Beatrice looked up. "Oh. Wow."

Set on a low rise, the enormous white house reminded her of the aunts' house in *Practical Magic*, with a wide, wraparound porch, peaked windows, and an actual turret. The paint may have been yellow at one point, but it had faded to a creamy shade of butter. "This isn't where Cordelia lives, is it?"

Reno only jerked her head. Was that a yes? A no? She led Beatrice down a path through an overgrown flower garden, stuffed to bursting with dahlias and coreopsis and zinnias and begonias and roses. Bees danced among the blooms, and robins hopped along the crushed shell pathway.

The tips of Beatrice's fingers tingled. "Is Cordelia here now?"

"Not sure. If she is, she's sleeping off last night."

That's right, the birth Cordelia had assisted with. "What about Astrid?"

"She's at the shop."

Whew.

Instead of heading up the porch steps, Reno wound around the house and through another gate, this one made of black iron. She led them into a gigantic backyard that held an overflowing vegetable garden, two long wooden tables, dozens of cheerfully painted mismatched chairs, three heavy umbrellas, and a fire pit. It looked as if a party was about to descend, and everything about it was welcoming. A small white motor home sat on the fence line.

Past the fence was a graveyard.

An old one, by the look of the overgrown weeds and the leaning stones. Dozens of them, placed haphazardly on the hill under the huge, dark trees. Despite the fence separating the yard from the grassy, tomb-filled area, it somehow all felt connected. Peaceful. Beautiful even.

Reno was still moving. At the bottom of the backyard, just on the edge of the graveyard, stood an outbuilding painted to match the bigger house, and just as faded. It had its own tiny gated garden, which bloomed just as riotously as the front one. This last gate Reno pushed through was under a jasmine arbor so heavy with blooms, the air itself felt sweet and thick. The shed-like building had a small porch with enough room for two small rocking chairs.

The door of the shed stood wide open, and inside, Minna was sunk into a battered orange couch, her eyes on her phone.

"Hey, kiddo." Reno's voice was gruff.

Minna scrambled up. "Oh!" Light scudded across her face and then her expression fell, along with her gaze.

Feeling a tug she refused to ignore, Beatrice beelined past Reno toward the girl. "I owe you a huge apology. I'm honestly not the biggest hugger in the world, but I'd like to hug you. Would that be okay?"

Minna hurled herself at her.

For a long ten or fifteen seconds, Beatrice held her niece, and for those seconds, her mind was blank of every single thing except the feeling of this girl in her arms, the fingers that dug into her back with a tiny, sweet pulse of pain.

Finally, Minna pulled back. "Hi."

"Hi back." Beatrice took a deep breath. "Minna, I'm so sorry that you thought I had any judgment about you. I *do* have a shitload of judgment, yes, but *none* of it is about you. You're nothing but lovely. I'm just currently furious at my father. And my husband."

"And at Gran?"

How could she have left Astrid off the list? "Oh, yeah. Her, too."

"Why your husband?"

Beatrice shrugged. “He let me down in a pretty big way.”

“But... you’re not mad about me?”

The look of yearning on Minna’s face came close to breaking Beatrice’s heart on the spot, and she shook her head so hard, her neck cracked. “*Never.* I feel so lucky that I met you, that I have a niece, that you just happened to be in the grocery store when I was there. I’m so happy about that.” She hadn’t even known it was true until she said the words out loud.

Her niece gave a soft sigh. “I’m glad.”

“Me, too.”

Minna sat back down on the couch and, with a shy smile, patted the spot next to her.

As she sank into it, Reno moved to a woodworking area, where a half-built kayak sat on a pair of sawhorses. She had already tugged on a pair of headphones and picked up a plane. Her arms moved precisely, patiently, sending long curls of wood to the floor. She kept her eyes on her work, but Beatrice could *feel* her paying attention to her and Minna. Reno wasn’t going anywhere, obviously. She still didn’t trust Beatrice, and Beatrice didn’t blame her in the slightest.

Next to the woodworking area was a small collection of tools she didn’t immediately recognize, all gathered onto a rolling multi-level tray, the side of which was covered with stickers of Disney princesses. Some boxes held needles, according to their labels, and a red sharps container sat on the top shelf. Cords trailed from several electric tools—maybe Reno was a tattoo artist? And also a fan of Moana, Elsa, and Merida? That part didn’t quite jibe somehow.

The couch Beatrice and Minna sat on was broken in and comfortable, and the blue blanket at its foot looked cuddly. There was a miniature kitchen with a small stove and a half-size fridge. The open door let in the town’s salty air along with dusty rays of sunlight, and the whole place just felt *snug.*

"Okay." She turned to face Minna and firmly pushed away any thought of her life outside this room. There was just this girl, this one right in front of her, the one with the perfect winged eyeliner (seriously, what brand was that?) and eyes that, even so piercingly blue, reminded Beatrice of her own boring, round brown eyes. How was that possible? She wanted to stare at Minna for hours. Days. She wanted to examine each finger, the curve of her ear, the crook of her elbow. She was perfect.

No, cut it out. Minna wasn't a baby, and Beatrice didn't want her brain to freak out even more than it already was. "I can't believe I get to talk to my *niece*. Can I ask you some questions?"

Minna smiled hugely and nodded.

"What's your favorite color?"

Her response was instant. "Green."

"Me, too!"

"You're *kidding*."

Warmth spread in Beatrice's chest. "I would never joke about something like that. What grade are you in? I mean, at the end of summer, what grade will you go into?"

"I'll be a junior."

"Do you like school?"

"I hate it with the fire of a million exploding stars."

"That's a lot of fire. Favorite subject."

Minna squinted at her. "Art."

"Oh! What kind of art?"

Her face remained cautious. "Um. I draw."

"I used to draw." About a million years ago. Dad had hated it so much that she'd eventually stopped. "What medium do you use?"

"Ink? Yeah, ink."

"Cool. I used pen and ink, too."

Minna folded her lips tightly, obviously trying not to say something.

"You can tell me anything," said Beatrice, meaning it.

"Eep! Okay. In school, I do pen and ink."

Interesting. "And... out of school?"

Minna looked across the room. "Reno?"

Minna's voice wasn't loud, but Reno tugged an earpiece out. Maybe the headphones were just for show. "Yeah?"

"Can you show her my art?"

One slow eyebrow lift. Then a nod.

Reno pulled up a low leather ottoman and straddled it, slipping off the red plaid she wore over her T-shirt.

Tattoos in a deep blue ink wrapped around her forearms and up her biceps, accentuating the hard musculature below them. The lines were intricately drawn—the overall impression was one of climbing vines, but when Beatrice leaned closer, she saw each leaf was actually a curved line drawing that held something else. A key in one, a star in another. Some lines looked like letters, as if words were climbing Reno's skin, but she couldn't read them.

"This is your art? You drew these for her to get tattooed?"

Minna's smile grew. "Um. Kinda?"

Reno flexed her forearm, and a tiny rabbit inside a letter *G* seemed to move. "Her. She did it."

Surprise jolted Beatrice into a laugh. "No. You're fifteen!"

Reno shrugged back on her shirt. "She knows what she's doing."

Beatrice got it. It was on her to prove that she meant Minna no harm. "Obviously, yes. I'm just amazed, that's all. It's incredible work. How long have you been doing it?"

Minna said, "Drawing? My whole life. Since I could hold a pen, probably. My dad was a tattoo artist, a famous one. Taurus Diaz? Maybe you've heard of him."

She hadn't, but she nodded encouragingly.

"I inherited his tools, but Mom won't let me ink anyone but Reno until I'm eighteen, not even myself."

"Especially yourself," said Reno.

They shared a smile, and Beatrice felt a sharp pang of longing. "What about your mom? Can you tattoo her?"

Minna laughed. "Oh, Mom would rather *die*. She didn't even let Taurus ink her—she'll never let me."

"You inherited his tools. So... he died?"

Another smaller nod.

"I'm very sorry."

"Yeah, well. Me, too." Minna examined a torn fingernail. "He fell off a ladder when I was little. I don't even remember him. This place was his favorite place of all. He called it his hideout, and now it's where I like to hide, too. Me and Reno."

"So, are you—"

Minna interrupted her. "Can I tattoo you?"

Beatrice started. "Oh! I don't know about that. Your mom..."

"She wouldn't care if it was what you wanted."

"I don't have any tattoos, either. Just like her." *Just like my twin.*

"How long are you going to be here? Can you stay awhile?" Minna's gaze was made of hope.

"I wish I could."

"Why can't you?"

Reno leaned against the countertop with folded arms. Her eyes were so dark they were almost black.

"I live in LA."

Minna said, "No one lives in LA. The best they do is survive."

"What?"

She giggled. "I watch *The Real Housewives of Beverly Hills.* You can't tell me those women are okay."

Beatrice snorted in appreciation. "Fair. But I do have a life there."

"You're mad at your husband, right?"

Lightly, she said, "It seems I might not have one of those for much longer."

"Oooh. Sorry about that." Minna paused. "But not *that* sorry. Wouldn't that make it easier for you to stay?"

"I have a job."

"What do you do?"

"I'm a CPA and tax preparer." She balanced books and gave tax advice for a living, working for her father's small accounting firm, as she had since she'd graduated college. Dad gave her a tiny raise every year—oh so proudly, with a grin and a hug—and Beatrice would rather jab an ice pick into her own shoulder than let her father know that he paid her less than the newest stock clerk got at Whole Foods (she'd heard them talking about it when she'd been buying fair-trade organic raspberries). She made a sixteenth of what Grant did. So, when she was done with her work, Beatrice was the one in the house who made sure Grant didn't run out of his favorite Timor coffee or the brand of hand soap he liked best. Once or twice a year, it annoyed her, and she told him she wasn't a fifties housewife and he should get his ass to the grocery store and pick up *her* favorite milk, which, to his credit, he always did, with a laugh, delivering her a milk product that was almost what she'd asked for. If *he* had to pay the power bill? The lights would go out first. They both knew it. He was fabulous at his job. And at having fun. She was better at doing literally everything else.

Minna fell backward into the couch. "Sounds *boring*."

"I love it." It might be boring but it was true. Beatrice adored the way the numbers fit into each other, except when they didn't, which was almost better in a way, because then she got to sink deeper in and untwist them.

"Can't you work remote? Everyone does now."

She could. But she knew her father wouldn't want her to, and it was still his business. She'd made most of the major decisions for the last few years, and she'd be the lead on their client pitch on Monday, but she was still, technically, his employee.

Though, honestly, fuck him. "Mmm."

"You could just stay for a while. In the rental unit!" Minna's expression blazed with hope. "You *said* you'd stay with us if you were staying longer."

"Is this the rental unit?" Something about this cozy space *was* attractive to her.

"Oh, no. That's in the house. Like I said, it's got its own entrance and everything and, like, really nice sheets. *This* is just Dad's hideout, but sometimes I sleep up there." She pointed at a loft. "You could buy a house here! If you have the money, that is. Do you?"

She had to admit, Minna's eagerness was adorable, if a little exhausting. "Not enough for a house, no." Would she and Grant sell their home? Would he want her to buy him out?

"What about a houseboat? Hector Vino is selling his—I heard him talking to Marion at the library about it yesterday. He says it doesn't leak at all, and it's really pretty, blue and yellow."

"A houseboat?" Not leaking at all didn't quite sound like the most exciting recommendation.

"It's called the *Forget-Me-Knot*. Wouldn't you love to live on a houseboat?"

Beatrice glanced at Reno, but she was proving to be no help at all. "I'll think about it."

Minna's head thunked backward onto the sofa's edge. "Well, shit."

Reno said, "Minna, leave it. She said she'll think about it."

"Yeah, but she's Mom's *clone*. What does Mom mean when she says she'll think about it?"

"She means no."

"Like, *no*, no."

How funny, that this girl could know Beatrice, sort of, because Beatrice's twin was her mother. Beatrice said, "So, that's kind of a cool superpower you have, huh?"

Minna looked startled, her gaze flying to Reno. "What?"

"Just that you know your mom so well, and apparently, we're a little bit alike, so that means you kind of know me."

"Oh. That. Yeah."

Reno and Minna blinked at each other.

"What did you think I meant?"

"Nothing! Nothing. Will you tell me more about you?"

Beatrice sighed. "I promise you, I'm very boring. You, on the other hand, are *not* boring. Oh! How did the birth go last night?"

Minna's brows drew together. "Huh?"

"Your mom. She's a midwife, right? That guy dragged her out right before I left. Was the baby okay?"

"Oh." Minna and Reno shared that look again. "No one was having a baby."

"Then..."

"She's a death doula."

Beatrice choked. "Pardon?"

"She helps people die. Sits with them and helps them."

What had the man said? *She—it's all happening so fast, this can't be normal.*

"Shit. Sorry." She had to stop swearing around Minna. Then, "I wouldn't have guessed that. Like hospice?"

"Um." Minna's gaze slid sideways. "Mom says that hospice provides medical care. A death doula is more like... spiritual care. Actually, that's how she and Reno got to be friends."

Frowning, Reno turned and headed toward the door. Without saying good-bye, she left, winding her way through the garden. As she reached the jasmine-covered arbor, she raised her hand to touch the vines, and then she was gone.

"Okay, she's... intense," said Beatrice, trying for neutrality. Maybe Reno had simply decided that Beatrice could be trusted around Minna?

"Don't worry—that's normal Reno behavior. She built that arbor and planted the jasmine for her wife who died."

Damn. "Oh, no. That's awful."

"She died on the same day my dad died, actually, just years later. Mom helped her go."

What was she supposed to say to that? "Ah."

"Mom helped a *lot*."

Something rippled under Minna's voice, but Beatrice didn't know what it was. "So, if she built the arbor and planted the jasmine, does Reno live here?"

"Kind of? She just really likes building things. Did you see the motor home in our yard, next to the cemetery? That's hers. She's like the—what would you call it? The guardian."

"The groundskeeper?"

Minna said carefully, "Yeah... that's it. She's not as weird as she seems, I promise. She's just gone through a lot, and she's not the best at small talk. That's okay, though, neither am I."

"Small talk is overrated."

"Exactly! Mom says we all have broken bits and Reno's damaged pieces just show more on the outside than others." She wriggled sideways on the sofa, and her tone turned fierce. "She's family, though. She'd do anything for me or for Mom. Gran and her can't stand each other, but Reno would take a bullet for her, too. Although she'd be hella irritated about it."

God, it all sounded so *pure*. "I'm glad you have each other."

Hugging herself, Minna said, "And now we have you. I know Mom's gonna be *so* jealous when she finds out that we've already talked so much. I think she's probably still sleeping in from her late night, but you want to go wake her up?"

"Oh." Beatrice stood. "No, I definitely don't want to do that. I should get back to the hotel, honestly. I have to—" What? What did she actually have to do? Nothing. Except to try to be brave in this situation she didn't understand at all. "Would you all like to have dinner with me tonight? You think your mom would be free then?"

"Yes and yes. She's always free," said Minna simply. "Unless someone dies."

CHAPTER ELEVEN

People ask me all the time if we reincarnate to be near the ones we've loved in a past life. I don't know, but I do know that there are people in this world I love beyond reason, people I'd be happy to learn I'll get to see on the next part of the ride.

—*Evie Oxby,* People *magazine*

Beatrice meandered back toward the hotel, feeling stronger in her bones than she had all day. Somehow, the conversation with Minna had shored something up in Beatrice, as if she'd gotten a good nap and a big sandwich instead of just time with her niece.

Her *niece*.

Would it be too incredibly weird if she already loved Minna?

She wouldn't—couldn't—admit it, of course, to anyone, but could this be a tiny sliver of what new mothers felt when they held their babies for the first time? This sudden *thump* of love, shoving her just like she'd been pushed yesterday (was it only yesterday?) in front of the café.

Midday sunshine fell onto her shoulders, and instead of turning toward the hotel when she passed the tree house and gazebo, she took a left and walked out past where the grass and trees ended, onto the rocky sand. She was on an island. She should do island things.

So she sat and stared at the water. Weren't you supposed to do nothing on a beach?

Grant had always said, *You always have to get up and do things. You never sit in place. Why don't you just relax?*

Why? Because someone had to make sure there was extra toilet paper in the downstairs bathroom—that was why. Someone had to make the list and then cross the things off the list.

But she could try to do nothing now. Far across the water, Seattle was visible through a haze. A light wind tousled the tops of the waves breaking gently on the shore.

Beatrice made it three minutes before calling Iris, who answered on the first ring. "I don't want to go home."

Iris gasped. "Then don't."

"Are you working out or something?"

"Hell, no." Another panted breath. "I would never. I just ran in from the car to get the ice cream into the fridge before it melted. It's like a million degrees in LA today. You don't want to be here."

"No, I have to go home. But then I'll have to deal with both Dad and Grant. But it's not like I have a choice, you know?"

"Or... you could stay there."

The light sparked off the water creeping higher on the sand. "I can't. This isn't some holiday fantasy where you look up house listings and pretend you'll stay forever."

"Bullshit. You can do whatever you want, and this *isn't* a holiday fantasy. You found a fucking family."

"Well, that's good, since I just lost one."

"You'll recover from Grant."

Was it possible she was already starting to? Beatrice found that when she poked at the raw, bloody part of her heart, it felt firmer than she would have expected. Coagulating already? Or was that just fresh new anger plumping it up? "I can't stay. I've got a huge pitch on Monday and, like, twelve clients this week."

"And you really feel like honoring your father's business reputation?"

Augh. No, she didn't. But even in the middle of multiple bewildering betrayals, she couldn't drop all the balls she was supposed to keep in the air. Keeping plates spinning was what she did for her clients, for Grant, and yeah, for herself, also. "It's my reputation, too."

"Damn it, Beatrice. What if you really *are* fucking dying?"

Beatrice shivered in the sunlight. "Not helpful. Besides, we're all dying. I could be hit by a falling airplane wing, et cetera."

Iris sighed. You know you can come here if you want to, right? Stay with us, and we'll get you so fucking lawyered up, you'll have to scrape bonus lawyers out of your ears with a Q-tip. Fuck Grant. I told you to stick with girls. Didn't I tell you that? We can still get you back in that house if that's what you want. He's the cheater—he should be the one to leave. Even though you went to your dad's house, it's only been a couple of weeks. We can still get you back in."

"I *hate* his house." She picked up a thin piece of driftwood. The stick was smooth and cool in her fingers. Comforting.

"I thought you loved it."

"I loved that it was close to you and work. I loved that Dad moved just down the street and that I could be there for Naya at the end. I loved that it was a four-minute walk to Trader Joe's.

But everything else? I've *always* hated living in that minimalist greige box." How had she not ever really admitted that to herself? Anger lit the backs of her eyelids red.

"Seriously?"

With the stick of driftwood, Beatrice leaned forward and drew a house in the sand. "I wish that house would burn to the ground."

She drew a flame leaping from above the roof. It felt so strangely *good* to be drawing something, even if it was just lines in the sand. "You know Dad never let me draw?"

"Huh?"

"I remembered it today when I was talking to Minna. I used to do this thing where I'd draw words. He caught me doing it once and knocked the pencil out of my hand."

"Okay, Mitchell is letting me down more and more, so fuck your dad, and second, what are you talking about?"

"I'm not sure I can explain it." Beatrice dragged the stick through the sand, the top loop of a *B* darting through the roof of the house. "I'd make the letters into lines that *felt* like the letters I wanted them to be, but no one else would have been able to read the word. Looked like spaghetti. Very, very pretty spaghetti." The *U* ducked down and into a window, the *R* came out the back. Then she curled the *N* under the porch.

"Huh. So, have you called your dad yet?"

"No."

Iris's voice sounded worried but she didn't push it. "When can we pick you up at the airport? Burbank, right? You want us to bring you a big ole burrito to eat in the car?"

Beatrice added a dashed line around the image, little sparks flying away from the house. "I can't remember when I land tomorrow. I'll have to look it up."

A wave bigger than its little friends flirted with her, coming closer than any of the others had. Beatrice stood, backing up as another one encroached on her drawing. The roof was taken first, and then the rest of the house.

Sudden heat flooded through her. Anger? Grief? Whatever it was, it felt like it was ripping her heart in half. "I just don't understand any of this. What *if* it's all true? What if I'll be dead soon, after five more miracles happen? What the hell have I been doing with my life? How am I supposed to figure all this out?"

"Sometimes we can't—"

She bent forward, stabbing the stick into the now-wet sand. "Don't you dare tell me that sometimes we can't figure it out. We can always learn more and increase our understanding. We figure it *out*."

Iris was silent.

"I can," said Beatrice. "You know I can."

"Understanding things is your superpower, yeah. But maybe you can't—"

An electrical pulse rippled through her chest. "What if I did stay?"

"*Now* you're talking."

"What if there's more to life than Excel spreadsheets and Sunday night sex and saving money for a retirement that might never come?"

"You're preaching to the choir, you know that, but I'll point out that you *love* saving money. It's like a sickness."

True. It felt like a game, one that she could win. At college, she'd started a savings club with three other CPA-minded friends. She'd thrown a *party* when she found a bank with an interest rate that was .25% higher than anywhere else. A literal party. Everyone wore golden crowns and whoever collected the most Monopoly money hidden around the house won. And it had never been about having a lot—she'd never needed to be "rich." It was why she'd never completely pooled her money with Grant's bigger accounts. She'd just wanted to be safe, no matter what.

Safe.

What the hell did that even look like? What did it feel like?

Maybe being safe was overrated.

She clutched her phone so hard, she heard it take a screenshot. "Screw taking a couple more days here. I could just *stay* stay. I could change everything, right now, in this minute. I could change my life."

"Um—"

"Are you happy?"

Iris's voice was a squeak. "Me?"

"Yes, *you*."

There was a pause the length of time it took for two gentle waves to roll in and complete the destruction of Beatrice's drawing.

Then Iris said, "I am. I love Jess. I love our messy house and the fact that I'm the only person in LA who can't grow a tomato, and I'm happy to get old with her, and I love complaining about traffic to her. Saturday nights with her on the couch that cost way too much but fits us perfectly—it's heaven."

When was the last time she had *wanted* to spend an evening on the couch with Grant? They were always going somewhere, doing something, always looking outward. When had they last held hands just because their bodies were close enough to do so?

Idiot asshole dickwad Grant.

Grant, the cheat.

Grant, the man she'd thought was the perfect fit for her well-planned life.

Stop. There were things more important than him; that was for sure. When was the last time Beatrice did something just because *she* wanted to? Her calendar was so time-blocked that no light could filter through.

"I'm not happy," Beatrice said with a thump of shock. "I'm not happy? I had no *idea*. Did you know?"

Iris snorted. "Do you even remember why we broke up?"

"Of course I do!"

"You don't."

"Okay, I don't."

"You weren't happy. You said you were fine, but you only wanted to be either at work, all curled up inside your columns of numbers, or at night, reading about how tax legislation was changing. When I called you on it, you *said* you were happy, but you were full of crap. I thought I could help, and you pushed me away. You spent all your time trying to fix problems that didn't need fixing. So I left. And to be honest, you didn't seem to mind."

Beatrice wished she could protest. When Iris had moved out of her condo, she'd been glad that she wouldn't make Iris sad anymore by being so boring. "But I wasn't actually unhappy. I wasn't depressed."

"Are you sure?"

She scooted backward as a wave ran at her. "Is happiness something people actually go out and try to get?"

"Christ on a Popsicle stick, you try to prove to everyone that you know everything, but you don't know that much, do you?"

The accusation hurt. She hated being called a know-it-all, but sometimes (often) she did, in fact, know more than others. "Come on."

"With all that knowledge you've got, I sometimes can't believe you're a human being. Said with love. Yes, dummy. Everyone goes out and tries to catch happiness with their butterfly net."

Beatrice swallowed her pride. "How do *you* catch it?"

"Huh!" Iris sounded surprised. "Sounds dumb, but meditation helps me, I guess. Acceptance. Also, in obvious news, I like to have fun. You should try it sometime. Make one of your spreadsheet lists. I would suggest this to no one but a freak like you. Make a Fun List."

Beatrice breathed for a moment, listening as Iris popped open another Coke Zero on the other end of the phone.

She thought.

The list formed in her mind, finally. "I've got it. The list."

"Speedy. Tell me."

She closed her eyes and read it to Iris as it unscrolled behind her eyelids. "First, I'll stay for a while." She'd check out of the Skerry Cove Lodge with its overly aggressive housekeepers and check into the second-best hotel in town. She'd leave the reservation open-ended. "Second, I'll do what I want to do, when I want to do it. Third, I'll spend money on things that delight me. Fourth, I'll try to figure out what a miracle is, and if it exists. If it does, it should be provable, right?" Maybe trying to prove a miracle wouldn't sound like fun to anyone else, but Beatrice felt her blood sizzle at the idea.

"Okay! Now *that's* a list! One through three, anyway. Good luck with that last one, you freaking monster."

The sound of Iris's cat quietly yakking came over the line. "Taylor Swift again?"

"Yep. She's three-quarters hairball."

"Are you less worried about me now?"

"Hell no. You just said that you want to spend money frivolously, so I'm worried you actually *are* dying. Should I call you an ambulance?"

CHAPTER TWELVE

Spirit loves a curious cat.

—*Evie Oxby,* Cat Fancy

If Beatrice didn't know better, she'd think Astrid—she couldn't think of her as her mother—was trying to get her drunk.

"More wine?" Astrid asked sweetly for the third time.

Again, Beatrice covered her glass with her hand. "I'm really okay."

"Mom," hissed Cordelia. "No means no."

Minna took another piece of chicken off the platter. "What we're looking for is enthusiastic consent, Grandma."

Astrid snapped, "I don't know what that means. Everyone's so careful with their drinking now, but I always say if you're not an alcoholic by forty, you'll never be one!" She raised her eyebrows at Beatrice. "I can't remember if your father had addiction in his family?"

In a tired voice, Cordelia said, "Please leave her alone."

Beatrice had no intention of answering the question. Astrid's sour attitude was okay, though. Kind of funny, honestly. Maybe she felt that way because she was sitting in her sister's house.

To be precise, she was sitting in her sister's *gigantic* house. The inside matched its gorgeous outside, with huge rooms lined in dark wooden bookshelves. The air smelled of rosemary and garlic from the chicken, and underneath, dust and candle wax. Every spare surface held something interesting: a yellow vase painted with a red hummingbird, a saucer that contained three bone-white rocks, a rusty harmonica, two corgi figurines so small they could both sit in a child's hand.

In front of her sat an unexpected home-cooked meal. When she'd texted earlier to confirm where she would take them for dinner, Cordelia had texted back, I've already got a chicken brining, and I got the prettiest sweet potatoes at the farmer's market. We both had a strange birthday yesterday—let's celebrate being forty-five tonight!

So now, Beatrice sat at a rustic farmhouse table marred with the nicks of everyday life, surrounded by her very own family.

Cordelia was obviously used to entertaining, comfortably throwing the roasted vegetables into an orange bowl and sliding the platter of carved chicken, still steaming, onto the table. Candles, dozens of them, scattered dancing shadows around the room as the sun set outside.

But a thin tension hung above the candlelight, perfectly invisible but still noticeable. Did they, too, feel the strangeness, the *bigness* of this? Beatrice peered at her sister and her niece through it, and they peered back, and *that* was why she didn't want any more wine. One glass was enough—she needed to keep her mind focused.

So far, Minna had carried much of the conversation, affirming the unspoken agreement the adults had made to let her do it. First, she tried to insist that Beatrice stay in the room for rent, but Beatrice rejected this in no uncertain terms. She'd booked into a three-star bed-and-breakfast and dropped her bag on the way to Cordelia's, glad to be in a completely neutral place. Minna eventually let the idea drop, and then she chattered about a Cooper's hawk she'd seen in the woods on her way home from the library, where apparently she volunteered in the summer. She shared opinions about two kids who had been caught smoking weed in the library bathroom—one of the boys' mothers was a librarian and she'd been livid. Minna hoped neither of the boys would be in her homeroom in August because they were idiots. "They think that trans kids don't really exist. Also that manga is a foodstuff."

Beatrice's stomach tightened, but Cordelia said easily, "They don't sound smart enough to read manga. You okay, poppet?"

Minna nodded, her face relaxed. "Totally. Haters just help me know who to avoid at lunch."

Was being different that easy for her? It couldn't be. Could it?

Minna shifted into peppering Beatrice with questions, but they were easy ones that she could answer without taking her attention from the way Cordelia's face moved and how the lines around Astrid's eyes creased deeper as she laughed with Minna. *I have a Mini Cooper*, Beatrice said. *Red. Yes, it's a convertible. No, I don't cook much. My favorite ice cream flavor is peanut butter chocolate.*

Beatrice tried to ignore the emotions that kept sneaking into her heart. Yes, she was deeply angry with Astrid in ways she knew she probably couldn't even understand yet. But that was something for another day. Tonight was for fact-finding. Anger would only get in the way. She wanted to study each one of these people, making mental notes of each quirk and tic so she could look at them later under the microscope of memory.

Should she tell them about Winnie's prediction? About what Evie said?

No. She didn't believe it herself—why worry them with something so ridiculous?

Minna said, "Why don't you have any children?"

Whoo. When she married Grant, she was so hopeful that his boys would love her, that they'd make one big happy family. After Josh and Lucas moved to live with their mother, she talked Grant into trying for a baby, not an easy sell. She had a miscarriage at fifteen weeks. What a lightweight phrase for something that had sent her to bed for a month.

Grant hadn't wanted to try again. She'd been fine with that.

Okay, mostly fine.

She laced her fingers in her lap. "Never got around to it."

"Do you still want to have one? How old are you?" Minna laughed. "Oh, ha. You're forty-five, duh." She raised her fork high, not seeming to notice the piece of sweet potato that bounced off it and onto the wooden tabletop.

"When's *your* birthday?"

Minna didn't fall for it. "Forty-five is old, but not *too* old. Halle Berry had Maceo when she was forty-seven, and she swears it was a surprise."

Cordelia gaped at her. "How do you even know that?"

"Googling to see if you were too old to give me a sister."

Pressing her hand to her chest, Cordelia said, "Oh, trust me. I am way, way, *way* too old for that."

Minna pointed her fork at Beatrice. "So, any plans on that front? I would accept a cousin."

"No plans. No desire." Beatrice's phone buzzed in her pocket, but she ignored it. "If it helps, I'm pretty stoked I just inherited a niece."

She grinned. "What about pets?"

"None at the moment. But I did used to have a three-legged cat with seven toes on each paw."

"Whaaaat?" The way Minna's face scrunched up in confused delight set off fireworks in Beatrice's chest.

Her phone buzzed again, and then once more. "I'm sorry, I don't usually look at my phone at the table."

Cordelia pulled her knitting out of the pocket of her apron and made a go-on motion with her hand as Astrid *tsssk*ed.

Grant: there was a fire -

Beatrice's heart froze solid in her chest.

everything's okay, Josh put the air fryer too close to a pizza box and forgot about it but your dad was going by on a walk and saw the smoke coming from the window and went in

She couldn't stab the screen fast enough. Is he okay?

I'm on my way home now, Josh says it went out on its own but he used the fire ext so I'm sure it's a huge mess. Yr dad doesn't need to come in anymore, can u pls tell him to give me the key back

The image of the house she'd drawn in the sand rose in her mind. The flames around it.

A warring text came in from her father. Grant's idiot son almost burned your old house down. We have to get your important paperwork out of there. I can get it all for you, just tell me where it is. I still have the key.

Carefully, Beatrice swiped away her father's text.

Then she typed back to Grant, Tell him yourself.

"Is everything okay?" Cordelia's fingers twitched as she added more stitches to whatever it was she was knitting.

Beatrice tapped the Do Not Disturb button and slipped her phone back into her pocket. "Small fire. Dad, um, helped, and it's apparently all okay."

"Losing the plot, is he?" said Astrid with satisfaction. "Unsurprising."

Screw that—no matter how angry she was, this woman didn't

get to criticize him. Only Beatrice had earned that particular right. "He's the smartest person I know."

Astrid narrowed her eyes and stared at her. "We all knit. Do you?" She made the abrupt change in subject sound like an accusation.

"No."

"I'll teach you."

Beatrice had always wanted to learn, but she'd rather learn from a YouTube video in a language she didn't understand than learn from this woman, who had broken her heart by dying and, then again, by being alive.

Cordelia placed her knitting on the table and stood. "Beatrice, would you mind helping me in the kitchen?"

Minna leaped up. "I'll help, too! I've *got* to hear about the three-legged cat."

Touching her daughter's face, Cordelia said, "Thanks, lovey, but you pulled back the curtain on my crafty ruse. I'm just trying to get her alone for a minute."

Minna sighed, but sat.

In the kitchen, Cordelia held up a bottle of mineral water. "Yeah?"

"Please." The kitchen was as welcoming as the rest of the house. Colorful bowls and well-used-looking kitchen tools covered the long counters. The walls were blue and purple, and violet gingham curtains hung at the large window that looked out into the garden, now lit with white twinkle lights. A honey jar and three boxes of tea sat next to the blue-and-white crockery, stacked in friendly piles on a mosaic-tiled island, and a slab of yellow butter rested on a matching plate.

Cordelia poured the sparkling water into a green glass. "Mom can be a bit much. I'm sorry."

"It's okay."

"So can Minna, obviously."

"She's perfect."

Cordelia's expression softened. "She is." She handed the glass to Beatrice, and then leaned against the island. Her hair swung forward to hide her face, her white stripe bright under the rustic wagon wheel chandelier.

Beatrice waited.

Cordelia's shoulders rose once, and then again, before she raised her face. "Do you remember the mirror?"

"The mirror?" Beatrice could have sworn that as the words left her mouth, she had no idea what her sister meant, but by the time they hit the air, she did. When she'd been very small, all the mirrors in her father's house were boring, everyday mirrors, showing her the plain old Beatrice she saw every night as she brushed her teeth in front of the toothpaste-spattered glass.

That mirror, though, the one hidden at the back of the closet—that one was special. It had been round and chipped at the edges like a mouse had been nibbling at it in the dark. The closet light overhead had been just right, dim and yellow, so that when she'd crawled in to sit in front of the mirror and talk to herself, she could imagine that the little girl she saw was someone else. A real friend, someone who laughed when Beatrice laughed and seemed to love Beatrice's stuffed elephant as much as she had.

Her little friend that no one else could see, the one she'd chatted to in the mirror so long ago. "Oh, my god."

"You do remember the mirror."

"That wasn't real."

Cordelia just raised an eyebrow.

Beatrice reached out to lean on the counter. "Holy... shit."

"Yeah."

"It was round, and kind of worn, like the glass itself was rusted somehow. And you—"

Cordelia nodded. "I was there. You were, too, on the other side."

"No." The girl Beatrice had babbled to in the mirror hadn't been real. It had been a reflection. A small face, just like hers.

But the lips had moved with words Beatrice herself hadn't said, and if she leaned as close as she could, she could hear the girl speak. *Can I see Mrs. Lumpy?* Beatrice would hold up her old stuffed elephant and the girl in the mirror would laugh, then *she* would laugh, and it didn't matter that they never said much of anything. It was enough to be able to see her. "No."

Cordelia's gaze was soft. "The elephant. Do you still have it?"

"This isn't possible."

"Miss Lumps. Ms. Plumpy?"

Something crashed inside her lungs. "Mrs. Lumpy."

"That's it." Cordelia's face fell. "What happened? Where did you go?"

"Daddy broke the mirror."

Astrid's voice came from the doorway. "That idiot. That is *exactly* why I took Cordelia and ran. Breaking my best scrying mirror. Never could take a spot of magic, that man."

CHAPTER THIRTEEN

It's not hard to believe. Just shut off everything you've ever learned about logic. And by that I mean, hell, yes, if you struggle to believe, you're *normal*. You're human.

—*Evie Oxby, guest appearance on* Queer Eye

Beatrice gave a laugh that felt more like a wheeze. "There's no such thing as magic." Enchanted mirrors existed only in movies. The only magic wand she'd ever held was her vibrator.

Somehow, she was shepherded back to the dining table. Astrid poured her another glass of wine in a fresh glass. "Just in case. You never know around here."

Cordelia slid a slice of apple pie in front of her. "Eliza down at the bakery is a genius. Should I get some candles for us to blow out?"

"No, no, that's fine."

Minna joggled up and down in her chair as her arms first punched the air and then wrapped around her waist. Her face glowed. "If Gran can mention magic, we can, too, right? Mom!"

"Be patient, honey. This is a lot for Aunt Beatrice."

"Beatrix," muttered Astrid.

Cordelia held back the plate of pie she'd been about to slide in front of Astrid. "Mom, you agreed you'd play fair."

Astrid said, "I *am* playing fair. I'm just using her real name."

"Playing fair?" The frustration burst out of Beatrice before she could think what she'd say next. But the words were all there, lined up and ready to go. "How is any of this fair? What did you mean, that you took Cordelia and *ran*? Does that mean my father doesn't know about any of this?" A wild hope rolled through her. Was it possible he was as clueless as she was? Had he, perhaps, been searching for his lost family for decades?

"Oh, he knows," said Astrid darkly. "And he was glad."

"Explain." Her father wouldn't have just thrown away a *child*.

Astrid's fingers fluttered on the stem of her wineglass. "There was an accident—I didn't lie about that. He was driving. The car crashed."

"More." Beatrice pulled out her accounting *I just caught you embezzling funds so don't even try* voice. "Right now."

"Hoo boy." Astrid's gaze flicked upward. "Okay. It was dark and icy. He took a turn too fast, and we hit the guardrail of the bridge, but it didn't hold. We went over."

"Whoa." Minna's eyes were huge.

"The impact of hitting the water should have killed us all, but it didn't. The car slid under, and I couldn't get my seat belt off. Mitchell hit his head on the wheel, so there was blood everywhere."

Her eyes focused on her knitting, Cordelia said evenly, "This is where you always said that he and Beatrice died. Can't wait to hear this new version."

"You weren't ready to hear it."

"You mean you weren't ready to tell it."

"*Anyway*, even with the blood, he managed to get into the back seat and pry both of you out of your car seats. Both of you were laughing." Astrid's face twisted into a smile. "Like it was the funniest thing that had ever happened to you. I still couldn't get my seat belt off. He yelled at me to break a window, to let the water fill the car. Then the pressure of the water would let him open a door, and he'd swim you both up. Then he'd come back for me. I knew he wouldn't, of course—I wouldn't have, either. He'd have been too busy taking care of you both, making sure you were breathing. There wouldn't have been enough time for him to come back for me."

Beatrice wanted to protest, but there was no air in her lungs.

"So I reached for your hands, and I got them. In my right hand, I held one little Cordelia fist and one little Beatrice fist. With my left hand, I made a sign. I don't know what happened next. I promise you that's true. All I know is that one minute we were inside the car, and then next all four of us were on the shore, all of us dripping. You were both bawling by then, and I think Mitchell and I were, too."

None of this made sense. "I don't get it."

Astrid shrugged. "I'd honestly never seen anything like it, and I've seen a lot. I just took it for what it was, but it scared the living shit out of your dad. He'd put up with how you blew feathers out of your pillows and into the air, and with what you did with the mobile above your bed—"

Minna leaned forward. "I don't know that one. What did they do?"

Astrid beamed, as if she was reporting that they'd learned to read at two. "Oh, it was glorious. It was the moon and stars and sun, and they could make the whole room go into sunrise and then sunset, and once, I swear to god, there was a meteor shower under that thing. He hated it, threw it out. The two of you, together—you've always had it. But the way you got us all out of the car... he couldn't handle it. He blamed me for it."

But what the hell was *it*? A thousand questions filled her mind, so Beatrice grabbed the most important one. "Fine, so no one knows how we got to shore. Why did you leave with Cordelia?"

Her gaze slid sideways. "Shortly after that, not even a day later, she *took* the Knock from me. Grabbed it, really. She literally activated herself. After that, I had to leave to protect her. Cordelia was the strongest."

What did that *mean*? Had her mother decided Beatrice was bad at magic, of all things, and snatched the better kid? Awesome. But she needed to understand something else first. "How could Dad allow you to take her, though?" Her father had always been so obvious with his love, so generous with it. Nothing could convince Beatrice that he wouldn't have felt the same about her sister. Cordelia, she noticed, kept her eyes on her knitting, her mouth a thin line.

Astrid raised her shoulders and let them drop. "I'm not a monster. I didn't want to take both his babies from him. I thought I was doing the right thing, and I think he was just grateful I didn't take both of you. He knew I could have. I know you won't believe this, but it broke my heart to lose you, Beatrix."

Cry me a goddamn river. She was right—Beatrice didn't believe it. "And you never looked for me."

Astrid took a large bite of the pie. Around the mouthful, she said, "I didn't have that right. I was the one who'd left you. I figured you'd find me if you wanted to know me."

A mother who knew her own daughter was out there, motherless? Did that give her not only the right, but the responsibility, too? "But he didn't tell me anything."

"Seems to have worked out." Astrid gave a too-sweet smile,

revealing a piece of peel stuck in her teeth. "I knew it would. You found us."

Minna said, "*I* found her, actually."

That was true. That was important.

"You did, kiddo." Cordelia reached over and squeezed Beatrice's hand. "And then you brought her to me. Yesterday was one of the happiest days of my life."

Minna said, "The number *one* happiest day of her life was the day I was born. Dad's, too." A shadow crossed her face. "Mom always says..."

Cordelia smiled. "I always say he wanted nothing but you."

"But—"

"But nothing!" Cordelia's voice was too high, too light. "Beatrice, what do you think of the pie?"

The pie could have been stuffed with cotton balls and topped with shaving cream for all Beatrice had noticed. So far, she'd managed only one bite. Pushing the plate away, she took a breath, then she crossed her arms. She stared at Astrid. "You said you made a sign. In the car. What did you mean by that?"

"I drew a sigil in the air."

"And that is?"

Astrid sighed. "Your lack of knowledge is truly pathetic."

Anger lodged at the top of Beatrice's throat. "Thanks so much for that."

Minna looked at her grandmother. "Can I answer this?"

"Well. You can *try*."

The girl tugged her chair closer to the table, as if trying to get nearer to Beatrice from the other side. "You know Reno's tattoos?"

Beatrice nodded.

"You said they looked like words, but you couldn't read them."

Beatrice drew back sharply. "I didn't say that." She'd thought it. But she hadn't said it. It would have sounded too bizarre. "All I said was that I used to draw things like that."

Minna's eyes widened. "Oh, yeah. That's right. That's what you said. Anyway, do you ever do that nowadays? Do you still draw?"

"No." *The house on the beach, drawn in sand. The flames.*

"Why did you stop?"

Dad's face, furious in the lamplight of her bedroom. "My father said that artists were con artists and liars who made things up that didn't exist in order to exploit the generosity of suckers." It had been so startling coming from his gentle mouth that she stopped drawing immediately.

Liars. That was rich, coming from him.

"That's too bad," said Minna. "Sigils are cool."

Beatrice's heart flipped frantically. "But I still don't know what they *are*."

Astrid got up to rummage in a sideboard. "We'll show you."

"Mom—" Cordelia held out her hand. "We might want to wait?"

But Astrid ignored her and handed a small pad of paper and a pen to Minna.

"Thanks, Gran. Okay, I'm going to make a sigil right now, okay? It's just a little bit of magic, that's all."

"Magic doesn't exist." Beatrice didn't know how much she knew anymore, but that, at least, was easy. She lived in the real world, where numbers didn't lie. Only people did.

Minna nodded easily, apparently undisturbed by Beatrice's lack of belief. She moved the pen in a small circle on the page before closing her eyes.

The candle in front of Beatrice flickered.

Slowly and smoothly, the line Minna drew played out across the paper. One line and two loops, another loop, and then one that reversed back on itself. She looked like she was in no rush making what seemed like a doodle. A very pretty doodle, yes. But that's all it was.

"Oh, that's lovely," said Astrid.

Minna held up the paper. "So here it is. Just a drawing. Then I charge it with power." She glanced at Cordelia. "Can I? This once?"

"Fine." Cordelia nodded. "But use the can for safety."

Mystified, Beatrice watched as Minna rose and took a metal can from behind the door to the kitchen, and then placed it on top of the table.

She held the paper over a candle's flame. The page caught, the drawn symbol turning black and disappearing. Minna dropped what was left of the paper into the can.

The moment should have been mildly exciting. Perhaps amusing. Definitely strange and confusing.

But instead, Beatrice felt something.

A warmth spread inside her chest, a pool of something liquid and sweet. It felt *good*, like when you stood in a sunbeam on a chilly morning, or like pulling up the covers after a long, hard day. It came out of nowhere, and she knew it came from a place outside herself. *She* wasn't making herself feel like this, which should have been worrisome, but it wasn't. It was, instead, deeply comforting. Like being hugged but from the inside.

She pressed her hand to her chest. "What—Minna, what did you *do*?"

CHAPTER FOURTEEN

Honestly, I love that you asked me to comment on this, but I have to take issue with your terminology. Social-media terms like "witchling" and "baby witch" are at best, infantilizing, and at worst, gatekeeping. Don't other our new siblings. They're simply witches who are learning, and aren't we all? Call them a novice, or a novitiate, if you're feeling fancy. And remember: a novice's first spell is special. It might be wonky and misaligned, and lights that weren't meant to blink might flicker, but no matter what, it's always a lovely moment. Celebrate it.

—*Evie Oxby, "Advice for Baby Witches,"* Slate

Clapping, Minna laughed. "You felt it!"

An icy finger of fear traced the edges of the warmth. "No. Wait. Felt what?"

"I wrote your name, only it didn't look like that, I know. But each line and loop was a letter in your name, and then I added a word on top of that."

"What word?" The answer felt unbearably important.

"Don't laugh, okay? Love."

"Huh." The puffed syllable was inadequate—it couldn't hold both the melted warmth and the chilled fear coursing through her veins. *Love.*

As if she was overwhelmed, too, Minna said quickly, "And *that's* what a sigil does. Some people draw images, others do letters, but the point is the intention you put into them, followed by the energy you charge them with. For this one, I used the energy of fire to give it the boost it needed to work."

"How did you spell my name? Beatrice? Or with the *X*?"

"Beatrice, of course. No *X*." Minna looked at her carefully. "I would only ever call you what you want to be called."

The leg of Astrid's chair squeaked.

Minna continued, "A sigil is what you create it to be. There are sigils on the doorjambs, see? We put them in all the rooms."

Beatrice had noticed them, actually, delicate decorative symbols painted over the doors and next to windows. *What an artistic family*, she'd thought.

Once she was out of here, she'd lie very still for a long time, preferably with a cold compress over her eyes. A little spa music, perhaps. Some chocolate. And this would feel like the night she had the flu, took too much Nyquil, watched too many episodes of *Sabrina*, and ended up convinced that if she tried hard enough, she could snap her fingers and travel back in time to meet the dead mother she didn't remember.

The one who was in front of her now, quite alive.

True: everyone, at some point, wanted magic to be real.

Also true: everyone knew it wasn't.

But if Beatrice didn't say it now, she might not be able to say it later. "I think I drew one of—those—at the beach today. The house, where I live—I drew it in flames in the sand. I wanted it to burn to the ground. Then I got that text from Grant, and..." She held her breath for one tight second. "Did I *do* that?"

"No!" Cordelia set her knitting down so hard, her wine-glass sloshed red onto the tabletop. "You didn't. That was just a coincidence."

"Hmph! A pretty big one, if you ask me," said Astrid.

"You were too far away. And you didn't charge it with power."

The candle's flame had eaten Minna's sigil. "A wave washed it away."

Minna nodded. "That would work, right, Gran?"

Astrid narrowed her eyes at Beatrice. "The house didn't burn down, though, right? So you started it but didn't follow through because you don't—"

"Magic doesn't *exist*."

Cordelia and Minna's faces stayed open. Accepting.

Astrid, though, said, "Jesus, woman, what do you need? More proof?"

"Yes. Hell, yeah." That *was* exactly what she needed. "Prove it to me."

Her mother tossed her head. "You're not activated. There's no way to prove anything to you."

Beatrice opened her arms wide to the side. "So activate me."

Minna bounced up out of her chair and then back into it. "You want the Knock? Mom, she wants the Knock!"

Cordelia shoved her hair behind her right ear in the impatient way that Beatrice could feel she herself had just done. "Beatrice, you don't have to do anything right now. There's a lot to talk about."

Astrid glared. "This is her *heritage*. Hollands choose to activate."

Stubbornness warred with the recklessness running through Beatrice's bones. "Don't forget I'm not a Holland."

"You are. Hollands never give up their names. They never change them."

Minna said stubbornly, "Unless they want to, Gran."

"They don't want to," said Astrid. "Ever."

Beatrice said, "You sure have a lot of rules, don't you?"

Leaning forward, Astrid jabbed at the tablecloth. "Other people live by rules. We *make* them."

"I mean it. Give me that Knock, or whatever it is."

Cordelia's expression was tight. "You should understand what it is you're getting into—"

"Did you know?"

"Of course not. I was a baby."

"Think of this as my first instance of sibling rivalry, then. I want it, too." It wouldn't do anything, and she'd tell them that. It would be her own kind of proof. She'd show them she was immune to new age psychobabble.

"It's magic, Beatrice. Are you sure?"

Wow, they really took this nonsense seriously, didn't they? Astrid looked smug, Cordelia's face was tense, and Minna was practically vibrating with excitement.

But that still didn't make it real. "I don't believe in magic. So whatever you do, it can't hurt me."

"Mom," said Minna. "Can I give it to her?"

Cordelia's grip on her knitting was so tight, her knuckles were white. "It has to come from love."

Minna twisted in her seat to face Beatrice. "Obviously. That's easy."

Whatever they were talking about—it didn't matter. Minna had just said again—or at least implied—she loved her, and now Beatrice's insides had melted into hot chocolate, or something even sweeter.

"I'm ready," Beatrice said.

"Oh, my *god*, yay. It won't hurt, don't worry."

Cordelia said, "Remember, we talked about the speed of the flow…"

"I know, I know. Can I have your arm?"

Beatrice wanted to make a joke, to ask if the Knock was actually a tattoo she'd just signed herself up for, but something told her to hold her tongue. She leaned toward Minna, who placed one hand on the skin of her upper arm and the other on her lower arm, her fingers soft and cool.

"Close your eyes. Don't worry, I will, too."

Beatrice closed her eyes. Her breath quickened.

Minna's hands tightened and then squeezed suddenly, hard. It hurt but Beatrice didn't pull away.

She waited for whatever this "magic" was.

But Minna just let go.

When she opened her eyes, Minna and Cordelia were smiling at each other.

"Was that right, Mama?"

"Did it feel right?"

Minna nodded. Then, conspiratorially, she said to Beatrice, "That was my first time giving the Knock. I hope you don't mind that I didn't tell you that first. I didn't want you to worry."

"Of course," said Beatrice. She felt a strange, small twist of disappointment. Nothing had happened. Naturally. "Thank you?" No, not a question. She corrected herself. "Thank you."

Astrid, who'd been almost too quiet, reached for the pad of paper and pen, thrusting them at her. "Draw something."

Beatrice stared at her. "Excuse me?"

"Pick a word. Draw it, don't write it. Draw it. Let your hand show you the shape it wants to be."

It would have been so nice if she could say she didn't understand. *Nothing you say is making sense.* But she did understand, which felt... complicated.

Cordelia put a hand on the page. "You can move at your own pace. Or not at all. There's absolutely nothing you have to do."

Astrid pursed her lips. "Well, she has to stop being a little idiot like her father."

"I swear to god, Mother, I'll make you sleep in the chicken coop if you don't chill the fuck out."

"Sorry! I'm sorry. Bea*trice*, will you please draw a word, any word? Indulge me."

Beatrice picked up the pen. But—what word? For a moment, all words deserted her. Should she even do this?

A word. A word! Any goddamn word.

If magic was real (which it wasn't), Astrid would certainly be riding a broomstick. Maybe Cordelia would be able to fly, too, but Beatrice pictured her gliding through the air smoothly, not hurtling clumsily through the sky like the Wicked Witch of the West.

Flight. Wasn't that, after all, what Beatrice had wanted most as a child? The ability to lift off the ground, rising upward into the sky? She used to have such vivid dreams about it—she'd wake completely sure she knew the secret. The trick was to *want* it enough. She'd go out to stand on the stump in the backyard, and she'd arrange herself into the magical shape that was the preparation for liftoff. Then she'd wait for the magic to lift her to the clouds. The hours she'd spent standing on that stump must have added up to days. Once, hoping that the light of the full moon would provide what she'd been missing, she'd stayed out so late that her stepmother, Naya, had come out with a quilt to drape over her shoulders.

Fly.

She drew the F long and lean, lowercase with one loop up and one down. The loop of the L backed over the F, so it looked like a three-petaled flower, and then she hung the descender of the Y like a stem below it.

"Oh, that's so pretty!" Minna leaned companionably against Beatrice's arm. "Now you charge it."

"How?"

"You can burn it, or you can trace it in salt, or there are about a thousand other things you can do."

"What's the fastest way?"

Something small—maybe disappointment?—flickered over Minna's face, but she said, "Just put your hand on the word, close your eyes, and push energy and intention into it."

So, feeling like the idiot Astrid said she was, Beatrice touched the paper and closed her eyes.

When she opened them, she was not flying.

She was not floating.

She felt nothing, which was *exactly* what she'd expected, after all.

All of this was ridiculous. What was she, some kind of child, to even hope for a moment that magic was real? Because she could admit—she had thought about it for the flutter of a half second. *What if…*

But no.

The others still looked expectant, though, and she was almost embarrassed for them. "Well, that was fun."

She swatted at the bug that buzzed around her head. It landed on the piece of paper, right on the *F*.

A fly.

Minna squeaked, and Cordelia laughed.

"Oh, come on." They didn't really believe that was anything more than a coincidence, did they? "That's hilarious. But it doesn't mean anything. You know that, right?"

Minna gave an honest-to-god chortle. "You drew the fly. Get it? You drew it and *drew* it."

With a flick of her wrist, Beatrice shooed away the fly before picking up the pen again. She wound the letters around the other ones: *BUTTER*. Then she sat back. "So. You think a *butterfly* will land on this now?"

Astrid poked the table with a stern finger. "Put the energy in and see what happens."

Beatrice exhaled heavily but did it, holding her finger to the word and attempting to push energy (whatever that meant) into it.

Then she leaned back in her chair. She looked into the dark wooden beams overhead, to the heavy red velvet curtains that Cordelia had drawn when night fell. "I see no butterflies."

Crash.

Wordlessly, all four rose.

Shattered blue-and-white crockery lay smashed on the tile of the kitchen floor, yellow butter smeared against the shards.

With a bark of laughter, Cordelia began picking up the pieces. "Well, I wasn't expecting *that*, but I love it. Except for the broken dish part. I did like this one." From her crouch, she met Beatrice's gaze. "You have to admit it's funny."

Beatrice couldn't admit anything—her brain was going into free fall, somersaulting through space.

She backed out of the room, retreating to the dining area. With one hand, she propped herself against the table.

"The fly."

Minna propped open the door of the kitchen with her boot. "Yep."

"The butter flew."

Astrid didn't even look like she wanted to gloat. "It did."

"Was that—was that a *miracle*?" If it was, if they really did exist, then would that mean she had only four miracles left before she *died*? Holy shit—

"Oh," sighed Cordelia from the floor. "No. That was just magic."

CHAPTER FIFTEEN

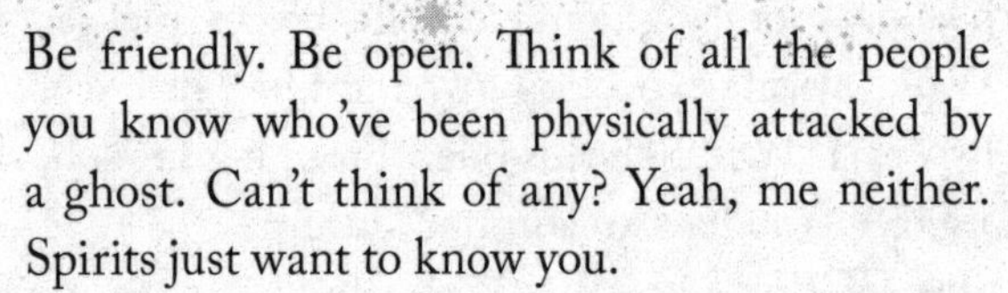

Be friendly. Be open. Think of all the people you know who've been physically attacked by a ghost. Can't think of any? Yeah, me neither. Spirits just want to know you.

—*Evie Oxby, Bluesky*

The next morning, Beatrice woke to the sounds of the bed-and-breakfast moving around her. She stretched, resting in the puddle of sunshine that shone on the foot of the bed. Something clunked closed, a cabinet maybe, and then two different voices laughed before murmuring words she couldn't quite make out. The sounds were so different from the noise of an all-male household, so much more melodious. When the boys were with her and Grant, the day started with bathroom clattering and shouts about missing items. When it was just the two of them, Grant always got up before the break of dawn and thumped out of the house, on his way either to the golf course or to work. He'd always said he liked to beat everyone to the office so he could work in peace. She'd never given that a second thought. When she'd realized that morning must have been his time with Dulcina (he didn't stay out late and liked to go to bed early), she'd felt like such an idiot.

The pain that came from thinking about Grant now wasn't sharp, like she would have guessed it would be. Instead, it was a sickness rising from her gut into her gullet, a roiling mass of anger bigger than anything she'd felt since Naya's death.

No, no, fuck Grant. He didn't matter.

(He did. He had. But she couldn't let him matter. Not anymore.)

Because she was changing *everything*. Today.

Starting now.

A tap whispered at the door and she opened it to find a silver tray waiting on the rug, beautifully set with a silver carafe of coffee, two different muffins (one chocolate, one poppyseed), a small plate of sliced cheese covered with a linen napkin, and a pot of peach yogurt.

She sat on the bed and ate, surprised by how hungry she felt.

New life, new start.

Staying in this town for a while was a preposterous idea. It was a huge and bold and terrifying idea, and the worst part was that there was no safety net. The low gut-roll of fear and elation felt like free-falling into a roller coaster's descent. How was she supposed to figure out which emotion was which?

She *would* figure it out. That was what she did, after all—she figured things out and managed them. Soon she'd call her father, and figure out exactly what had happened in the past and why he'd lied. It would all be new information, and potentially overwhelming, so she might wrangle it into a spreadsheet somehow.

Heck, even magic might benefit from a pivot table.

Magic.

Nope. She could almost hear the clang of the mental bars she dropped around the idea.

Later, she might think about things that didn't exist.

But now, she would explore the town, which was very real.

She left the bed-and-breakfast, walking the streets that slanted and turned, continually winding away from the water and then weaving back again. She stopped to admire a particularly riotous summer garden, filled with roses and zinnias, only to be shocked that when her eyes focused at the rear of the property, she was looking at the ocean yet again. Probably, on a small island like this, water views were the norm, not the exception, but she was used to the ocean being in one place, and one place only: to the west. Here, naturally, the town was surrounded by it, and the knowledge rushed through her with a surprising intensity.

It felt nice to be encircled by the sea. No, it was bigger than that. It felt *right* somehow.

The houseboat that was for sale, according to Minna, the *Forget-Me-Knot*, kept popping into her mind.

Which was ridiculous.

Wasn't it?

She supposed it couldn't hurt, though, to go down to the marina and look. First, though, when she reached the main street, she stopped at Java Express. She'd had only a quick swallow of the coffee on her breakfast tray, and she needed more caffeine, stat.

The barista with the bushy eyebrows who'd served her two days before was behind the counter again. Fritz, was that their name? They grinned as she entered. "Well, heck, you sure got me good the other day, didn't you?"

Smiling sheepishly, Beatrice said, "I honestly didn't mean to. I didn't even know—"

"I *heard*. Twins separated at birth? Can't wait for the Netflix series." They gave a wave. "I'm Fritz. Jackie of all trades, master of foam."

She waggled her fingers back. "Beatrice, master of the spreadsheet and lover of caffeine."

"Extra-hot cappuccino?"

"Good memory."

"It's on the house. I figure it's the least I can do after you almost died sitting outside my coffeehouse. Want a churro?"

That was the cinnamon smell in the air. "I'm okay for now."

"You sure? They're your niece's favorite."

Beatrice filed away that potentially useful fact. "Truly, I'm good."

Fritz looked carefully at her. "Really? No aftereffects?"

"Fine." She vaguely remembered them standing in the small crowd that had formed around her. She remembered the feeling of being pushed before the blade sliced through the air. "Did you...um, did you notice anyone around me? Right before it happened?"

Fritz yanked the levers of the shiny espresso machine. "Nope. Just glad you're okay. Having to clean up all that blood would have been bad for business."

"Jesus, Fritz!" The woman sitting at the table nearest them looked horrified. "She's not going to know you're joking."

The woman looked familiar, but it took Beatrice a second to place her. "You're the bookseller, right?"

Dark brown twists framed the woman's face, and multiple silver chains hung from her neck. "Sorry I tried to force the book Cordelia ordered on you the other day. You had me pretty confused, too."

Fritz offered, "Keelia is a good person to know. She knows, like, everything and everyone."

"Oh, stop." Keelia flapped a hand.

"Seriously. There are people in town who trust her more than the internet."

Keelia raised an eyebrow. "And by 'people,' you mean you?"

"Can you blame me? It's easier to call you when I need to know something than to type it into Google. Faster, honestly, because I don't have to sort through the ad results. Plus, you're nice."

"And that is why I let so many of my calls go to voice mail." But she winked at Fritz and said, "I'm Winnie's sister. The person you met on the boat?"

"Oh!" While there was no chance of Beatrice forgetting who Winnie was, she wouldn't have guessed on the first try that Keelia, with her dark skin and brown eyes, would be the sister of the pale psychic who had white-blond curls and an ice-blue gaze. Half siblings? Adopted? Oh, right. None of her business. "Sure. Yeah."

"Winnie's an amazing person, with a real talent I can't explain, nor do I want to try. It does *not* run in our family, thank god." Her gaze sharpened.

Beatrice fumbled with the cup Fritz handed her, tightening the lid. Did Keelia know what Winnie had told Beatrice? "It's a talent I'm not that familiar with, I guess."

Keelia's voice was mild. "She's setting up a side hustle in the annex of my shop, offering tarot readings and that sort of thing."

Fritz sounded surprised. "Wait, Winnie's staying?"

A nod. "She's decided to start her whole life over."

Was it in the water here?

"Why hasn't she come in for coffee yet? Did she mention me?" Fritz bent to glance at their reflection again in the side of the espresso machine.

Keelia barely glanced at them. "Anyway, Beatrice, I know she'd love to see you again."

"Did she tell you... um..."

"She doesn't read and tell. But—" Keelia paused. "I know she was pretty shaken up, whatever it was."

"Yeah, well, that makes two of us." Enough of that—she

didn't want to go there right now. "So. I'm dying to shop at your store. Books are my love language."

"We're open nine to six every day."

Fritz said, "You should do the Book Concierge!"

Keelia shot him a look. "Okay, thanks. But we don't push strangers into major purchases over coffee, okay, friend?"

They held up their hands. "I'm just saying. If it's good enough for Oprah..."

"Don't mind them," Keelia said with a smile. "They're my best marketer, but they get a little carried away."

"Wait, that's you?" That was why Keelia had been so familiar to her. Not just from the few seconds they'd talked in the bookstore doorway, but from the bookseller documentary she'd watched a few months ago. The Book Concierge was a service that, for an eye-watering price, the bookshop (which had looked adorable with its dark wooden shelves and high ceilings) would close the entire store just for you, and the proprietor (Keelia) would spend hours filling bags with books that suited your reading tastes precisely. Oprah Winfrey, Stephen King, and Jennifer Garner had used the service, and had waxed rhapsodic about it in the documentary.

"That's me! Let me know if you'd be into it."

She *would*. Books were a better escape than anything else in the world. "Sadly, I'm only here temporarily, and the carry-on I brought with me is small."

"I'm happy to ship, too." But Keelia's tone was light. "So, how temporarily? Are you staying with Cordelia?"

"No, I'm at a bed-and-breakfast."

"Will you move here, now that you've found each other?"

I have a life. But really, did she anymore?

"I'm just visiting." But then, as if her brain hadn't heard her own mouth, she found herself saying, "Someone mentioned a houseboat for sale in the marina?"

Keelia's fact lit up. "Oh!"

Fritz said, "That's Hector. *Forget-Me-Knot*'s a sweet little thing, although I'm not sure it's really the kind of houseboat that leaves her dock. Needs a bit of work, I think. Probably won't sink, though."

"No, I'm not going to buy it." But…maybe she could rent it for a week or two? The B and B was nice, but a houseboat sounded picturesque. "If I *did* stay down there for a little while, what should I be concerned about?" Was there a problem with crime in a place like Skerry Cove? Meth, of course, might come into play. In a town like this, there was probably a good amount of it—young people got bored everywhere, didn't they?

Keelia grimaced. "Friday nights can be difficult down there."

Oh, no, could there be gangs in a place this small?

"Yeah," agreed Fritz. "Avoid at all costs the southernmost boathouse on Fridays after six."

This was exactly what she needed to know. "Tell me."

"Cranky Al's ukulele jam. It used to be pretty mellow, but since he invited the accordion players, it's been a mess down there."

Were they kidding? Beatrice couldn't tell. Were they teasing her?

Keelia shook her head. "Right? They sure screw up the parking down there. For hours. I never knew there were so many accordion players in the whole world, let alone here in our little corner of the world."

Beatrice looked at Fritz. "You're *not* kidding."

They fist-bumped her. "Welcome to Skerry Cove."

"Seriously, I'm not buying a boat."

Keelia didn't look convinced. "I recommend earplugs."

CHAPTER SIXTEEN

There's no hurry. Take your time with your practice—it's called that for a reason. You're not going to get it all right, but you won't get it all wrong, either. Deep breath. Then, when you're ready, light the candle again.

—*Evie Oxby,* I Ain't Afraid of No Ghosts

Fritz gave her Hector's number, and he met her at the marina ten minutes later. Hector was a short, round man who wore a flannel jacket that looked like it had gone through two world wars, and by the looks of his beard, he'd had eggs for breakfast. But his smile was kind as he helped her on board with a warm hand. He warned her, "This gal's a ridiculous charmer, I'll have you know. A forty-foot legend."

"I'm not really in the market." Beatrice felt her cheeks flush. "Lookie-looing. That's all. I hope you don't mind."

His eyes twinkled. "Just you wait till we get inside."

The *Forget-Me-Knot* was a delightful boat, yes. That was, if she even *was* a boat. As Hector searched his pockets for the key, he explained she was more of a stationary houseboat, because she didn't really *go* anywhere. She was attached to the dock, almost growing out of it, and looked from the outside more like a tiny home than a boat. "It's why I'm selling her—I finally want to be out on the high seas. Run away to a far-off land, you know?"

Beatrice did know.

"You a sailor?"

"No," she said apologetically.

"Eh." He shrugged and two screws fell out of a hole in his jacket's pocket. "Better that way, honestly. Where *are* those keys?"

He found them, and they entered through the front door. (An actual front door proved that it was more house than boat, right?) The main cabin was lined in warm reddish wood, the ceiling curving up like the swell of a wave. Three skylights let in the sun. There was a tiny galley kitchen, and a table with four chairs in matching wood. A potbelly stove perched next to a soft-looking sofa, and the brass fittings gleamed. An armchair made for a person with very short legs looked like it was waiting for Mama Bear to come home. The space felt roomier than she would have thought possible. Seven or eight people could sit comfortably inside. If they liked each other.

She wouldn't—shouldn't—ask. But the words came anyway. "I know you're looking to sell, but would you consider a short-term rental?"

"Extended holiday, like?" His bushy eyebrows rose.

"Something like that."

A pause. Then, as if she hadn't spoken, he ushered her up six steps to the raised bedroom. The room was small but the bed was a good size. "The way she rocks you to sleep, you'll never know what hit you. Ever have insomnia?"

Beatrice nodded. "On occasion."

"Never again. I tell you, never again. Now, look here." He pulled a knob at the foot of the bed. "*More* storage!"

The bathroom (the head, he corrected her) was minuscule and didn't produce a lot of hot water ("just a wee twelve-volt heater") but it would do. The rest of the power came from a bank of four six-volt batteries.

The only thing it lacked were bookcases of any sort. But the space between two of the windows in the main cabin would be an ideal place for a built-in bookcase, wouldn't it? And at the end of the counter there was a bit of wasted space. Another bookcase could go there. And perhaps under the window seat? And next to it? Beatrice—or whoever bought the boat—would have to figure out how to keep books from getting damp on board. A dehumidifier perhaps?

Hector slapped a pile of battered-looking papers onto the galley counter. "Inspection report! Clean as a whistle!"

She wasn't buying a boat.

But even if she *were* considering anything this preposterous, shouldn't she get her own inspection report, at least, and not just trust his? What if the deed that was going through the vessel dealer fell through, or if there were liens on the property? It was a houseboat, not a house, but she should still follow proper protocol. *When everything is in perfect place, worry can be perfectly released.* She pushed her father's voice out of her head.

So what if it all fell apart? The money was just sitting in Beatrice's bank account, enough of it liquid to make this happen. Rather easily, in fact. She'd been saving for a rainy day. And if there was even a small possibility that she wouldn't live long enough to see that rainy day (just like anyone else—she wasn't special in this, she reminded herself), why not spend it on something she wanted?

I want this.

A shiver slipped through her. "Would you rent it to me?"

Hector fixed her with a knowing eye. "No. But I'll sell it to you."

I want to live here.

They agreed to the price on a handshake. Hector called the vessel dealer and his friend at the bank, who made a phone call (an actual *phone* call) to her bank in LA, and the cash flowed through the money pipes. Then he handed her the keys, even before he got the transfer confirmation.

Nine phone calls and three hours later, Beatrice owned a houseboat. Feeling rather green, she shook Hector's hand one last time.

"Thank you." What had she just done?

"She's all yours, and you won't regret it, my dear!" He spun around, gave the doorframe a friendly pat, and walked down the dock, whistling cheerfully.

Beatrice watched him greet someone in the parking lot, who nodded back to him politely. Reno, dressed in a black beanie and a well-worn jean jacket, headed her direction down the dock.

Beatrice watched her approach, surprised by how pleased she was to see her. "Hey, there."

Reno stopped at the foot of the gangplank. "I was over at the marina store. Heard a mainlander was looking at Hector's boat. Wondered if it was you."

She clutched the railing. "I think I bought a boat. Oh, shit."

"May I come aboard?"

"Yes! Of course."

Reno boarded easily, not even watching her feet. "You talk him down?"

Down? The boat had been so cheap, she hadn't even thought of it. "Well, no wonder he seemed so chipper."

"Now what?"

Beatrice held up her phone. "I've already got a guy coming over to haul away the old mattress." While waiting for the banks to do their things, she'd already called the one furniture store that sold beds. It had taken five minutes to tell the owner she wanted a queen mattress, firm, no springs. She'd been prepared to offer a hefty bonus for immediate delivery, but the woman had offered to deliver it herself that afternoon. "This town is a force of nature. Come in, please?"

Following her across the deck, Reno said, "When you live on an island, you take care of each other."

"That must be nice."

She pressed her thumb against a small nick in the wood next to the front door. "I can fix this if you want."

"Can you?" Beatrice was surprised by the offer—the woman was so quiet, she'd all but convinced herself Reno disliked her. Then she remembered the gorgeous wooden kayak Reno had been building in Minna's hideout. "Um. Do you build bookcases?"

Another nod.

"Are you hirable?"

Reno closed her eyes, squinching them up as if she was in pain.

Oops. Had she said something wrong? Or was Reno sick? "Are you okay?"

Reno rubbed her chest. "Yeah." She coughed. "Fine. And yes. Hirable. But..."

She waited a moment, and when Reno didn't finish the sentence, she said, "But what?"

Her gaze stayed down. "You would want to hire me?"

"Is there a reason I shouldn't?"

Reno shook her head.

Strangely relieved, Beatrice said, "Good. You're hired. Let me show you."

She pointed, and Reno made notes. Then Reno peered around the cabin and bedroom, determining the best place for the bookcases. Quietly, she took measurements using the tape she pulled out of her pocket and jotted numbers down on a small notepad that came out of another pocket. She was methodical and silent. Beatrice didn't get the impression Reno didn't *want* to talk—instead, it felt more like she didn't need to speak as much as other people.

Beatrice pushed down a jangled clang of nerves. "I've got to go buy some things. Sheets, a kettle, some towels. Can you tell me where I should go?"

"Housewares store on Main, three doors down from Keelia's bookstore."

Had she really just bought a houseboat? She looked at her phone for the time—she'd only just missed the plane she would have been on to go home. Soon her father would be looking for her to arrive home. He didn't even know she'd met Cordelia and Minna. And his ex-wife. All their talk of magic—had they put some kind of psychological spell on her?

What the hell was she doing here?

And how was she supposed to talk to her father about all of it?

Reno stopped making measurements and fiddled with a sticky galley drawer. Then she jiggled the handle of the small sink. "What?"

"Sorry?" Beatrice hadn't said anything out loud. Had she?

"You look... sad."

"I think I have to quit my job. Which involves quitting my father, I think. No, I know. That's why I have to quit my job."

After a few seconds of consideration, Reno said, "Sounds like you know what's right."

A tug, like the feeling Minna had put into her chest last night. "How do I know for sure, though?"

"You don't."

"I hate that." Beatrice looked under the galley sink and found exactly what she was looking for: a bottle of cleaning spray and a pile of clean rags. She sprayed the countertop and wiped it down. At home (at Grant's house), the counter had been so big that it had taken at least five minutes to clean all of it. This one was, what, twenty inches long? It took seconds. "Do you know how much I'd pay for a life manual? Like, why hasn't someone written a book with all the advice in one place? I mean, obviously, there's all the religious texts, but I don't mean that. I mean something bigger. Something that has *every* answer. You could input something and read the output, and that would be that."

"Would that be fun for you?"

Of course it would be. *So* much fun. She would always know what to do. She'd always get it right. But something about Reno's voice made her look at her sharply. "Are you teasing me?"

"Maybe." Reno rubbed the side of her neck where the blue tattoos spiraled upward. "Maybe not."

"I've just got some hard decisions to make."

Reno said, "Some people would say buying a houseboat is a hard decision."

True. And she'd done that without blinking, hadn't she? "Good point, yeah. Hey, can I ask you something?"

Reno's dark gaze remained locked on hers as she nodded.

"Do you believe in magic?"

There was a pause, not an easy one. The air between them was thick with something Beatrice couldn't name.

When Reno finally responded, her voice was low. "Don't fuck with them."

"Wait. What—"

"When you walked into the store—Cordelia's face... She's

been hoping for you her whole life. If you hurt either her or Minna, you'll answer to me."

It wasn't an idle threat. This woman would protect Cordelia and Minna; that was clear.

And Beatrice's heart, which it seemed was completely and intractably twisted up in this place now, approved of Reno's motivation.

Beatrice placed her hand on her chest as if she were saluting a flag. "I promise I won't hurt them."

A nod was all she got in return, but it was all she needed.

CHAPTER SEVENTEEN

Some will tell you not to work dark magic, but honey, you think Spirit can't handle the darkness? Who do you think is in charge of the light switches?

—*Evie Oxby, TikTok*

Hours later, Beatrice sat on her deck in one of the four new chairs she'd bought at the hardware store. (One for Minna, one for Cordelia, one for... Astrid? No, scratch that. It would be for Reno.) Every limb felt like it weighed double what it normally did, but the exhaustion was almost pleasant in its intensity. After buying the boat and talking to Reno, Beatrice hadn't stopped moving for hours, in a buying frenzy that left her debit card smoking and the interior of the boat looking like... *her.* Grant thought that cream was too aggressive a color, so their house had been done in muted shades of bisque.

Fuck Grant and his boring-ass taupe marble countertops.

The boat's cabin was now colorful. After her shopping binge, the main room had two fluffy orange rugs. The sofa held five new velvet pillows in yellows and reds. She'd traded out the old, battered toaster and coffee maker for shiny green ones, and she'd hung purple dishcloths in the galley. The bedding was red and purple, her towels bright blue.

She'd scrubbed the interior from top to bottom as well as she could. There were a bunch of things she didn't know how to work, like the radios and everything in and around the bilge pump, so she'd leave those alone until she learned what everything was for. At some point she'd understand every inch of the boat, from below the waterline to the wind vane that pirouetted overhead.

Working through the orange flares of sunset, Beatrice had declined separate invites to dinner from both Minna and Cordelia. She shoved a piece of cheese and bread into her mouth when hunger pangs threatened to slow her down.

So she deserved this cup of tea on the deck. When she was done with it, she'd take her first houseboat shower and crawl into the brand-new sheets. Tonight, Beatrice was sure, sleep would come easily.

As she picked up her phone to check email, a text from Iris landed.

Your dad's called me twice–didn't leave a message–need me to talk to him for u?

She typed back, No thx, might get you to box up some clothes and household stuff for me tho.

Then, as if her father had heard her thinking about him, her phone buzzed in her hands, his photo on the screen.

Instead of declining his call—again—she answered.

"Dad."

"Beatrice, oh, thank god. I thought you'd dropped off the face of the earth. Are you okay? Why didn't you call me? Or respond to my texts? That's not like you, Button. What's wrong?"

When he finally paused for breath, Beatrice said, "I quit."

"Quit what?"

"My job, Dad. I'm quitting my job."

She heard a cough of surprise. "I don't understand."

"I found Cordelia." The words slipped from her lips like razor blades. If she touched her mouth, would her fingers come away with blood? Each syllable was sharp. "I found your wife, too. Astrid. Did you even know you have a *granddaughter*?"

She didn't know until she said the words that she'd still held a thin shred of hope—that he'd say he had no idea, what was she talking about?

But she could almost feel the pulse of his panic beat through the line.

"Oh, no." His voice was a thin, thready breath.

"You lied."

"Beatrice—"

"My whole life, you taught me one thing. You said right was right and wrong was wrong. Numbers never lie; that's why they're so beautiful. Humans do, but we never should. But *you* lied."

"No—"

"And about the most important thing of all." Beatrice's chest hurt so much, she wanted to rip out her heart with her bare hands. "It was always me and you, until Naya came, and then it was the three of us. We were a family. Except we weren't, because a family knows each other. They love each other *because* they know each other. I have a twin sister, Dad. How could you?"

The air on her father's side of the line clattered, as if he was dropping things, many of them, one after another. "But I don't understand. How did you find them?"

A miracle. "Doesn't matter. Did you know they were here?"

"No. She never told me where they went. Listen very carefully to me. Astrid is dangerous."

"She says you *allowed* her take Cordelia away from us. You really let that happen?"

The silence told her everything she needed to know.

So, even though her voice shook, she poured out the gasoline. "You hid my sister from me." Then she lit the match. "I'll never forgive you."

Beatrice hung up as the life she'd known caught ablaze. It was too late to pull her heart from the fire.

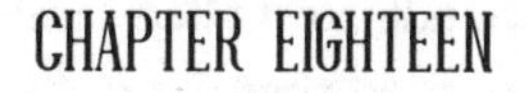

CHAPTER EIGHTEEN

Never look a gift synchronicity in the mouth.
—*Evie Oxby,* New York *magazine*

The next morning, Beatrice blew a fuse while making breakfast. It was her own fault—she should have realized that toasting bread while the electric kettle heated might be too big a drain on her mysterious electrical system, but when she couldn't even *find* the fuse box, her own internal electrics started to overheat, too. The internet company was coming later in the afternoon, but until then, she was making do with the shitty cell phone reception that came and went with the island wind. Pulling up houseboat diagnostics at the dial-up speed of the late nineties wasn't helping her irritation level.

Her mood probably had something to do with the fact that her life as she knew it was over.

Or maybe it had to do with the fact that she'd quit her job without warning. It got harder to breathe every time she remembered that. Yes, she had savings. But savings were supposed to be for the future, not for the *now.* That was the whole point.

Maybe her mood was bleak because she'd bought a boat? Who bought a *boat*? Sure, it was a houseboat that didn't like to be away from land. But still. She used to do the books for a sailing instructor who'd said the second-happiest day of a sailor's life was the day they bought their boat. She'd fallen for it, asking, "What's their first-happiest day?" He'd grinned. "The day they sell it."

Or perhaps this dire cloud of fear that had settled into her brain like a summer thunderstorm had something to do with the fact that she'd never noticed that her husband was in love with another woman, and had been for the duration of their marriage.

Beatrice tried to put peanut butter on her untoasted bread and succeeded only in ripping the slice to shreds. Fine. She ate the sticky pieces with her fingers.

Or maybe—just maybe—this dark mood had a little something to do with a prediction of full-on *death* after seven miracles, and that two of them might have already occurred.

She wiped more peanut butter on another sad, torn piece of bread.

A voice called out from the dock, "Beatrice? Are you home?"

Home. *Was* she home? When would she know that for sure?

Outside, Cordelia's hair hung in two braids, and her face was bright with hope. "Hi. Good morning. I didn't want to bug you, but I brought you something." She carried a red patchwork bag over one arm and held a to-go cup in each hand.

"Please tell me one of those has my name on it."

Cordelia thrust one cup forward. "Extra-hot cappuccino. Fritz says hello."

"Bless you both. Come in."

Inside, Cordelia put her bag on the galley counter and slowly turned in place. "This can't be Hector's old place. How did you do this in just one day?"

Every muscle in Beatrice's body ached. "It's possible I worked a little too hard."

"I get it. I'm the same way with a new place. Which reminds me, I brought you a housewarming gift." She reached into her bag and took out a piece of folded white cloth. "Here."

It looked like a simple handkerchief until Beatrice unfolded it to find the middle intricately embroidered. Three overlapping circles of red thread crossed two lines that resembled spears. Four thicker lines wove around seven French knots. It was stunning, equally pretty on the right side as on the wrong.

"Just a little protection. I sell kits for something similar at the store, but this sigil is just for you." Cordelia's smile was wide, her gaze open. "You, buying this boat... Beatrice, I can't tell you how happy it makes me. It means we have time. All the time in the world." She blushed. "That is, if you *want* that time. Here I go again, rushing in, assuming you're staying because of me, because of us, and I could be completely wrong. Maybe you're here for the golf. I hope I'm not. But I could be. I know that."

Emotions, too fine and too many to untangle, knotted in Beatrice's chest as tightly as the French knots on the cloth. "I hate golf."

She needed to tell her what Winnie had said. Soon.

"Oh, thank goddess."

Beatrice sank into the tiny armchair and gestured for Cordelia to take the small sofa. "Dude. I have *questions*."

"I bet you do." Pulling a thick book bound in dark leather out of her bag, Cordelia sat. "I'll do my best to answer anything you ask."

Okay, then. Beatrice folded the handkerchief tightly in her fingers. "What's the book?"

"Our family grimoire. Our book of spells."

The words tumbled out before she could stop them. "Are you a witch?"

"Mmm." Cordelia looked at her hands, which rested on top of the book on her lap. "You could call me an energy practitioner."

"And that means..."

"I manipulate energy, shaping it a bit, to make things around me and my loved ones a little better."

"That sounds really witchy."

"Okay, fine, I do call myself a witch, but I don't do it in the hearing of the nonmagical. Makes 'em nervous. Even at Which Craft, I play dumb if it comes up. I'm just one in a very long line of people who've learned how to harness an ancient gift."

She, Beatrice, was presumably part of that long line. It was nice of Cordelia not to push that. "So, is it Wicca? Is that what it's called?"

"No—Wicca was started in the forties and fifties, and while I respect it, I don't practice it."

Beatrice boggled. "As in the *nineteen* fifties?" She'd imagined centuries of women standing in circles in forests, calling upon—something.

"Yeah. While they've reclaimed some ancient traditions, we Hollands use magic that's somewhat longer in the tooth."

"And you keep your last name."

"We tend to keep it, yes. Matrilineally." Cordelia leaned forward. "But you can do whatever you want with your powers, including ignoring them entirely."

Maybe they'd circle back to that, but Beatrice's big questions were busy having lots of squirrely little question babies. "So, let's assume I buy that magic exists. Which I don't. But for the sake of argument, I'm going to pretend I do." She ignored Cordelia's look of satisfaction. "Is everyone in this town magical?"

"Not like us, no."

"Does everyone know about the family...talent?"

"Only those we've deemed safe to know. You can imagine that it's dangerous for the wrong people to learn about us."

"How much of this town knows?"

Cordelia shrugged. "I've never thought about it that deeply. Maybe forty percent of them?"

"How do you keep the ones who know from talking to the dangerous ones?"

"Spells of safety. And hoping for the best."

That didn't sound very safe, but Beatrice only said, "Why does magic work for you and not for others?"

Cordelia gave her a proud smile. "Good one. Magic is in the land and sea and sky, and it tends to puddle up where those things meet. Islands, like this one, are great for collecting it, especially if magic has been practiced in the same place over many years. Minna is the seventh-generation Holland to live in Skerry Cove."

"Really?" Beatrice couldn't even remember the names of her father's grandparents, all of whom had died before she was born. She couldn't fathom seven generations of her kin, all in one place.

"We'll show you at the cemetery. It's kind of astonishing. Anyone with a sensitivity to magic—and I believe that's most people, though Astrid would definitely disagree with me—can learn to use magic. It's just that, in some families, we've built up some extra talent, if you will. Just like the land has. When you combine pooled magic in the land with a familial gift, and if you know how to jump-start that talent—"

"With that Knock thing. Which didn't feel like a knock, by the way." It hadn't felt like much of anything.

"Yeah, I have no idea why we call it that. When you activate your strengths with it, that strength grows, fast."

"But what *is* it?"

Cordelia slipped a ziplock bag of oatmeal cookies out of her bag. "Mom made them, but I swear they're not poisoned. Okay, how to explain it. You know how the immune system works, right? It's just kind of hanging out, waiting for a threat to activate it. The Knock is like that—it's in your body but it can't really get to work until someone starts it up. Before you're activated, any magic you do is either accidental or the kind that nonwitches can do. Afterward, once it's been fired up... well, the sky's the limit, really."

"But I didn't feel anything. Did Minna? How are you supposed to know it worked?"

"You don't feel anything when the immune system turns on, either. It's autonomous, just happening, the same way your heart beats and your lungs breathe. As to how we know—we all saw it work when the butter flew."

"Technically, no one saw it." It still could have all been a coincidence. That wasn't out of the question.

"Mmmm."

"And this, this Knock, is just in our family?"

Cordelia lowered her eyes and pulled out a cookie. "Ours and some others."

"So if it's not for everyone, is it blood-borne? Or can you give it away to someone who isn't genetically related?"

Cordelia paused, appearing to choose her next words carefully. "You can, yes. It's not always... the best idea to do so. Someone for whom the knowledge is completely new often struggles with controlling that kind of power."

It still didn't make sense, but Beatrice's mind was full of questions ping-ponging in every direction. "So what's the difference between magic and miracles?"

"Whew." She smiled. "An easy one. Magic is the intentional transformation of energy to affect an outcome. A miracle, on the other hand, is an unearned gift."

"Huh." Beatrice sipped her coffee, relishing the way the caffeine slipped through her veins. "What about psychic predictions? Prophecies?"

"I don't receive them myself. But yes, some people get predictions of the future."

"Do you trust them?"

A careful shrug. "Depends. For every real psychic, there are five running around taking money for preying on people's grief."

"Do you know Keelia's sister?"

"Winnie? We've never met, strangely enough. But I know she's moving to the island, and I believe from what I've heard that her power is strong."

"You would trust a prediction from her?"

"From what Keelia has said, a hundred percent, yes."

Time to rip off the psychic Band-Aid. "She said I was going to die soon, but before I did, I'd experience seven miracles. And it was kind of backed up by Evie Oxby, if you know who she is."

"Ah." Cordelia sighed. "Well, *fuck*."

CHAPTER NINETEEN

> Surprises wouldn't be surprises if you saw them coming. So I can't tell you everything they say, not even about who's going to win tonight. I wish I could.
>
> —*Evie Oxby, to Rihanna at the Grammy Awards*

Beatrice frowned. "To be honest, that wasn't the reaction I was hoping for."

Her sister held up a finger. "The blade that flew off the wood chipper."

They hadn't talked about the incident at dinner. "How do you know about that?"

"Small town. Everyone knows." She held up another finger. "Us, finding each other."

"Could be coincidence."

Cordelia shook her head. "It was an unearned gift that took no energy from us. It was a miracle. Have there been any more?"

"No. I don't think so. I'd know, right?"

"Miracles tend make themselves known kind of obnoxiously.

Usually. Holy shit." Her eyes got a glossy sheen. "Did she give you a time frame?"

"She said she saw the number one. She didn't think it was one day or one year, but couldn't tell if it was one week or one month. Could have been one decade by that argument, right?"

Cordelia made a strangled noise that wasn't quite a sob, but her nose went red the same way Beatrice's did when she was fighting emotion. "Sorry. Shit." Cordelia held up a hand. "Sorry."

"So—" Beatrice's voice cracked. "So you believe it?"

The effort Cordelia put into pulling herself together was visible, her face relaxing and softening, her body language easing. "Okay, while some psychics can predict the future, it's only ever a guess. A suggestion, one that can be refashioned."

At Cordelia's calm words, Beatrice felt her own heart rate steady. Her sister helped people die, right? No wonder she was good at the whole calming thing. "Refashioned. Like, undone?"

Cordelia pulled the book closer to her on the table. "That would imply a prophecy or a vision could be erased, and while it can't, it *can* sometimes be turned into something else. We might be able to bend it a little."

Beatrice released a tight, stale breath. "So maybe I'm *not* going to die? Or can we find a way to block the miracles? Not that... not that I believe any of this."

Cordelia's smile wobbled. "Well. I hate to break it to you, but yes, you're going to die just like the rest of us, but maybe we can do something about the timing. Because I'm not going to be okay with losing you after I've only just found you." She closed her eyes, swallowing hard.

Beatrice's fingers worried at the edge of the paper cup. "You do this all the time, though, right? Help people die?"

"Not you. I refuse to help you with that, just for the record. Okay?"

"But how do you do…wait, what *do* you do, exactly?" And why wouldn't she do it for Beatrice? Was there something scary or bad about whatever it was she did?

Cordelia touched the book's cover with just one fingertip, tracing a decorative fold in the dark leather. "It's just about being present. Not letting anything else get in between the dying person and what's really in the room with them at that moment. Allowing whatever love is there to flow without interruption, ideally." She cleared her throat. "It's also about helping them understand what leaving this plane might feel like and sound like. Hospice often works with the families, and so do I, of course, but my job is to be there at the end, even when no one else might be."

An image of Naya's last few moments rose in Beatrice's mind. "How do you handle the rage?"

"Same as any other emotion. I let it move through and blow on out to the other side."

Beatrice's fingers tightened on the hanky as she remembered Naya making those terrible deep dry gasps that sounded like painful snoring. Her father sobbing. The hospice worker saying it was normal, telling them that Naya couldn't feel pain anymore. The snow globe from their Bryce Canyon trip on the shelf above Naya's head, the souvenir mocking them with the memory of happiness. The hospice worker saying, *Beatrice, put down your phone and be here with her now.* Her father begging, *Please, Button, just hold her hand.* But the hospice worker herself had said it—Naya was beyond pain, so she was beyond knowing who was in the room with her, which meant Beatrice could keep poking at her phone, keep looking for a solution for the terrible snoring sound. She could keep reading about agonal breathing, trying to find *any* source that said it was reversible, that Naya could be saved. She'd come through so much already. She could do it one more time, and Beatrice would figure out how to make it happen.

Only she hadn't. The snoring had stopped, and Naya was just...gone.

Now, she tucked the handkerchief into her pocket so she'd quit messing with it.

Her sister's gaze was kind. "You've watched someone you love die."

It took Beatrice a second to find her voice around the heat in her throat. "Naya. My stepmother. I'm still so angry."

"At what?"

Such a dumb, impossible question. But she had a dumb, impossible answer to it. "At life. For the whole death thing." She ripped another piece of sharp plastic from the coffee cup's lid. "My mother died when I was little. It was the truest thing about me. I was a motherless girl, and I was so mad about it for so long. I did everything I could do to understand it, to figure out what cancer was, and why it had taken her from me. The things that were important to me—I didn't get to keep them. I think I was just starting to get over it, honestly. My husband's kids weren't going to be some magic fulfillment for me, and we'd tried to have a baby, but it didn't work out. So maybe I was just about to accept that and—oh, shit, what am I saying?"

Cordelia waited.

"I guess I was about to accept that it was all going the way it was supposed to go. I didn't have a mother and I wasn't going to be one. It didn't have to mean I was broken. But then—Astrid is alive, and it *didn't* go the way it was supposed to, it just got fucked up, and now, if I end up believing in magic and miracles, I have to also believe that I have no time left?" The steaming fury built up into a scream inside her brain. "I just can't."

No to magic.

No to predictions.

The butter hadn't flown. That could have been an accident.

Wasn't that the only "magical" thing that had actually happened? She could have imagined the tug in her chest when Minna had written her name with the word *love* around it. In fact, she was feeling that same warmth now, just thinking about Minna's sweet face. Grant's house hadn't burned down. A butter dish crashing to the floor in another room, something that no one had actually witnessed happen? That was nothing. She hadn't even asked if they had a cat. They *totally* had a cat. She was sure of it.

Cordelia patted the back of her hand. "We'll figure something out. Together."

She wasn't getting it. "I don't believe in any of it."

"Okay, the truth is, you don't have to believe any of it—it'll still work."

Great. Yet another assumption, shot down. "You don't have to have, like, complete faith in magic?"

"Pffft. Please. Who has that?"

"I used to, when I was a kid." Beatrice wanted to turn the book toward her, so that she could see the symbols scratched on the pages Cordelia was turning. "I used to stand in the backyard, convinced if I tried hard enough, I could fly."

"Now, *that* would be a miracle."

It was stupid, the tiny twist of disappointment Beatrice felt. "Got it, no flying allowed."

"Think about it like this. We can't disable the laws of physics, because we're bound to the system that we all share. We live inside gravity, so we abide by its rules. But we can push and pull at it, at the edges. Ah, here."

Cordelia turned the book so they could both see. Spidery writing traced down the page, and at the bottom was a snarl of lines that could have been undecipherable letters. "Like I said, this grimoire is where our family has kept our spells for the last two hundred years. Before that, they were passed down orally.

This, right here, is a spell for a sick person. It pushes out the illness and pulls in healing, always in equal measure."

"So why don't you just heal the dying, then?"

"It's energy work, so it all has to equal out in the end. Every reaction, and all that. With the right tools, I probably could stop one person from dying, but it would be at the expense of my own life. But I *can* siphon off other kinds of energy and push them into my patients, giving them some relief when they need it. Likewise, I can pull out some pain, but it means I have to accept it myself."

"So, what, you just sign up for extra pain?"

"I get migraines. When I'm in one, it doesn't really matter if there's a little extra pain in there." She laughed. "I'm not a martyr. I've got good meds from both my doctor *and* from Maizie Marco, who distills the best cannabis tinctures on the island."

"So how did the butter *fly*?" Beatrice put air quotes around the last word.

"Your energy gave it a push, that's all. It wouldn't have taken much out of you—you might not have felt it at all, just a small muscle cramp in your calf for a second, maybe—and it's not like the dish rose into the air, defying gravity altogether, and whizzed in loops around our heads, right? It got pushed, then gravity brought it crashing down."

"Or your cat knocked it off."

Cordelia's smile was gentle. "We don't have a cat."

Well, damn. Taking a deep breath, Beatrice said, "So do you have a plan?"

"Absolutely not. I wish I did. But we can go through the book together and I'll tell you about what's in it, and maybe together we can come up with something. I think Mom knew something was wrong. She's a pain in the ass, but she's powerful. She told me as I left this morning that we'll be stronger if we work together. Honestly, she wanted to come with me, but I said you might have questions, and that you're probably not ready for her to answer them yet."

Cordelia was right, but it didn't take much intuition to figure that out. "I might never be. I've run away, except when I left, I didn't know I was running, so I'm hoping that my best friend can ship me up some clothes soon. I'm staying here for a while because you and Minna are here, and I'm... curious." What a lightweight word for the heaviness in her chest. "But Astrid? I have zero interest in her."

"I feel the same way about Mitchell."

A ridiculous urge to defend her father rose inside her. *He's a good man. All he cares about is his family. Naya and I were everything to him.*

Now he had neither.

But losing his daughter—both his daughters—was entirely his own damn fault.

Beatrice pulled the book toward her. Cordelia said she didn't have to believe for it to work, and that was a good thing. "So show me some things."

But they'd gone through only the first two pages (a method of encouraging bees to make more honey, and a ritual for full-moon house cleansing) when her sister's cell buzzed with a text.

"I'm so sorry." She tapped something back. "I have to go."

"A patient?"

"Yeah. I honestly don't think it's her time yet, but her husband is scared." She reached for the book, but Beatrice closed her fingers around the edges.

"Can you... can you leave it with me?"

"Oh, wow. No. I'm sorry, I couldn't do that."

"Why not?"

"It's... precious."

"And you don't trust me."

"It's not that—it's just that everything we know is in there."

"And I know none of it. Please?" The smooth leather warmed under her touch, almost as if it were alive. She wanted more of it, even though deciphering the wobbly script hurt her eyes. "I won't... do anything with it."

"Astrid wouldn't like it."

"That just makes me want to keep it more. Pretty please?"

Cordelia's cell pinged again. Blowing out a breath, she said, "Okay. But I need you to look in my eyes and promise with your whole heart not to open the page that's folded in on itself. The one in the middle that's sealed with wax."

A chill raced down the back of Beatrice's neck. "What is it?"

"I can't even tell you that much. I just need you to promise that you won't unseal it."

"I promise I won't."

"Thanks. It's really important. Okay, make a list of the new questions you come up with, and we can go over them tomorrow. Come by Which Craft when you can? Shit, I *have* to run."

Unexpectedly, she kissed Beatrice on the cheek.

Long after the door had shut behind her, after the boat had stopped its tiny movement from her disembarking, Beatrice could still feel the kiss there, warm against her skin.

CHAPTER TWENTY

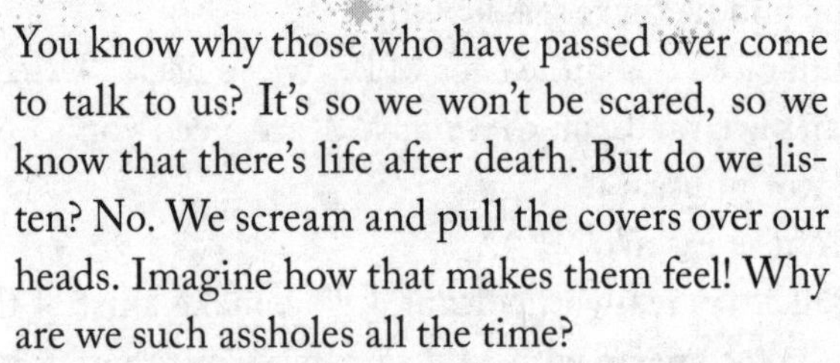

You know why those who have passed over come to talk to us? It's so we won't be scared, so we know that there's life after death. But do we listen? No. We scream and pull the covers over our heads. Imagine how that makes them feel! Why are we such assholes all the time?

—*Evie Oxby to Stephen Colbert on* The Late Show

Confusion was too clean and simple a word for how Beatrice felt after Cordelia's visit. Questions stacked in her brain, growing more bewildering the harder she thought. She sat with the grimoire for an hour, but every page she turned deserved dozens more Google searches, which were almost impossible without Wi-Fi. She did her best to ignore the sealed page, only running her finger along the waxed edge once.

Then Beatrice tucked the grimoire into a bag and headed out for the civilized world. She'd almost made it to the library, where she planned on setting herself up with the book and some of that sweet, sweet high-speed internet, when someone called her name.

"Beatrice!" Minna stood in front of the barbershop across the street. She looked both ways and then scampered across, giving Beatrice a hug that was a full-force flop of bodily joy. "I'm so glad to see you!"

"Well, I'm glad to see *you*. You look adorable."

Minna had draped a lacy red capelet over a black tank top. Black-and-white-striped pants came up high on her waist, and the flat black boots that laced up to her calves were painted with silver sparkle. "I do, right?" She tugged her hand through her black hair. "Thanks. Good thrifting a couple of weeks ago. You ready for that tattoo yet?"

Beatrice laughed. "Not yet. But thanks."

"Always worth a shot. What are you doing right now?"

"I thought I might do a little reading at the library. Later Reno's going to work on a bookcase for my new houseboat, but I gave her the spare key yesterday, so I might spend all day here reading—who knows?"

Minna pressed her hands dramatically over her heart. "You bought the *Forget-Me-Knot*. You're *staying*. I knew it."

"For a while, yeah." If staying meant getting to know this kid better, there was no better reason to stay. *Even though I might be dying.*

No, come on. She wasn't. She'd have to make sure Cordelia didn't mention the prediction to Minna. It wasn't real, but Minna would probably genuinely believe it.

"Wait, and you *hired* Reno?"

"Yep."

"Seriously?"

Uh-oh. "Should I not have?"

"No, she's the absolute best, but... she just doesn't trust many people. It's kind of a big deal she agreed." Minna's eyes widened. "Which I think is *great*."

"Well, I'm glad."

"And you trusted her. Just like that."

"You're making me worry now."

"*No.* Don't worry. There's just some people in town who say shit about her. But she's literally the best and you did the right thing. Anyway, forget reading in the library. Mom texted that she left our grimoire with you. She made me swear not to tell Gran." Her eyes lit up. "Your plans just changed. I'm taking you to my favorite place, and I'll *show* you what's in that book."

Minna's favorite place was the graveyard. Of course it was. When Beatrice was her age, she liked the one near her father's house, but it was a rather boring, flat piece of grass-covered land, each marker either set flat into the ground or tastefully upright and regularly cleaned. Very mundane.

This?

This place was different. Set into the undulating hillside behind Cordelia's house, just past Reno's motor home, the graves wandered up through the grass. Through overhanging trees, the sun dappled enormous blocks of chipped stained marble. A cool breeze came off the glinting water in the distance. The space was friendly. Mostly. Maybe in the darker spots it looked spooky and spine-tingling, but not actually frightening, which was a distinction Beatrice had never had to make before.

Minna leaped from broken flagstone to grassy hummock. "That's where my second-grade teacher is buried. She died in her sleep of old age, which my mom says is the best way to go. And that's the guy who invented a machine that makes paper clips. See the paper clips etched all around the stone?"

In some places, the grass grew high, more weeds than plants, and a few of the old stones were broken and crumbling. "Do they still use this place for burying people?"

Laughing, Minna jumped off the edge of an old, dry fountain. "Use is kind of relative, right? Are these bodies using it? But no, there's a new town graveyard closer to the highway, and it's covered in boring grass that's mowed once a week and they *throw out* the flowers you leave after a week. It's way more respectable than this old place, which is why I love it here. Hey, speaking of relatives, check this out!"

Minna led her down a row of aboveground crypts that looked like small marble houses. Some were ornate, with open doors that allowed the breeze to push leaves through. Peeking into one, Beatrice saw a grime-covered stained-glass window at the back, and a vase holding plastic flowers tipped onto its side. On either side were plaques with names, and presumably, the original owners of the names were lying behind them.

"Look." The crypt Minna led them to wasn't huge—maybe half the size of a single-car garage.

Holland was carved grandly at the top of the door's arch.

Beatrice inhaled sharply.

Her family, right here.

Engraved in smaller letters was *Anna Holland, daughter of Valeska Holland.* The next line: *Rosalind Holland, daughter of Anna Holland.* Decorative fleur-de-lis wound over the marbled sides. The tomb had one door, also marble, which looked firmly closed. There was no handle, nor anything else that suggested an entrance, just a single slot that might fit a key.

"Gran really wants to get permission to be buried in there with her mom and grandma. She also wants me and Mom to be shoved in there, too, although honestly, that's not her business, is it?"

Mutely, Beatrice shook her head. She had a living will in

which she'd stated she wanted to be cremated and placed in Grant's prepurchased plot at Forest Lawn. *That* was going to have to be amended. Sooner might be better than later.

Minna went on, "Gran wants to get in and clean in there, too, but we've never been able to find the key, and no one at the city council seems to know what to do next about getting permission to remake one. Anyway, over here, I have something even better to show you!"

Her niece hooked her hand around the top of a stone pillar and swung herself around it so that she was facing the lettering. "Here we are. Meet your earliest foremother to live in Skerry Cove."

Xenia Holland, b. 1827, d. 1919. Below that, carved into the marble in a light script: *She who sees must share her vision.*

Minna crossed her ankles and sank to the grass, patting the ground next to her. "Sit with me? We'll spend time with the ancestors. First with the ladies. My dad's here in the graveyard, too, but I'll show you his spot later."

Ancestors. Her very own. "So who is this?"

"Xenia is my great-times-five-grandmother, so she's your quadruple great. She came to the island in 1851 with the first wave of white colonizers. Even though Xenia's husband left to hunt for gold in California, her daughter Valeska was born here in 1857, and she refused to leave. Valeska married Theodore Velamen in 1877." She shot a quick glance at Beatrice. "He wasn't a good man. She's not buried in this graveyard because of him. Gran won't tell me much about them, but I'll get it out of her someday. Valeska's daughter is Anna, who's in the family crypt I showed you, with Rosalind, her daughter. Rosalind was Gran's mother. I met her when I was a baby, apparently, but I don't remember."

Beatrice sat, the grass's coolness rising through her jeans.

She reached forward to touch the marble, and of course, it was cold, much colder than the grass. But she also felt an odd banked warmth, like the side of a cold mug when you've just poured the coffee in, the second before the ceramic heats. Maybe the sun had warmed it all morning, even though there was no sun overhead now, just dark, looming clouds.

Minna nodded as she unzipped the top of her backpack. "You can feel it, right?"

Beatrice yanked back her hand. "What?"

"That weird warmth."

She wasn't going to admit it. "Xenia and Valeska. Not common names."

"I think they're Slavic, maybe? I'm not sure if we know where Xenia's family came from, but we know they were both powerful AF. I've been trying to get Valeska to talk to me for *ages* but nothing yet. Don't tell Mom, though. She worries."

Beatrice sank her fingers into the grass. "And by getting Valeska to talk, you mean..."

"Oh, Aunt Bea." She looked shy suddenly. "Can I call you that? I want to, but I won't if you hate it."

Even though the sun was still hidden behind the clouds, the top of Beatrice's head warmed. "I love it."

Minna gave her a brilliant smile. "Yay. Oh, my god, Aunt Bea, we've got a *lot* to go over."

Beatrice opened the grimoire, flipping through it until she found the page that had been folded back on itself, almost to the very center of the book. In the two-millimeter gap where the edge of the page touched the middle, a thin layer of wax had been laid down, sealing the page to itself. "Can we go over this?" She pulled at the half page to see if she could peek down into it without breaking the seal.

"*No.*" With a look of horror, Minna yanked the book out of

her hands. "We don't open that page. Ever. Unless it's the end of the line."

Beatrice felt chastened. "I was only teasing."

"Seriously, we don't even joke about that."

"Okay."

Minna's expression was fierce. "I mean it."

When had Beatrice turned into the kid and Minna the adult? "Fine." She tried to believe it really was, in fact, fine. "Tell me some things about magic."

"Tell you? I'm going to make you *do* magic."

For the next two hours, Minna tested Beatrice, getting her to say and do things that made no sense. Minna would open to a page, then she'd give Beatrice a collection of words to say, sometimes in verse, sometimes just a jumble of disparate phrases that felt ragged in her mouth.

Then a solid block of *nothing* would happen.

As the morning wore into afternoon, the clouds overhead darkened, and the scent of impending rain rolled in. They stayed seated, though, Minna correcting Beatrice's pronunciation.

Still, nothing.

Beatrice found this unsurprising, but every time she did a magic belly-flop, Minna seemed flummoxed. "Huh. That should have been an easy one. Okay. This one—you'll totally be able to do this one. I could do it when I was five. This will make the grass move."

When Beatrice said the words, the grass did move.

"Good job! You did it!"

Beatrice licked her finger and held it up. "The grass moved because: wind."

"But maybe—did it blow the opposite way for a second?"

No. It hadn't.

That morning, when she'd sat with Cordelia in the galley of

the boat, Beatrice could admit that she'd felt a poignant tug of hope. Silly, of course, but anyone might have. It had been a fresh new day, the book had looked so beautiful, and who didn't want magic to be real?

But now, she was sitting in the real world, humoring her real niece, and she didn't want to keep disappointing Minna. "Maybe that's enough for one day? Try again another time?"

Minna looked up from a page covered in red and black ink. "You still don't believe. You need more proof."

She sighed. "Minna, I'm a math person. I'll always need more proof until I can see for myself that something is true. It's okay, I believe that *you* believe it." Even as the words came out of her mouth, she regretted them. What a stupid, unhelpful thing to say.

Minna frowned. Then she closed her eyes. Her lips moved, but what she said was too quiet for Beatrice to hear.

"I'm sorry—"

Minna held up a hand. Her lips kept moving as her eyelids fluttered, as the wind lifted and dropped her hair.

Fine. Beatrice would wait for whatever this was, then she'd praise the girl for whatever she eventually said, and then she'd go check to see if Reno needed her for a bookcase consultation, before returning the grimoire to Cordelia at the store.

Minna's eyes flew open. "In your home, you have a secret shrine to the woman who was your alternate mother inside a blue suitcase that you keep at the top of a closet."

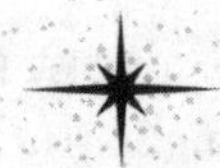

CHAPTER TWENTY-ONE

Experiment. People think they're going to accidentally open a portal to hell, but I hate to break it to you, it takes a lot of training to do something like that. The worst that might happen is you could poison a few people. The hellmouth worry is overblown. Just play.

—Evie Oxby, to Martha Stewart at her Skylands home

Beatrice's whole body jolted, as if Minna had reached out and slapped her.

The girl continued, "You take out the suitcase every year on her death day and let yourself look at it for exactly fifteen minutes. You literally set a timer. The suitcase holds only one thing—I can't quite figure out what it is. It's round and clear, like a snow globe with no snow. Like, red rocks instead? I don't get it but that's what I see. Then you zip up the suitcase and you try not to think about her again until the next year rolls around, but you always fail."

"What the fucking *fuck*."

"Ooof." Minna leaned forward, looking a tinge green. "That one hurt a little."

"How did you do that? Who told you that?"

"I asked someone."

"Did I put that on Instagram or something?" As far as Beatrice knew, she'd never put the globe on social media, but maybe she'd just forgotten?

Minna shook her head. "What's the thing with the red rocks? Is it really a snow globe?"

A million years ago, when Beatrice was a junior in high school, Dad and Naya had taken her to Bryce Canyon. One morning, Dad slept in while she and Naya went to Inspiration Point before the sun came up. It was late in the season, and it started snowing as they waited. When the sky streaked purple with the sunrise, the red pillars glowed through the floating snow. Beatrice had laughed at how hard Naya cried at the beauty of what she called a miracle. Later, in a gift shop, Naya bought a snow globe, tiny limestone columns rising inside it. Instead of fake snow inside, it held reddish sand. After Naya died, it was the one thing Beatrice had asked her father for.

She exhaled roughly. "Snow globe, with sand. But—how do you know about it? You've got to tell me because you're freaking me *out*."

"A guide told me."

"A *guide*." Beatrice couldn't keep the heat, the panic out of her voice. "I don't understand. This doesn't make sense."

Minna scooted closer. "You have to stop trying to make it make sense. It's not going to. Not really."

A blast of cold air struck Beatrice's face. "Minna. *Tell me how you knew*."

"Okay, okay! I chanted an incantation that gets me into contact with someone who can connect me with dead people."

"Someone?"

"I told you. A guide. I've worked with them before. And no, I didn't connect with your mother figure herself."

"Naya. Her name was Naya." Even saying her name still hurt.

"I didn't connect with her, and my guide didn't, either, but—okay, this is kind of hard to explain. It's kind of like that game you play in grade school. Telephone, you know, but I don't hear things, I see them instead. Naya must have given someone the image of the suitcase, and then the image of the snow globe, in order to prove to you that it was her, and then that someone sent the image to my guide, who sent it to me."

"So you see images in your head." No, Beatrice couldn't believe this. She didn't want to believe it.

Or did she? Could it be possible Naya was reaching out?

If she was—if that could be true—what would that *mean*?

"Yeah, I'm a clairvoyant medium. In training, I mean. And I only see images when I ask for help in seeing them—it's not like I'm getting images from the dead all the time. Which is good, especially during the school year, because that would seriously mess with my homework."

"Oh, my god." A warmth crept through Beatrice's bones as if she'd been covered with a heated blanket—could Naya really be thinking of her?

If so, it would mean Naya still existed somewhere.

The taste of salt rose at the back of Beatrice's throat.

Life after death, come on. No one in the history of the world had ever *proved* it, and certainly, if it were a true thing, someone would have managed to. Which meant it was all crap. But—how to explain the red rock snow globe?

The warmth she felt shifted to a chill as the wind blew colder against her face. "It could just be coincidence."

Minna rolled her eyes. "The front pocket of the suitcase is broken, and there's a red ribbon tied to the handle."

Wrong. "Red bandanna. Not a ribbon."

Holding up her hands, Minna said, "Fine. You got me. You're right—all of this is just a big fat hoax. Jeesh. In the meantime, I want you to try it."

"Try *what*?"

"The incantation."

"No."

"Because you're scared?"

"Absolutely not." But fear laced through her veins like a poison.

"I'll be right here with you."

"Fabulous. Protection in the form of a fifteen-year-old girl."

"Almost sixteen. And you've sucked at all the other incantations anyway. You really think you're going to get this one right? What's the harm in trying?"

She did have a point. "Fine."

Minna took out a notebook and pen from her backpack and handed them to Beatrice. "Mom used to make me write them out when I was learning. Maybe it'll help." She opened the grimoire again, to a page on which the writing had grown faint.

"Is that...a coffee stain?" A brown half ring marred the page.

Smiling, Minna touched it. "You know when your favorite page in the cookbook gets all effed up because you use it so much? Same thing. Okay. I'll read it to you, and you write it out phonetically, so you get it right."

"It's not a rhyme, like the others?"

"It's not a rhyme, and it's not in English. Well, it may be Old English or something, but it doesn't sound like anything I know."

The syllables were odd and didn't fit in Beatrice's mouth.

Piece by piece, she said them slowly, writing them down and putting them together, one after another, until Minna finally said, "Good. You've got all the bits. Now say it all at once."

"And then what?"

"Then you listen. Or you see. Or whatever." Minna's voice was cheerful. "Anything could happen."

Beatrice took a deep breath and sat up straighter. "This isn't going to do anything."

"Noted."

She began to mutter the words.

As each syllable slipped through her mouth, the phrases got easier to say. By the time she'd spoken the three gibberish lines, the pen in her hand heated up, as if it had been plugged into a wall socket.

"What the—?"

But before she could finish asking, everything dropped away. She could see Minna's outline, but it was blurred, as if Beatrice had put on someone else's prescription glasses.

In her mind rose the image of an old fountain pen, the nib of it nosing into the keyhole of a rusted padlock. A vibration roared in her ears, and she only wanted one thing: to scrape the pen's tip against the paper in the notebook. As the ink trailed out—dark blue against the ruled pages—it was the only thing that stayed clear.

It felt like scratching an old mosquito bite, the kind that's mostly healed but wakes you in the middle of the night with its phantom itch as fresh and new as the day you got it. Impossible to resist. She didn't *want* to resist. The only thing that mattered was drawing the lines. Nothing in Beatrice's consciousness told her how to move the pen—it was an urge that she followed without questioning, like drinking a glass of water when she was thirsty. It was right. It was good.

Snap.

With an audible pop, the buzz in her head stopped its whine.

The plastic barrel of the pen, which had felt like hot metal just two seconds before, was cool again. Just a plastic Paper Mate. The air was heavier and colder, and thunder rumbled close by.

Minna swam back into focus—her mouth was slightly open, her eyes wide. "Whoa. What did that feel like?"

Feel like?

Beatrice hadn't felt. She'd just *been*. Sometimes, when she was working on a particularly thorny tax problem for a client, she'd look up to find an hour had passed instead of a minute. It had been like that—the knowledge of herself had vanished, and she'd—somehow—become the blue line on the page.

"What did you write?" Minna was clearly working hard to control herself, but her fingers twitched as if she wanted to grab the notebook right out of Beatrice's hands.

Beatrice read from the page: "*Norman, the key is in the g/f pizza box in the freezer.*"

"Huh?"

She read the next line. "*K–M and J send love and out of season peppermint bark. Don't worry. We're watching O. Froggy carries our kisses.*"

"What does that mean?"

Beatrice blinked at her. "You think *I* know?"

"And what's that one?"

"*Patrick, you'll be forgiven but not yet. Andy says be patient.*"

"This is so great. And the last one?"

Beatrice read it out, "*K is here with me. We are together. At the same time, I've never left your side, nor has he. He knows his blue hanky will always catch your tears. He still loves salt and vinegar chips dipped in Nutella, and he says you never have to let him go. I'm sorry I said you did. L.*" Good grief. This was ridiculous.

"Nothing for you, specifically, though?"

"I mean, I have no idea. But they're not my initials..."

Minna's voice got smaller. "And nothing for me?"

Oh, no. "Come on, we can't read anything into this. It's like playing with the Ouija board, you know?" When she was a kid, she'd talked Naya into playing with one after she'd found it at a garage sale. The planchette had rocketed around the board, but the words it spelled had never made sense. Naya had said her father could never know, which was weird, because surely Naya had been the one pushing it.

Minna's eyes were huge. "The Ouija board always tells the truth."

Just because Minna presented herself like a small adult didn't mean she wasn't just a kid. "It's a board game made by Hasbro, and this—whatever this is—is a game, too."

"Bullshit." Now Minna did yank at the notebook.

Beatrice let her have it. She passed the pen back, too, before picking up the grimoire and slipping it into her bag. The sooner she returned it to Cordelia, the better.

"You *know* it's real. You can feel it. I saw your face—you felt the power."

"Power? I just scribbled junk on a page because..." *Because why?* "Because I wanted to buy into it. To make you happy."

"You're *so* full of crap!" Minna blinked rapidly, her nose scrunching up, looking like she was on the verge of tears. "You've probably known you could do this since you were little, and you've been shoving it back inside you, too scared to let any of it out."

"I swear to you, I don't believe in magic, and I never have."

"Don't call it magic, then. Gran sometimes calls it divine intention, and you *can't* deny that you want things. You can't tell me you wouldn't put energy and intention into something you were desperate to have. What do you want to do with your intention?"

I want to live.

So that just made her exactly like any other human on the planet. Not special. Definitely not magical. "Fine. So what do *you* want to do with your intention?"

Tears rose to Minna's eyes. "I want to talk to my dad."

CHAPTER TWENTY-TWO

When in doubt, look to the sky. There's more up there than we can ever know. Besides, it's pretty, isn't it? What do *you* see in this cloud?

—Evie Oxby, Instagram

Beatrice's heart creaked. "I understand—"

Minna threw the pen against Xenia's headstone. "You do *not*. You're pissed at your father, but he's alive. Mine isn't. Wanna know what the worst part is? He wanted a boy. Did he get a boy? Yes. Was he the happiest man on the planet because he had a baby boy? Yes, he was, and I know that because he told my mother a million times. And because he died falling off that stupid ladder before I was old enough to remember him, my mother spent the first ten years of my life telling me how *thrilled* he was that he got what he wanted: a strong, smart boy." She plucked at her red capelet. "But he didn't get that, did he? He actually got a girl. And my mother stopped telling me he wanted me because she tries not to lie straight to my face. I know she and Gran love me the way I am. But my father? I want to talk to *him*. I want to tell him—I want to see if—"

Beatrice did get it, though. Even after Naya had come into their lives, the empty *mother* spot never truly filled.

Minna's voice broke as she hung her head. "Mom and Gran say they can't talk to him because of stupid reasons, like they're too close to the situation, and I can sometimes get images through my guide but never from him. And then you just—you just tap into the actual words of people on the other side? Just like that? But you don't want to? You don't want to even try to learn how to control it?" With a strangled groan, she flopped backward on the grass. "It's too much."

The words came before Beatrice could stop them. "I'll try."

Minna's head popped up. "Huh?"

"Tell me what to do, and I'll try it." It might be ridiculous, but Beatrice felt as if she'd try anything for this girl. "I don't believe in magic, or in divine intention or in whatever word you want to dress it up in. But I believe in *you*. So tell me what to do."

Minna waggled her arms and legs in the air like an upside-down water bug and then scrambled up. "Oh, my god. Thank you. Just one more try. Thank you." She shoved the notebook back at Beatrice.

Beatrice took it and reached for the pen from where it had landed in the grass after bouncing off the headstone. "Should I read it again? Out loud?" She touched the nonsensical syllables she'd written out.

Minna nodded and looked up as the first cold raindrops hit the leaves overhead. "I'll hold the umbrella over you."

"What else?"

"Set the intention. His name was Taurus." Her spine straightened. "He's buried around the corner—should we go there? No, wait. This feels right. Here with our ancestors. Just think of me. Then reach for him and see what comes through."

It felt cruel to get Minna's hopes up, but somehow it felt crueler to deny her the attempt.

So Beatrice began to read the sounds out loud.

"Bent canth ilno trill—"

The image of the fountain pen clicking itself into the old padlock flashed back into her mind, and she wasn't even halfway through speaking the first line when something rose in her chest—a need that was as strong as her need for oxygen—she needed to write right *now.*

Her brain folded itself out of the way, leaving her hand to move on its own. She had as much control over it as she did the rain, now coming down harder, smacking against the umbrella Minna held over them both.

A second—or an hour—later, she blinked, and she was back in control of her hand, her breath, her brain.

run to the tree house get them out don't wait run and then run more go NOW

Minna met her eyes.

Then, together, they ran.

Minna was younger, with longer and stronger legs, but somehow Beatrice kept pace with her niece as they raced through the rain. As she frantically wiped water from her eyes, fear blazed through Beatrice's limbs, fueling her speed. Out the gates of the cemetery, down the residential side streets until they hit the main drag—then they skidded around the corner and dashed across the street, dodging cars, ignoring their outraged honks.

Through the park, past the gazebo, and then they were there, at the base of the tree house where the busker had stopped on Beatrice's first day in town.

Rain lashed down, and the wind howled through the limbs. Minna gasped for breath as she pushed back her dripping hair. "What do we do?"

Beatrice threw herself at the ladder nailed to the tree's trunk. On another day, she'd probably have taken some time to think about how to climb it without hurting herself, but now, she flew up as if she'd done it a hundred times. She pushed her way past the hanging oilcloth to crouch inside the tiny space.

Inside, where it was still dry, three girls read comic books. None of them could have been more than ten years old. The noise of the pounding rain was a roar.

"Out," yelped Beatrice. "You have to get out."

"What?"

"Who *are* you?"

"Throw them down if you have to!" Minna shouted from the base.

"It's not safe. Get out, *now*!"

Her roar was enough to terrify them into motion, and they leaped around her and out, tumbling down the ladder, Beatrice scrambling down after them.

run more go NOW—she could almost hear the words she'd written reverberating in her ears.

"Keep going! To the gazebo!" The five of them ran the fifty yards, Minna in front, Beatrice bringing up the rear.

Once in the gazebo, out of the rain, the tallest girl demanded answers Beatrice didn't have. "What's your problem? Now we're soaked." She held out a comic book. "And so are these!"

"I'll buy you new ones," mumbled Beatrice, feeling sick to her stomach. The smallest girl's lower lip was trembling. What *had* Beatrice been thinking? Had she just kidnapped these kids?

No, that required keeping them, right? She'd merely forced them quickly to a new place, but that was probably some kind of crime, too—

CRASH.

The sky lit up—everything did, going white-bright, the noise so loud, it was almost soundless, registering only as pressure and a terrifying heat.

Just as quickly, the light and heat and pressure were gone.

And the tree that held the tree house just...disintegrated. The lightning must have destroyed the trunk itself from the inside out, because instead of simply burning, as the tree house was doing—flames leaping from all sides—the trunk began to crumble, and then, with a thunderous *whoomp*, it collapsed into itself, the biggest limbs cracking as they hit the ground, the smaller limbs catching fire.

Two of the girls burst into tears. The tallest one walked to the edge of the gazebo's platform and threw up neatly into a trash can.

The handkerchief Cordelia had given her was in Beatrice's hand, but she didn't remember taking it out of her pocket. She gripped it so tightly a French knot indented the tip of her finger.

Two women and three men hurtled out of Fritz's café, throwing themselves at the girls, shouting in confusion, their voices merging with the siren that rose in the distance.

If Beatrice had arrived a few minutes later, the parents clutching their kids would have had no one to hold.

Fritz arrived, followed by Keelia. A girl Minna's age detached herself from Keelia's side and wrapped her arms around Minna.

Beatrice didn't notice her legs were giving out until Reno, who had arrived along with the parents, guided her to sit crossed-legged on the gazebo's wooden floor.

"It's okay," said Reno.

"But—" Beatrice clutched at Reno's warm, strong hands. "What if I hadn't—what if—"

"It's a *miracle*," said the woman holding the tall girl.

It couldn't be a miracle. She and Minna had simply done something, something that had given Beatrice information that she couldn't have had any other way, information that had allowed her to save those kids.

Had that been . . . a *really* big coincidence?

No, of course not. Coincidences didn't work that way, written on paper in some kind of bizarre fugue state.

That was—it had to be—magic.

But magic didn't exist.

CHAPTER TWENTY-THREE

Starting to learn about your own psychic power is like being alone in a tiny boat in an immense sea. During a hurricane. And your boat's just sprung a leak, your period's just started, you have no tampons, and your cell phone just went overboard.

—*Evie Oxby,* Come at Me, Boo

So for the second time in four days, Beatrice found herself telling a fire official what had happened, how she (and this time, three others) had escaped certain death. Without discussing it, neither she nor Minna mentioned exactly how they'd ended up in the right place at the right time, and people seemed to accept her explanation. *The storm was starting to rage—I just didn't think it was safe for the girls to be in there.*

Then Cordelia was there, and before Beatrice knew what was happening, she and Minna had been herded into Which Craft.

Cordelia flipped the Open sign to Closed and locked the door. Then she moved three afghans and a basket of yarn from the sofa. "Sit. Breathe. Then tell me everything."

Astrid appeared from the back room, sweeping out in a long black linen tunic, her white hair piled artfully on top of her head. "You'll tell *us* everything. And only us." She raised an eyebrow at Reno, who was behind the counter, pulling waters out of a mini fridge.

"Reno is us, Mom. You should know that by now."

"Oh, *fine*." Astrid sank into the largest armchair. "What happened? I saw the tree fall and the fire start, so lightning, yes? But all that screaming—a little dramatic, don't you think?"

Cordelia sat next to Minna, draping an arm over her daughter's shoulders. "Mom, how about we let them tell us? In their own words?"

Reno handed each of them a water, and then, instead of sitting in the spare chair, she sat next to Beatrice. Her dark curls fell over her forehead as she glanced at Beatrice. In a low voice, she said, "Still okay?"

Was she? Maybe. She nodded.

Cordelia pointed at Minna. "Okay, my darling. Go."

Minna's words tumbled quickly from her mouth. "Okay, so we went to the graveyard because I wanted to introduce her to the relatives. We saw Anna and Rosalind's crypt, and we sat with Xenia, and then we tried some things from the grimoire and no offense, Aunt Bea, but Mom, she wasn't good at *anything*, and then I—" She broke off and stared up at her mother.

"You're not going to get in trouble."

"Okay, so I talked to a guide—"

Cordelia's jaw tightened. "I told you not to do that without me."

"—and it showed me this image sent from Aunt Bea's stepmom, and then she kind of believed me a little more, and then *she* tried it, and oh my god, you should have seen it, she reached for my pen and then she was writing—"

Astrid started. "She wrote in our grimoire?"

"She wrote in the notebook I'd brought because I'm not the dumbass you sometimes think I am, Gran, and then she went super red in the face and wrote a bunch of things, and none of them make sense, but I bet they *do* somehow, we just don't know it yet, and she still didn't really believe, so I told her—" Minna broke off.

Cordelia squeezed her shoulder. "Yeah?"

"I. Um. I asked her if she would try again, as a favor to me. Um."

Cordelia's eyes narrowed. "Why would you want that?"

"I know I shouldn't have. But I wanted to hear from Sienna."

Beatrice stared at Minna—no matter who Sienna was, that wasn't the truth.

But Minna gave her a miserably piteous look, the look of a lost kitten taking shelter from the rain under a truck's rusted bumper.

So Beatrice shut her mouth. For now.

Astrid said, "Who?"

Cordelia stroked Minna's hair. "Her friend who drowned last year, remember, Mom? Baby, we talked about that. I know you're sad, but Sienna's just fine where she is."

"I know. I mean, I should have remembered. But then—this is the weirdest part—Aunt Bea didn't even get to the end of the incantation. Maybe not even halfway! So I don't get that, but she did it again, went all red like a tomato again and wrote down—wait, I have it here. Look." Minna shook the notebook out of her backpack and flipped it open.

run to the tree house get them out don't wait run and then run more go NOW

"So we ran."

Cordelia traced the words on the page with her index finger and Astrid demanded they be read aloud to her. Minna did, and then said, "Beatrice scaled the tree like a cat, I swear, and then the kids came out so fast, it was like she'd turned the whole thing upside down and shook it."

The kids. Minna was still a kid herself, and she'd been near the tree, way too near—what if she'd been struck? Beatrice's pulse juddered in her throat again.

Next to her, Reno tapped the back of her hand, then pointed to her own chest. She took a deep breath in, then let it out just as slowly.

Gratefully, Beatrice mimicked the motion.

"So that's the story. The end. Magic for the win. I told her about divine intention, Gran, but maybe you can explain that—"

Astrid shook her head. "That wasn't magic. That wasn't divine intention."

The cap of Beatrice's water bottle slipped out of her hand.

Cordelia folded her lips as if she agreed but didn't want to.

Astrid continued, "Magic requires intention and energy. A miracle is a gift. Plain and simple."

Now Beatrice was confused. "I did say the spell. I put intention into it."

"But you didn't finish saying it?"

Dumbly, Beatrice shook her head.

Astrid's expression looked almost kind. "There you go. You were given the gift anyway. I'm not sure why you look so upset. Miracles are good things."

Miracle number three.

In a very quiet voice, Minna said, "Do you think, maybe, the person we were trying to reach—Sienna, I mean—was the one who told us to run?"

Cordelia leaned forward as if her stomach hurt. "I don't know, baby."

"Oh."

Cordelia looked at Beatrice. "Three miracles down."

No, Minna didn't need to know about the prediction. "Don't—"

"Only four to go."

Minna's expression was horrified. "Wait. What's going on?"

Beatrice had no idea what to say.

"Mom?"

Gently, Cordelia said, "Keelia has a sister named Winnie who's just moved to town. I haven't met her yet, but I know from what Keelia says that she's the real deal. Aunt Beatrice received a prediction, from her and another psychic. She—um—might be dying, but before she does, she'll experience seven miracles."

It took Minna only two or three slow blinks to digest it. "That was the third miracle? The tree house?"

I don't believe in any of this. But something kept Beatrice from saying the words out loud.

"It might have been." Cordelia took her hand. "We'll figure it out, though. Stronger together, right?"

Astrid had gone so pale that her skin resembled the undyed fiber in the basket perched next to her. "Winnie said that?"

Cordelia nodded.

Astrid glared at Beatrice. "Who was the other psychic?"

Reluctantly, Beatrice muttered, "Evie Oxby."

"Oh, *no*." Minna bit her lip and stared at Beatrice as if she was going to kick the bucket right then and there. "We'll figure it out. We will!"

That was nice. But none of them had to deal with the rising existential panic that threatened to choke Beatrice, did they? No, that was hers, her own dire gift bag of terror.

I'm young. Youngish, at least. I'm healthy.

At her last routine physical, the doctor had said, "Whatever you're doing, keep it up. You've got the blood pressure of a twenty-year-old runner and your labs are gorgeous."

I'm youngish and I'm healthy.

A chill swept through her, cooling the sweat that had broken out along her spine.

Reno bent to pick up the cap of her water bottle for her. When she pressed it into Beatrice's hand, the kindness of the small gesture made tears rise behind her eyelids.

Cordelia turned to Astrid. "We *are* going to figure it out. Right?"

Instead of answering, their mother rose.

"Mom?"

Astrid went to the front glass door, unlocked it, passed through, and with a key she withdrew from a pocket in her coat, relocked it again from the outside. Then she was gone, down the sidewalk.

Beatrice's throat knotted so tightly, she could hardly breathe. Yep, that was just about what she'd expected from a person who'd abandoned her as a baby.

Minna sighed. "She's just pissed all the action isn't happening to *her*."

But Cordelia shook her head. "There's more to it than that. I think it's guilt. And fear."

Bullshit. Astrid didn't fear losing her. How could she? She barely accepted the reality of her.

Besides, the reality of Beatrice wasn't going to last very long at this rate. Nausea rolled through her at the thought. "Fuck," she said softly.

Reno spoke. "What about those other things you wrote?"

Cordelia threw her a grateful look. "Of course. Start with what we have."

Minna flipped back a page. "Here." She let Cordelia read the page first, and then passed it to Reno.

As Reno read the words, Beatrice skimmed them again.

Drivel. All of it.

Except…

It had felt the same to write the sentence about the tree house.

So, what if it wasn't drivel?

Minna listed names on her fingers. "Norman. Do we know a Norman? And Patrick—isn't that the name of the new butcher at the store? And those initials, *K*, *M*, *J*, and *O*."

"Keelia and Olive?" said Reno.

Beatrice scanned that one again.

K–M and J send love and out of season peppermint bark. Don't worry. We're watching O. Froggy carries our kisses.

Cordelia said, "Keelia's mother's name was Margaret, right? What was her dad's name?"

Minna's mouth formed a circle. "Olive was just talking about her grandpa on her mom's side. Grandpa Jackson."

At the bookstore, Keelia was ringing up a customer. The girl who had put her arms around Minna in the gazebo was behind the register also, perched on a stool, reading a thick romance novel. She must be Keelia's daughter, Olive.

Minna said to her, "Hi, you."

Olive said, "Hi back."

Something swam in the air between the two girls. Beatrice looked at Olive and then back at Minna. *Oh.* Okay, that was damn cute. Maybe she'd get a chance to ask Minna about it later.

When the customer had left the store, Cordelia said, "Keelia, this is going to sound really weird—will you trust me?"

Keelia tipped her head to the side. "The last time you said that, you made me get a mammogram that showed stage one breast cancer, so you think I won't trust you now? Spit it out, though. Am I sick again?"

"*God*, no. Absolutely not. Sorry to scare you like that. This is different. What does peppermint bark make you think of?"

Keelia's laugh was relieved. "I didn't expect that." She shot a look at Olive. "We love that stuff. My parents used to give us each a box of it at Christmas, and Mom would always buy two extra boxes, put 'em in the freezer. She'd give them to us in July, as a half-Christmas surprise."

Spit caught at the back of Beatrice's throat as she choked.

"What were their names again? Margaret, right? And..."

"Jackson. Margaret and Jackson." Keelia sighed. "Oh, we miss them, don't we, honey?"

Olive nodded.

Cordelia slid the notebook across the counter. "Beatrice did some automatic writing. That means that—"

"I've been your friend a long time. I know what it is," said Keelia, pulling the notebook toward her. Olive stood behind her, and together, they read the words.

Beatrice held her breath. This was nothing. It meant nothing. That's what Keelia would say, right? Any second now.

"Well." Keelia thumped down onto the stool behind her. "Okay. That's... something. That sure is something."

Good god. What was happening? Beatrice stepped forward. "It actually makes sense to you?"

"Every word of it. Mom used to watch Olive when I was here at the store, on the days I couldn't bring her in, do you remember that? And when Mom was dying, what, six months after Papa passed? She said she'd always watch her. That they both would." Keelia rubbed her cheeks. "And Olive still has Froggy on her bed, the one they gave her when she was a baby."

CHAPTER TWENTY-FOUR

Pain comes and goes. When you're in it, you think it'll last forever. It won't. Think of yourself like that kitten in the Hang In There poster. Cheesy as hell, but sometimes all we can do is hang on a little longer. Spirit's got a reason for you still being here. That much I know.

—Evie Oxby, Facebook Live

The next day, Beatrice went to the library to use the Wi-Fi. At the table that was rapidly becoming her favorite (next to a window that looked out on the town center's grassy lawn), she pulled up the medical results from her last routine physical. Her doctor had told her she'd been in great shape, but what if she'd missed something?

For an hour, Beatrice examined the labs that had come back. She didn't understand all the words, but when she cross-referenced her levels against what Google said were normal ones, Beatrice did, in fact, look to be in great shape. Perfect blood pressure, normal blood sugar levels, a low (but still normal) resting heart rate.

A clean bill of health.

Did that mean her death would be unnatural? Violent?

Beatrice squeezed her eyes shut and pushed her laptop away from her. Enough of this. She'd go back home and work on figuring out the houseboat's battery storage thing.

As Beatrice walked through town, she remembered what her doctor had said the last time she'd seen her. *Enjoy your good health.*

So, was the prediction one of those self-fulfilling prophecies? Would she be so worried about dying that she wouldn't get off the tracks in time to avoid the train?

If something *did* happen to her, it would kill Dad to lose her. With his own health issues, and after losing Naya, it would be the final straw for him.

Of course, he'd apparently handled losing Cordelia just fine.

In front of the market, she almost tripped over a crate of apples being unloaded from a truck double-parked on the street. "Be careful, lady," admonished the delivery person.

Good idea.

She was careful not to glance into Fritz's café as she passed, nor did she look into the bookshop window. She didn't want to talk to anyone right now. She just needed to get back home. Hopefully Reno would be done working on the bookcases for the day and Beatrice could—what? Bully herself into believing the majority of psychic predictions were bullshit? She already believed that. Why the hell was she feeling so shaky?

Which Craft was just a few doors up, so she crossed the street and kept her face averted. In the grassy park at the center of the village, a group of children was racing around the playground, and a joyful golden retriever bounced after a ball thrown by its owner. The rubble of the burned tree was almost all gone, tidily spirited away at some point, but there was no hiding the blackened grass. She could still smell the char of it.

The same busker she'd seen her first day in town was leaning against an oak tree near the gazebo, playing an old song Dad liked. A Townes Van Zandt tune, maybe? She caught a few words: "I tried to kill the pain, bought some wine, and hopped a train, seemed easier than just waitin' around to die."

Beatrice stopped in the middle of the sidewalk. What *wasn't* easier than waiting around to die?

She closed her eyes and tried to feel anything wrong inside her body, but all she felt was her heart, thumping along like it always did. Maybe a little faster than normal, but no pain. Just fear.

Open your eyes.

The words were insistent and almost audible in her head—neither male nor female, just there. Fair enough. If she wanted to remain unnoticed on her walk back to the houseboat, standing with her eyes closed in the middle of the sidewalk wasn't the way to do it.

So she opened her eyes.

Just in time to witness a very small boy dart in front of a fast-moving car.

CHAPTER TWENTY-FIVE

Sometimes there are no answers to our questions.
And that's why the Universe made TikTok.
—*Evie Oxby,* CBS Mornings

The double-parked delivery truck had obviously blocked the driver's vision, and in what felt like a hundredth of a second, Beatrice saw the driver's face contort with shock. But no matter what, no matter how quickly the woman slammed on her brakes or spun the wheel, there was no way to prevent the impact. She was going too fast, with no one close enough to the boy to grab him out of the way.

There were no screams, no sound. Not yet. There would be soon. For now, Beatrice was the only witness.

A blast of heat roared through her and suddenly she was toppled, crumpled to the cement.

Then the boy was in her arms, slammed into her body like he'd been thrown at her, which, essentially, he had been.

Because he'd flown.

She'd watched.

One instant, he was about to be mown down by the woman driving the red car, the next it was as if he'd sprouted wings, his small body bent backward as he was shot through the air into her arms. Beatrice looked down at him. His nose was bleeding. His mouth was wide open for three, four, five long seconds, and then his wail matched that of his mother's, who dropped to the cement next to Beatrice.

"How—I saw him—*Dario*, Jesus." The dark-haired woman wiped away the blood with her hand. "Dario, baby, are you okay?"

The boy launched himself out of Beatrice's grasp and into the arms of his mother.

The driver, an older woman wearing a bedazzled denim jacket, raced toward them, her car abandoned in the roadway. Beatrice could still hear the squeal of her brakes echoing in the air.

"Did I hit him? I swear I didn't touch him, but how did—*did I hit him?*"

Beatrice shook her head. "He wasn't hit."

"I saw it," stammered Dario's mother. "I *saw* him fly. To you. It was a miracle. You performed a miracle." She held the boy in one arm, and with her free arm, she grabbed at Beatrice's hand. It wasn't until the woman was pressing her lips to Beatrice's fingers that she understood what she was doing.

Beatrice yanked her hand away. "I didn't do anything!"

The driver had tears running down her face. "I swear I didn't hit him. There was no impact."

Dario was bawling normally now. The nosebleed had already stopped, and he pulled at his mother's shirt, trying to hide his face.

"It was a miracle," his mother said reverently.

A small crowd was forming around them. (Was this Beatrice's lot in this town?) A man said into his phone, "Yeah, send an ambulance."

The driver covered her face with both hands. "I can't bear this. I'm so sorry."

Beatrice stood. She said the truest thing she knew. "Your son is just fine."

That had been a miracle. Of course it had. It had taken no energy from her. It had been an unearned gift.

It had been a miracle, so the boy would be okay.

The fourth miracle.

Through the static zapping through her brain, she said, "I'm going to get some wet paper towels, okay?" She pointed at the public restroom. "I'll be right back."

"Wait—"

But she didn't wait. She hurried toward the bathroom as if she had an important task to carry out, as if wet paper towels were exactly what was needed.

At the restroom's door, she turned and looked at the knot of people clustered on the sidewalk. Everyone was staring at Dario, and at his mother, who was just starting to shout at the driver. So instead of going inside the restroom, Beatrice went around it. On the other side, she could see the marina, just a block and a half away.

She ran.

CHAPTER TWENTY-SIX

The Universe speaks in shouts and whispers. The whispers are fine, but I honestly think it's got some work to do on its inside voice.

—*Evie Oxby,* Come at Me, Boo

A startled-looking Reno stood on the deck of Beatrice's houseboat sanding a long piece of wood as Beatrice raced down the dock.

Reno took one look at her face. "Just about done. Leaving now."

Beatrice waved her hand in what she hoped was a *Don't worry about it* motion but didn't wait to see if it was received that way.

She boiled water for a cup of tea, watching her hands shake as she waited. Strangely, they didn't feel connected to her body. It was as if she were watching someone else move through the boat. These were her hands? Really?

She peeked out the blinds—Reno was already heading up the ramp, away from the boat, and that was probably for the best.

Then she flipped on the lamp, got in bed, and opened her laptop.

Miracles were fucking real.

And Beatrice was going to die.

She was going to *die*, as in she would die *soon*. Everyone was going to die, yes, and everyone knew that, but Beatrice had never realized until this very moment how much she'd enjoyed the denial she'd cultivated. Decades in the future, yeah, she'd known she would die. But it wouldn't happen until she was old, until she was tired, until she was ready. It had never been anything to worry about, not really, even though at any moment of her life so far, her breath *could* have been snatched away unexpectedly. A drive-by shooting, a medication mix-up, a subway derailment.

So nothing had changed, not really. She even had a clean bill of health, something that should have reassured her. But all possible reassurance had been stripped from her when Dario had flown into her arms.

Impossible things didn't happen. That was simply their nature. Unless they were miracles.

After a lifetime of nothing impossible occurring to her, Beatrice had experienced four miracles. Numbers were important; numbers made sense. To zoom from zero to four? Miracles were real, and numbers didn't lie. That meant three miracles remained. Then her own death.

Beatrice opened a new Google Sheet, poising her fingers over the new, blank cells. Spreadsheets were where she could lay her brain down, setting each thought into its own discrete block so that she could fly up and look down on everything from a great height. It worked so beautifully with math—when each number was contained in its perfect little box, she could see where the problems were. Then she could make them work better, or best case, fix them entirely.

It wasn't just addition and subtraction. Even though Iris had teased her mercilessly for doing it, when Beatrice had been trying to decide whether it was a good idea to marry Grant, she'd used a spreadsheet to enumerate the pros and cons. She'd assigned each pro a number between one and ten, and had done the same thing for the cons. Pro: they had good, rambunctious sex. That earned an eight. Con: he was a man, and she honestly preferred the clean softness of women. That got a six. Pro: Naya was sick, and she and Dad wanted to live closer to Beatrice than ninety minutes away. Grant helped them find an affordable house just a block away from his place. That was a huge ten in the pro column. (It would have been an eleven if Beatrice exaggerated in columns, but she never had, and she never would.) Con: after a year of trying to engage with Grant's boys, the closest she'd come was when she learned to lace a lacrosse stick and Josh had said, "Not bad. For a girl." Four.

In the end, the pro column had 101 points, the con column had 97. So she'd married Grant.

And even now, the numbers probably still held. Numbers were never at fault. Grant had changed, that was all. No, wait, *he* hadn't changed—she'd simply failed to notice that Dulcina had claimed a higher numerical ranking than Beatrice had. And that, had she known it, would have earned a big fat ten in the cons, which would have put her final total at 101 pro, 107 con. With that result, she *wouldn't* have married him.

So. Could a spreadsheet help manage mortal doom?

There was only one way to find out.

Beatrice took a too-large sip of her tea and typed, *Life Expectancy Checklist.*

In the first column, she typed, *How many years left?*

In the second column, she typed, *Things to do with this time.*

Out the window, a sailboat chugged past under motor power, and her bed rocked slowly in the light wake. The tea in her cup moved gently in the same rhythm.

Okay, it was always better to start with the focus dialed all the way out. Zoom out and up, then look down from a bird's-eye view. She was forty-five. Her doctor had said she was healthy. Did that mean she could live to a hundred? Not very likely, but if she didn't factor in the prediction, it wasn't totally impossible.

Under *How many years left?* she typed, *If I have 55 years left.*

To the right of that, she started her list, each item getting its own vertically centered, left-justified text box.

Travel to every continent, including Antarctica.

Learn to draw.

Be able to play two instruments well and one badly but with enthusiasm [guitar, ukulele, and accordion?].

Have a strong community around me that I love, a community that loves me for who I am.

A whole community? How did someone get that? How was it made?

In school, it came built in, she supposed, though she never saw the people she went to high school or college with anymore. Presumably it happened at the workplace, but for her whole career, she'd been employed by Barnard Family Finance in their two-person office. Other than Dad, she'd never had workmates with whom to gather around a watercooler. She'd never been tasked with bringing a carrot cake for a coworker's birthday. True, she'd always enjoyed that she didn't have to deal with annoying associates she couldn't escape. But maybe bringing donuts and huddling in a break room had a greater purpose?

It had been easier when she and Iris had been together. Iris couldn't walk into a café without running into a best friend or ex-lover, and she couldn't walk out without making a new pal destined to become another bestie. She and her buddies had included Beatrice in the things they did. Then Grant and his group had done the same. Beatrice was forty-five, and had never had to build her own circle of friends.

Idly, Beatrice typed into an empty box, *Dulcina, go fuck yourself.*

Delete, delete, delete.

Building her own community would probably take fifty-five years. At least.

Next up: *If I have 25 years left.*

She'd be seventy when she died—okay, that was creeping into the age range she'd consider actually old. When she'd been twenty, seventy wasn't old, it was *ancient.* (And forty-five was old then.)

To the right, she slipped new goals into their tidy text boxes:

Visit beautiful places I've never been. Sublist: *Venice, Paris, New Orleans, Rio de Janeiro, Istanbul, San Miguel de Allende.*

Read one book a week for pleasure, not for learning.

Take a pottery class.

Make one new friend a year.

Beatrice sighed and pushed her feet more firmly under her new down comforter. The duvet cover was dark purple with bright red poppies. Grant would have hated it, but that's not why she'd bought it. She'd bought it because she loved it.

She typed: *If I have ten years left.*

If she died in ten years, she'd be fifty-five.

Learn to braid my hair like Cordelia's.

Ice skating lessons.

Live in a home filled with things that make my heart happy, no justifications needed.

Beatrice looked around—could this be that home? Some of the old timber still needed fixing and painting, and there wasn't a single knickknack on any surface, and anyway, she had none to place on a surface even if she'd wanted to. What *had* happened to her tchotchkes? Maybe she had a box of them somewhere. Grant had hated clutter—he'd always wanted his home to make anyone feel welcome. *Like the best kind of hotel, neutral and inclusive.*

The problem was that "neutral and inclusive" equaled

absolutely zero personality. Fuck that. Maybe she'd go to a flea market or thrift store this week and actively search out something just for *her.* Minna would surely know the best places to go—perhaps she'd come, too? Would Cordelia have the time to go with them? She could see it: Cordelia poking through a rack of polyester blouses, pulling out a pair of linen overalls covered in avocados, holding them up with the non-ironic intent to buy them. Minna with a book on sailing the West Indies under her arm and a cracked incense burner in her hands, peering eagerly at the creepy doll Beatrice would joke about buying (but would never), approving of the small blue paperweight Beatrice would buy instead.

Soon, hopefully, Reno would install the bookshelves that Beatrice would fill with things she loved: funky lamps from the sixties, framed postcards of places she'd explored, maybe a glass frog that was objectively ugly but meant something to her because of how she felt the day she found it.

That was, if she didn't keep running Reno off like she just had.

And if Beatrice lived long enough.

She shook her head.

Next: *If I have five years left.*

Know where I belong.

Know who I love.

Be a good friend.

Be a great family member.

Why was this exercise getting scarier?

She didn't want to think about the answer, so she rushed ahead to the next one: *If I have one year left.*

Help Minna decide on colleges to apply to, if she wants to go.

Help Cordelia with a problem. Any problem.

Learn how Reno takes her coffee and surprise her with a cup.

Do that Book Concierge thing at Keelia's shop.

Accept Astrid's offer to teach me how to knit.

Slowly, Beatrice double-clicked Astrid's name and replaced it with Cordelia's. She wasn't ready to want anything from Astrid. Maybe in a year. But maybe not.

A boat's horn blared outside. She jumped so much, she spilled tea into her lap, just missing the keyboard.

Then she typed the next time frame:

If I have one month left.

What would she do, honestly, if she knew for an absolute *fact* that she had thirty days to live?

Beatrice closed her eyes and breathed, trying to still the throb that rose in her chest.

If she had just one month left, would she curl her body into a fetal shape and cry with the covers over her head? Would she take up smoking and drink herself to sleep each night? Why *wouldn't* she?

Slowly, she typed:

I would tell Cordelia, Minna, and Reno that I want to know them.

I would try to be myself with them. Truly myself.

I would try to be brave.

I would try to be open.

Okay, this was definitely the most difficult spreadsheet she'd ever made, even harder than the taxes she'd filed for the ex–gambling addict who'd come clean after forty-one years of dodging the IRS.

If I have one week left.

She took what was perhaps the deepest breath of her life.

I would ask each of them (Cordelia, Minna, Reno, maybe even Astrid) to spend as much time telling me their stories as they could spare.

I would listen.

I would—

She deleted the words in the box.

Then she typed the full phrase.

I would let myself love them.

Her chest thudded—was this a heart attack? Would she even live to type another line? Would she ever get used to this fear?

Then:

If I have one day left.

But her fingers gave up. Beatrice couldn't fill in the boxes to the right.

Nothing came except stupid words like *Maybe* and *If I could just*, ridiculous words she erased, one by one, words with no attached phrases.

She couldn't do it.

Beatrice closed the laptop and then her eyes.

What if…

She let the big thought come.

I got myself into this mess.

All of her best thinking had gotten her to this exact place. She'd worked her whole life to do the right thing, making sure her sums were correct, but now, after all that careful work, she'd lost her husband. She'd lost her home. She'd lost the person she'd thought her father was.

With all of the best, most thoughtful plans she could make, *this* was where she'd ended up. In a houseboat that for all she knew leaked like a colander in the winter.

Alone.

For a person who needed proof, this seemed pretty indisputable. Her old way of thinking and living hadn't worked.

Up till now, she'd needed proof to believe in something. But what if wanting proof that something existed was simply a different *kind* of belief, just the belief it didn't exist?

What would happen if, instead of insisting on evidence, she did the opposite?

For once in her goddammed life, what if she decided to believe in things until they were *disproved*?

Miracles—she'd seen four of them happen right in front of her.

So...until someone could show her how they *weren't* miracles, what if she just believed in them, too?

A psychic prophesying her early death?

What if she chose to believe it unless it could be proved false?

If Cordelia said that magic existed, what if Beatrice believed in magic until she was shown actual hard proof that she shouldn't?

This meant that there *was* an action item she could take now, if she decided to do this.

She could learn everything there was to know about magic.

If she believed in it, she would need to understand it.

Beatrice flipped open the laptop again.

If someone told her she had only one day left...

Fuck.

No, she still had no idea what she'd do.

But—if magic and miracles existed, if the dead could speak to the living, that meant that there was an order to the universe that she didn't understand.

Did that, in turn, imply that there was a greater, orderly force in charge of it all?

What if that force could hear her?

In the box to the right of *If I have one day left*, Beatrice typed one simple word.

Please.

CHAPTER TWENTY-SEVEN

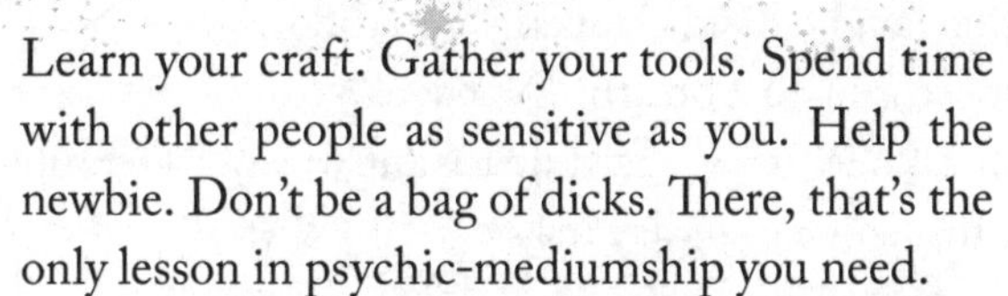

Learn your craft. Gather your tools. Spend time with other people as sensitive as you. Help the newbie. Don't be a bag of dicks. There, that's the only lesson in psychic-mediumship you need.

—*Evie Oxby,* Palm Springs and Bat Wings, *Netflix*

For the next few days, Beatrice studied.

She studied alone on the houseboat when Cordelia and Minna were busy, and she made lists of questions to pepper them with when she got to see them. She'd managed to talk Cordelia into letting her keep the grimoire for a little longer, and now that her internet had been hooked up, she could cross-reference some of the language used in the family book of spells with what she found online.

Previously, she'd thought the internet was made up of equal parts kitten videos, porn, and political memes, but it turned out she'd missed a whole huge segment of it: witchcraft. Minna came over one afternoon after her library shift and showed her the reputable sites. She made Beatrice put TikTok on her phone and told her the best witchtokers to follow, warning her away from the ones who just wanted to sell her fake crystals from China.

That same afternoon, Minna happened to witness Beatrice's first verifiable, tried-for spell. It was small, simply spinning a plastic spoon as it sat on the galley table, but Beatrice *made it happen*. On purpose. She used the right words for a tiny push and then felt the cramp of energy move out of her body through her fingertips. The spoon spun six inches to the left. Nothing touched it. The windows were closed. Not so much as the wake from a kayaker rocked the *Forget-Me-Knot*.

Minna laughed and clapped. "You did it!"

Beatrice gulped a breath. "Not a..."

Minna knew what she didn't want to say. "Definitely *not* a miracle. Just some everyday magic."

"I did magic!"

"You're, like, one of us, Auntie."

Beatrice felt her cheeks redden with pleasure.

Other days, when Reno was on the houseboat quietly working on the bookcases, Beatrice got out of her way, spending time at the library with her computer and all the metaphysical books Keelia could load her up with. With the books at her side, Beatrice watched YouTube videos and made notes in a *Magic* spreadsheet. On it, she tabulated both what she learned (the assemblage of herbs, incantations, and energy work) and the time she spent learning (tracked in fifteen-minute increments, categorized into *Reading*, *Watching*, *Written Reaction*, and *Questions for Further Research*).

Slightly embarrassingly, the book she enjoyed most was Evie Oxby's recent memoir. The psychic's tone was conversational, and she came at the subject with an edge of disbelief, one she herself was battling, and one Beatrice recognized. Her favorite part so far came from chapter 7: "How can this be true? I can see that lighting a candle's wick with a few words and a bit of my energy should be technically impossible. Yet, I can do it. I know that the man speaking to me in the dark died two hundred years before I was born. That makes me desire to know more, and at the same time, I distrust anyone but myself to tell me anything about how the universe works. But since I can't remember to move my laundry from the washer to the dryer until it smells like mildew, I'm not sure I should trust myself this way."

Not that Beatrice would ever tell Grant she was a new fan of his famous client. She was trying not to tell Grant anything at all, which was difficult with his near-daily text messages. Apparently he was sticking with his belief that they could split "amicably," because so far he'd asked her: where the laundry detergent was (shockingly, above the washer), where the dishwashing pods were (had he really not looked under the sink?), and her absolute fucking favorite, when trash day was. Beatrice hated that as a proud bisexual feminist, she'd fallen prey to outdated binary gender roles, but yes, she'd been the one to remind him every Monday night to roll the trash and recycling to the curb for their Tuesday collection. She'd honestly thought he just forgot each week, not that he didn't even *know* what day it was.

No one could possibly fault her for telling him trash day was Wednesday. It would probably still take him a few weeks to figure out why the garbage was piling up.

Meanwhile, at the bookstore, Winnie had posted Beatrice's auto-writings from the cemetery on a billboard in her fortune-telling annex. According to Cordelia, who Beatrice had coffee with every morning, two of the messages had already been claimed by townsfolk who recognized themselves. Norman, whoever he was, *had* needed to know that the key to his deceased wife's safe-deposit box was in the freezer inside the gluten-free pizza box. Patrick admitted he did need to be forgiven for something, and he was willing to listen to Andy, who'd said to wait. The message about Nutella and potato chips still hadn't been claimed.

"Word's getting around," said Cordelia. "Winnie hasn't told anyone you're the scribe yet, but she's been clear with people that it isn't her. Someone is going to want you to do more of it at some point."

"I'm not ready."

"Yeah, well, it can be really hard to turn away people desperate for help. In hard times, people look for certainty." Cordelia touched the pile of colored Post-its that Beatrice was organizing into questions in a companion notebook to her *Magic* spreadsheet. "Isn't that what you're looking for?"

Beatrice exhaled before nodding.

"So…when will you have enough of it?"

"No idea. I just want to learn what to avoid. The last time I auto-wrote, I triggered a miracle."

Cordelia dropped the small pink block of Post-its. "Oh! But you didn't auto-write before the other three miracles, right? Could that just be a coincidence?"

"I have no idea. About anything, really." And that was why she would keep studying. "What if there are multiple miracle triggers? Like trip wires. Auto-writing is one, and um, sitting with coffee, and looking into traffic…" No, it didn't make sense.

"Auto-writing is magic, not a miracle. I think you might be trying too hard to make connections that might not be there."

"Hang on," said Beatrice. "My sister, the actual *witch*, is telling me I might be getting carried away?"

It felt good to laugh with Cordelia, but still, if all of this was true, Beatrice had only three shiny miracles left. She needed a shit-ton more certainty about all of this before she got cocky. Feeling that little jolt of her own energy moving a plastic spoon was more than enough to keep her happy for quite a while.

And it felt good, honestly, to dive so deeply into something new. She loved being on her boat, and she loved seeing Cordelia and Minna almost daily. And it was so easy to avoid Astrid that the evasion must have been mutual.

One evening, when she arrived home after having dinner with Keelia at the diner, Reno was still there in the dimness, finishing up her work on the deck. She wore a headlamp, and she was bent over a sawhorse, sanding a long plank.

Beatrice stepped on board. "Hi." The light of the headlamp dazzled her.

"Sorry." Reno switched off the lamp.

But there was still enough light dropping from the sky to see the work Reno was doing. The edge of the wood was marled and unique, perfectly smooth and stained a deep reddish-brown to match the paneling inside.

"This is gorgeous. You're a magician."

Reno shook her head. "I just like wood."

"It's going to be beautiful."

Reno looked out at the water. The lights of the mainland were visible, the clearest Beatrice had seen them yet. "It'll be nice, yeah."

Beatrice remembered what was in her bag. "I got you something." She rummaged under the pile of her research books and pulled it out. "Keelia said you were looking at it the other day."

Looking startled, Reno said, "You bought me a book?"

"I love Nick Offerman's voice. I've never worked with wood in my life, but I read this when it came out and loved it." The more she said, she sillier she felt. Not everyone responded to everything in life by reaching for a book.

"That's... really kind." Reno gazed at the cover with a serious expression, and then her face melted into a slow, warm smile. "Thanks."

Her words were simple, but they felt good to receive. Beatrice rocked on her heels awkwardly. "You're welcome."

"I'll get out of your way now."

A line from Beatrice's *Life Expectancy: If I have one month left* checklist flashed through her mind. *I would tell Cordelia, Minna, and Reno that I want to know them.*

Before she could second-guess herself, Beatrice said, "Would you like a glass of wine?"

A pause. "I don't drink. Anymore."

Crap. Maybe she shouldn't have asked. But she had. "Tea?"

That slow smile again. "I like tea."

After Reno tidied her tools and Beatrice brought up two cups of tea, they sat in Beatrice's new chairs and watched the marina close itself up for the night. Most of the sailboats were in, their sailors coiling lines and battening down sail covers. A low, squat fishing boat chugged past, heading out for the night. A man on board waved at them, and Beatrice's heart lifted as her hand did.

Then it was quiet.

"So—" started Beatrice.

At the same time, Reno said, "Are—"

"You first," Beatrice said.

"You're staying? Not just a summer person?"

"I... yeah. I'm curious about what it's like to live on a houseboat in winter." *If I make it that long.*

Without hesitation, Reno said, "Cold."

"You live in the motor home at the cemetery, right?"

"Technically it's in Cordelia's yard."

"Why do you stay there?"

"What do you know about me?"

Startled, Beatrice said, "Nothing." *Except that Minna said people don't trust you.*

"Mmm. I like to keep an eye on them." She didn't have to specify who.

"Does the motor home get cold in winter, too?"

A nod. "I can help you get your stove to work more efficiently. If you want."

She did want. "Yes, please." Something about Reno—she wanted this woman around.

Reno tilted her head back to look at the sky, and Beatrice followed her gaze to the first star glimmering overhead. Or was it a planet? She couldn't remember how to tell the difference, but it didn't matter. The glint of light was pretty. Knowing what it was wouldn't make any difference in the way it looked. "Can I ask you something?"

Reno kept her gaze up. "Yep."

"How did your wife die?"

Reno's profile remained the same, but something shifted in her posture.

Crap, she'd screwed up. "Sorry. Forget I asked."

"No. I like to talk about her. I do. I try not to think of that day very often, that's all. But Scarlett was..." Reno pointed upward. "She was like Venus. Glowed. Didn't twinkle. Solid. She could hold up the weight of the world and also laugh about all the hard stuff. She was little. Not even five feet tall. People underestimated her. Men especially. Then she'd come out swinging and could knock them all down with a couple of words."

"How did you meet?"

"Teaching. High school. She taught English."

It surprised Beatrice to think of Reno standing in front of a classroom. "What did you teach?"

"History."

This quiet woman had talked to students all day? "You're kidding."

"I just...like knowing what came before."

"Why did you stop teaching?"

Reno turned her head and met her eyes. Slowly. Deliberately. "After Scarlett died, I drank every day."

Was it a test to see if Beatrice would act like an asshole about it? She stayed silent. Waiting.

"After a year or two, I couldn't stop. Got so I couldn't trust myself to do anything right, but I didn't care, either. Went to class. Taught that way. Blacked out in front of my AP class. Twice. I was teaching, still talking. My eyes were open, but I wasn't in the driver's seat of my brain. Second time, they gave me a warning. Did it again, got filmed by one of the kids, who put it on YouTube. *Drunk History* but not funny, just slurring about Watergate and then I passed out, splitting my head open on a desk as I went down." She spread out her hands and looked at them as if her fingers held answers. "Bled all over the homecoming queen. I heard she used the trauma of it as her college-entrance essay. Good for her, honestly. Lost my job. Lost respect. And lost friends."

Beatrice just nodded.

"People in this town, they have long memories. There's a lot of people who don't trust me in this town, and a lot of days, I'm one of them. But I got sober. Stayed sober with the help of some good folks. Not the long-memory kind. They were there for me. So was Cordelia, who drove me to every one of my first twenty or so meetings. I owe her my life." Reno took a choppy breath. "I'll never be able to repay that debt."

"How long were you and Scarlett together?"

Reno closed her eyes tightly, her mouth drawing into a slim line. She rubbed her chest with a closed fist.

"Are you okay?"

"Just a sec." Her voice was low and ragged.

Was she ill? Should Beatrice call someone?

But instead of moving, she waited, and in another moment, Reno opened her eyes with a gasp. "I'm fine. Sorry. What did you ask? Oh, yeah. Twelve years." Her words were slow but becoming more even. "Couple of rough ones in there. But the rest? Never perfect, never dull, and everything I ever wanted."

Beatrice let the pause lie open between them.

Eventually, with her chin still tilted to Venus and the stars joining it, Reno said, "We went on a hike. She got bit by a rattlesnake."

"Oh, my god."

"Seemed like it was going to be fine—they got a helicopter to pull us out, they had antivenom on board, and they got her to the hospital pretty quick. But she was allergic to the antivenom, and even though serum sickness usually passes, hers didn't. She died of shock two days later."

Beatrice reached for words—any words—but could only come up with the worse-than-useless "I'm so sorry."

Reno nodded. She took another sip of her tea. "Cordelia was there at the end. Scarlett was with me one minute. The next, she was with Cordelia."

Beatrice blinked. "Sorry?"

"You know. How she talks to people after they pass?"

"Um. No. I do *not* know."

Shuffling her boots, Reno said, "Crap. I shouldn't have—"

Jesus, if this was true, why hadn't Cordelia told her? Of course, with the death doula work—that would fit. Beatrice made a keep-going motion with her hand. "You can't stop now."

"It's why she does what she does. So she can be with them on both sides, helping them over. She can hear them, talk to them for a while. They're not alone."

"Wow."

"All three of them do that. Talk to the other side in some way. Minna gets images."

"Her guides. Right. Clairvoyant, she said."

"Yeah. And Astrid, she can hear them in her mind, and I think she can do even more, but I try to stay out of her way so I'm not sure exactly what other skills she has. And you, you've got the writing. Right?"

Holy crap. Presumably, she did. "Wait, so is that, like, their special flavor of magic? Talking to dead people? Or is that something that all, um, witchy people can do?"

"No clue," Reno said. "I didn't know what Cordelia could do, either, until about ten minutes after Scarlett died. I'm sitting on the bed with my wife, not even able to cry, and Cordelia's holding both our hands. She tells me that Scarlett's fine where she is."

But anyone would say that, right? It was what everyone needed to hear. If someone had said that to her when Naya's hand was still cooling in Beatrice's own, she would have done anything to believe it.

Reno apparently saw the look pass over her face. "No, it was more than that. Cordelia gave me Scarlett's words. *I love you, Popper. I'm fine. I'll be with you whenever you need me.*"

"Popper?"

"Jalapeño popper—she was half-Mexican and teased me for being unable to handle even Tex-Mex spice." She held out her arms. "I'm darker-skinned than she was, but my heritage is mostly Italian. Northern Italian, at that. I don't do heat."

"So Cordelia must have heard you call each other that."

She shook her head. "We'd only known Cordelia for about a year then. And Scarlett hadn't called me that in years. I'd totally forgotten it until that moment. Scarlett was telling me she was still there." Reno looked up at another star so bright and still, it must have been a planet. "That she's still here."

"You believe that."

Reno put her hand on her chest, as if she was rubbing away heartburn. "I do."

"But *how*?" She was unable to keep the frustration out of her voice. "How does it work? If it actually does."

"You still don't believe?"

Beatrice wiggled her jaw to unclench it. "I do believe. I'm *choosing* to believe. I mean, I'm trying like hell. But I need to learn so much more. Why *my* family? What are we supposed to do with it? What's behind it, and how do we affect it?"

Reno only shrugged. "I don't understand how electricity works, not really. But I know enough to respect it. I don't need to know much to be able to flip the light switch."

Funny that she put it that way. In the darkness, each word Reno spoke seemed to spark a tiny flame inside Beatrice. Was it desire? Simple curiosity? Sudden loneliness?

Whatever it was, though, the feeling wouldn't help her understand magic.

"Yeah, well." Beatrice wrapped her arms around herself as a chill crept over her. "I want to be a master electrician."

CHAPTER TWENTY-EIGHT

Feel free to be creative in how you seek Spirit.
She's tougher than you think.
—*Evie Oxby,* I Ain't Afraid of No Ghosts

Two days later, Cordelia didn't look the slightest bit surprised when Beatrice entered Which Craft in the late afternoon and acted from her *Life Expectancy: If I have one year left* checklist: *Accept Cordelia's offer to teach me how to knit.*

Within minutes, Cordelia had cast on and knit a row for her. "I can't in good conscience let any baby knitter learn how to cast on first—it's a ridiculous way to learn. Get the hang of the knit stitch and *then* I'll teach you how to cast on."

So Beatrice knitted. From time to time, Cordelia would walk past and peer over her shoulder.

"There. You're doing it!" Cordelia's voice was warm, and the tension between Beatrice's shoulder blades melted the smallest bit. Of course, holding the needles and peering down at them ratcheted the tension back up, but she *was* knitting. Well, she was doing something with yarn anyway.

The yarn in question was light purple, thick, and strong, and the dark wooden needles had already warmed in Beatrice's hands. Cordelia had opinions about them, too. "Straight needles are good for beginners, but soon I'll move you to circular needles. Better for everything, including healthy wrists. Making things is powerful, you know. That's why we have this store. We put energy into intention and help others to do the same."

Beatrice would have knitted asbestos rope with ski poles if Cordelia told her it was the best way to learn. Did she care about knitting? Apart from it being something to bring her closer to her sister, nope. Not in the slightest. She didn't care if what left her needles was a scarf or a bath mat.

She just wanted to be here. Near Cordelia.

Which meant being near Astrid, of course, but even that felt easier now, as if the edges of the woman had been sanded off a little. Now, when she looked at Astrid, it was as if a subtle Zoom filter had been turned on. The way the woman clattered around the shop—greeting customers with a piercing, singsong, "Tell me if you need help deciding Which Craft to tackle!"—was actually kind of funny. Colorful. If Beatrice had been a tourist in this town (like she had been just two weeks ago), she probably would have found it charming.

And perhaps Cordelia had cautioned their mother against overwhelming Beatrice, because Astrid hadn't ordered Beatrice to do or be anything yet. Today, she'd given only a small wave when she'd entered, and then she'd floated past behind Beatrice's chair twice, both times saying, "Oh, you're a natural, aren't you?"

Beatrice *wasn't* a natural—that was a lie. (So maybe Astrid was being herself.) The needles felt clumsy in her hands, and as she wrapped the yarn around the right needle, she used her whole body to do it. Her core muscles tightened, as did those in her neck and upper back, not just the fingers of her right hand.

Wasn't knitting supposed to be relaxing?

She glanced at Cordelia, who was ringing up a young woman purchasing a skein of yarn that would apparently knit up into rainbow-striped socks. As if she felt the gaze, Cordelia smiled at Beatrice. *I'm so glad you're here.*

Beatrice jumped.

Had Cordelia's lips moved?

No. That was silly. But it felt like she'd heard Cordelia's voice in her mind. She hadn't, of course. She played it back. Her ears had heard nothing in the room but Astrid showing a woman where the size-10 needles were.

"Did you say something?" Beatrice asked, feeling immediately ridiculous. Still at the counter, Cordelia was obviously too far away to hear her over the classical music on the stereo and the chatter of a small cluster of shoppers looking at a spinning wheel.

She'd just read the sentiment on Cordelia's face; that was all.

Had this been part of the way they'd communicated as kids? Through the mirror? More came back to her now, a thin memory of watching Cordelia's lips move, and just *knowing* what it was the other little girl was saying, even though she couldn't always quite hear her. Once, she'd fallen in the garden, skinning her knees. She'd showed her sister the cuts and bruises, and Cordelia had blown kisses toward them through the glass. She'd been able to feel the cool air on her knee, and together, they'd laughed.

Who would she be *now*, if Dad hadn't smashed the mirror? If she'd known Cordelia her whole life?

A stitch jumped off her needle and slid into invisibility, no doubt gone forever.

The bell jingled on the door. Minna raced through, her face

tight, her expression stormy. She marched to the counter and thumped her backpack to the floor.

"I locked myself out."

"Again?" Cordelia reached under the counter and pulled out a ring of keys. "You were supposed to put the extra one in your bag."

Minna's outfit of the day was varying shades of bright pink and deep green. Whatever could be dipped in glitter (hair band, nails, earrings, purse strap, shoes) had been. "I did. But apparently, it didn't stay in there."

"Ah. It just jumped out on its own?"

A muscle jumped in Minna's jaw. "Good, be a jerk about it. Excellent choice."

Cordelia sighed. "You okay? How was the library?"

Minna's back was so straight, she almost vibrated. "*Fine.* Fantastic. I had to do story time because Miss Liesl didn't show, so I'm covered in kid snot, and all I want is a shower, but instead, I have to come beg my *mother* for a *key* and be *mocked* while I'm at it. So yeah." She snatched the key from Cordelia's fingers. "I'm just great. Thanks for asking."

She stalked toward the door, noticing Beatrice at the last moment.

Beatrice raised her needles, and two more stitches leaped to their untimely death.

"Hi, Auntie. Bye, Auntie." Her voice was almost as surly as it had been toward Cordelia.

And Beatrice freaking loved it. Apparently there was nothing better in the whole world than being snarled at by your teenage niece. "Hey—um. I could bring you a churro from Fritz's after your shower?"

Minna nodded as she yanked the door open. "And a hot chocolate. Extra marshmallows. *Please.*"

A sharp stab of happiness ran through Beatrice, and she set down the three inches of knitted travesty. What she'd just done to that yarn was probably illegal in some countries. No more knitting for the day.

Her niece needed marshmallows, and by god, she would have them.

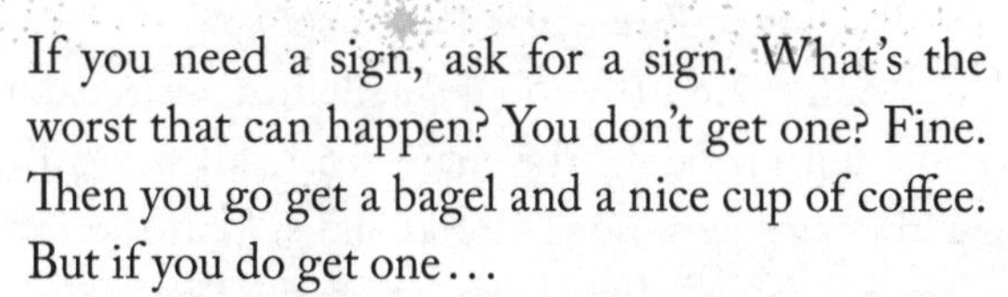

CHAPTER TWENTY-NINE

If you need a sign, ask for a sign. What's the worst that can happen? You don't get one? Fine. Then you go get a bagel and a nice cup of coffee. But if you do get one...

—*Evie Oxby, in conversation with Lisa Ling, on CBS News*

It's really that bad at the library?" Even though Beatrice had been spending so much study time there, she rarely saw Minna, whose summer intern job had something to do with archiving in the basement.

They'd already finished the churros and most of their hot chocolate. Minna's hair was still up in a towel, and she'd changed into a green-and-black argyle robe (which, in a masterful feat of textile engineering, was also glittery). The angry tightness of her body had softened, and she slumped so low on the sofa that she might slide right off into a sparkly argyle puddle.

"It's not bad at all. I'm just in a stupid mood." Her eyes were shut tight.

Surely, Beatrice hadn't been so self-aware, so clear about how she felt, at that age. "Is there anything that might help you feel better?"

Minna opened her eyes. "We could do manicures. I mean—oh, never mind."

"Why do you sound so sure I wouldn't love that?"

"Gran and Mom think manicures are dumb, and your nails look like they haven't been polished in a year. No offense."

"None taken." Beatrice held them up. At least she kept them filed and rounded. "But you're wrong—it's been way longer than a year. Six years, I think? I had them done for my wedding day."

A small screech. "Six *years*? That is so *sad*."

Ten minutes later, the room smelled of acetone and polish. Minna insisted on being the manicurist, allowing Beatrice to touch neither her own nor Minna's nails. "I'm the expert here. Let me do my thing." They both sat on the floor, Minna on the opposite side of the coffee table. The afternoon sun streamed in, lighting the top of her black hair with a brightness that glowed almost blue. Outside, the afternoon shadows lengthened, and inside, music poured from Minna's phone through the living room speakers, a dark techno-pop Beatrice didn't know but liked immediately.

Then Minna said, "Have you been thinking about your tattoo?"

Beatrice felt almost drunk as she watched Minna wield the nail polish brush. Maybe she was high on the fumes? Her body felt relaxed and warm, her limbs heavy and content. "Not much." It wasn't a no.

A bright flash of a smile was Beatrice's reward. "I've been working on a couple of new designs. But of course, you could design it if you wanted. Or I could help you."

"You mean a sigil tattoo?"

"If that's what you wanted."

"Like Reno's."

"Lots of people have sigil tattoos. They just don't always know it. You know that if you get someone's name tattooed in a heart on your upper arm, it's a kind of spell, right?"

I choose to believe in spells now, unless someone proves otherwise. But she couldn't help asking, "How do you explain such a big laser removal market, then?"

"Good point. Maybe the people doing the spells aren't very powerful."

"You're powerful." Beatrice didn't mean it as a question.

"Yeah. I think maybe sometimes Mom gets scared because of it, but that's dumb. She's more powerful than I'll ever be, and I can tell that when the two of you are together, that's even more off the charts." She paused. "I wish *I* had a twin."

"But you're unique. There's no one like you in the entire world, not a single copy of you anywhere."

"Ha. That would be too much of this fabulosity for the world to handle."

"I'm sure it would. So what are the designs you're working on?"

A look—was it slyness?—crossed Minna's face. "I *want* to tell you. I'm just not sure I should."

"Why not?"

"Because I can't trust you."

It stung only a little. "I get it. We met two weeks ago. That's fair."

"Nooo." She closed her eyes and groaned. "I know I can *trust* you, like, I get that. I just can't trust you not to go to Mom with something I tell you."

Beatrice longed so much to have a secret with Minna that the tips of her fingers ached with it. "As long as it's not illegal and you're not going to hurt someone else, I promise I won't tell your mom."

Minna peeled one eye open. "Hmm."

How should she play it? Did Minna want to be persuaded to share? Or would that make her clam up? Beatrice inhaled the tang of the polish and said, "I'd love to know. But only if you're comfortable. There's no hurry. I'm not going anywhere." It felt both good to say and scary as hell—she couldn't guarantee its truth.

But they were the right words. Minna pulled herself closer to the table. "Okay. So. I found some old pictures of my dad, and I had them blown up so I can see the tattoo he had on his forearm. It looks like a sigil, but it's blurry, even blown up, and I'm *rabid* to figure it out. If I do, I'm going to ask Mom if I can *please* get my first tattoo. I'll even go to a professional, if that's what she wants me to do."

"She must have known what his tattoo was—can you ask her?"

Minna's gaze dropped. "She won't talk much about him, says it hurts too much. I just think—no, I hope—that if he and I shared the same tattoo—" She broke off.

"Then you'd hear him? Wait, that's your grandmother who hears the voices. You hope that you'll get an image from him?"

Minna frowned. "How do you know all that? Did Mom tell you? She said we weren't supposed to talk about it until you were ready."

"Reno."

"She told you? *Reno* told you? She trusted you like that?" Minna reached over the table and, in a surprise move, grabbed both of Beatrice's hands, apparently confident her nails were dry. "Do you—holy shit! You do! You believe us now!"

Beatrice let Minna gaze into her eyes for two long, uncomfortable seconds, then she pulled away. "Maybe." What a cop-out.

"Yes. Why not, right? I'm trying belief on for size. Can't hurt, right?" *Unless it can.*

Minna gave an adorably fierce fist pump. "Thank *god.* I wasn't sure how you were going to help me out if you didn't believe."

Beatrice's cheeks warmed with the thought that Minna wanted help from her, but first, she had some questions that felt like they'd been piling up inside her. "Hmmm. Real quick, is talking to people who have—uh—passed on, is that the family magic?"

"What do you mean?"

"Are Hollands special that way? Or can anyone who can do magic do that, too?" Oh, this kind of question felt so strange coming out of her mouth.

"Mediums aren't unicorns or anything, but I'd guess they're rarer than your average street-level psychic."

"What's a street-level psychic?" She'd have to add it to her spreadsheet.

Minna shook her head. "Just made it up. Don't even know why I said it. It's like this: All mediums are psychic. But not all psychics receive information from the dead. Some just read tarot or dreams or tea leaves or get weird feelings and cross the street right before a safe falls out of a window."

"Why does our family have the medium part of it? Is it something you earn? Or work up to?"

"It just kind of... is, I think."

"And it's not just our family."

"No way. Lots of us out there."

"Do you all know each other?"

"Of course. *Massive* Facebook group."

"Really?"

Minna gave a joyful hoot. "You're so gullible, oh, my god. Your face!"

"Minna!"

"Honestly, some elder witches probably *do* have a Facebook group, but that doesn't seem very smart. There are meetups, though."

Beatrice narrowed her eyes. "Now I don't know whether or not to believe you."

"Seriously. Like huge camping trips, with lots of us. Music all night, and spells in the woods, and honestly, a bunch of meetings that require unanimous agreements and a bunch of truly mind-numbing bylaws. I skip those as much as possible."

"It's okay if I ask you more questions as I think of them?"

Minna's eyes crinkled with pleasure. "I want you to. It makes me feel smart. And I'm *so* happy you believe us. So now, will you help *me*?"

"Nothing illegal, right?"

"One thousand percent."

Beatrice lifted a polka-dotted fingertip. "As your accountant, I must point out that a thousand percent is an impossibility."

"It's one hundred percent legal. I just want you to try your writing thing again."

Beatrice should have seen that coming. Minna had seemed so brokenhearted when nothing from her father came through the week before. But then she'd lied about it to her mother. "Why did you say that about your friend? Sienna, right?"

Minna heaved a sigh. "Because whenever I bring Dad up, Mom ends up crying. Sometimes she even gets headaches. Migraines. Then I feel like it's all my fault. But it's not fair, that she gets to know everything about him, while I know literally nothing."

But could Beatrice risk it? She had only three miracles left, and what if Cordelia had been wrong about auto-writing being simple magic and (probably) not a miracle trigger? "I don't think that's the best idea. It didn't even work last time, honestly."

Her niece spoke quickly. "I know we didn't hear from him, even when I asked you to think about him—you heard from randoms instead, and that had to be hard. But I'm wondering if your mediumship doesn't rely on something physical from the person who's on the other side to make that connection. Like, Evie Oxby—have you seen her Netflix series?"

Beatrice hadn't watched it yet, but she didn't feel like admitting to Minna that by now she practically had certain sections of Grant's client's latest book committed to memory. She knew exactly how Evie Oxby felt about holding objects while reading for a subject. "No."

"She's real deal as fuck, and a lot of the time, she holds something to call the spirit. You could try that? Maybe get a leftover vibration, right?"

And that, exactly, was what Beatrice had been trying to untangle for the previous couple of days. It *almost* made sense to her. It wasn't just a hippy seventies idea: According to Einstein and everyone who came after him, all physical objects actually did vibrate at particular frequencies. If a person had an object they loved very much, an object that was frequently close to their body, then it made a certain sense that the object and the person might have shared a frequency overlap.

Beatrice had dived down this rabbit hole so deeply in the last three days that, yes, she probably did know enough about it to move forward. And if she understood it, she could keep control of it. Surely she could prevent another miracle.

But there was one problem with Minna's logic. Beatrice kept her voice gentle. "What about those others I heard from?" Holy shit, she was admitting *out loud* that she'd written words that came from dead people. "I wasn't holding anything that belonged to them."

"Yeah, I know, but you could try, right? Would you do that? For me?"

I'd sleep in the snow wearing a swimsuit for you. I'd jump out of a plane with no parachute and build one on the way down out of my hair if it helped you in any way at all.

I'd die for you.

"Yes," Beatrice said.

CHAPTER THIRTY

You know better than anyone else what the voice of your loved one will sound like. If you hear them, you can trust you've tuned into the right radio station.

—*Evie Oxby,* All Things Considered, *NPR*

Minna wanted to try their experiment in the hideout—it had been Taurus's favorite place, after all.

Beatrice expected Minna to prop the door of the shed open—it was stuffy inside, still holding the day's heat, and outside, the dropping night's air was cool. But Minna pulled the door shut behind them. "If Reno comes home, we don't want her just popping in to see what we're doing."

They didn't? Why not? "Okay, let's ignore for a moment that I'm supposed to be a grown-up. If you're saying we have to hide from the grown-ups, that's not really inspiring confidence in me that this is a great idea."

"No! I don't mean that! She just worries too much. I don't want to upset her."

Reno did seem to be a worrier. "Okay. But I'm going on record as saying I'll shut this down the second I feel weird about it."

"I get it, I get it." Minna flicked on the light and went to the cart that held her tattoo equipment. "Here's a notepad."

Beatrice dropped into the couch. She held out her hand. "Sharpie."

As if it were a scalpel, Minna slapped it onto her palm. "Sharpie."

"And...what's the thingie I'm going to hold?"

Minna turned to the workbench. "This. Obviously. Coil machine, old-school."

The tattoo gun was silver steel with blue accents. Its power supply cord dragged against the old red rug as Minna handed it to her, and the barrel was cold in Beatrice's hand.

She pushed herself deeper into the battered orange cushions. "I'm worried you're going to be disappointed." She didn't want to let Minna down, but hey, with all she'd learned, Beatrice felt a solid five percent hopeful that this would work. Maybe six percent. Better than zero, right?

"Aunt Bea. Haven't you figured out that I'm disappointed, like, all the time?"

Oh, crap.

Minna's face, though, was twisted in an almost-laugh.

"You're kidding."

A three-quarter smile broke through. "I'm almost sixteen. Mom says it's my job to start being more disillusioned soon, and while her attempt at reverse psychology is kind of adorable, yeah, I can admit that I'm only disappointed like once or twice a day, max."

"That number might rise."

"It might," Minna said with equanimity. "But right now, I'm

just happy you're going to try. Oh! The incantation! We need the grimoire! Do you have it with you?"

Beatrice tightened her grip on the tattoo gun. "I left it in my bag in the house. But I think I remember the words." Ha. She didn't think, she *knew* she remembered the words. She could have recited them backward.

"You sure? Gran says it's better to read from something than to risk screwing it up."

"I'm good."

Minna's eyes brightened as she sat in the rattan chair opposite. "I'll shut up now." She mimed locking her lips closed.

Shutting her eyes, Beatrice sat up as straight as she could, the tattoo gun firmly held in her left hand. She took one long breath in and let it out again. Just as she had last time, she imagined the fountain pen fitting into that old-fashioned padlock.

Then she said the words of the spell out loud.

She opened her eyes and held the Sharpie over the blank page with her right hand.

Nothing came to her.

No words at all.

She took another breath as she poked around inside her mind, but found it curiously blank. She supposed she could make up some words. Didn't every girl simply want to hear loving words from her father? Surely Minna would eat up anything she wrote. *I'm close by. I'm proud of you.*

Crap, what if the treacherous thought was written on her face?

She couldn't do that to Minna.

So this was what happened when she finally decided to believe in magic? It ceased to exist? What a cruel prank. She shouldn't have—

The tattoo gun jumped in her left hand. "Fuck!"

Minna jumped. "Did you do that?"

The gun was buzzing now, jittering against Beatrice's palm. She dropped the Sharpie and grabbed the tool with both hands. "I don't—I don't know!"

"It's—it's not connected to the power supply." Minna kicked at something that looked like a foot switch, which wasn't plugged into anything at all.

Then the buzz finally rose in her ears, as it had in the cemetery. She set the gun down on the rug, where it immediately quieted, and picked up the pen to scratch the itch flaring under her skin. Only writing would soothe the wrenching ache that curled inside her wrists.

She wrote.

Time moved and stretched around her as the hum turned to a kind of strange ocean song, roaring against her eardrums, enchanting and exhilarating and somehow instantly recognizable, as if she'd always known *this* song, *this* movement, *this* need.

She heard a quiet *pop*. And she was back.

"Auntie?" The raw hope on Minna's face was terrifying in its immensity. "Did it work?"

"Hang on." She needed to read it first, to make sure there was nothing in it that might hurt Minna.

> My darling. I can't believe you'll get to hear me—I've been trying to reach you for so long—can you really hear me this way? My darling one, you must know, first, how much I love you. When I first held you, I told your mother that you were the only reason I lived—millennia of ancestors, all of them leading straight to you. The first man who held fire in his hand, the first woman to give birth and create language with the sole intention to proclaim aloud

she loved her child—all of history has led to you. I'm sorry I had to leave you so early. I'm right here, just around the corner, trying to get back to you, always.

"Oh, Minna. Come look."

Minna hurled herself at the sofa, pressing her body against Beatrice's side.

Then she made a gulping noise as tears ran down her face. "Mama *said* that. That he said the earliest cavemen had evolved just so she could give birth to me. You couldn't have known that. She didn't tell you that." A pause. "Did she?"

It was somehow comforting to know that Minna, too, wanted proof. "No. I didn't know that."

"It was him." Minna stroked the page. "Daddy was here. He *is* here."

"I . . . " She didn't know what to say next.

"I can't believe it. I can't. This is the best day of my *life*."

"I'm so glad."

Minna jolted, as if she'd remembered something. "You can't tell Mom, though."

"Wait. What?" Not that Beatrice had been planning to run straight to Cordelia to tell all, but Minna not wanting her to made her feel like she probably should.

"Or Gran."

"But this is a good thing, right? Exactly what you wanted. Don't they deserve to know?"

With horror in her voice, Minna said, "*No.*"

"Tell me why not, then." And it would have to be a *really* good reason.

"It's not a big deal."

Oh, yeah, there was more here. "That's what people say when things *are* a very big deal."

"I just...I don't know if you want to hear this."

Beatrice turned to face her more directly. "Try me."

"Mom's cool. You know? You know. But she's not always *that* cool."

"Am I going to have to pull this out of you splinter by splinter?"

"Sorry. Okay, when I came out as trans to Mom, she didn't get it. She didn't believe it."

"Oh."

"I knew Gran would be a problem, because that's, like, printed on the box she comes in, you know? Gran has opinions, and she doesn't care who knows. But Mom—it was so bad. So hard. She'd always talked this big talk, like love and tolerance for all. She made rainbow yarn displays during Pride Month, that kind of thing. That was before I came out, though. When it came to me, and who I was, she just kind of refused to see me for a long time." A deep sigh. "A really long time."

Well, damn. Beatrice would have bet good money that Cordelia had been the kind of mother who'd said, "Really? How wonderful. As if I couldn't love you more," before gathering Minna to her chest and ordering *Protect Trans Kids* T-shirts for the whole family. Beatrice had mentioned Iris to Cordelia a few times, calling her "my ex." Had Cordelia needed to guard her expression when she'd learned her twin was bi?

That thought hurt.

"How long did it take for her to come around?"

"About six months. Me running away helped."

There was so much family history Beatrice didn't know, wasn't there? "Where did you go?"

"Just to Portland. I didn't have a place to go, and the shelters were okay, but there were some super-skeezy people in there, so for most of those months, I usually slept in this abandoned house with some other kids."

"Jesus! How old were you?"

A shrug. "Twelve. It was fine. And when Mom found me, she was beyond pissed but it *really* chilled her out, so it was worth it. Oh, my god, your face! Nothing that bad happened."

Beatrice wanted to roll Minna in bubble wrap, leaving just her head poking out. If that's what she wanted to do after knowing Minna for fourteen days, how had it felt for Cordelia? "But what does that have to do with your dad?"

"She has this stupid belief that the people we love most are the ones we shouldn't hear from once they go through the veil, or we risk never letting them go. I get that. But it's *not* fair—she got plenty of time with him, and I got none. She thinks if I obsess over him, it'll be bad for me and my 'psychosocial development.'" She put air quotes around the last two words. "I just don't want her overreacting again, like she did when I came out. That was really hard."

The catch in Minna's voice ripped the air from Beatrice's lungs. "I get that."

"But..."

"What?"

Minna's voice was so thin, Beatrice had to strain to hear her. "But he didn't say if he's okay that I'm a girl."

"Oh! No, Minna, he said he loves you. That came through really clearly, didn't it?" *A ghost told a girl he loved her using my hands to write his thoughts.* Would Beatrice ever get used to this? Would she have time to?

"He was talking about me as a baby."

"He said he's with you now, though, so I'm guessing he probably noticed your gender. Or maybe genders don't matter where—where he is?" Wherever the fuck that was.

Her niece turned her wide wet eyes to her. “Could we ask him?”

She took a deep breath. “No. You have your answer. He told you he loves you now. Sometimes answers take a form that’s different from what we want, but that’s not less of an answer.”

Minna laced her fingers together under her chin. “Please? *Please?*”

Beatrice had no skills at this, zero parenting techniques, no resources or muscles built up that would help her refuse this girl. “I’m sorry. No.”

Minna grabbed the tattoo gun and thrust it at her. “I knew using this would work, and I was right. You *have* to.”

Beatrice shook her head.

Minna dropped the gun into Beatrice’s lap.

And it twitched again.

Minna saw it jump. “Auntie Bea!”

Beatrice breathed, trying to recapture her resolution, her firm *no*, but it felt far away. Instead, she imagined the tip of the pen entering the keyhole, thought about the tumblers inside it moving.

She thought the words of the spell, hearing them inside her head, stuck like an advertising jingle.

The tattoo gun twitched harder, still open to whatever it was channeling. It still had something it needed to say.

Fine. There was obviously something going on Beatrice didn’t understand. Without looking at Minna, she picked up the tattoo gun, ignoring Minna’s quick indrawn breath.

Should Beatrice address Taurus directly? “Your daughter wants to know—do you accept her as the girl she is proud to be?”

The hum built inside her, and it was almost as if there was a flavor to this feeling, or a scent just beyond her nose’s ability to comprehend. Taurus was here—she recognized the same feeling she'd had just a few minutes before. He gave her the same impression, as if she were shaking hands with someone in a dark room. Just as she'd know her father's own handshake even if blindfolded, just as she'd know Grant's, and Iris's, she was now learning Taurus's.

The tattoo gun whirred, as if in confirmation.

Then something ripped the gun out of her hands and hurled it through the air, violently smashing it against the wall.

And the buzz growing inside Beatrice changed—the feeling of Taurus was gone, a thicker, bleaker *something* backfilling into the space where he'd been. The vibrating drone went dark and cold. The noise of it spiraled upward as a tornado crashed through her mind, her thoughts buckling into rubble at the sound of a thin scream.

CHAPTER THIRTY-ONE

> Spirit isn't always predictable. Would you really want it to be, though? Life is so damn expected. Let Spirit shake you up a little.
>
> —*Evie Oxby,* Yoga Journal

Reno's voice was soothing. Why, exactly, did Beatrice like Reno's voice so much? Listening to her was like drinking a hot toddy, all warm and sweet and smoky. It was so comforting, a weighted blanket of words. She could just lie here and let the sounds wash over her—ah, yes, so nice. She didn't even have to understand what she was saying.

But Beatrice's feet were cold. Was there a blanket maybe? Could she ask for one? Because it wasn't just her feet; her whole body was shaking. Freezing. God, she was *freezing*, and Reno's voice, warm as it was, wasn't warm enough.

She heard Minna's voice, too—shit, what was happening?

With what felt like a mighty, groan-worthy effort, she pried her eyelids open. She was lying flat on the sofa in the hideout, a pillow under her head. Reno's big brown eyes were inches from hers. She looked so *relieved*.

"S'up?" Beatrice's throat felt sore, as if she'd been smoking. Or screaming.

"Aunt Bea!" Minna grabbed at her arm. "What did you see? What happened?"

It all flooded back—Minna's request, the lock's keyhole, the crash of the storm in Beatrice's mind, the sound that dragged her away... Taurus *had* been there.

Then he'd been shoved out by something—someone—else, and that feeling... no. "I don't want to do that again."

"You shouldn't." Reno's gaze was steady, but there was a shake in her voice. "That was bad."

The door of the shed slammed open. Astrid and Cordelia tumbled in, both of them panting.

"Got your text," Cordelia said to Reno. "Are you sure?"

Reno nodded.

Astrid strode to Beatrice. When she spoke, icicles hung from her words. "Get up."

Beatrice struggled to sit up. "What—"

"Not here." Astrid's fingers dug painfully into her upper arm. "We have to be in the house for this. Move quickly through the dark and don't look back."

In the parlor, Cordelia lit candles, placing them on every surface—the big table, the windowsills, on the broad wooden arms of the chairs. She directed Minna to the kitchen to turn on the kettle while Astrid disappeared somewhere with a threat-like promise to return in a moment.

Reno said to Beatrice, "They know what they're doing."

I thought I did, too. "What *are* they doing?"

Reno rubbed her sternum with one hand but said nothing.

"How did you know to come?"

Still Reno didn't answer.

Astrid reentered the room carrying a small carved wooden

box. "Sit." She nodded toward the smaller table, the round one surrounded by five dark wooden chairs.

Minna carried in a tray with a teapot and five cups. She placed it in the center of the table.

"Good girl," said Astrid. "Everyone, take a cup."

Minna looked hopefully at Beatrice from the seat she'd taken. "Sit by me?"

Beatrice wanted to hug the girl and, at the same time, to yell at her for insisting they do whatever it was they'd just done. But she took the chair next to Minna. "Should I know what's going on?"

Astrid's glare was sharp. "Of course not. You know literally nothing, as you've just so magnificently evidenced."

Beatrice's spine prickled. "Considering that you left before teaching me *shit*—"

"Enough, both of you." Cordelia finished placing the last of the candles and switched off the overhead chandelier, plunging them into a wavering yellow light. She slid into the chair between Astrid and Reno. "Yarrow and yellow dock for repelling fear and negative forces." She poured each of them a cup.

Minna opened her mouth, but Cordelia interrupted her before she could speak. "If you ask for sugar, I swear to god, Minna."

Minna's mouth snapped closed.

Opening the wooden box, Astrid pulled out a small bundle wrapped in purple cloth. She unwound its red ribbon to reveal a deck of cards. The edges were worn and soft-looking, and they made a shushing noise as Astrid shuffled them.

Beatrice tucked her fingers under her thighs.

She was choosing to believe until proven wrong. And these women knew what they were doing. Even in the darkened room with the heavy atmosphere emanating from Astrid's dark expression, Beatrice felt a bump of hope. She sent a small, private smile in Minna's direction.

Unfortunately, Astrid caught it. Her shuffling remained even and rhythmic as she said, "You were a fool to come to this island."

Cordelia shifted in her chair. "Mom, you said you wouldn't."

"It was *wrong*. And it's even worse for all of us that she's stayed. Reno knows."

But Reno said nothing. She rubbed her chest with one hand and kept her eyes on the candle in the middle of the table.

Astrid went on. "We'll cast a circle of protection that will last until Beatrice leaves the island."

"No, she's staying! She bought a houseboat. Please don't make her go," said Minna. "It isn't fair."

As if Astrid could make Beatrice go anywhere.

But Astrid smacked the deck so hard against the tabletop that they all jumped. "She contributes to the darkness being called to us. Do you not feel that?"

Minna's shoulders folded in on themselves.

Was that true? Could darkness be summoned by someone who *thought* she knew what she was doing, but could probably use some more training? "How are any of you going to help me with this—whatever it is—if you send me away? Astrid, you and I have to come to some sort of resolution."

As if Beatrice hadn't spoken, Astrid shoved the box across the table to Cordelia. "We will sew."

With a nod, Cordelia reached her fingers into the box and pulled out a small white paper packet. She tugged silver needles out of it, handing one needle to each of them.

Astrid kept shuffling as her nostrils flared in the candlelight.

Passing Minna a spool of white thread and a small pair of scissors, Cordelia said, "Lovey, can you cut me off five lengths?"

Minna nodded. "How long?"

"Double your forearm."

Beatrice worried the needle, testing the sharpness against the tip of her finger. "Did you even hear me, Astrid? We've got to come together. I think we both know that."

"Silence!" The word was a roar, and under any other circumstances, it probably would have cowed Beatrice.

But these weren't normal circumstances. She was being silenced by the mother who'd abandoned her, and that went far beyond bullshit and all the way into completely un-fucking-acceptable.

"No."

Astrid's fingers fumbled the cards, and two of them spilled out of the deck onto the table.

For one second, Beatrice felt powerful. "You have no right to tell me what to do. None. Are you getting that?"

Silence. Astrid stared at the table.

"Hello? I need you to hear me. You may not order me around, you can't tell me what—"

Astrid reached forward for the two cards that had leaped from the deck. "The Tower."

It didn't look good, people leaping from a burning building.

"And the three of swords. The card of heartbreak."

Beatrice was pretty damn sure that any of the cards that Astrid pulled out of that deck were going to tell the story that *Astrid* wanted to tell. No objectivity. Obviously. "Whatever you say. I'm sure it's all very terrifying. I'm not an idiot, and I can see that something's going wrong here. But you're the idiot if you think you can shut me up and shove me off the island. I've found my family." Her throat tightened, and she reached for more courage. "Meanwhile, does someone want to tell me what happened back there? Reno, why did you arrive, like, out of nowhere?"

Two deep furrows creased between Reno's eyebrows and she leaned forward slowly.

But Minna spoke instead. "Mama, I have to tell you something."

"Heaven help us, that can't be good." Cordelia turned to face her daughter. "Okay, midge, tell me."

"You're going to be mad."

"I'm going to be most concerned about keeping you safe. If mad gets mixed up in there, that's because I love you. You know that. Tell me."

"I asked Beatrice to contact Sienna again. You didn't know it, but before she died, we were dating."

Cordelia's mouth dropped open.

So did Beatrice's.

Astrid wheezed, "Impossible."

Okay, now was when Beatrice should refute Minna's words—she knew she should. She was the adult, and Minna the child.

But what if Minna hadn't told her mother about Sienna because she'd been scared of the same rejection she'd faced when she'd come out as trans? Beatrice hadn't had a chance to ask Minna about the vibe she'd picked up on when Minna and Olive were together. Maybe Minna was scared that being both trans *and* gay would be a step too far for her mother to accept?

Still, things were getting out of hand. "Minna—"

"Aunt Bea started to hear something from Sienna. We think." Minna's voice trembled. "But then Reno busted in."

Cordelia said softly, "You shouldn't have... *Oh*, honey. That wasn't safe."

"You always say we can't reach the close ones, but they're who we want to talk to. I don't understand the problem."

Beatrice finally found her voice. "Minna needs more information. I do, too."

Cordelia held up her hand. "We're trying to protect you both, and you don't know enough about this yet, sister. Respectfully."

Respectfully? That was rich. "No one here has earned that from me yet." She corrected herself quickly. "Except you, Minna. You're good."

Astrid, apparently tiring of this line of chat, turned to Reno. "What did you feel?"

Reno kept her eyes on the table. "A darkness. An enormous energetic shadow."

"How big?"

"Bigger than I've ever felt. It was like a whole terrible continent of blackness."

Beatrice hadn't known it was possible to feel more lost, but apparently it was.

"Oh, no," breathed Cordelia.

"It's them." Astrid held up the deck, passing it over the three flames in the center of the table.

Minna shoved her cup, sending a wave of tea onto the wood. "It's them *who*? I'm not little anymore. I'm almost a woman. You have to tell me. What's going on?"

Cordelia looked at Astrid.

The older woman gave a tight nod. "I suppose it's time you tell her." Astrid flicked her gaze at Beatrice. "And *her*."

CHAPTER THIRTY-TWO

Some souls play such important roles in our lives that we can't escape them. Would we really want to?

—*Evie Oxby, in conversation with Glennon Doyle on the* We Can Do Hard Things *podcast*

Was it okay to stab an old lady with a silver needle? Because Beatrice really, really wanted to. It was a thin needle—it wasn't like it would kill her.

Cordelia picked up a length of thread and ran it through her fingers. "Okay, then. I'll try to make this as clear as I can. Here goes. Many years ago, Valeska Holland fell in love with Theodore Velamen, marrying him in 1877. The Velamens were a prominent family on the island, owning many of the shops, the sawmill, and most of the local farmland. Valeska didn't know that the Velamens were also sensitive to the magic puddled here in Skerry Cove. She'd kept her own power a secret from him because Theodore's father was vocal about persecuting non-Christians.

Which was really rich, given that his father could also summon lightning. Then she gave birth to twins."

"Twins!" Minna looked gobsmacked. "But I only know about Anna."

Cordelia pressed her fingertips into the table so hard, her nail beds striped pink and white. "Twin girls. Anna and Louise. There's no way you would have known, honey."

"But it's not in the book—"

"Let me finish, okay? Not everything's in the grimoire. There are some things we pass on orally. One of those things is that the power of Holland twins is immense. The power is multiplied by more than just a factor of two."

Beatrice's hands and feet tingled painfully, as if they'd fallen asleep without her noticing.

Her sister's voice was strangled. "And... we're back to Theodore. He was a—"

"Just tell them," said Astrid.

Cordelia shot a look at Minna. "We don't know how she found out, but Valeska learned that Theodore had a terrible plan for their daughters. He... oh, crap, I don't want to say this." She took a deep breath. "He planned to have children with their daughters when they grew up, so that their combined familial powers would multiply exponentially."

Minna blanched. "That's the worst and *grossest* thing I ever heard."

Cordelia inclined her head. "Then Valeska and Theodore disappeared. Not long after they left, his remains were sent back in a pine box to his family on the island, along with a rather murky story about him contracting an unnamed infection, but Valeska didn't come back with his body. She never returned to the island."

Sitting forward, Minna said, "What about the babies? Anna and Louise?"

"They were only thirteen months old. Valeska left them with her mother, Xenia."

The same age I was when Astrid left. Beatrice shifted in her seat.

Cordelia continued, "From the grimoire, we know a couple of things. Most importantly, we know that Xenia stripped the Velamen power out of her granddaughters, attempting to keep their powers solely of the Holland lineage."

Beatrice's head ached. "How?"

"We don't know that exactly, but we think that whatever method she used went badly for one of the babies. Louise died shortly after her parents disappeared. The power Xenia removed from the girls is probably the power she put into the forbidden sigil that's sealed in the book. We also know that she kept teaching Anna, and that Anna became more powerful than her grandmother. Anna eventually married and gave birth to Rosalind"—Cordelia looked at Beatrice—"our grandmother."

Astrid said, "My mother, Rosalind, was the strongest one. Until I came along. Hollands get stronger as our lineage lengthens. So then... then there were you two."

The twins. What had Cordelia meant by the power of twins multiplying? If that were true, why couldn't Beatrice do more than shove around a plastic utensil and occasionally write for the dead?

"And then there was me," said Minna in a small voice.

Cordelia squeezed her daughter's hand. "And all that time, the Velamens were growing stronger in their hatred of the Hollands for what they believed was the murder of Theodore Velamen, and the theft of their power."

Minna's eyes were huge. "Theft?"

"It's not like we actually stole it. The power that Xenia stripped from the twins and put in the grimoire was energy they never got back, but the thing is, the Velamens tend to have big, loud energy, and they burned themselves out, wearing their magic down like an eraser until all that was in them had bled back into the land."

Bluntly, Beatrice asked, "Are they all dead?"

A nod. "The last one, Otis Velamen, died six years ago."

Minna blinked. "Wait, Otis, the shoe repair guy?"

Cordelia nodded.

"But he was so nice. He was always offering to shine my shoes for free. *That's* why you wouldn't ever let me talk to him?"

"Remember how I always made you wear a friendship bracelet?"

"When it would fall off or get too small, you'd make me another one." Minna rubbed the skin at her wrist. "I just thought you stopped wanting to make me one. Like maybe you were embarrassed of me when...But it was charmed. I should have known."

Cordelia shook her head sharply. "I would never be embarrassed of you. Never."

Really? What about when Minna had come out and Cordelia had rejected her? Beatrice kept her mouth shut, though, and her ears open.

Astrid leaned forward. "The bracelet was a bit of light magic, but it was enough to keep you safe until Otis was gone. In other, older times, according to our history, we knew that evil could move through ether, that evil could be called back to earth via the undead."

"Zombies?" said Beatrice. "Come on."

Astrid continued, "Families like the Velamens have been eradicated before, only to fight their way back to this mortal plane by twisting and using the energy of their enemies. Once banished, they tend to stay stuck unless a huge amount of their enemy's energy is gathered in one physical location. If they manage to pierce the veil, they can suck from that energy and return."

"Zombies *and* vampires. Oh, my." It was getting more and more ridiculous.

The glare Astrid shot her scorched her skin. "That crossover has been a real danger in the past, but in this generation, we didn't have to worry about accidentally drawing the Velamens back, because... Well, we weren't as strong as we used to be. Until now."

A thunk from something falling over in the wind outside made Beatrice jump. "What does that mean?"

Astrid said through gritted teeth, "It means that the prodigal daughter fucked everything up by coming here. *You're* to blame for the danger threatening my family now."

It was a tragedy that half of Beatrice's genes came from Astrid, the woman who would never quit rejecting her apparently. "Well, *you're* unbearable." It was a childish retort, but it was better than telling her to fuck off, which felt like her only other option.

Reno, silent until now, held up a hand. "May I?"

Cordelia said, "Go ahead."

Focusing her dark gaze on Beatrice, Reno said, "I told you that when Scarlett died, Cordelia talked to her."

I choose to believe. Even when it sounds like a fairy tale, I choose to believe. Slowly, Beatrice nodded.

"She was a close one, as they say. I shouldn't have wanted more than just that single, short connection. Cordelia made it clear that Scarlett's soul would always be close to me, wherever I was. But I wanted to feel her more. So one night, I got Cordelia really drunk."

Minna's eyes widened. "What? Have I heard this story?"

Reno looked ashamed. "I didn't want you to know. It was a shitty thing for a sober person to do. I got her really, *really* drunk and then I started crying and saying that I wanted a family again. She said that we were family, and I insisted it wasn't enough. I talked in circles around her, asking her questions until she told me about the Knock." She took a breath. "She was so out of it, I managed to convince her to give it to me."

Cordelia said, "It was my fault. Even blasted out of my gourd, I should have known better—"

"Mom!" Minna's body was rigid. "After everything you've told me about consent. A drunk person can't give it! It wasn't your fault."

Reno looked physically ill. "She's right. I'm never going to stop regretting that I asked you to do that."

"Oh, please," said Cordelia impatiently. "You got the short end of that shitty stick; you know that."

Minna said, "*That's* why you get those feelings. And why you can't control them."

The more they said, the less Beatrice understood. "What feelings?"

Reno looked at her. "I told you. Astrid hears voices of the dead, Cordelia communicates with them right after they pass over, and Minna sees images they give her. Me—I feel them."

"What do you mean?"

She rubbed her sternum again. "I feel their emotions. Sometimes I feel what they felt when they died. Other times I feel their current emotions."

"Who?"

"Anyone. Anyone dead. I can't block it, and I can't choose who comes through. Can't even tell who they are, usually."

"So," said Beatrice, "you're, like, emotionally possessed?"

Astrid scowled. "That's a ridiculous way of saying it."

"Exactly right," said Reno. "But I'm protected in this house and in the hideout."

It made sense now. "The sigils over the doorways. But only here and the hideout, not in your motor home? Which you park just outside a *graveyard*?" She turned to Cordelia. "Why don't you protect her in her vehicle? Or draw a sigil like that on her body?"

"You think we haven't tried?" Cordelia pointed at the tattoos writhing from below Reno's shirtsleeve. "It only works where we live, where the power's the highest, we think. And she refuses to stay with us in the house."

Reno said, "I prefer it out there. The dead don't actually like hanging out in the graveyard, unless that's where they spent most of their time when alive. They tend to go to where they lived, where their emotions were the most intense. If they do come through the cemetery, their emotions pass through me like wind."

Minna snickered, and the sound of it lightened the tone of the room. The candle in front of Beatrice flickered more brightly.

"Okay, yeah. I pass spirit gas." Reno smiled. "Anyway, I was in the motor home, and I felt this total blackness roar through me like a hurricane of the soul. This one wasn't like the others; it had a direction. A physical one. I was just in the way. It was headed right for the hideout. So I ran at it. Astrid, what you told me about how it would arrive—you were right."

"Mom?" Cordelia stopped twisting the thread in her fingers. "What *is* it? We know it's bad. And now we know you warned Reno, which, no offense, Reno, you know I love you, but Mom, that's not cool. You should have warned all of us."

Astrid drew herself up straighter and rubbed her upper teeth as if wiping off lipstick. "I knew she'd feel it coming first."

Cordelia snapped, "You do know that the canaries in the coal mines were sacrificial?"

"I don't mind." Reno looked at her hands, the fingers interlaced tightly. "As long as I get it right."

With a shake of her head, Cordelia said, "You know you can trust yourself. We trust you, and—"

"*I'm* the one who got it right," said Astrid. "Thread your needles. All of you."

"Mother! Tell us!"

Beatrice fumbled with the thread—it had been years since she'd picked up a sewing needle. Maybe decades, come to think of it. The eye of the needle was so small, difficult to see in the low, flickering candlelight. This might take a while.

"The Velamens know the Holland power comes from its aggregation."

"Can you put that in English, please?" Minna also seemed to be struggling, tilting her hands toward the light.

"Pfft." Astrid snapped her fingers, and when Beatrice looked at her needle again, it was threaded. So was Minna's needle. And Reno's. "Together, we Hollands have our full power. Twins, like you, make that power even greater. Together, we have what they desire most, what they feel cheated of. When we're together, they'll do anything to get across the veil to us. Because we've been involved with them for so many generations, our strength calls to the strength they used to have. Separated, our family's power is fractured. Separated, they ignore the Hollands. They'd almost forgotten us; I could feel it."

"Oh, my god." Cordelia stared. "Mother. *That's* why you split us up?"

CHAPTER THIRTY-THREE

That connection you feel when you sing with a group? That's Spirit. When you laugh together, that's Spirit. When you worship as a collective in any direction at all, whether to Jesus or Buddha or Allah, you're calling Spirit. And you might have noticed, Spirit loves a party.

—*Evie Oxby, in conversation with Beyoncé and Jay-Z*

Well, hell.

If what Astrid had just said was true, if she'd separated Beatrice from her sister in order to keep them safe, that was almost... understandable.

It might even explain why Astrid had been such a bitch since Beatrice had arrived.

"Why didn't you just tell us that?"

In a similar tone, Cordelia growled, "Not once in the last forty-five years did you think to mention this to me, Mom?"

Astrid's lower lip trembled. "I thought I'd done enough to protect you. To protect all of us."

"Well," said Cordelia, "you didn't. And now we're together, and apparently, we're stronger this way, so what do we do now? I'm assuming we're canceling the Un-alive party tomorrow night?"

Beatrice stared. "The what now?"

"Shoot." Cordelia touched her forehead. "I keep meaning to tell you about it. It's a party where we celebrate all the dead things."

"Seriously?" A dead-anything party was probably something best avoided by a person with an imminent death sentence.

"It's the anniversary of not only Minna's dad's death, but Scarlett's, too. Same day, eleven years apart. We usually hold a little memorial gathering. Everyone comes to honor their un-alive things, their people, their pets. This year, though—"

Astrid clapped her hands. "This year, of course, it's more important than ever. We will present a united front, and invite our friends into our home. Then we will honor the dead and insist they stay that way. And now? *Now* we will invoke the blood ward upon us."

That sounded unhygienic. Beatrice said, "Look, what are we trying to prevent here? I'm still not getting it."

Astrid's jaw was tense. "If the Velamens manage to get one of us to join them, then they'll be able to cross back to this plane."

Clutching her tiny needle like a dagger, Cordelia demanded, "What do you mean by one of us joining them?"

"By choosing to cross to them on the other side of the veil."

Cordelia said, "Why would we do that, though?"

Before Astrid could answer, Beatrice said, "So your plan was to abandon one of your daughters, leaving her alone, without a clue about any of this? With no defense?" Astrid was many annoying things, but Beatrice hadn't thought she was stupid until this moment.

Astrid's eyes narrowed to angry slits. "If you weren't activated, they wouldn't find you. Nor would they have any reason to look. And without one of us joining them, without taking our power, their own leftover power isn't strong enough to make the leap."

"Leap? What does that even mean? Into what kind of body?"

"I don't... know."

Astrid didn't *know*? "Oh, my god."

"Reanimation is complicated, but no, they wouldn't use their actual cast-off bodies, if that's what you mean."

Beatrice didn't actually know what she meant. "What do they *want*?"

Astrid shrugged. "What does anyone want?"

Minna ventured, "Netflix? Ben and Jerry's?"

Astrid's frown deepened. "They want power. Control."

Beatrice was so confused. "And by one of us, crossing over to them—do you mean as in, choosing to die and go to them? So, since that's ridiculous, it shouldn't be an issue, right?"

"Our families have been linked a very long time, and the Velamens have many wiles. If one is in enough pain, one might agree to anything."

Trying not to lose what little composure she had left, Beatrice said, "Them wanting power tells me nothing. What do they actually want to *do*?"

"Their main desire is to avenge Theodore's demise, to destroy the Hollands completely. Our power is like that of the island—it pools in places. And our power pools matrilineally. Theirs is patrilineal, and therefore weaker."

Minna's expression fell.

Continuing, Astrid said, "But they've been biding their time, accumulating their rage for a long time."

"That's... terrifying."

"To be very clear, because I'm worried you're not truly understanding this, they want to do more than simply kill us. When we are subsumed by death at their hands, they absorb the strength of our power. All humans carry some magic—that's what souls are made of. So if they take our soul, there's nothing left of us. At all. We disappear from all planes of existence. Permanently."

Beatrice could actually see the color leaching from Minna's cheeks.

"Well," said Reno slowly.

As one, they turned to look at her.

"Fuck *that*."

Crisply, Astrid said, "Quite right, Reno. Though I hoped we wouldn't ever get here, this has gone past simple sigils. We need bigger magic. So. All of you. Pierce the meat of your thumb with the needle."

"Pardon?" Surely Beatrice hadn't heard that correctly.

With a sigh, Cordelia said, "Just do what she says. It's almost always easier than arguing with her about spells. She's infuriating but usually right."

"I can hear you, Cordelia, in case you forgot that I, too, have ears. Everyone, now. Pierce all the way through. We need actual blood for this one. No faking, Minna."

Beatrice watched as Cordelia pushed the needle through the pad of her thumb without even wincing. Minna gave a little squeal but did it, too. Reno, like Beatrice, was moving more slowly toward the idea, holding the needle to her thumb as if trying to imagine what it would feel like.

"Do you want me to do it for you, like I threaded your needles?" asked Astrid.

Beatrice yelped, "No!" as Reno shook her head.

It didn't hurt that much—the difficulty was more mental than anything else. A quick punch, and it was done, the needle going through the skin and some of the meat of her thumb and out again.

Now what? Was Astrid going to make them sew themselves to each other? Because that would be too much.

"Now pull the thread through. Slowly. You need to bleed on it. If you don't, you'll just have to do it again." Astrid waited.

When they all held up the stained threads, she said, "Give them to me."

Shuddering, Beatrice pulled hers out of the needle and handed over her small biohazard.

Astrid draped all five strands over her right palm, then rolled them together into a small ball, whispering words under her breath that Beatrice couldn't quite hear.

"Thread of red, bind the dead." Astrid looked around the circle of the table, her expression stern enough that she didn't need to explain what she wanted them to do.

Together, they chanted, "Thread of red, bind the dead." Then they repeated it. And again.

It felt a little ridiculous. Maybe a lot ridiculous, honestly, smacking as it did of standing in front of bathroom mirrors on sleepovers and calling for Bloody Mary. That apparition never rose, but the idea of her was always scary enough that at least one girl had to phone their mother and go home early.

Astrid frowned at Beatrice. She'd missed saying the last two words on that round.

"Sorry. Thread of red, bind the dead." Surely Beatrice's wasn't the only rapidly beating heart at the table.

After a dozen more times through the phrases, Astrid raised her arms dramatically. "With my hand, I burn the strand, now burial ground, repel the bound."

She thrust the ball of thread into the flame of the tallest candle on the table, and instead of simply catching and burning, it flashed bright white and made a startling *pop*. Then it flared red and disappeared into a wisp of black smoke.

Something enormous smashed against the side of the house, shaking the walls and the floor.

Beatrice grasped the table with one hand and grabbed Minna's with the other.

Then a lawn chair crashed through the window. Minna screamed at the shattering of the glass, and Beatrice tightened her grip. Reno went pale.

Cordelia nodded, seemingly unruffled. "I'll get the dustpan."

"Well." Astrid gathered her cards, blew out the candles, and reached to collect their empty needles. "That went better than I expected it would."

CHAPTER THIRTY-FOUR

> It's not a bad thing that I can't pick who comes through to me. Sure, I'd be a better medium, but I'd probably be a worse human.
>
> —*Evie Oxby,* Come at Me, Boo

Beatrice's dreams were full of screams, breaking glass, and flashes of light reflected against the sheen of monsters' teeth. As she gasped awake, she could still see the sewing scissors rising into the air before plunging into Astrid's left eye.

But between the nightmares, she surprised herself and slept, the bed warm, the sheets soft, and the water below a rhythmic lullaby.

In the morning, when she rolled to her side to squint at her cell phone, she found a text from Reno. Ten okay?

Apparently, what happened in this town was you worked a protection spell (against what, exactly, undead hotheads?) one night, and then got right back to work the next morning.

Beatrice could respect it even if she didn't understand it.

She had, of course, asked Cordelia to explain why, exactly, a chair had sailed through the window after what was supposed to be a spell of protection. She hadn't felt very safe in that moment. We're just trying to prevent anything worse. Glass is easy to replace. The answer had been both unsatisfying and chilling.

Now, at the café, Fritz made her an extra-hot cappuccino without being asked. "Justin said he's going to Cordelia's to fix a smashed window this morning. I thought the Un-alive party was tonight. Did you kick it off early?"

That had all been real, then. The chair through the window. The blood on the threads. "Is that how Holland parties normally go? Chairs through windows?"

"Not normally, but that was before you came to town, raising our Holland quotient." They dropped a wink before turning to the espresso machine.

Fritz thought Beatrice was one of the Hollands.

She had no idea how to feel about that.

"Beatrice!" Keelia raced in from the street. "Oh, thank god, someone said they saw you come in here. We need you."

"Now?"

"Now."

Fritz called, "I'll keep your drink warm."

Winnie's fortune-telling annex was draped with dark velvet curtains, and as they pushed into the dimness, Beatrice could just make out the form of an older woman sitting at the table with Winnie.

"Come in!" Relief laced Winnie's voice. "Mrs. Jumai, this is Beatrice, the one who wrote—the one who received the message."

Mrs. Jumai resembled an old chair, creased and wrinkled and smooshed with a few too many pillows. She wore a beige blouse and brown slacks, and she wore slippers instead of shoes, as if she'd left her house in a hurry.

"You? You wrote this down?" The woman tried to stand but only got halfway up before her pins started to wobble.

Winnie said, "Mrs. Jumai, how about you just stay where you are? I'll trade places with Beatrice."

It was obvious that Winnie, with her rapid blinks and intent gaze, was trying to telegraph something to Beatrice, but if Winnie was trying to psychically communicate with her, it wasn't working.

Clueless, Beatrice sank into Winnie's seat and tried to pull her face into something appropriate. "So. You're saying this had specific meaning for you?"

Mrs. Jumai pushed a wrinkled piece of paper across the table to her.

> K is here with me. We are together. At the same time, I've never left your side, nor has he. He knows his blue handkerchief will always catch your tears. He still loves salt and vinegar chips dipped in Nutella, and he says you never have to let him go. I'm sorry I said you did. L.

The woman's eyes overflowed with tears. "I need to know if you—no, I will do anything. I will give you all the money I have in the world—"

"Oh, hey." This couldn't be good.

"Anything." Mrs. Jumai fumbled with a chunky golden bracelet at her wrist, but it appeared to be stubbornly resisting her efforts, so she grasped the diamond-encrusted ring on her wedding finger. The woman tried to slide it off, but it looked as if it hadn't moved over her rheumatic knuckles in years. Meanwhile, her movements got jerkier and more frantic. "My ring? You'll take my ring?"

"I will absolutely *not* take your ring." Maybe a distraction would work. "Mrs. Jumai, can you tell me what this note means to you?"

Mrs. Jumai stopped pulling at the ring and touched the paper again. "*K* is for my Kumail. Leukemia. He was thirteen. Two years after he died, my husband said I had to let Kumail go or he would leave me, too." A sob broke through. "I tried. I really did. And then my husband died last winter, and I can't let either of them go, and this says... does this mean I don't have to?"

Beatrice reread the words. *You never have to let him go.* "I'm so sorry, but I don't know. I don't know how those words came to me. I wish I did."

"Do it again. Please. Do it again?" Mrs. Jumai tugged at her ring again.

The thought of that howling dark wind rose in Beatrice's mind. "I can't."

"You must. I have to apologize to my husband."

"It doesn't work that way. Look. Let's be logical about this." Even with the panic flopping around in her stomach like a hooked carp, Beatrice was pleased to hear her accountant's voice emerge. "If we look at this paper, we can extrapolate several things. Shall we go through them point by point?"

A hiccupped sob sounded like agreement. Hopefully.

Reading upside down, Beatrice touched the words on the paper. "This says they're together. That by itself means something incredible. Life after death. A continuation of the soul."

"I already believed in that."

It must be nice to be so unsurprised. "Okay then, it also says that not only are they together, which is amazing, but they're with you. That chip and Nutella thing—"

"Why didn't the message talk about my white chocolate chip cookies? He loved those. The Nutella thing was always so disgusting," said Mrs. Jumai.

"No matter what, it's confirmation for you, that this is your message."

A nod. "And the handkerchief. I cry into it every day—it was the one I made him take to his T-ball practice before he got sick. He always laughed and stuffed it in his back pocket."

"Wow. Okay." Chills spread over Beatrice's arms. "Here it says you don't have to let your son go. By extension, if they're together, you don't have to let your husband go, either."

Impatiently, Mrs. Jumai said, "I see that. I get that. But I want *more.*"

Suddenly, Cordelia and Astrid's rule about not reaching to close ones made sense. When did the desperate craving for more leave? Did it? Could it?

"I lost my stepmother two years ago," Beatrice said. "I know it's not losing a son—no loss in the world can compare to yours—but I miss her every day. Before she passed, she told me grief is unexpressed love."

Touching her ring again, Mrs. Jumai sniffed. "What does that mean?"

"I think she meant we only grieve the people we still want to show our love to but can't, because they're gone. And when that love we still carry around can't be used, can't be given to them, it hurts."

Winnie, who'd been standing motionless behind Mrs. Jumai, made a soft noise in the back of her throat.

Beatrice leaned forward. "I get a lot from thinking about her saying that. I'm so sad that I can't tell her I love her every day, like I used to. But if I didn't feel sad about that, it would mean I'd spent all my love and didn't miss her anymore. Would we want that?"

The woman wiped her tears from her face with the back of her sleeve. "Never," she whispered.

"I don't need to do another reading for you. They don't need me to." She recalled an Evie Oxby technique she'd thought was particularly smart. The bereaved, she said, would know exactly what their loved one would say. Possibly, they'd be able to tune to the right "radio station" and hear them. And if they didn't, if it came from their own mind, that was okay, too, if it brought comfort. "Ask yourself what they would tell you. Right now."

"Me?"

"What would they say?"

Mrs. Jumai closed her eyes. After a moment, the deep line between her eyebrow eased, and her eyes flew open. "Oh! I'd forgotten something that Leon always said to me. I'd forgotten it till right this minute."

"What was that?"

"'Woman, unless you're running from a bear, there's no need to be in such a bloody hurry.'" A smile bloomed below her damp cheeks. "Oh, I'd forgotten that. I swear, I can hear him right now, telling me to slow down. There's no hurry to get to my boys."

"So now you know they're together in the afterlife. And you know you'll join them, but only when the time is right." Beatrice could barely believe she was saying this, that she was *believing* it, but she was. And she had one more thing to say. "Don't hurry. They'll wait for you."

Winnie sighed. "That's beautiful. And it's not accidental that you remembered. That's a gift they just gave you."

Mrs. Jumai touched the paper. "*This* is a gift. You must let me pay you for it. Both of you." She looked tearfully at her wedding ring. "The proper way. Do you take Visa?"

"No." Beatrice shook her head firmly. "But I do like white chocolate chip cookies."

CHAPTER THIRTY-FIVE

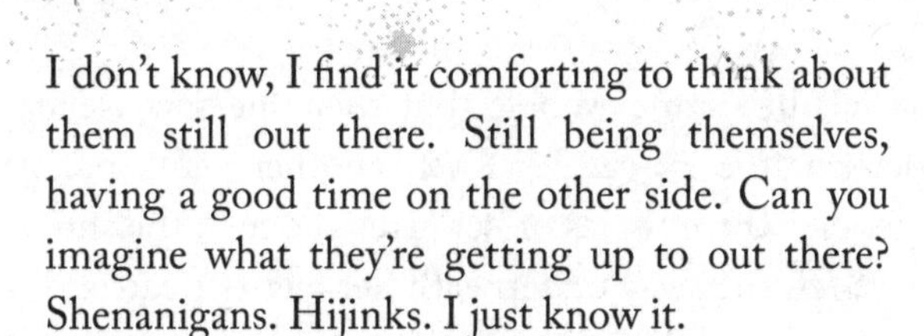

> I don't know, I find it comforting to think about them still out there. Still being themselves, having a good time on the other side. Can you imagine what they're getting up to out there? Shenanigans. Hijinks. I just know it.
>
> —*Evie Oxby,* Us Weekly

Her cappuccino hot in one hand, a latte in the other, Beatrice wandered back to the marina, a new lightness in her bones. She'd helped someone! That was real! Who in the world would mix salt and vinegar chips with Nutella? Okay, granted, the world was really big, and surely, a *couple* of other people probably did. But the initials, *K* for Kumail, and *L* for Leon. The blue handkerchief. Put together, the truth was incontrovertible, right?

It was proof.

And more: She'd known enough to handle the situation the right way. She hadn't done more auto-writing. She hadn't triggered another miracle. Nor had she inadvertently invited the pissed-off undead to throw chairs through windows.

She had simply made Mrs. Jumai feel better.

All of it pointed to one thing: She was figuring this shit out, and if she figured more shit out, maybe she could forestall future miracles. Maybe she could keep being alive.

The gate to her dock was wide open, and Beatrice felt a smile spread across her face.

Reno was good people. Somehow, she knew it. Was it possible that Beatrice really could make a home here? Would Reno be her first real friend? Cordelia and Minna didn't count—they were her family. (Her heart gave a zing at the thought. Again.)

But friendship took time. Something she might not have much of.

She felt her smile wobble, but then she saw Reno on the wide deck of the *Forget-Me-Knot*, another plank balanced on her sawhorse. The muscles of her arms shone in the sun, and she must have felt the sway underneath her feet as Beatrice boarded, because she turned. She didn't smile as much as... brighten.

That brightening? Better than any smile.

Feeling suddenly too warm, Beatrice held out the cup. "Brought you something."

Reno did her head-duck thing. "Oh."

Their fingers brushed.

Something danced in Beatrice's stomach. "Cordelia said you like a latte."

The brightness got even brighter. Joy looked so good on Reno. "I do."

"Fritz guessed it was for you and added two sugars."

She touched the lid. "That's... really kind of you."

This was where Beatrice would normally wave away a gift with a quick *Oh, stop, it's nothing*. But if she did that now, she'd brush off this moment of—what was it? Connection? Whatever it was, it felt good. "I know you're working, but do you want to take a break? We could sit on the bench over there and just..."

Reno's eyebrows rose.

"Sorry. That's silly. I'll let you get back to work." Surely Reno had enough friends already.

"It's not—"

Beatrice tried to grin. "Enjoy the latte. I'm going to go to the library and let you work in peace."

Reno, though, was looking over Beatrice's shoulder. "You have company."

Beatrice turned.

Then she dropped her cup. The lid flew off, and coffee splattered up her jeans.

"Hi, Button."

Her father insisted on buying her a replacement cup of coffee, which was fine, because that meant she didn't have to invite him into the houseboat. Fritz had obviously wanted to ask questions, but a small rush of customers flooded in, so all Fritz said was "Do my eyes deceive me? Do I see a family resemblance here?"

Before her father could answer (and he wanted to—he always wanted to brag about his daughter to anyone who would listen), Beatrice said, "Wow, look at all these people! See you tonight at the party!"

On the sidewalk, her father said, "Party? Settling right in, huh?"

She couldn't even dignify that with a response. "Beach walk?"

"Of course."

Beatrice led him past the marina and around the gazebo, past the charred remains of the stump of the lightning-struck tree. Sunlight glinted from his bald head—he should be wearing a baseball cap, but he always forgot to. Naya was the one who'd reminded him.

Only one fisherman wearing chest-high waders was on the deserted beach, two buckets at his side.

Her father's voice was tentative. "Gorgeous day out here, yeah?"

Fury stopped Beatrice's throat. She nodded.

"Good flight, not too bumpy. That ferry was something, though. Worst nachos of my life."

It physically ached not to agree with him about the fake cheese.

"Don't blame Iris. I brought the stuff you asked her to box up. It's all at the hotel. I hope I brought the right things."

Oh, Beatrice *would* blame Iris. She stomped through the sand, refusing to worry about his high blood pressure and whether he'd be able to keep up with her. He would or he wouldn't. Not her problem.

"Button, we have to talk."

Did they, though? Two weeks ago, she would have agreed with that wholeheartedly. But now, really, what was there to say? If Astrid had been telling the truth last night, there had been a good reason to separate the girls, to keep their power from gathering in the same place. Her father, though—he should have fought to keep Cordelia in his life. And he should never have lied to Beatrice. "Maybe you should have talked to me a long time ago."

"I always wanted to."

"Oh, my god. Don't."

"I'm so sorry. I wish this had never happened."

Beatrice stopped walking, keeping her gaze on her bare, sand-covered toes. "You wish *what* had never happened, exactly?"

"You coming here. Finding them."

"They're my family."

"They are *not*!"

His shout jolted her—Dad wasn't a man who shouted. The adrenaline that spiked through her wasn't fear, though. The jolt of it only bolstered her anger. "Care to explain that claim?"

"Who raised you?"

"You did."

"Damn straight I did. Me and Naya, no one else."

"How could you possibly have let Cordelia go?"

He looked up at the sky as if hoping the answer would be written in the clouds. "She said she'd take you both if I fought her. And I knew by then what she could do."

"You knew about the magic."

"Trickery, you mean. She was good at the sleight of hand. Astrid abandoned you, never forget that. She left you behind without a backward glance."

It still stung, but not in the way he was probably hoping it would. "I admit you and Naya did a good job of bringing me up."

"We did."

"You always said family was the most important thing. Me, you, and Naya."

"Yes." Her father scowled. "I know what you're trying to do. Don't bother."

But she kept going. "If family was the most important thing, why keep me from half of mine?"

"I chose the best mother in the world to raise you."

"I thought my own mother was dead. Because you lied. Then you substituted another woman in her place." *Sorry, Naya.*

Her father's neck turned red, and then purple. "Naya was everything to us. You know that. You're just trying to make me feel like I did the wrong thing."

"By not telling me I had a mother and a *twin sister*? You did the wrong thing. Do you have any idea how I grieved Astrid?"

"You didn't even remember her."

"I knew how her absence felt, though. You wouldn't even tell me how she died. It took me begging for you to even tell me she'd had cancer."

At five years old, when she'd asked how her mother had died, Dad had said, *When you're older, I'll explain it to you.* At ten, he'd told her that Mom had cancer. At thirteen, he'd told her it was lung cancer.

Her father rubbed his jaw. "I hated lying to you."

"Yeah, well, I hate that you did, too. You have no idea how much I knew about lung cancer as a thirteen-year-old." Beatrice had insisted that Naya and Dad get the house tested for radon and had held her breath when she walked past people smoking on sidewalks. When she was a high school sophomore, James Reyes had offered her a cigarette. She'd batted it out of his hand and said, "The risk for lung cancer is twenty to forty percent higher in smokers than non-smokers, and tobacco use is responsible for seventy-nine to ninety percent of lung cancer." He'd said in response, "Give me fifty cents for wasting that smoke, you little freak." She'd had a three-inch binder full of research on somatic mutations in the TP53 and EGFR genes, filing each new bit of information by date of publication in plastic sheet protectors.

"Oh, Beatrice."

"Did you even love Naya? Or were you just trying to find me a mother so you could have less guilt over keeping the secret of my mother and sister from me?"

He looked stricken. "I can't believe you would say that. You know I worshipped that woman."

Dad had thought Naya hung not just the moon, but also the sun and probably every single star, too. No one knew that better than Beatrice did. Why, then, did she keep twisting the knife? She couldn't help herself, though—the words just kept coming. "I'm not sure about any of your motives anymore. You're so careful with money—maybe you just didn't want to pay for a nanny for me. Easier to marry someone?"

"Button, no."

"My name is Beatrix. Isn't it?" Would claiming her birth name give her distance from this man, the one who'd ostensibly taught her that honesty was key?

"No." He ground the word out. "You can't use that name. That's her name. Please, please use the one I chose for you. You're my Beatrice. My Button. That's why I'm here—"

"You said that you came to bring me my stuff."

"I did."

"Could have FedExed it."

"Guess you're right." He frowned into the sky again. Wrinkles cut deeply across the face Beatrice had always thought handsome. When had he gotten so old? Sure, he'd been slowing down, but Beatrice realized that if a stranger looked at him, they'd just see an old man in wrinkled chinos.

Beatrice stopped walking and turned to face him. *Don't cross your arms. He always knows when you're nervous.* Helpless to stop herself, she crossed her arms. "You let a woman steal my sister from me. You let a daughter *go.* Did she matter that little to you? I don't know who you are anymore, and I'm not sure I ever did."

His eyes gleamed with unshed tears. "You've always known me. I'm the one who loves you most."

"Did Naya know?"

"No. She... suspected I was hiding something. But I never told her."

Beatrice gave a half laugh. Was she glad that Naya had also been kept in the dark? Of course she was—maintaining that kind of secret would have eaten Naya alive. But oh, how heartbreaking. "So she never knew who you were, either."

"Both of you knew *exactly* who I was. Who I am. A man who would do anything to protect those he loves." His gaze fell to the sand. "I'll never forgive myself for the shame of letting Cordelia go, though."

"Nor should you." She walked away from him.

"Beatrice—"

Her stride didn't slow, even when she tripped over a piece of driftwood. She wheeled her arms, keeping herself upright and moving fast. When her father caught up with her, when he grasped her arm, she was panting. He must have had to run.

"*Please*," he panted, his face streaming with tears.

She pulled her arm away sharply, but she slowed. Then she stopped, digging her toes deeply into the sand, finding the chilly dampness under the top layer of warmth.

This hurt—it hurt so much, and honestly, she could admit that this betrayal was small compared to some. Her father had just loved her very much. The one he'd truly betrayed was Cordelia, not her.

Still, her very soul ached.

He breathed heavily, recovering.

This was on him. This was *all* on him.

Finally, when he'd stopped wheezing, her father said, "What's it going to take, Beatrice?"

"For what?" There was no reason to make any of this easy.

"For you to forgive me."

Beatrice couldn't help it—she laughed. "You think you can snap your fingers and I'll just forget the fact that you lied to me about everything for the entirety of my life?"

"Just tell me what it will take."

"A fucking miracle, Dad."

He glanced to the left, where the surf was breaking. "Watch out."

A wave larger than the others crashed, racing up the sand toward them. It wouldn't have been big enough to knock either of them over, but instinctively, they dodged backward.

Beatrice felt something cold and hard catch her heel just before she went down with a thump. Any other day, the fall onto her backside would have made her laugh. Today, though, the jolt felt like just another slap in the face.

Her father reached out his hand. "Need help?"

"Absolutely not." She brushed the sand off her palms. What had she tripped over anyway? It hadn't felt like driftwood or seaweed... Scrabbling at the place her heel had caught, she felt it. Rounded glass, partially buried.

Naya had loved finding old glass on the beach, the sharp edges worn down. She'd even resembled the glass at the end, something Beatrice had thought but never said. Her sharp elbows and knees had softened, her chiseled jaw melting. Her brown skin, always soft, had felt like the lightest silk. Only her voice, always sharp and bright with love, had never dulled.

Beatrice pushed more sand aside.

"Careful. It could be broken."

She didn't look at the man who'd lost the right to tell her how to do anything.

The glass was buried deep, but at least it gave her something to do for a minute or two, a reason to avoid looking at him. It was a squat beer bottle, remarkably still whole, though the green glass was worn and clouded. Wedged in the neck of it was a cork, but the bottle felt empty and light.

"Wouldn't that be something," her father offered, "if there was a message in there? You remember that day we sent those messages out?"

The memory flooded back. The three of them on Venice Beach on Mother's Day. She'd been what, fifteen? Sixteen? Naya had just started struggling with chronic bronchitis and various respiratory infections that never really cleared up, even though the COPD wouldn't kill her for another twenty-seven years. Beatrice had been so scared—looking back, she realized they must all have been. It had been Naya's idea, of course: the green bottles, the yellowed paper with the artfully burned edges, the quill pens they'd dipped into a pot of purple ink. They'd each written letters, corked them, and tossed them into the water off the pier. Beatrice's letter had been a kind of prayer for Naya, she remembered. Also, she'd mentioned Tony Valdez and the hope that he'd kiss her someday, even though he'd never spared her a second glance in the quad.

The poignancy of the memory felt too intense. She didn't want this.

But she did want to pop out the cork to see if someone on the other side of the world had put a message in this particular bottle. She had a tiny corkscrew attached to the house key she was still idiotically carrying.

Her father plopped onto the sand next to her.

The cork crumbled, but then it was out. This was silly—it was just an old beer bottle, right?

She held it up and peered inside.

"Anything?"

Beatrice swallowed. "Paper."

"Seriously?"

Her first finger was *just* long enough to fit down the neck, if she pushed and twisted—yes, here it came. Here they came, rather.

Two sheets of yellowed paper, burned on the edges.

At the top of one page, *Mitchell, my love.* And on the other, *My darling Button.*

Scanning the end of the first page, there it was: *Love, Naya.*

Beatrice's own words rang in her head.

A fucking miracle.

CHAPTER THIRTY-SIX

> Angels? I don't know. Maybe? For sure, though, our loved ones are watching over us. I adore that about them. Unless I'm naked and doing something I don't want them to see. Then, I gotta admit, yes, the idea creeps me out. But they get it. I hope.
>
> —*Evie Oxby,* Out *magazine*

Her father didn't even try to bluster his way through his disbelief—how could he, when he had the proof in front of him?

Silently, they read their letters.

My darling Button,

Now, I don't expect to go anywhere for a while yet. I have a feeling I'll beat this. But in case I don't, I know one thing, and I know it truly and surely and deeply—I know it in exactly the same way I fell in love with you about three seconds after I fell in love with your father. You are my daughter. Yes, your birth mother loved you—of course she did. Sometimes I swear I feel her near me, her hand on top of mine as I touch your hair, like she's a ghost, but alive? I know that doesn't make sense. Anyway, you having had a birth mother doesn't mean you can't have two moms, and thank you for letting me be that to you. You are the delight of my soul, the lyrics to my song, the brilliant burst of color in everything I see. No matter where I am when you read this, I'm with you. (Because you will read this someday. Isn't it silly that I believe that? But I do.) Tell your father nothing bad will happen if he widens his own beliefs. Contrary to what he thinks, it won't kill him. If I'm not around, tell him to get a girlfriend. He's not the kind of man who should live alone. Cheese sticks and apples with peanut butter shouldn't make up more than one meal a day. And you, my love: perhaps your beliefs are already widening? The truth isn't relative, but it's more expansive than some people think. My deepest truth is that I have loved you with my whole heart. I always will, for eternity. Can you feel me now? I'm right here. I'm always here. Love, Naya.

There was no use in trying to stop the tears, so she didn't bother. "She said to stop eating cheese and peanut butter apples."

Thickly, her father said, "Oh, yeah? She said for you to fall in real love."

Beatrice's heart thunked. "Well, she said for *you* to get a girlfriend."

"Is this…is this real?" His hands shook as he held up the paper. "Honey, what's happening?"

She took a deep breath. "I was told by a psychic—"

"Your *mother*?"

"Someone else. Listen, Dad. I was told that I was dying, and soon, but that I'd experience seven miracles first."

He puffed out his cheeks. "Impossible. We know that's impossible. You're not *dying*."

"What are the odds of me tripping over a bottle that your dead wife cast into the ocean a thousand miles and almost thirty years ago?"

He opened his mouth.

"And *do not* say that I could have set this up. Because you know I didn't. And I'm sure she put something in your letter that only you could know was true."

A slow nod. Then he said, "I'm not saying I buy into any of this, but out of nothing more than morbid curiosity, what number miracle would this be? If it were one?"

"Five."

"Five." His voice was strangled. "And then you... We have to get you to a doctor."

"I had a physical recently. Fit as a fiddle." A seagull swooped at a group of sandpipers with a scream. "I didn't believe in miracles before I got here, Dad. But there are just two left."

He kept his gaze on the seagull. "Your mother and all her magical nonsense. You were better off without her."

"Maybe she should have taken both of us." It was a low blow, and she regretted the words as soon as they left her lips.

"Does *she* know about this miracle stuff?"

This was just too hard. "It's probably time you went home."

"Jesus, as if I would. What kind of doctor did you get that physical from? Some quack on this undeveloped island? We'll get you a better one, they can find what's wrong, *if* there's something wrong, and fix it. The best treatment in the world. I'll start making calls this afternoon."

And because Beatrice knew exactly how her father ticked through life, she knew that, by the end of the day, he'd have his own spreadsheet started. *Management of Beatrice's Optimal Health* or something. Every potential step would be plotted out. Within a month he'd be one of the leading experts on middle-aged female life expectancy, and the knowledge would give him a bit of peace.

But . . . would it?

When Naya was dying, her father had abandoned his spreadsheet with its lists of medications and the best internists ranked by country.

He'd sat by his wife's side, leaving only to bathe and take an occasional walk outside. He was with her, fully, in every moment of those last six months.

Beatrice had been the one lost in spreadsheets, unable to let go of the hope that they could beat it. If she, the last person to believe, let go of that hope, if she stopped searching for a miracle cure, then Naya would die. So she *couldn't* let the hope go.

She'd failed, of course.

Dad's face was still animated. "And I'm not going anywhere until I talk to my ex-wife, until I explain to her that the only truth is verifiable and provable. She's been running from reality for too long."

Cordelia's little face in the mirror. "You already know what's real, Dad. That's why you broke that mirror."

He had the grace not to ask what mirror, but he grabbed a fistful of sand and thrust it at her. "No, *this* is real." He grabbed a small piece of driftwood and pointed at the water. "This wood is real. That ocean is real. Real is what you can see and what you can touch."

"What about love? How do you prove that?"

Her father scowled. "I love a good pastrami sandwich, too. I don't need to prove that."

Beatrice touched his letter, still gripped in his other hand. "So I could rip this up? You don't need this proof?"

"*No.*" The look of grief that smashed across his face would have knocked her to the sand if she hadn't already been sitting on it. He dropped the stick and clutched the paper with both hands, bringing it to his chest. "Please, no. This is mine."

"I'm sorry. I didn't mean to..." Her chest ached like she'd run uphill in a snowstorm. If she died—*only two miracles left*—her father would be so very alone. He'd barely recovered from losing Naya.

Picking up the driftwood he'd dropped, she wrote Naya's name in the sand, curling the Y's tail to blend with the N.

Minna had said, *A sigil is what you create it to be.*

Beatrice could receive miracles.

She could also do magic.

Around Naya's name, she drew the shape of a bottle, then she connected the letter *M* and the letter *B* in long loops around it. Three hearts, one for each of them, and then a large circle to enclose them all, to keep them close together.

She closed her eyes and imagined the ache in her chest moving into the sand, filling the ridges the stick had left.

The scent of gardenia filled the air.

Beatrice's eyes flew open.

Naya had filled the house with gardenia candles, and wore gardenia perfume every day. Her garden had been full of them, and when the bushes bloomed, she could always be found lying on a blanket next to them with a book, her nose constantly twitching rapturously.

Beatrice's father sat up straight, sniffing the air. "That's—do you—?"

"Yeah, I smell it, too."

"But—is that another miracle?"

Slowly, Beatrice said, "No. Miracles are unearned gifts." She touched the piece of paper she'd rolled and stuck halfway back into the bottle. Then she pointed at the sigil. "That's magic."

"So it's not real. She's not here."

I'm always here.

"I think she is. I think the gardenias are a sign that she sent because she saw my drawing." Beatrice pulled out her phone and took a picture of the sigil. Then she turned the phone around and held it up, grabbing a quick selfie of the two of them, her father managing a small smile.

He drew a shuddery breath. "You've changed."

"I'm just trying to learn new things." A wave of lightheadedness washed over her, and she changed the subject. "How's Grant?"

"He looks fine when I see him, which isn't often. I've only glared across the street at him a couple of times. How are you doing with the idea of him? The marriage?" He waved the letter in the air. "Et cetera."

"I'm furious with him. But I'm not brokenhearted."

"What? You should be!" he blustered. "If you're not wrecked to leave him, how could you have loved him enough to marry him?"

"It made sense. I do love him, as a person. Statistics show that marriage reduces things like depression and emergency room visits. People who marry have greater longevity and enjoy better physical health, on average. Plus, you liked him a lot. I figured it was time."

"Statistics? You can't be logical about *love*."

Down the beach, the lone fisherman was packing up his poles. Beatrice leaned sideways and nudged her father's shoulder with her own. "Well, you always made logic look pretty good."

"Blaming me, then?" But there was a smile in his voice. "I'm looking into a condo in Lakewood. Get a little farther away from him. No need to be on his street if you're not there. Might even start thinking about retirement."

Beatrice took a breath. "What about looking up here for a place? Cheaper cost of living, I'd think."

He blinked once. Twice. "But... don't you hate me?"

"At the moment, yeah. A bit."

"So..."

"So what? I'm trying to believe in more things than I used to. I believe you love me, even though you had a really shitty way of showing it. And I love you, even though you fucked up."

Her father's smile bloomed slowly, and then all at once. "Oh, honey. But oh, lord, if I lived on an island with your mother—yeah, there might not be enough room in the whole Pacific Northwest to..." He trailed off.

"Fair enough." She would let him do what he needed to do, when he needed to do it.

"So." He got that nervous look, the pinched one he'd always gotten before she'd driven anywhere in her first car, a beefy Volvo he'd bought for her. "Do you think I could come to that party with you tonight? She always told me I'd go bald early. I want to show her I look good this way."

CHAPTER THIRTY-SEVEN

> Ancestry is less important than we think in terms of connection to the other side. Blood is overrated—what matters is the connections we forget on this earthly plane. But if you have witches in your lineage, do let me know, okay? A little backstory in our heritage doesn't hurt to know about.
>
> —*Evie Oxby,* City Arts and Lectures

An hour later, Cordelia sent a text: SOS if you have time to help with party setup?

Of course she had time. Her father was settling in at the Skerry Lodge. With no job other than reading every single one of the approximately four million books published on magic and mediumship, Beatrice had nothing *but* time. Unless she didn't, ironically.

At Cordelia's house, she knocked and waited, admiring the way the porch wrapped around the side, as if the rails from which the paint was gently peeling were hugging the house. The flowers in the garden almost shouted with joy, the purple hollyhocks waving their arms above the even more chaotic petunias.

She heard a muffled thump followed by Cordelia's voice, but no one came to the door.

So Beatrice let herself in. She just *did* it. Pushed the door open as if she had every right to do so, as if she'd done it a million times before.

What would it have been like if she'd had decades of letting herself into her twin's home? What if Cordelia had carried a duplicate key for Beatrice's house on her key chain, even though they lived in different cities? Would that have changed who she became? Would Beatrice being around have smoothed Minna's transition and Cordelia's acceptance? It was obvious Cordelia loved her daughter with all her heart now, but what if Beatrice had been around when Minna had run away—what if her niece had been able to run to *her*?

Fresh anger at both Astrid and her father rose in her throat, but it dropped away when she found Cordelia in the kitchen, moving so fast, she was practically a blur.

Cordelia smiled and gave her a bone-crushing hug. "I missed you. Honestly, thank god you're here. I'm making a huge mess of Mexican food and I've got the beans going already, but I need to start the mole, and I'll need help with chopping a zillion things soon—"

"Dad's in town." The interruption felt harsh, but Beatrice didn't know how to sugar-coat it.

"Oh." Cordelia stilled. "Huh. That's interesting."

"He wants to come to the party. I'll tell him no, though—"

"Of course he can come." The smile she pushed onto her face was fake but bright. "Dang it, though, I've done almost no decorating at all. Can you make a start on that?" Smelling of onions and cumin, she gave Beatrice a quick kiss on the cheek before muttering something about harvesting cilantro, and zooming back into overdrive.

Beatrice spent the next hour or so draping the house in Halloween decorations, even though it was mid-July. Spiders hung from the staircase railing, and webbing covered the legs of chairs and tables. In one of the cardboard boxes Cordelia pointed her to, she found an entire family of dead things, related only by the fact that they'd been reduced to skulls. She thought one might be a fox, another a possum, which had surprisingly sharp teeth. There were four or five bird skulls, and one that might have belonged to a cat, though she didn't want to think about it too much. She set the skulls on top of any free space she found, placing silver candelabras next to them (Cordelia had so many candle holders!) and making sure their candles were fresh and ready to be lit. Through the parlor's window, she saw Astrid on the back deck, carving jack-o'-lantern faces into watermelons. As if she felt Beatrice's gaze, Astrid looked up. Their eyes met and then broke apart with a snap.

But something had shifted between them—was it the way Astrid had done the thread spell, obviously trying to protect them? Whatever the reason, the anger Beatrice felt toward her was burning lower, just like her anger at Mitchell.

She might manage to forgive her father, someday, for lying to her. She loved him, and it was that simple.

Astrid, on the other hand, she loved not at all. Not one bit.

Damn. She cut her finger on the sharp edge of a tea light.

"Beatrice!" Her sister came out of the kitchen, wiping floury hands on a dishtowel.

She wrapped her lightly bleeding finger in a tissue. "Yeah?" Cordelia would want more info on their father, of course. And if she wanted Dad not to come to the party, Beatrice would tell him he wasn't invited. Cheerfully.

But Cordelia only said, "Can you please track down my wayward daughter and remind her that she's in charge of the deviled eggs? I need, like, fifty of them, so if she doesn't start the water boiling within the next sixty minutes, I will personally melt all the way down, and then she'll be in charge of the entire party, and I assume she doesn't want that."

"Absolutely. I'll do that right now." She'd do any chore her sister wanted her to. Especially if it had nothing to do with their father.

Minna wasn't upstairs in her room, and presumably she wasn't at her library job, so that meant she must be in the hideout or in the cemetery. A joyful thought struck her: she knew enough about Minna to have an educated guess as to where she might be. Hugging herself, Beatrice let herself out the front door, the better to avoid Astrid on the back porch, and went around through the side garden, under the jasmine arbor, and in the gate of the separate hideout garden.

The door of the shed was open, and Minna was flopped backward on the orange sofa, staring at the ceiling, her hands lying open at her sides.

"May I come in?"

A shrug was her only response.

"Are you okay?"

Another shrug.

"Are you high?"

Minna snorted. "I look that couch-locked?"

"You do."

She wriggled into an upright position. "While it's true that many of my friends are budding professional potheads, I don't actually enjoy feeling paranoid."

"Yeah," said Beatrice easily. It was nice, this camaraderie. "I never really liked that, either."

Minna made a face. "Yeah, yeah. That's what adults say. All buddy-buddy, all *hangovers suck so bad am I right?*"

Okay, being lumped in with clueless adults didn't feel quite as good. "What's wrong?"

Minna laced her fingers together and stared at the white-and-red polish. "I can *feel* my dad trying to reach me. It's like he's so close...but he just can't get to me." She threw herself backward on the couch again. "I'm so frustrated."

What was Beatrice supposed to say to this? "I'm sorry. That sounds hard."

"You're not sorry."

Ouch. "I am, actually. Don't you think I understand what it's like to not know a birth parent?" Whoops, she still sounded like a know-it-all adult, didn't she?

Tears filled Minna's eyes. "Last night, he was in a dream I had about being at the library, but it wasn't a visitation dream, it was just a stupid one where he was trying to return a book and I wanted to give him a hug, but he didn't have any idea who I was and pushed me away. Gran always says that you know when it's a visitation in a dream. And that wasn't one."

"How do you know?"

"She says they're short and sharp and clear. Maybe you just see the person for a few seconds, or you hear them say one really direct thing, and you know your brain isn't making it up. But last night, it was totally stupid. He rode off on an elephant, and then the whole building turned into a chocolate factory, and I was in charge of roasting the almonds. *Idiotic.*"

"That would be a good-smelling job, though."

Minna rolled her eyes. "Can you try the writing for me again?"

Nope. Her gut didn't like that one bit. "Why don't you ask one of your guides?"

"They won't talk to me about it."

"Huh." Seemed like a pretty good indication it was a bad idea, then.

"Please try the writing?"

This time, Beatrice's response was instant. "No."

"Please."

"Hey." She needed to distract Minna, get her mind off this. "Your mom sent me to wrangle you into the house. Within the hour, she wants you to start making eleventy-million deviled eggs—did you know that?"

Minna reached for the tattoo gun. "You don't even have to hold this. I can hold it. I think that might work."

A bigger distraction was called for, then. "You know, I actually might want a tattoo from you at some point."

It was like releasing a mouse into the middle of the room. Minna gave a little scream, bounced into the air and then back down, all while clapping. "Yes. *Yes!* What do you want?"

"Wait, I didn't mean right now—"

"No time like the present!" She jumped up and started clattering tools on the work cart, arranging bottles of alcohol, boxes of needles, and wipes. "I'm a good artist, so you can basically tell me whatever you want, and I'll sketch it—wait." Minna spun to stare at her. "Oh. You already know what you want. It's a sigil, isn't it?"

Beatrice lost her breath. She hadn't, actually, known what she wanted until that exact second. "Maybe."

"Show it to me."

So Beatrice pulled it up on her phone. The photo of the sigil in the sand.

"Ohhh," breathed Minna. "That's pretty." Without asking, she reached forward to flick to the next photo.

Beatrice gasped. She hadn't looked at the photo after she

took it. In it, she and her father smiled at the camera. A nice, normal photo of a father and daughter at the beach.

What wasn't normal was the light. A blinding ray of blue-white sunlight hit the top of her father's head. Another one lit the top of her own head. The rays streaked down from the top right of the shot.

But judging by the shadows cast by the streetlight on the sidewalk behind them, the sun had been to their left.

CHAPTER THIRTY-EIGHT

Don't overcomplicate magic. Keep it simple, sister.
—*Evie Oxby, on* Radiolab

Minna grinned. "Amazing."

"That's..." Beatrice zoomed in, then out again. "Why...why would the sunlight do this?"

"It wouldn't. That's not sunlight. That looks like *love* to me." Minna extended the word out long, almost singing it. "What—or who—was the sigil for?"

"My stepmother. His wife."

"Her light's super pretty."

"Holy shit."

"So." Minna held up the gun. "Black ink?"

"Don't be silly, Minna. We have to get ready for the party."

"I can do line drawings like this in my sleep. Fifteen minutes, and done."

Beatrice bit her bottom lip. She wasn't actually considering this, was she?

Permanently marking the sigil on her skin, the sigil that had proved Naya was always near? The very idea felt lovely. "Really, fifteen minutes?"

Minna nodded, her face bright. "Then I'll make one squillionty deviled eggs."

"Your mother won't kill you?"

"She'd kill me if I tattooed myself, or anyone else under voting age, but I can tattoo adults."

"Like Reno and who else?"

"Okay, like only Reno so far. But that's because I've only asked you and Mom, and Mom always says no."

It was silly to feel so flattered, and yet, she did. Beatrice held out her arms. "Where should I get it?"

"Wherever you want, maybe somewhere you can see it easily and remember her? Your forearm, or inner wrist?"

Why the hell not? "Inner wrist." She'd never gotten one before because of pure vanity. How would a tattoo age on her? How it would look on wrinkled, crepey skin? But if her skin never had the time to wrinkle...

And what was the big deal about a little ink in memory of a woman she'd loved, who'd managed to send her a letter through the years on the ocean's waves? Even Naya herself had a tattoo on her left shoulder, a goldfinch lighting on a gardenia flower to commemorate her own mother. "Purple was her favorite color. Can you do it in that?"

Minna squeaked. "Can I ever!" She pulled out a drawer and then muttered, "Whoops, can I? Hang on." Then she triumphantly held up a plastic bottle with a purple pointed top. "Yes, I can!"

The prep went quickly. Minna asked Beatrice to draw the sigil while she sterilized the tattoo area and her tools. Then Minna made a stencil sheet of the design and pressed it against Beatrice's right wrist. She pulled the paper away, leaving behind light purple lines. "You like the placement? We can move it, or make it bigger or smaller, whatever."

"It's perfect."

Minna sniffed. "That's a gardenia flower, right? Is that what I smell?"

There it was, again, that sweet perfumed air. *Wow.* "Yeah."

"She sure smells good." Minna held up the gun. "This won't hurt very much. And if I'm lying, at least it won't take very long."

But Minna wasn't lying. The tattooing hardly hurt at all. The pain of the needle wasn't like any other pain Beatrice had ever felt, actually. If someone were holding her down and tattooing her against her will, it probably would have hurt like a son of a bitch. But as it was, it felt like a weird, scratchy itch, one that she'd chosen. It felt good.

As she worked, Minna kept up a steady stream of chatter, as if she were trying to distract her. Beatrice listened and responded, but the words didn't feel important.

Nothing felt as important as being here with Minna, getting the symbol of Naya (and of her, and of her father) inscribed upon her skin.

The gardenia scent bloomed, getting more and more heady, until Minna finally said, "There. Done." She wiped away a small bit of blood welling to the surface. "Look as much as you want, and then I'm going to wrap it in plastic for the night, okay? Tomorrow you can let it air out and I'll show you how to take care of it. Do you like it? How does it feel?"

It felt *right.* As if Beatrice's skin had been waiting for this, exactly. "I love it. It's weird..."

Minna took off her gloves and reached for her phone. "I'll put on a new pair before I wrap it, but I want to get some good shots now—is that okay?"

"Sure. The scent has faded, right?"

Minna nodded. "I have a theory."

Did it match the question running through Beatrice's mind? "The smell went into my skin with the ink?"

"That's what I think."

"Oh." Beatrice felt warmed from the inside out. "She's inside me."

Minna held her phone over Beatrice's wrist, taking multiple shots. "Well, to be fair, she already was. But yeah, stuff like that's important. Reno's got Scarlett's ashes in a couple of her tattoos."

"Oh, my god, people do that?"

"It's not a big deal if you do it right. Which I do. I wish I had some of my dad's ashes, but he was buried. If I did, I'd use them in the sigil I'm trying to copy from that photo of him—do you want to see it?"

"Of course I do."

Minna flipped open a notebook to a sketch of a bold T surrounded by slashes and lines made through two conjoined circles. The effect was strong, almost leaping off the page.

"I love it."

"I'm getting closer. I know I'm missing something, but I can't tell what it is."

"It'll come to you."

With a sly look, Minna said, "Or *you* could help me figure it out by auto-writing. *He* could tell me."

"Nope." Okay, rejecting her niece's bad ideas was getting easier with practice apparently.

Minna huffed out a breath. "I keep trying. I say the spell perfectly but nothing happens. What's wrong with me? Why can't I do it?"

The image of the fountain pen entering the padlock rose in Beatrice's mind.

"Oh!" Minna exclaimed. "You figured it out!"

"What?"

"You just figured out what's special about the way you say the spell. I *saw* you realize it, don't even lie. Tell me. It's not like I don't have the spell, not like I'm going to give up trying. This way, I'm doing it right instead of wrong, you know? Doing it wrong could be dangerous, and I know you wouldn't want that."

Attempting to think clearly, Beatrice tried to ignore the blatant manipulation attempt. It couldn't be as easy as visualizing something, could it? Beatrice looked down at her tattoo, glowing with purple heat.

Evie Oxby said, *Share what you know, and a deeper knowledge will return back to you.*

As if Minna could hear her thinking about Oxby's advice, she said, "We share what we learn with each other. That's, like, Holland code."

Well, shit. "If I tell you, you'll try it."

"I won't."

"Oh, yeah?"

Minna clasped her hands at her chest. "I promise I'll try nothing alone, without telling you or Reno or Mom. Come on, Auntie Bea. You're a Holland at heart, I know that. Share with me? Please?"

The girl was good. "You swear. You *swear* that you'll tell me or your mom or Reno before you try it?"

"On my father's grave." Minna licked the tip of her finger and drew a cross over her heart. "I swear it."

If I had one month left: I would try to be brave. I would try to be open.

"I imagine a pen going into a lock."

Minna lifted and dropped her hands. "Why didn't you just *say* that?"

"Because I didn't know it was important! You keep forgetting I have no clue what I'm doing!"

"What kind of pen?"

"Fountain pen, long and skinny."

"Old-school. I like it. What kind of lock?"

"Also old-fashioned. Heavy, dark metal. The kind of lock you'd picture on the gate of an old cemetery. Or hanging off a bridge in France, you know?"

Minna nodded. "Got it. So. Can we try it tonight? At the party?"

"*Excuse* me?"

"I'm telling you! I promised I would tell you or Mom or Reno!"

Beatrice's heart sank. "But that whole 'close one' thing? Your mom seemed pretty serious about that. And the other night, when I tried it, and that...whatever it was chased us into the house?"

"Tonight is the *best* time. Not to be an asshole about it, but if we're in some kind of danger, wouldn't my father be even closer than normal to protect me? And since today's his deathiversary, I was already going to try to reach him at midnight during the party. I usually try to contact him, but this time, it might work. Thanks to you."

Something churned low in Beatrice's gut. She scanned her mental inventory of the *Magic* spreadsheet—why didn't she have a *Protecting Others* column? What was this dread? What was she missing? "I don't like this."

"Come with me, then."

"Maybe. And your mom, too?"

Minna slammed a package of nitrile gloves onto the workbench. "She doesn't get me. Only you do."

Through the dread, Beatrice felt her heart expand a notch. This girl trusted her. "I hear you."

"So you'll come?"

"Yes." And she would tell Cordelia, too. She'd convince her sister to keep it a secret but she'd also get advice on how best to help Minna and keep her safe. It was too important now to get it wrong.

Minna's shoulders relaxed. "Good. I'll be careful. Plus, you'll be there, so it'll be fine. I know what I'm doing."

That makes one of us.

CHAPTER THIRTY-NINE

Magic is so plentiful, it's hard *not* to find it. And believers, in the same way, are everywhere. You have to look, though. I say this with love, sugar: put down your phone, m'kay? Time to get out there.

—*Evie Oxby,* Palm Springs and Bat Wings, *Netflix*

The party was packed. It was fun. And it was beyond intense.

It felt like everyone had arrived at one time, en masse, carrying plates. The food tables groaned with the weight of lasagnas, sushi, chana masala, and cupcakes. The drinks station was staffed by a giggly Minna and her friend Olive.

Just outside the covered porch was a table laden not with food, but with framed photographs of guests' deceased loved ones. The images mostly showed older people, but there were also a few heartbreaking photos of children, as well as some adorable pictures of dogs and cats (and one iguana).

Beatrice directed traffic as Cordelia had asked her to, and during a brief lull, she studied the photos. She touched the edge of a silver frame that held the image of a woman with flame-red hair, who grinned so brightly that it was impossible to believe she wasn't alive anymore.

This time next year, would Beatrice's photo be on the table?

"Here, dear."

"Thank you." Beatrice placed the photo of a tabby next to the other cat pictures.

"Oh, you *are* the spitting image of Cordelia, aren't you? My word!"

"That's what I hear."

The comments kept coming. *Look at you! Can you believe it? What's that like, finding a twin? A whole family?* There wasn't an easy response to any of them.

Beatrice handled it well for about an hour. Then she found an excellent hiding spot, the little space behind the largest two planters on the patio.

It took her sister just ten minutes to find her. Cordelia grinned as she wiggled into the spot next to her. "So this is where you went to. A bit much?"

Embarrassed, Beatrice set down the empty beer bottle she'd been clutching like a life preserver. "It's a lot." She peered around the leaves. "It has to be the whole town, right?"

"And then some." Cordelia pointed. "Those three are from the mainland, and that guy came all the way from Idaho."

"And you know them all?"

"Most of them, yeah."

"Tell me about them." She needed to tell Cordelia about Minna's plans, but first, Beatrice just wanted to listen, to let her sister's voice wrap around her in the middle of the party.

Cordelia smiled and obliged, telling her about the fishmonger and his wife who ran a ship-to-shore community-supported fishery, about the head librarian who was supposedly vegan but had been spotted in Seattle eating churrasco in a Brazilian steakhouse, and about a man with broad shoulders who'd been Cordelia's latest sexual escapade. "If he looks like he could chop an enormous log in half with one swing of his ax, I can confirm that you're right. And no, I won't tell you about that night until I'm thirteen percent more drunk, but then I'll tell you *everything*."

Beatrice laughed. "You're such an extrovert."

"And you try to fool people into thinking you're one, but you're not." Cordelia bumped her shoulder with her own.

"Is it that obvious?"

"I don't know. It's hard for me to tell how other people see you."

Beatrice picked her bottle back up. "How do you see me?"

"You'll laugh."

"I promise I won't."

"I still see you like I saw you in the mirror. I always knew Mom wasn't telling the truth about the car accident. She tried to tell me that the girl in the mirror was just a trick of my imagination, but I knew it wasn't. So now I see you like . . . " She paused. "Like I'm looking at my best friend, the one who's always been there for me."

It hurt to know that she hadn't been. Beatrice glanced out at the crowd to reassure herself that no one could see them. "I hate that you felt I was out there. That you had to carry that amount of hope with you for so long. That must have been awful."

"I guess. But at the same time, I would never have traded it for what you had, that not knowing."

"What you don't know can't hurt you, right?" Ha. She didn't believe that—why had she said it? Cordelia didn't know about the messages in the bottles, the fifth miracle, yet. She needed to tell Cordelia about the tattoo Minna had given her, and sharing the image of the lock and key with Minna. Most importantly, she should tell Cordelia how obsessed Minna was with hearing from her father.

But if she told her all those things, she might make Cordelia's glowing face fall. And her sister looked so *happy*. There would be time for sharing those worries later, after the party.

Cordelia said, "Oh, look at Fritz."

The barista was balancing on the balls of their feet, their gaze pinned on Winnie's sequined tank top.

"Did they ever date?"

"In Fritz's *dreams*. At least, that's what Keelia told me. I like Winnie, what little I know of her. I think they'd be good together." Cordelia looked at Beatrice, her eyes alight. "Hey, you want to learn a little spell?"

"Yes." It was true. She'd love another spell to add to her *Magic* spreadsheet. But what she wanted even more was just to sit here while her sister continued to narrate the party to her. She'd never known this was a thing to want, and now she did, and she might never recover from this loveliness.

"Mom taught it to me as a Push-Pull, but Minna called it a Push-Me-Pull-You a long time ago, and that stuck. First, you pick two people that you want to move toward each other. Or alternately, that you want to keep apart."

"Fritz and Winnie."

Nodding, Cordelia said, "First, we ground ourselves. Feel your feet and imagine you've got roots going into the earth like a tree, but the roots go deeper. They go through the crust of the earth, through the mantle, through the pockets of air and water deep inside, down through the molten outer core, and into the very middle of the earth."

Beatrice could almost feel it, the heat of the earth rising into her, strong and elemental.

"Now that your roots go to the super-heated solid iron and

nickel core, you imagine them pulling that stability upward, closer and closer to you. At the same time, you're looking at your targets." Cordelia shot her a quick wink. "Iron ore at the core, feel the pull you can't ignore."

Winnie, who'd been speaking to a woman holding a newborn, twisted her head in Fritz's direction as if someone had tapped her on the shoulder.

Fritz took a step toward her.

"Then," said Cordelia, "if you want to play around, you can reverse and do the push part. Imagine that you're at the center of the universe, as if everything you know about astronomy and physics is wrong, and it's literally you—your body—that the universe is expanding out from. Push energy from your center out past your skin, up through the top of your head, into the stratosphere and then the exosphere. Then push your power into space, out past the planets, past our sun, past the next galaxies, and all the way out to the farthest edges of the universe."

A chilled, metallic stream of raw power surged through Beatrice's limbs.

Cordelia said, "Power out, space them out." She nudged Beatrice.

"Power out, space them out."

Winnie turned back to the woman holding the baby. Fritz took the same step backward, shoving their hands into their pockets.

"Into the ground again, into the core. Ready?"

Beatrice focused. Her roots actually *trembled* in the center of the earth, a tickling roar that raced up her legs and into her own core. Together, they said, "Iron ore at the core, feel the pull you can't ignore."

Fritz took all ten steps needed to get to Winnie, who turned around to face them just as they reached her. They smiled at each other so broadly that Beatrice could practically warm her hands at the heat they exuded.

"So it's a love spell?"

Cordelia jumped. "Oh! No. We don't use those. Ever."

"Really?"

"This is just a fun little party trick, moving around the energy that flows between people." She shook her head. "But never a love spell."

"Do they actually exist?"

Cordelia narrowed her eyes. "Is this for your exceedingly anal spreadsheet? Why are you asking?"

"Absolutely zero reason except curiosity, I promise." Reno's face rose in her mind, and just as quickly, she blanked it out.

"Love spells exist, yes. But they're not for Hollands. Trust me."

Did she want to dig deeper? Absolutely. But she wouldn't, not yet. Hopefully, she'd earn the right to hear about that at some point. "So we can push and pull a little for fun, though."

"Oh, yeah."

Fritz glanced at the band that was playing old-time and honky-tonk tunes from the makeshift stage under an enormous oak tree. The group had just swung into a slow waltz, and while Beatrice couldn't hear Fritz's words, their body language made it clear they were inviting Winnie to dance.

Please say yes. Wishing wasn't magic, was it? Beatrice couldn't stand the idea of watching Fritz's face fall.

Winnie nodded, and they joined the other dozen couples already out on the grass. Some did the correct steps, one-two-three, four-five-six. Other couples merely swayed. Fritz and Winnie did some kind of hybrid move, and the look of hope on Fritz's face was enough to make Beatrice sigh. "That's adorable."

"Oh, shit." Cordelia clutched her arm. "*Look.*"

Dad had Astrid by the hand, and with a practiced twirl, they entered the group of dancers. And they looked like they knew what they were doing. Not even the fact that Astrid was wearing a full-ass black cape seemed to get in their way.

Holy crap. When Beatrice and her father had arrived, Astrid had been out of the house, making a run for more ice. Then she'd lost track of him entirely in the swirl of partygoers and hadn't seen Astrid at all until right now. "Did you talk to him at all yet?"

"No," said Cordelia. "I keep dodging him every time he gets close. But I suppose I should talk to him at some point. I want to."

Funny. She didn't know Cordelia at all, but she knew when she was lying. "You don't have to. You owe him absolutely nothing."

"He's our father."

"I love Mitchell. I worry about his high blood pressure and his diabetes. I worry whether he's going to the doctor often enough and if he remembers to take his pills. I'm weirdly glad he's here, even though I'm furious with him. But he's a stranger who let you go, and who hid you from me for our whole lives. If you feel about him the way I do about Astrid, you're allowed to go as slow as you like. Even if that includes never getting to know him at all."

"But... I feel like I should at least say hello."

"You make every rule. Every single last one."

Cordelia pressed her hand. "Thank you."

Together, they watched the dancers. The tempo slowed as the band shifted into something more romantic. Some couples broke apart, laughing and thanking each other.

Fritz and Winnie kept dancing.

"You sure that was a Push-Me-Pull-You and not a love thingy?"

"I'm sure. Those only last a second or two. If there's a stirring in their loins, we didn't do it." Cordelia's gaze was glued on Mitchell and Astrid. "Look at them. I've never seen Mom dance when it didn't involve a moon ritual. She doesn't dance. Not like that."

Naya had loved to dance, but Mitchell had always claimed two left feet. At weddings and parties, Beatrice was always Naya's dance partner. "Well, Dad *doesn't* dance. Ever."

But together, their mother and father moved like a thawing river finding its course. If she hadn't known them, Beatrice would have been charmed by the sight of the two tall, white-haired people gliding through the crowd of other dancers, moving as if they'd danced together for decades, as if they'd never been parted. "That cape she's wearing is a whole mood. Drama." Something struck her. "Shit. Did we parent-trap them by accident?"

"Ew," said Cordelia.

"Triple ew. I'm not okay with this." Astrid might kill him. If not with a spell, then with her terrible attitude.

"Me, neither. I know he's your dad and you love him, but he's a liar."

Beatrice tilted her head. "Yeah, well, your dad's a liar, too, you know."

Cordelia sent her a crooked grin.

Suddenly, Astrid and Mitchell stopped dancing. Rather, Mitchell stopped, and Astrid whirled against him with a thump. Their words didn't carry far, but their rigid body language was clear. Beatrice knew when her dad was pissed, and Astrid was a pretty easy read, too, with the way her cheeks flamed red and her crimson lips thinned.

Cordelia moved a ficus branch to see more clearly. "Trouble in paradise, you think?"

Beatrice snorted.

Astrid swept through the dancers by herself, and Beatrice

would have felt sorry for her abandoned father if he hadn't looked so furious himself. A moment later, he stormed off in the opposite direction.

Cordelia turned to face Beatrice. "Can I admit I'm relieved?"

"Hoo, boy. Me, too."

Her sister flapped a hand in front of her face. "I don't want to think about them anymore. What about you? Talked to Grant yet?"

Beatrice had told Cordelia a few days before that she'd wanted to get the ball rolling on the divorce. "Not yet."

"Are you all right?"

She flexed her ankles. "Fine."

"It's okay." A tinge of hurt colored Cordelia's voice. "You don't have to tell me—"

"No, I actually mean it. I'm fine. I'm hurt and sad, yes. But at the center of it all, I think I might be relieved." It turned even truer as her words hit the night air. "I had no idea I wanted out, but apparently, I did. I must have, right? Otherwise... I should be more upset, I know. And I *am* angry at Grant, and at the woman I thought was my friend." She thought for a moment, testing the weight of her words. "But the anger is—oh, how do I explain this? It's the same kind of anger I feel at Dad. It's hot but not boiling. Does that make sense?"

Cordelia nodded slowly.

Scoville. Heat radiated from the tattoo hidden under her long sleeve, and in the dark, she could almost see Naya's smile. "Oh, my god, I just remembered. My stepmother Naya had a scale for this—I'd totally forgotten. The Scoville Anger Scale. You know, like the heat in peppers." It had been one of the many things her father and Beatrice had loved about Naya—that she quantified and listed everything, just like they did. Their household shopping lists alone could have brought peace to warring nations.

"How did it work?"

Leaning back against the wall, Beatrice said, "If I couldn't find my homework because I put it in the wrong bookbag, that was bell pepper mad. Jalapeño mad was when I was in high school and forgot to call her to tell her where I was. Cayenne was getting a D in physics in college because I hated the professor and didn't withdraw in time. Ghost pepper was the time she found out I drove home after a party, still buzzed."

"Was that the hottest it went?"

Beatrice grimaced. "No, there was always pepper spray. I don't even know what that would be for, but I bet Dad felt it a couple of times."

"So your husband cheating on you with your friend feels like..."

"I *think* it should be somewhere between ghost pepper and pepper spray, but it's actually a little lower than jalapeño. Maybe sriracha sauce?"

"You could eat it with a spoon, in other words."

"I'd rather not, but yeah. I could."

"Oh. Well, that's good, then. I know your feelings around it are going to be complex, and they might change, but..." Cordelia smiled. "I have to admit, I'm selfishly pleased when people I love are single at the same time I am. Makes going out on Friday nights way more fun."

People I love.

The band started playing a faster song, and Beatrice's head whirled like the fastest dancer.

Her sister loved her.

She wanted to say it back—she wanted to grab Cordelia and hug her tight and tell her the same thing. But she couldn't.

Instead, she said, "I don't want to die."

I don't want to lose you.

Cordelia clasped her hand. "I know."

"We're up to five miracles now."

Her sister didn't even ask what the miracle was. It didn't really matter anyway. "Fuck."

"You know that sealed page in the grimoire? Do you think it could help us?" Every time she opened the ancient book to study, her fingers played with the edges of the wax seal.

Shaking her head, Cordelia said, "The opposite. Don't do it. Remember that it's the Velamen power Xenia removed from her twins. It can't do anything but hurt us."

She felt seasick as a low swell of fear rolled through her. "You're the expert in dying. Anything I should know?"

"I..." Cordelia took a deep breath. "No matter what, I won't let you be alone."

And it turned out that was enough. For now. It was enough to sit there with her sister in the dark, holding hands.

Beatrice wasn't alone.

She wouldn't be alone, no matter what happened.

That was plenty.

A minute or an eternity later, Cordelia stood, brushing off her skirt. "I wish I could hide in here all night with you."

"I wish you could, too." Her throat felt thick. "Wait, I have a few more things to tell you about."

"Oooh, secrets?"

"Maybe. About Minna, and what she wants from her guides. I'm a little worried..."

Cordelia glanced at her phone. "Oh, them. They want the best for her. You think it can wait? I didn't know it was so late already. The ceremony's about to start."

Minna was smart, and she trusted Beatrice. "Sure. It can wait."

"Hey, have you seen Reno?"

Confused by the subject change, Beatrice stammered, "Not in a while."

"Huh." Cordelia's voice was light. "Maybe you should look for her. She likes to hide the same way you do. You have a lot in common."

CHAPTER FORTY

You can think of emotion like a fire. Grief is the center of the flame, as painful as it gets. It's destructive and terrible and absolutely necessary for life. I wish I could tell you how to go through it, but each person's fire burns differently.

—*Evie Oxby, to the Duke and Duchess of Sussex, Harry and Meghan*

The bonfire roared, the high red flames gnawing on the inky black sky. Children awake long past their bedtimes raced around it, and small groups of laughing people shifted as the smoke changed directions and chased them.

Honestly, none of it felt very safe.

But it wasn't Beatrice's job to police any of this. Okay, true, she *had* allowed herself to prowl the edge of the house until she found the hose, so that if anything caught fire, she'd be able to race for it. That was it, though. She wasn't responsible for anything else here.

That included her father. He'd apparently made a couple of

friends, other older men who liked fly-fishing as much as he did. She heard them chattering on about dead drifts and hollow hairs and hackles—were they working spells, too? He gave her a wave as she passed by.

She'd forced herself to come out of hiding, but she wasn't sure how much longer she'd be good for. It was already after eleven, and the party seemed in no danger of sputtering out like she was.

Minna, freed of the drinks table duty, raced past wearing a short black dress and blue sneakers, an identically dressed Olive on her heels. "Aunt Bea! Someone brought red velvet cupcakes! Don't forget to meet me at midnight! Ceremony of the Dead's about to start!" In a blur, before any of that made complete sense, they were gone.

Shit, meeting Minna in the graveyard. She'd almost forgotten. She should never have agreed to that. She'd grab Cordelia as soon as this ceremony—whatever it was—was finished, and no matter what, she'd tell her about Minna's obsession with hearing from her father. Then they would both meet her in the graveyard. Minna would be pissed, but she'd have to get over it.

The sound of a gong being struck rang through the night, the noise shivering through the air and raising goose bumps on Beatrice's arms. Everyone turned, moving in their small, shifting groups toward the bonfire. Beatrice followed.

At the front, Cordelia climbed up onto a picnic table that had been set perhaps a little too close to the bonfire. Minna scrambled up to stand next to her mother.

Reno moved through the crowd. She didn't get up on the table, but she sat on the bench at their feet, keeping her gaze directed up at the stars that blinked above the sparks.

When the guests finished forming a semicircle around the fire, and when all eyes were focused on Cordelia, Minna, and Reno, the three of them raised their hands into the air.

Then firmly and at the exact same time, they clapped once.

As one, the crowd clapped once in response.

Beatrice's hands went together too late, softly. Silently. Not knowing it was coming, she'd missed the moment.

"Greetings! Welcome to our Celebration of the Dead!" Cordelia put her arm around Minna. "Tonight marks fifteen years since I lost my husband and Minna lost her father. Tonight it's four years since Reno's wife, Scarlett, died. This night has come to mean a lot to a lot of people, not just us, and I'm grateful you're all here."

She made a shooing motion with her hands. "Now, y'all know what to do, and if you don't, someone will tell you. Goddess bless, let's burn some shit!"

The crowd murmured and began moving.

Someone touched Beatrice's elbow. "You burning something?" asked a man quite young to be so bald.

"I don't know."

"You can write a note if you want." He pointed at a table she hadn't noticed. "To your people."

"Oh. Thanks."

Dad was already there, bent over a scrap of paper illuminated by a gas lantern.

"Hey."

"Hey." He folded the page.

"I want to, too."

He passed her a piece of paper.

"Thanks."

But when she picked up the pen, her mind went blank. What to write to Naya? Carefully, she pressed her fingers against the fabric of her long-sleeved blouse, feeling below it the plastic wrap covering the tattoo at her wrist. How could she possibly respond to the letter she'd received the day before?

So she just wrote, *Thank you for teaching me about anger.* Naya had always said that no matter how much it hurt, the pain from a pepper, or from anger, would eventually stop. Faster with a glass of milk or a beer. Chocolate milk worked, too. *Thank you for teaching us about love.*

She turned back toward the crowd.

A large woman with dark, glossy hair that fell to her waist was herding people into rows. "Three years? That line. Seven? Over there. See? Between six and five. Clever, right?" She beamed at Beatrice. "Ah, Cordelia's twin. How gorgeous you are. What time zone, love?"

"I'm sorry, I don't understand the question."

"That's right, you're new to this. How much time since your loved one died?"

"Oh. Two years?" Why had it come out of her mouth like a question?

The woman touched her shoulder. "I'm very sorry for your loss. Now go stand with Horace over there, in time zone two."

The line for the forty-one-year time zone was the oldest one, and it went first. There were only two people in it, a man and a woman. They held hands at the edge of the fire. Cordelia, still standing on top of the picnic table, raised her arms.

On this cue, the man and the woman each threw a note into the flames. The fire was so hot, the paper flared for only a split second.

Then, conducted by Cordelia, the entire crowd clapped exactly forty-one times.

Who were the couple remembering? By the way they never let go of each other's hands, Beatrice guessed it might be a child. A lump rose in her throat, one that only got bigger as she looked around and saw her father behind her, in the same two-year line, watching the couple at the edge of the fire.

Then, line by line, people walked forward. They threw their items into the fire. Most of them tossed in notes, but Beatrice saw a teddy bear, and a T-shirt, and three or four bunches of dried roses. One woman threw in a whole chocolate cake. After the items were thrown and Cordelia raised her arms, the crowd clapped the appropriate number of times, and now that Beatrice knew what was happening, she clapped so hard her palms stung.

When Cordelia and Minna walked forward, arms around each other, something about the way the crowd clapped those fifteen times made Beatrice want to howl into the night sky. Instead, she bit the inside of her mouth and tasted salt at the back of her throat.

Reno didn't toss anything into the fire when she went forward with the four-year time zone. She just bowed her head and folded her hands over her chest, keeping them there as the claps resounded through the garden.

And when the two-year line moved forward, Beatrice waited for her father to join her. She didn't want to hold his hand, or have his arm around her shoulders—and thank goodness, he seemed to know that intuitively—but she did want to be near him. Together, they leaned forward, and as their notes caught fire, the paper with their words flew upward, twisting and dancing together, before flaming out, the blackened ashes falling back down into the pyre. She watched their flight so closely, she realized she hadn't even heard the claps, and her chest ached as if her heart would break in half.

Then, the one-year line moved forward. It was too long a line, at least twenty or twenty-five people. *Car accident*, Beatrice heard someone say. *Dougie would have been a senior. So loved.* Three teenage girls held hands and put into the fire a poster with a large red 37 painted on it. One was crying so hard, she couldn't have been able to see. But what threatened to break Beatrice's heart in half was the expression of the woman who was obviously the mother. Her face was somehow both blank and, at the same time, totally wrecked. A man on either side of her held her up, and after she threw in a red-and-black flannel shirt, she stepped back, her head low, her knees buckling.

There was a long pause, all eyes on the woman.

Finally, she straightened, raising her head. Her shoulders rose as she drew in a shuddering breath. Cordelia, as if she'd been waiting for her to breathe, raised her arms.

The crowd gave one single thunderclap.

Just one heartbreaking crack of loss.

Beatrice thought she might die from all of it. Fuck the two other miracles—how did any heart keep beating after witnessing love like this?

Then the moment—all the moments—were over, and people turned to each other, some hugging, some laughing gently. A man wiped the tears off the cheeks of his two young boys, and an older man threw his arms around a woman who had rushed at him with an overjoyed shriek.

Her father waved and closed the gap between them. "That was good, huh?"

"Yeah. Really good." Her voice was thick.

"She forgives you, you know."

Beatrice's jaw dropped. "What?"

"Naya didn't need you to write an apology letter."

But—she hadn't.

"I know she forgives you. You were doing your best, trying to save her. She knew that. It was okay that you weren't there for her at the end. I hope you truly, deeply know that, Button." He gazed over her shoulder. "Ah, there's Astrid. And I've thought of a few perfect things to say to continue our fight from earlier. I'll see you in a bit?"

"Dad, no! I *was* there for her."

But he was already gone, leaving Beatrice gut-punched and alone in the middle of a crowd that was somehow celebrating the loss of their loves.

Her head swam with confusion.

She'd been there for Naya.

She *had*.

Dad was simply wrong. Maybe she hadn't supported Naya the same way he had, but she'd been there the only way she knew how to be, with spreadsheets and research and action points.

A screaming kid ran past, wearing a ghoulish skeleton mask that was dripping with blood.

How, exactly, did people survive loss and death and then throw a party for it?

How could Cordelia and Minna and Reno bear this every year? Or did having this celebration every year on their terrible day make it easier? She spotted Minna sticking marshmallows onto a skewer with Olive. Next to her, Cordelia shot the wide-shouldered man a look that Beatrice resolved to quiz her about later. Astrid stood beside them, handing out chocolate bars for the s'more making. Her father was already sidling in their direction, and Beatrice tried very hard not to care.

Reno was nowhere to be seen.

And the space where Reno should have been was the thing that suddenly made Beatrice feel like she really might cry, if she didn't get away from this cloud of celebratory grief.

CHAPTER FORTY-ONE

Spirit is just waiting for you to ask. Didn't you know that?

—*Evie Oxby,* Come at Me, Boo

Out. Beatrice needed *out*. Her feet carried her through the crowd, and her face cooperated with her flight, smiling politely at people who smiled at her, and then, yes, thank god, she was on the edge of the party, and then she was in the garden that led to the hideout.

Beatrice pushed open the low gate, passing under the jasmine-laden arbor. The twinkle lights twined through the white flowers and along both sides of the fence. Overhead, the blackness of the sky was studded with pinpoints of light, and even though she couldn't see the bonfire from here, the smell still clung to the night air.

The door of the shed stood open, and there Reno was. Of course. She stood at the workbench next to her wooden kayak. Her back was turned, and she spoke without turning around.

"Was wondering when you'd come find me."

Oh, god, was Reno hoping for someone else? Would she be disappointed? "It's Beatrice."

Reno turned slowly, setting a piece of sandpaper down on top of the workbench. At her feet curled a pile of wood shavings. She was wearing a thickly knit black beanie and her red flannel shirt, making her look like a sailor home from the sea. "I know exactly who you are."

The air in Beatrice's lungs got caught somewhere near her heart. "Oh."

Half a crooked smile laced across Reno's face, but she didn't offer anything else.

"What are you making?"

"A gift. Want to see?"

Beatrice nodded, moving closer.

Whatever it was, it was small and thin, maybe four inches wide and two inches long. There was a hole drilled in the middle, and on both sides, it curved out like an elongated eye. The wood was dark red and already looked soft as silk.

"It's beautiful," said Beatrice.

"Do you know what it is?"

"Not a clue. Oh, wait! Is it a pasta measurer? You put the pasta through the hole and that tells you…um, that you need more pasta?"

Reno shook her head. "Nope."

"I have no idea."

"Book holder."

Beatrice remained puzzled. "How?"

"One-handed." She reached for a book on the closest bookshelf. It was a hardcover, something about building wooden boats. Reno held it out to her. "Open it."

She did.

Then Reno reached for her hand, slipping the piece of

wood onto her thumb. Beatrice wasn't sure what felt better, the smoothness of the freshly sanded wood, or the warm touch of Reno's fingers against hers.

The point of the wood fit exactly into the seam of the book, and the flanges, curved as they were, rested against the pages. With her other four fingers under the book, it was easy to hold the book open one-handed.

"You like books," said Reno simply.

"You...you made this for me?"

A nod. "Did I get it right?"

Beatrice's voice came out breathier than she'd expected. "I love it."

With relief in her voice, Reno said, "Good."

"Thank you."

"You're welcome." Reno tugged off the hat, rubbed both shaved sides of her head, and then shoved a hand through the dark curls on top.

Could she be nervous, too?

Reno opened the door of the small fridge. "Ginger ale?"

"Yes." Not that she was thirsty—she'd already had a beer and three lemonades. She just wanted to agree with Reno. About anything. She'd have accepted a glass of warm milk spiked with bathtub gin; she didn't care.

"Outside?"

Outside, inside, upside down, it didn't matter. The day was catching up to Beatrice and nothing had made sense for a while, but this? Right here? This made sense.

In the garden, they sat on a wrought iron bench.

On the other side of the gate, a group of children holding sparklers ran over the grass without glancing in their direction. The roses and hollyhocks were high enough that Beatrice felt hidden again, as she had with Cordelia.

Only this was different.

Reno's thigh was so close to hers that she could feel the heat of it.

This was *really* different.

But she was probably imagining all this—Grant had always said she was too prone to flights of fancy.

She had to say something. She had to break the silence. "It's dark out here." It wasn't really, not with the twinkle lights hanging above. But it was something to say.

"Are you scared?"

"No." That wasn't quite true. "Maybe." Out there, past the garden where the cemetery began, that was the darkness that chilled her. A low film of dread filled her as she thought about meeting Minna there at midnight. But Cordelia would be with her by then, and maybe they could recruit Reno to come, too. She needed to keep her eye on the time, make sure she got back to the party to tell Cordelia first about Minna wanting to contact her father, then—

"Hey." Reno spoke gently. "I'll know if something really bad is coming. I've had a couple of waves of something unpleasant roll through tonight, but they pass by quick. I don't think we're in danger."

Beatrice frowned. "It's not that." But her words came out rough, and she could almost feel Reno retract into herself.

Looking straight ahead, Reno said, "I get it. I wouldn't trust me, either."

Oh, god. How could she fix this? Somehow, she knew she'd trust Reno with her life. "No, I swear. It's not about you. I'm just—just a little overwhelmed with everything." But it wasn't enough. She wanted to give Reno something real, something tangible, as sturdy as the carved bookholder. Something to show that she trusted her. "Minna gave me my first tattoo today. Cordelia doesn't know yet, and I guess I'm a little worried."

It worked—Reno's shoulders relaxed. "Ah. Wondered why it looked like she'd been cleaning her tools. Show me?"

Beatrice rolled back the sleeve of her blouse. "Am I allowed to pull back the plastic?"

"If you're careful, yeah."

Her heart beating faster, Beatrice said, "I'm right-handed, so I'm not sure I'll do a great job with my left hand. Would you?"

Reno's eyes caught hers, smoky with heat. As she unwrapped the plastic, her fingers were so gentle that Beatrice's stomach flipped. The tattoos that covered Reno's arms seemed to move in the dimness, swirling on top of her skin, blue lines blending and shifting. Beatrice's eyes traced each one.

Then her own tattoo was revealed.

"It's good." Reno tilted Beatrice's wrist slightly toward the strings of white lights above them. "It's really good."

"For my stepmother."

"You loved her."

"She was the mother I knew best."

"How does the ink feel?"

Through the string of lights, Beatrice saw a star wink down. "Like I was missing it before. Like I didn't know I needed it until the ink was inside my skin."

Reno carefully rewrapped the plastic, her touch still incredibly gentle.

Then she said, "I want to show you one of mine." She reached for the top button on her flannel, undoing it and the one below it. And the one below that.

Electricity sliced through Beatrice's blood as Reno parted her shirt.

"This is my most important tattoo."

There, just above the edge of Reno's black cotton tank, was

the letter *S*, done in a curling, lovely script. It was bright red, almost the color of blood against Reno's deep olive skin.

Beatrice didn't have to be told that this was the tattoo that held Scarlett's ashes in its ink. "Scarlett…oh, my god." Should she say it? "It's a scarlet letter."

A rich laugh was her reward. "Not everyone gets it that fast. Scarlett always joked that I should get one, so I did."

Bravely, Beatrice looked closer. To the left of the *S* were two bright little yellow things with wings. Against Reno's skin, they glowed. "Are those fireflies?"

"She grew up in Tennessee. Loved her fireflies. She hated the fact that we didn't have them here."

"I don't think I've ever seen one in real life."

"Yeah, I'd never seen one before we went to visit her family. They were pretty magical. To me, she was the brightest firefly of all."

Beatrice's hand rose, as if she were going to touch that brilliant letter inked over Reno's heart. *Shit.* Horrified, she raised her hand higher and tucked a nonexistent strand of hair behind her ear. Her pulse throbbed in her ears and her face flared red-hot. What the hell was she thinking? Surely it was wrong to be so attracted to a woman who was literally telling her about the love of her life?

But then Reno caught her hand and drew it to her skin, pressing it gently against the *S*'s red ink.

Under Beatrice's fingers, Reno's heartbeat raced as fast as her own.

Beatrice wasn't alone in this feeling. Was she?

Summoning all the courage she had, Beatrice reached for Reno's other hand. She turned Reno's palm to rest flat against her own chest. She covered Reno's hand with her own.

Reno's gaze went smokier. "These fucking damaged hearts, huh?"

"What's the prognosis, you think?"

"Inevitably fatal, I reckon."

She was right, of course. "No cure."

Slowly, ever so slowly, Reno released Beatrice's hand. The air that hit her palm felt like ice after the touch of Reno's skin. Matching her, Beatrice let Reno's hand drop from her skin.

Reno said, "There never was going to be a cure, though, right? Immortality's hard to come by these days."

"What about magic?" She knew it was silly to ask, but she asked anyway.

Inclining her head, Reno said, "Magic's always got a surprise up its sleeve, yeah. But... that thing I felt crash through me, when the darkness blasted through here with you and Minna." Beatrice almost felt the shudder she saw ripple through Reno's frame. "It was big. Bigger than I could even explain to Cordelia. It scared me."

"You think it was the Velamens?"

She shrugged. "I guess maybe? They're the ones who want to take the Holland power, so I'd think so."

"Astrid bound the power, though. The thread and the blood. *We* bound it. Right?"

Reno shook her head and looked out into the darkness on the other side of the gate. "I don't think it's going to stop."

Fear clacked down the knobs of Beatrice's spine. "Then we'll do more magic. Astrid will figure something else out."

Reno smiled. "Who *are* you?"

"No one is more surprised than I am, believe me."

"Damn, woman." The word was a velvet endearment. "Who else are you?"

"Apparently someone who's stronger with her family around her." Beatrice only realized it was true as she said the words.

"So where did your strength come from before?"

That was easy. "From me. Myself. My understanding. From learning. Studying."

"You like knowing everything."

"Merely saying yes would be one of the greatest understatements of my life. But yes. I do."

"Huh." Reno kicked out her boots in front of her, crossing her legs at the ankles. "I don't think I know anything at all."

She seemed so accepting about it, which made no sense. "So…how can you stop something if you don't know the truth about it? If you don't know how it works and why?" Beatrice wasn't sure if she meant the Velamens or death itself.

"I'm not sure we can stop anything. Not sure we have that kind of control."

Heat rose in Beatrice's lungs. "But you can *try*. You can *learn*."

Reno put her arms over the back of the iron bench. "What do you want to learn?"

If Beatrice leaned back just a touch, she'd feel Reno's arm behind her. "Everything. Especially now."

"Like?"

"If…" Oh, god, was she ready to sound *this* stupid to Reno? Maybe. "If there's…more…out there." She stopped herself and recalibrated. "Okay. Magic is real."

Reno smiled.

She went on, "I never knew that before. Nothing I'd ever learned had been able to prove it to me. But now—if the dead can still talk to us, then that means they don't just disappear. Doesn't that mean that maybe there's a reason for things, and that there's an order to the universe that I never understood before? I mean, I know this is super existential, but…"

"It's called an existential crisis for a reason."

Fair enough. "What do you think happens when we die?"

The look on Reno's face was so kind, it made Beatrice want to cry. "I have no idea what happens, but I know we keep existing, and that it's good."

"So, heaven?"

She shrugged. "I feel happiness move through me sometimes, but it's not angels-singing-in-a-choir type of shit. Honestly, when that kind of joy rolls through, it feels like it's on its way somewhere, stoked to be doing something awesome. The way you feel when you're on your way to the beach maybe. It doesn't last long, because I think the ones passing through are busy. If that makes sense."

It did not, not even a little. "What about the other emotions you get? The bad ones?"

Reno touched the top of the *S* on her chest. "Those…are heavier. They feel stuck. The lighter ones move through and are gone. I don't know where they go. The darker ones are muckier. Kind of the difference between walking through a stream and walking through a mud puddle. The stream is clear and moving fast, and you walk out clean. The mud, though. It sits. And sticks."

Beatrice rocked forward impatiently. "So does that mean there's someone in charge out there? Because I've never believed in God, some dude with a white beard who's pulling the strings and making us dance. I refuse to believe in that now, unless someone can *prove* him to me, which I hope they don't. But—oh, fuck. Should I believe in him? I don't know what I'm saying." She waved her hands in the air ineffectively before letting them fall back into her lap. "What do you think? You think there's someone driving the bus?" This time, she did lean back, Reno's forearm solid and warm against her upper back.

"Sal."

"Excuse me?"

"Sal's the truck stop waitress of the universe. Everyone thinks she just works in the joint, but she owns the place, never makes a big deal about it." Reno's voice was a low vibration in Beatrice's ears. "You ever been served by one of those waitresses who can do it all, keep it all in her head? Sal can manage everything all at once—she's got your refill of coffee, and she's about to bring you the piece of pie you didn't even know you needed. At the same time, she's wrangling a civil war over on table fifteen and handling a star going supernova in the corner. You ever hear a song come on the radio at exactly the right time? Like it was just for you?"

"Yeah."

"And then you think, well, that's a stupid thought, because this song really *is* playing for thousands of people, so it's not about you, but it *is* about you, and the next line in the song means something else to four hundred other people, and at the same time, she's brewing another pot of decaf 'cause the old one got stale."

"I love that."

A quick nod. "Yeah. And it's wrong."

Beatrice blinked.

"If I knew what the power spinning the universe was, if I understood it, it wouldn't be a very big power, would it? For my tiny brain to be able to get it? So I just choose to call it Sal. Short for the Spirit of All Life. And that's good enough for me. Honestly, I don't care what it is, as long as I don't have to rely on myself to be the power making things happen."

But I do make things happen.

Somehow, Reno must have seen, or felt, the thought crash through Beatrice's mind. And she laughed, which was kind of her. "That's right, you've got magic now. And those miracles. Had any more of those lately?"

She didn't pull out the letter from Naya, but she could almost feel it in the back pocket of her jeans. "I got a letter from my stepmother yesterday. It was in a bottle that washed to shore, a bottle I tripped over. She wrote it when I was sixteen."

"Holy *shit.*" Reno's face got softer. Sadder.

"Yeah."

"So you get letters from the dead in a couple of different ways." Reno sat up straighter, bringing her arms off the back of the bench and rubbing her hands together as if she was suddenly cold.

What Beatrice *wanted* to do: kiss Reno. She wanted to take away that look of pain, lock it far away.

Iron ore at the core, feel the pull you can't ignore. It wasn't a love spell, right? It would just be a little nudge? She could try it—

But no.

It was obvious Reno wanted something different. Grieving a wife—that was something Beatrice couldn't and wouldn't get in the way of. She didn't have that right.

But still, something stirred inside her, a recklessness she didn't understand. She didn't even know what she was going to say until the words were leaving her mouth: "Do you want me to try contacting her?" She didn't have to say who.

CHAPTER FORTY-TWO

> The dead loved just as hard as we do now. Think about that, how many people have been loved over the millennia. Isn't that the most gorgeous thing you ever heard?
>
> —*Evie Oxby, in conversation with Hilton Als*

How quickly Reno's expression changed, hope skating across her eyes, her mouth—and then, just as rapidly, the hope was gone. "Nah. She's not the type."

"What do you mean?"

A shrug. "Dunno. Just think she'd make it to wherever it is they go, and get pretty busy doing things. She'd be loved. Popular. Probably on three committees and managing a minor galaxy or something. I don't want to bug her. Besides, she's a close one, and I get it. We don't fuck around with them."

Reno rubbed her sternum, and another cloud passed over her face.

"What is it?"

She closed her eyes. "That darkness keeps rolling through,

like some kind of ominous lightning storm. It was here for a second, and now it's gone. I didn't think it was anything but…I don't like it." She rested her hands flat on her knees and stared forward into the darkness.

"That scares me."

Reno nodded. "Me, too."

Mustering all the courage she could, her breath high and tight at the top of her lungs, Beatrice placed her hand on top of Reno's.

She felt it then—the fear receded, followed by a quick piercing joy and a wave of heat. Could Reno feel it, too?

"Welp." Reno patted Beatrice's hand in a friendly way, so kind that it almost felt paternal. "I think I'll go check on Cordelia and see if she needs help with anything."

Ah.

So the answer was a very clear no. Reno felt nothing between them.

Beatrice swallowed the bitter taste of disappointment, and worse than that, shame. How ridiculous she was. What a fool.

She stood as Reno ambled to the gate with her hands stuck in her pockets. She'd wait until Reno was safely up the path and then she'd go find her father—it was getting late, and she would need to get him back to his hotel. Quiz him about his meds.

But Reno had stopped moving, her back rigid. Through the dimness, Beatrice could see her hand shake on the garden gate's latch.

Get over yourself. Reno was obviously having another wave of ghost feelings swamp her—the least Beatrice could do was swallow her hurt feelings and check on her.

She hurried down the path. "Can I help?"

Reno's jaw stayed clenched, and she looked straight ahead, out to the edge of the cemetery.

"Is the feeling back?"

Reno shook her head.

And something about the way Reno was holding herself made Beatrice ask, "Is it Scarlett? Do you... feel her?"

Reno gripped the top of the gate and gave a low rumble in the back of her throat.

"How can I help? What's going on? Should I go find Cordelia?"

Instead of answering, Reno held out her hand.

There, resting on her ring finger, was a firefly. It fluttered, glowing unsteadily.

Beatrice gasped, wordless for a moment. Then, "But—you said they don't exist here."

"They don't," Reno whispered.

It glimmered there for a few more seconds, blinking its tiny light off and on in some kind of code Beatrice didn't understand. Then it rose. It flew from Reno's finger and landed on Beatrice's ring finger.

It was so lightweight, she couldn't feel it. Was it even real? Could it be a shared hallucination?

Beatrice squeezed her eyes shut. When she opened them again, the firefly was still there.

Then it flew up into the night sky, blinked twice, and disappeared.

"Reno—"

Reno spun toward her. Putting both hands behind Beatrice's neck, Reno looked into her eyes for one long, stunned moment.

Then she kissed Beatrice.

Hard.

Long.

Devotedly.

The kiss—how had Beatrice lived her life this long without

being kissed like this before? It was rain falling on a hot day. It was a lightning strike in a dry forest. It was a new country, one Beatrice didn't know existed and had never wanted to travel to, but now, it was the only nation she wanted stamped on every single page in her passport.

The kiss burned with sex and heat, but also, Reno's lips were so soft, Beatrice wanted to write an ode to them. They, by themselves, deserved to be worshipped. Suddenly, she felt more religious than she ever had in her life. At the same time, impure thoughts made her want to sacrifice herself to a creature with devil's horns.

She pressed closer to Reno, feeling the shape of her breasts beneath her shirt, the hardness of her hipbones against her own softer hips. As their mouths tangled, the way Reno's fingers moved through her hair made Beatrice's breath catch, and the more she panted against Reno's lips, the tighter Reno pulled her against her body.

Then Reno gasped, and it sounded different—it wasn't a gasp from something Beatrice had done to her.

Beatrice opened her eyes.

Reno was gazing at the garden around them—the roses, the violets, the hollyhocks, and the dahlias—no matter their normal color, they'd all gone white. And they *glowed*, each bloom seemingly lit from inside. Their luminescence put the twinkle lights hanging above them to shame. Beatrice could almost see them breathing, exhaling the opalescent light that swirled up and around them. No, she wasn't imagining it—they *were* getting taller, reaching for the sky, growing inside the glow. The arbor of jasmine that Reno had made for her Scarlett was the brightest of all, each tiny white flower expanding to shine with the light of the stars above.

Reno said, "You."

It wasn't just the flowers. Reno's skin radiated a pale blue gleam that made no sense at all against her normally warm skin tone but turned out to be the most beautiful thing Beatrice had ever seen. She followed Reno's gaze to her own body, and she, too, was emanating the same blue-silver shimmer.

And wherever Reno's wondering fingers touched, a soft trail of pearlized light was left behind, as if her fingers were sweeping through a sea's bioluminescence rather than touching the skin of Beatrice's arm.

Beatrice leaned forward to kiss Reno, softly. A test.

The brightness on Reno's lips intensified, and in almost exact measure, so did the glow of the flowers. It was as if the moon had dived out of the sky and moved under their skin, into the petals, into the very air around them, the air that trembled with something bigger than just desire. Bigger than just need.

"What is this?" Reno raised her hands, palms up, as if testing the air for rain. The jasmine arbor above her head seemed to sigh with pleasure. "Is this..."

"A miracle," breathed Beatrice. "I think so."

"Shit." Reno pulled her against her body. "What number?"

"Six." Beatrice ran her finger over Reno's bottom lip, and the white-blue glow increased. The color should have been cold, but it wasn't. It was *life*.

"It can't be."

She knew. She agreed. "But... it might be."

How can I be falling in love?

Reno said, "I think I've been waiting for you."

"Me, too." Beatrice closed the gap between their lips.

The light filled each tiny pocket of air between and around them. For a few moments, as they kissed, the light *was* them. They were the roses that gleamed, they were the shimmer, the brightness, the hope.

Keeping her hand on the side of Reno's face, Beatrice whispered, "But it doesn't make sense."

Reno's gaze was equal parts hope and fear. "Hasn't anyone ever told you that things don't have to make sense?"

Of course things have to make sense.

She opened her mouth to speak, but before she could, a sharp cry rose in the dark—a thin wail of pain that went on much too long.

Minna.

CHAPTER FORTY-THREE

Don't forget that you're part of the Universe. You have a responsibility to the magic that already runs in your veins.

—*Evie Oxby,* I Ain't Afraid of No Ghosts

The glow snapped off as if a light switch had been flipped.

"What time is it?" Beatrice tugged at the gate in the dark, desperate to open it. "I told Minna I'd meet her at midnight in the cemetery. I was going to tell Cordelia—"

"I should have felt it. Why didn't I feel it?" Reno glanced at her watch as she ripped at the latch, flipping it up. "Twelve ten."

"Shit. *Shit.*" Beatrice broke into a run, not caring that the moon wasn't bright enough to light the ground under her feet—if she fell, she'd just get up and run faster to make up for it.

Reno matched her pace step for step. "We need Cordelia."

"She's coming." She felt it somehow. Cordelia would be right behind them. "Can you lead me to Minna's father's grave?"

"Of course."

Cordelia was already running through the dark toward them, her face serious and pale.

Reno turned on her phone's flashlight. "Stay close to me."

With so many trees, even with the light, the cemetery seemed pitch dark to Beatrice, but Reno obviously knew exactly where they were going. "Step. Jump. Hole right there. Watch that root."

Cordelia panted next to her. "*Hurry.*"

What were they hurrying to? All Beatrice knew was that it was bad.

Very bad.

They raced through a line of bigger mausoleums and took a left on a path lined by white shells.

Then there she was.

Minna squatted in the dirt of a grave, her fingers digging deeply into what looked like fresh soil. It couldn't be her father's grave, could it? This must be a place where someone had been newly buried, the ground still torn and naked at Minna's bare feet.

"Honey." Cordelia lurched toward Minna but halted at the edge of the grave. "Stop."

Minna didn't even look up. Her entire right hand was buried in the dirt. She was sweating as she scraped through it, and her clothes were covered in the same soil.

The headstone read, *Taurus Diaz, Beloved Father and Husband.*

But the fresh dirt...

Then Beatrice saw them: the clumps of grass that had been ripped out by the handful. The whole grave had been denuded, presumably by Minna's bare hands.

And now she was drawing in the dirt, using her fingers as a stylus. Blood showed at her knuckles, but she kept scraping:

"Minna, can you stop for a minute?" Beatrice reached a hand toward her.

Cordelia, though, grabbed her arm. "*Don't.* Don't touch her."

Reno swayed on her other side, rubbing her sternum, her face a grimace.

From out of the woods strode Astrid, her giant black cape billowing behind her. "What is the *meaning* of this? Minna, cease this nonsense at once!"

But Minna didn't look up. She still hadn't engaged with them or even glanced once in their direction. Beatrice wasn't sure she even knew they were there.

"Is it him?" Astrid stopped at the edge next to Cordelia.

Wordlessly, Cordelia nodded.

Nausea roiled in Beatrice's stomach. There was something going on that she didn't—couldn't—understand. But she was starting to figure out what Minna was doing in the dirt.

She was drawing a sigil, dragging it deeply through the earth above her father's body. A long vertical line was slashed through by a horizontal one—obviously the *T* of Taurus's name. Now she was working on adding something to it, a rounder shape, but the dirt was packed hard, even after she'd ripped the grass out of the plot. Sweat stood out on her forehead, and she grunted with the effort.

Under her breath, Astrid began whispering words, casting sibilance into the cold night air.

Cordelia said, "Minna. You have to listen to me."

"*No.*"

"Minna—"

"He *talked* to me. I *heard* him." The girl's head whipped up, her eyes glinting in the moonlight. Her fingers stopped dragging in the dirt, blood blooming along her knuckles and at her fingernails.

"Honey, he's not who you think he is."

"I just need him to tell me the rest of the sigil. Mama, I'm so close. I had a little of it, and I used Aunt Bea's spell to get this next part of it from him, but then he left—because *you* came."

"I have to tell you something—"

Minna shrieked, "*STOP IT.* I just need to do the spell one more time to get the rest of the sigil. I know that's all I need." Tears filled her eyes. "Please go. Please let me finish this. He won't come to me if you're here, I know he won't."

Astrid's whisper increased in volume, becoming a mutter. Reno was bent in half, her breath coming in harsh gasps.

But Cordelia's voice stayed calm. "He'll hurt you, sugar. He—"

A silent explosion—that's all Beatrice could think that it was—ripped through the air in a *whoomp*, a clap of noiseless pressure.

A voice that was more boom than actual sound filled the space around them. "*MINNA, RUN.*"

Minna leaped to standing, gave one terrified look at her mother, and bolted, deerlike, leaping over grassy hummocks and headstones.

Beatrice was frozen.

Completely.

She tried to run, but some force locked her legs in place. She tried to shout but the yell struck in her throat. She couldn't even blink, couldn't control her eyelids. What the *hell* was going on? Her flesh was solid and unmoving, and no matter how hard she tried, she couldn't move a muscle.

Her heart crashed inside her chest, so she obviously wasn't dead, but she couldn't even move her gaze—it remained stuck in the direction of Minna's running form. Minna got smaller and smaller, then she darted left and was lost in the dark. In her peripheral vision, Beatrice could see Cordelia's hand still raised, unmoving, reaching toward her now-gone daughter. She was frozen, too.

The cemetery was soundless. The trees had stopped rustling in the wind, and Astrid's mutterings had fallen to silence. Reno's gasping breaths had ceased.

Fear rose through Beatrice's body in a great red tide, cresting and breaking, sucking out, and rushing back in, as her body remained entirely fixed in place.

Help.

She couldn't even whisper it.

CHAPTER FORTY-FOUR

I'd love to tell you that you can't make a mistake when it comes to practicing your craft. But you can. Be careful. I'd hate to lose any of you.

—*Evie Oxby, Bluesky*

The clap of pressure resounded again, a cold, hard punch to the gut.

Beatrice's legs collapsed under her as she fell to the ground.

Reno, too, had dropped, but Astrid and Cordelia remained upright, swaying and gasping.

Beatrice sucked in a huge breath and hauled herself back up to standing. "What *was* that?"

"That was Taurus." Astrid's voice was acid.

"We have to go after her!"

Reno clambered up on her knees. "That kid runs twice as fast as any of us. She's gone."

"Oh, Cordelia—" Beatrice broke off at the look on her twin's face.

Cordelia's eyes flamed. "What did my daughter mean, the spell *you* gave her?"

Confusion twisted in her chest. "I didn't!"

"She said you gave her something."

"No! It wasn't a spell. I only remembered what I imagine when I do the auto-writing. I told her because she was so frantic to hear from her dad again."

The last word dropped into the space between them with the force of a ten-ton calving iceberg plunging into a frozen sea.

"Again," said Cordelia.

"I was going to tell you."

"She's a *child*. Who needs protecting."

Beatrice raised her hands. "Wait, why? Why is it so bad for her to talk her own father? I know he's a close one, but I get it, about wanting to know your parent. He's her father. Surely that counts for something. What do you mean that he'll hurt her?"

"This is the worst thing you could have possibly done."

"How would I know that, if you keep refusing to tell me anything? What's going *on*?"

"When she comes back—" Cordelia shot a look at their mother. "Oh, god, Mom, she'll come back, right? She has to come back."

Astrid rubbed her eyes and didn't respond.

Touching her chest, Reno said, "It's gone now."

Astrid nodded. "Okay. Okay, then. We'll go home, we'll reset the wards on the house, and we'll do a recall spell." She jerked her chin in Beatrice's direction. "Unfortunately, it'll be stronger if she helps. We need the twinship energy."

"Of course I'll help!"

"Absolutely not." Cordelia's eyes clouded. "Mom, what if Minna gets too close to him?"

Reno said, "She's never run away before. She'll be back by dawn."

Hold on. Beatrice didn't exactly want to remind them about

it—she didn't want to be that dick—but she said it anyway. "You can't just conveniently forget about Portland, though."

Cordelia stared at her. "Portland?"

"Oh, come on. Minna's not a baby, and she's obviously good at taking care of herself on the streets."

"*Excuse* me?"

"When she came out as trans? And ran away?"

Unbelievably, Cordelia laughed. "You're kidding me, right?"

"You rejected her. You found her living in a squat in Portland?" A sick feeling rose in her gut as a realization rose. "Oh, my god. That didn't happen."

Cordelia's voice crackled with fury. "The night my daughter came out, she was hysterical, thinking I was going to kick her out of the house, or worse. I got in her bed and spent the next three hours holding her, telling her how loved she was and how grateful I was that she felt safe enough to share her real self with us. We threw her a coming-out party twice as big as the one we threw tonight, and I didn't complain once that the party was Disney princess themed. For fuck's sake, Beatrice. A squat? She was twelve. How could you just believe her? How could you be that gullible?"

And *this* was why you couldn't believe things until you had proof. How could she have gotten this so wrong?

An owl called in the distance, and the darkness felt heavy and cold on Beatrice's skin. "I'm so sorry. She just wanted to talk to him, and I didn't know if he'd come through, and then he did. His words to her were so lovely and she seemed thrilled. I was just glad I knew enough to help. Tonight she was going to try it herself, and I was supposed to be with her. I was going to tell you and bring you with me." She shot a glance at Reno, who didn't meet her eyes. "But I got sidetracked."

Astrid smacked her hands against the folds of her cape.

"What's done is done. He's got some part of her. Now we have to get her back. Before it's too late."

"I don't understand! What's happening?"

"Her father is a Velamen," said Cordelia.

"But—" She looked at the headstone that read, *Taurus Diaz.* "I thought they were gone. Didn't you say that?"

"They're gone from here, from this island. There are more out there. He was a fourth cousin to the last Skerry Cove Velamen, a connection so distant, I never felt it. That's exactly the way they'd planned it. He'd played the long game, thinking he'd have time to talk Minna into joining the side of his people when she got old enough. When he fell off that fucking ladder—" Cordelia put her hand over her mouth.

Beatrice held her breath as she waited.

"When they said he might not make it, I did exactly what Mom told me not to do. He was unconscious in the hospital bed, and I'd put the sleeping Minna on his chest, to try to comfort him, to bring him back to us. I was so desperate to save him…I gave him the Knock while he was lying in that bed, pushed it into him with barely a thought. I would have done anything in that minute. When all that power flowed into him, he couldn't hide his own, the power he'd managed to hide from me for two years. His strength shone out at me, coming through his skin with this terrible sick glow, bile green and blinding. I snatched Minna off him, and his eyes flew open—I swear to goddess that if his heart hadn't given out at that exact moment, he would have tried to rip our baby out of my hands." Her voice trembled, but she kept going. "I would have had to kill him with my own bare hands. But his heart stopped, probably because of the increased power. His heart monitor screamed almost as loud as I did, and nurses ran in, pushing me and the baby out of the way. They were too late."

Beatrice tried to pull breath into her lungs. "Cordelia…"

"I didn't stop screaming until I was sure he was all the way gone. He's been trying to get back to her ever since. If he gets her, he'll take all her power, killing her and destroying her soul in the process. And now, the twin energy on the island has drawn Velamens back toward us with a vengeance. They've been reminded of everything they lost and have double the drive to get through."

So Beatrice had given Minna the last piece of the puzzle she needed to reach Taurus. "Does Minna know?"

"Of course not." Ice cracked in her sister's voice. "She still has too much to learn. We had a *plan*. And you—you ruined everything coming here."

A chilled slice of wind whipped Beatrice's hair against her cheek. "I didn't mean to. I thought I knew what I was doing—"

"You knew fuck all."

"But that's not my fault." Oh, how stupid the words sounded coming out of her mouth. "I've been trying to learn, trying to absorb everything you teach me, but with your secrets—I swear to you, I didn't mean to hurt her." Beatrice took a shaky step toward Cordelia, but her sister stumbled backward, holding up her hands.

"Don't come anywhere near me. You—what? You simply believed I was a bad mother to Minna when she came out? You *liked* Minna looking up to you. I saw that. I was *fine* with that. She'd gotten an aunt who would love her, and my kid deserves every scrap of love she can get in the world. But you should have told me about her contacting Taurus. You did the one thing that might not only kill her, but destroy her eternal soul in the process, *do you understand me?*"

That was the problem. All of this was so huge, and Beatrice didn't understand the slightest fraction of it. "What can I do?" There had to be something she could do.

"You?" Her sister glowered. "You think you can study what

we do, that you can learn it by heart, line it up on a grid and make it nice and neat, but you could spend the rest of your life trying to understand, and you'd fail. A normal person without a magical bone in their body would have known what *not* to do."

Cordelia straightened. She seemed to get bigger, wider, taller. Now she was the one to step forward this time, and Beatrice was the one to fall back. "If I lose her because of you, you will rue the day you came to this island."

Sharply, Astrid said, "Cordelia. She was stupid, but not malicious. She didn't know what she was doing. We'll be so much stronger with her. We need her."

Wheeling to face her, Cordelia said, "I don't give one single goddamn fuck. We can't trust her. I don't want to see her again. Ever."

The coldness of her voice chilled Beatrice to the core. "Astrid's right. I had *no* idea what I was doing."

Reno's voice, though quiet, would have carried through a hurricane. "Then you never should have done anything. What the hell is wrong with you?"

Everything, apparently.

This was all her fault.

Beatrice's heart fell to the clods of ripped-up grass at her feet, and as they turned to leave, she remained where she was. Stuck again, this time by her own stupidity.

One last try. "Please let me help find her."

Without turning around, Cordelia said, "Goddess forbid you try."

CHAPTER FORTY-FIVE

> Sometimes Spirit asks that we try again, that we try harder. Other times, we've fucked up so royally that we should just go to bed for a while and stay there. Ask me how I know.
>
> —*Evie Oxby, in conversation with Barbara Walters*

So Beatrice went home. With nothing more she could do, she got in bed and pulled the covers over her head. Her dreams made the scant hour or two she slept hardly worth it: pitch-black cemeteries, bony fingers writhing up from damp earth to claw her down into the mud, the padding of feet, the quick-moving shapes of girls running fast to a bloody, fiery doom. When she woke up in the morning, she couldn't have felt worse if she hadn't gone to bed at all.

A text waited from her father: At the cafe.

Nothing else, nothing about Minna.

She called Cordelia, but it went straight to voice mail, so either her phone was off or she'd blocked her. Probably the latter.

Quickly, she dressed, and then hurried down the dock and toward the café.

Minna's fine. Of course she's fine. She'd probably turned up an hour later. Maybe she'd tried sneaking into her bed, only to be caught by Cordelia. They'd probably had a good heart-to-heart before Minna fell asleep, wrung out from emotional exhaustion. Cordelia would still hate Beatrice, but nothing mattered beyond Minna being safe.

Surely Minna was safe.

She had to be.

Mitchell sat in the back corner of the café, a newspaper and a becrumbed, empty plate in front of him. She waved and got in line.

When it was her turn, Fritz said, "Your order, please?"

Funny that this would be the thing that undid her. Struggling not to choke on her tears, she said, "Extra-hot cappuccino, please." They nodded, shoving the credit card reader at her, before moving toward the espresso machine, their face blank.

Keelia and Olive sat in the other corner. She hadn't noticed them when she came in, but their heads leaned together as they glanced in her direction and whispered.

She could do this. Using the last tiny dreg of courage she had, she walked to their table.

"Have they found her?"

Keelia pressed her lips together, as if trying to decide whether to speak. Then she shook her head.

Olive, bless her, took pity on her, though. "No, but everyone's searching. They set up a headquarters at her house. We're going to bring them a box of coffee and all of Fritz's donuts."

Everyone. She wanted—needed—to be part of that. "How are they doing it? Are the police involved? They'll need a lot of people, right? I couldn't fall asleep, obviously, so I did quite a bit of reading about grid searches, and if they make sure to lay it out from the cemetery in the direction of—"

Keelia rose. "Fritz, that box ready?"

Fritz pushed the coffee box across the counter, along with a carry bag and three donut boxes. "All the milks, soy, almond, and regular, plus sweeteners. Cups and lids are in there."

Beatrice almost dropped her phone as she tried to wrestle her credit card out of the attached wallet. "Let me get this. Please. It's the least I can do."

Keelia raised an eyebrow. "It's the least, all right."

Fritz just shook their head as they slid her cappuccino halfway across the counter, as if they couldn't stand to get any closer to her. "As if I'd charge them for this. You really aren't from around here."

And you never will be.

Straightening her spine, she turned away and moved toward her father, who, of course, had witnessed the whole thing. Great. She was going to have to explain it to him, and she wasn't sure she was going to find the right words. But she needed to try.

"Dad. I'm not sure how long you stayed at the party after I slipped away—" Beatrice could almost smell the roses, could almost see the unearthly moonlit glow of them blooming around her and Reno. The most perfect moment of her entire life, followed by the most devastating one.

He raised a hand. "I'm all caught up, don't worry. How you doing? You must feel pretty shitty."

"How? *How* are you caught up?"

"Astrid."

"Have they heard anything from Minna?"

"Not yet."

The deep thud of disappointment was followed by a jolt that shot through her. "Wait, go back a second. *Astrid?* I mean, I know you danced, but..."

He stiffened slightly. "She was my wife, Beatrice."

"Yeah, well, she's not the wife I ever saw you with. When did you talk to her?"

With a shrug, he said, "Last night. This morning."

Something small and metallic frizzled in Beatrice's head. "You—no. You didn't. No."

"She needed comfort. She was upset."

Should Beatrice laugh? Should she cringe? "I can't believe you."

"Fair enough. She can't believe you, for what it's worth."

"Whatever." Great. Now she sounded as old as she felt, which was considerably younger than Minna. Next, she'd be lying on the floor, forcing people to step over her while she howled.

"She said you're exactly like her."

"Excuse me? No."

"And I have to agree."

How was this getting worse? "You think I'm like the woman who abandoned me as a baby?"

"You're both stubborn as an exhausted geriatric mule."

"I get that from *you*."

"Maybe. But unlike me, both of you think you can control the universe. Both of you think that if you have enough facts backing you up, that you're right."

But that was basically just science. "If the facts back us up, we *are* right."

A long, unfillable pause stretched between them. Then her father said, "Besides letting Cordelia go, the worst thing I ever did in my life was teaching you to rely on information."

"Instead of what, exactly?"

"Instead of your gut. Your heart. Anything but your brain."

Too angry to speak, she sipped her (cool) cappuccino.

After they had finished their coffees in uncomfortable silence, Mitchell said he had to get back to the house. He didn't need to say which one he meant.

"I'll walk you there."

With a chagrined look, he said, "You might not be, ah, very welcome at the moment."

"I can handle it." What was the worst Cordelia could do to her? Okay, fine, truthfully, she didn't know the answer to that. *Could* she turn her into a toadstool? Curse her to knit straw into railroad tracks?

Some of this, yes, was Beatrice's fault. But Minna had lied to her, and neither Cordelia nor Astrid had trusted her with the full truth. Beatrice had to at least try to help find Minna, to make sure she was safe. She had only one goddammed miracle left and she couldn't leave Minna without—no. Unable to even think it, she walked next to her father, passing the bookstore and the butcher and the pocket park next to the elementary school. *I will do this. I will figure out how to help.*

She continued her affirmations right up till the very moment she opened the bottom gate and looked up at the porch.

Reno leaned against the railing, despair etched on her angular face. She was wearing the dark watch cap she'd worn the night before, and her shoulders drooped with exhaustion.

But when Reno saw her, she straightened. Slowly.

Her eyes flashed like a lighthouse's beam.

Up until this exact moment, Beatrice had always thought of lighthouses as comforting. They were emblems of safe passage, weren't they? A welcome sight on a stormy night.

How wrong she'd been.

A lighthouse was the direst warning of all. *Dangerous rocks. Unnavigable terrain. If you value your life, stay far away.*

To her father, Beatrice mumbled, "Call me if you hear anything."

Then she fled.

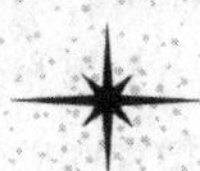

CHAPTER FORTY-SIX

They say it's darkest before the dawn, but that's a load of horseshit, ain't it? It's dark when there's no light. So quit whining and light a fucking match, okay?

—Evie Oxby, in conversation with Dax Shepard on the Armchair Expert *podcast*

Hours passed. The only place Beatrice could think of to be was on the deck of the *Forget-Me-Knot*. At least there, she could look at the long stretch of shops on the main street—she could view tourists eating ice creams and locals getting their groceries, going on about their business as if the world wasn't ending.

If she kept her gaze fixed firmly enough on the street, maybe she'd see Minna slipping through the clumps of people.

She kept her phone tightly in her hand.

Every thirty minutes or so, her father sent a text in response to her nagging. Nothing yet.

No, still nothing.

No, honey, still nothing. Yes, people are looking.

Then, Someone said they might have seen her near the river but

A terrifying pause was filled only with the bubbles that said her father was still typing.

but it was a just kid fishing who looked like her.

On the houseboat to the right, a man was scrubbing the film of salt off the windows. Three kayakers paddled past. The woman in the back kayak screeched at two teenage boys that they were doing it wrong, though she was the only one wobbling enough to be in danger of falling out. Because of what Beatrice had done, had said, Minna was running toward a father she thought loved her, but who would kill her and destroy her soul for his own gain. Maybe he'd already gotten to her. But what would that look like, what did it actually mean? Would he take physical form if he took Minna's energy? How would he do it? Who would protect Minna if she was up against him, alone?

And Beatrice couldn't even assist in the search.

She squeezed her phone tightly, then brought up Grant's face in Contacts. She stared at him for a moment. That crease in his cheek, almost-but-not-quite a dimple. At one time, she'd loved touching that with the tip of her finger. It felt like a really long time ago.

She pressed Call.

The hope in his "Hello? Beatrice?" made her even sadder than she'd been twenty seconds before. *Why* did he want this to be amicable? Why didn't he want to scream and fight and burn what they'd had to the ground?

"Why did you marry me?"

To his credit, he rolled with it. "Because I loved you." A breath. "I still do."

Somehow, she managed not to snort. "Okay, but that's not what I mean. I guess, why did you love me?"

"I love you because you're kind and smart and—"

"Can you tell me the truth, please? Like, cut the obvious canned answers. Tell me something that would apply to our relationship, and no one else's." She paused. "And be as honest as you can."

She heard him take a deep breath. Then he said, "I loved you because you knew everything, and because of that, nothing ever seemed difficult when you were around. I'd been so overwhelmed with everything when I met you—you remember how it was."

She remembered. He'd had half custody of his kids when they'd met, and his place had looked like a frat house the day after a tailgate. Laundry moldered in smelly, towering piles. Wet towels hung from bedposts and lamps. She'd found a pile of overdue bills next to the toilet once, and he'd sworn he had no idea how they got there. "I remember," she said.

Would Dulcina remember that Grant's toothbrush head needed to be replaced every ninety days? Would she know to purchase his favorite kind of boxers every year? Or would she be sensible and tell Grant to do his own shopping, the way Beatrice should have and never had?

"With you by my side, it meant I could shine at work and be a fuckup everywhere else."

"You were never an actual fuckup. More like a... careless pinball."

"Yeah. I'm sorry about that."

It sounded sincere. "Thanks."

"I'm... Even though me and Dulcy are happy... Shit, I miss you. I think I'm brokenhearted."

For a second, she almost felt sorry for him.

Because she knew how he felt.

She just didn't feel it about him. If grief was unexpressed love, like Naya had said, then it was official—this wild knot of unmanageable grief in the middle of her chest proved she did love Minna. And Cordelia.

And Reno.

But not Grant.

She realized he was waiting for her to respond through the silence. "Can you give me Evie Oxby's number?"

"Oxby? Like, her personal cell?"

"I know it's a big ask. But we talked at your party. She won't mind."

"I don't know, Bea."

She let more silence flow down the line. It wasn't as though she thought he owed her. Life was life, and this was where they were.

But if he believed she might think better of him for giving her the number, she'd take it.

Finally, he groaned. "Got a pen?"

Evie Oxby, unsurprisingly, was confused as to how she'd gotten her private number. "You're who, again?"

"The elevator. Seven miracles. Then I die."

"Oh, yeah. My lawyer's wife?"

"Soon to be ex-wife."

The sigh was heavy. "Soon to be ex-lawyer, too."

Trying to shake off the feeling of foolishness, Beatrice said, "I'm really sorry, but it turns out that I'm part witch or something, and I did something really wrong, and now someone's in danger."

She heard Evie say to someone in the room with her, "See? This is why I don't answer numbers I don't recognize." Then back to her. "You're not part witch."

"Pardon?"

"You're more powerful than that. The shit you're sending down this line into my ear is actually painful." Evie sounded bored.

It had been a mistake to call. Evie probably said the same thing to everyone. She was probably full of it, making up everything she said. She'd probably had no experience with anything really magical—

"You want to know where the girl is."

Could be a lucky guess.

Evie sighed as if in pain. "Holy Hierophant. You call me, but you want me to prove myself? I'm literally in the middle of making a chocolate ganache. It's the first day off I've had in two months. You're sitting on some kind of a dock, except it's also a house. I don't get it, but honestly, I don't care. You recently found a matriarchal figure you thought you'd lost, and a woman who looks like she could be your twin is also looking for the same girl."

"Jesus."

"Not in my world, no. Can we get to the point, please?"

"Can you help me find her?"

"Mmmm. No."

"No? Just like that?"

"She's cloaked herself somehow. She's a strong little thing, too, huh? That's good, because she's in danger. But you knew that already. You also know who's after her. Look, I don't get why you even called me. You didn't believe me on the elevator, and I can't help you."

"I'm sorry I didn't believe." Frantic, she said, "Can you just tell me how this works?"

"Pardon?"

"I'm new to this. All of it. I've been doing my best to learn, to study, and I really appreciate both your books, but I just need to know how it all works." If Evie could just point her in the right direction, maybe she could find Minna and fix what was broken. "Can you just tell me? Since I'm kind of like you?"

"It's different for everyone. You know how people's fingerprints are unique? Magic is like that."

"How is that possible?"

"Who are you to think you should know?"

Beatrice gripped her phone tighter. "Excuse me?"

"Seriously. What makes you so special? The world's been trying to figure this shit out for millennia, but you think *you* should be the one to figure it out?"

"You've figured it out."

"Are you kidding me? I'm twenty-nine. Twenty-four years of seeing ghosts and I still can't tell if there's one in a hotel lobby with me or if it's a bellhop in an old-fashioned costume. I have nothing figured out, except that I need to get a new phone number."

"I'm sorry."

Her sigh was pained. "What actually matters to you?"

Dad. Iris. Minna. Cordelia. Reno. "My people."

"Why do you love them?"

"I...just do."

"You'll get no extra control from knowing why you love them. You might have less. What happens when you just accept how you feel?"

"I get terrified."

"So the fuck what?"

She opened her mouth but nothing came out.

Evie went on, "Who *cares* if you're scared? We're all scared. Not everyone has the power you do, though. Use it. Act on it."

"How do I know what to do? And then, how do I decide to act?"

"Sometimes we have to act before we think. Sometimes that means we get arrested for indecent exposure, but other times it means we're following Spirit. There are times when the only thing to do is to act before thinking a single damn thought."

"But—"

"Don't even ask. You were born knowing how to do it—you just have to find your way back there."

Beatrice wasn't born knowing how to do anything except pine for a mother who'd abandoned her without glance in the rearview mirror. "You really can't tell me where my niece is? Her life truly is at stake."

"So many times. So many *goddamn* times they say that to me." A pause, another long, indrawn breath.

She waited. The neighbor next door finished washing the last window and went inside without glancing at her. A seagull landed on the railing of her deck, eyeing her nervously.

Then Evie said, "No. Nope. I'm not getting anything. This one's gonna have to be all you."

Beatrice spoke quickly, before she lost Evie entirely. "I'm so sorry I bothered you. I'm very grateful for your time, I swear. Just one last question: Do you... do you think I know enough to do this?"

"Shit, I have no idea. All I know is that my ganache just broke. Tell Grant that if I don't fire his ass, he owes me three free billable hours, because if I'd been watching this like I should have, it never would have separated."

CHAPTER FORTY-SEVEN

Be brave, new witch. We all had to start somewhere. Trust your gut. Especially if that gut says you need black-and-white striped stockings. Who doesn't need those, am I right? Some things never go out of style.

—Evie Oxby, at Paris Fashion Week

On the little table in Beatrice's galley kitchen stood five candles. All were lit and flickering. It was midafternoon, but she'd drawn the curtains in an attempt to set a helpful mood.

As if she knew how to do that.

She'd already lit incense and rung a small bell four times, to the east, west, north, and south. In front of her, she'd set a notebook, a pen, and a small, sharp knife. Every book and website she'd read had different ideas on how best to ground oneself before spell casting, so she was taking a little of each and hoping for the best. Beatrice breathed deeply, and just as Cordelia had instructed her, she tried to feel her roots sink down through the boat's hull, through the water, and into the rock below, moving down through the layers of the earth.

I can do this.

I know enough.

Was she really feeling her roots spread into the earth? Was that the cool energy she felt spreading through her? Or was it the placebo effect?

Did it matter? The placebo effect worked, after all.

"I know enough," she whispered to herself while flipping the pages of the grimoire. "I know enough."

At the doubled-over folded and sealed middle page, she paused. She fingered the waxed edge.

No, she couldn't do that.

There was *something* in here on an unsealed page that would help. Surely.

Quickly, she flipped through. No, not a casting-off spell, not a mending—

Wait. Would this one work? She read over the words of a finding spell, and something about its words rang a bell.

Beatrice scrolled through her *Magic* spreadsheet (the computer was the least magical thing on the table, but she needed it). In one of the cells she'd written: *Sympathetic magic uses the power of like calling like, e.g. cave drawings of animals made to lure the hunted close.*

It couldn't hurt to give it a try.

Well.

She hoped it wouldn't hurt much.

Like-to-like. Okay, so who was like Minna? Her mother. Cordelia had given Minna fifty percent of her DNA.

From the research she'd done recently, Beatrice knew identical twins shared most of their DNA.

Which meant that her own body was very like Minna's, too.

She took out the handkerchief Cordelia had embroidered for her. Cordelia had said it was for protection, not for finding, but Beatrice was pretty sure she knew how she could make this work. She scanned another webpage she'd bookmarked, flipped through Evie's book to a highlighted passage, and then cross-referenced her spreadsheet.

Yes. This *should* work.

Beatrice took out a blue ballpoint pen. She held the tip against the cloth, next to the embroidered sigil her sister had made.

She watched the flames wobble for a count of three, and then she closed her eyes. Evie said the simplest spells were the strongest. The fewer words spoken, the fewer she could screw up.

"One, two, three, show Minna to me."

Then she opened her eyes and drew her own sigil on the handkerchief. An *M*, tall and sharp and sweet, just like her niece. She drew a circle around it for the sun, then she drew wavy lines to symbolize the sun rising in an unmissable ball of brightness. To make it really clear what she needed—this had to reveal Minna's whereabouts—she drew below the sun a line of water, connecting that line to a jagged rock. The sun, rising above this island, to show where Minna was.

Carefully, she connected the last line to the embroidered sigil, so that both she and her sister's energy were connected.

It would take energy to activate. Serious energy. No more fucking around.

Without hesitation, she picked up the knife and cut the tip of her first finger deep enough that blood rose in a sudden bloom.

"One, two, three, *show Minna to me.*"

She squeezed a drop of blood onto the white of the hanky, and the reaction was almost instantaneous: the blue inked lines of her design began to glow a bright red, as if she'd drawn the whole thing in blood, as if the sun itself were glowing behind it instead of just the candlelight.

The lines of her sister's embroidery glowed red, too.

Beatrice's heart hammered painfully in her chest—she'd known it would work, but that didn't quell the fear.

She kept her eyes on the handkerchief. Any minute, Minna's location would be revealed, and Beatrice would be the one to find her. She would save her.

The boat jolted violently, as if an enormous wave had hit it. She jumped, but kept her gaze on the glowing fabric. She waited.

Then the door crashed open.

Through it came water and all Beatrice could think was that the houseboat was suddenly sinking, but not in the slow way of a leak. It was as if it were *already* underwater. Had the house been hit by a cruise liner? What could possibly—

Waves smashed through the windows then, and before she could even stand up from the table, the entire cabin of the galley was not just taking on water, but was *full.* The seawater was dark and green, and her lungs strained, holding the deep breath she'd taken just as the freezing flood hit her body.

Another surge of water hurled her against the wall. She managed to catch one quick breath before another wave slapped her sideways.

Her brain flew into overdrive. The computer didn't matter—the spreadsheet was in the cloud. None of her paper notes were consequential enough to die for, and the library books were just books. But the hanky that had been ripped from her fingers—she needed that. And the grimoire. She had to get the grimoire.

She could just see it, six feet below her, giving off its own reddish glow. Her lungs burning, she kicked her way down into the frigid water, but the closer she got to the book, the smaller it became, as if the galley of her boat were getting bigger and wider as she got smaller and weaker.

From the corner of her eye came a brighter glow. When she

turned her head, she saw the handkerchief floating just a few inches from her face. She made a grab for it, her motion sluggish in the water.

Her hands went right through it. It wavered as if it were water, too.

An illusion.

Somehow, she'd conjured an illusion. Whatever like-to-like she'd meant to call, she'd done it wrong and gotten this instead.

Help.

But there was no one to call, no one to protect her. And the water in this illusion was very real, very cold, and very drowningly wet. She surfaced an inch from the ceiling and sucked in a breath that was half seawater.

As she choked on the brine, the only sigil of protection that she could drag to her mind was the one her sister had embroidered—but how could she draw it now? How could she charge it? How was she supposed to know what to do in this kind of emergency?

You were born knowing how to do it.

She'd rejected the idea when Evie had said it.

But what if she wasn't wrong?

Beatrice heaved in another breath and then went back under.

In one long blow, she drew her sister's sigil in bubbles, feeding the sigil her own oxygen. It was all she had left to give.

Another crash shook the boat. This was it, then. This was when she would die.

Then came another thump, but that was her own body crashing to the floor of the galley.

The houseboat swayed as a slight swell passed below it.

The interior of the cabin was dry. The five candles on the table still burned. The spreadsheet on her computer still displayed its regimented, orderly boxes.

Beatrice sat up, her clothes as dry as the floor. The only wet thing in the whole cabin was the handkerchief on the floorboards next to her. She lifted it, heavy and dripping. The sigil she'd drawn in blue ink was smeared, almost gone.

Beatrice put the edge of the handkerchief to her tongue: salt.

As she stood, her legs trembled. The grimoire was still on the table, too, smack-dab where she'd left it.

Only one thing had changed.

Instead of being open to the finding spell, the pages had been flipped.

The book was now open to the sealed page. The one she'd promised Cordelia she'd never look at.

Even if it made her sister and everyone else hate her even more than they already did, there was only one thing to do.

CHAPTER FORTY-EIGHT

I should clarify. I said to be brave, new witch. Not stupid.

—Evie Oxby, at New York Fashion Week

Beatrice touched the wax seal at the edge of the page. How long had it been since someone had opened this? Had Cordelia ever seen what was inside? Did Astrid know what it was? Or did the secret of its contents go back farther, to her foremothers, Rosalind and Anna and Valeska and Xenia?

As Beatrice's shaking fingers touched the edge, ready to unfold the page, she paused.

The promise she'd made to Cordelia not to look was from before.

Before Beatrice had learned so much, before she'd spent hours and full days studying magic.

Before she'd really, truly believed.

And crucially, before she'd broken everything by teaching Minna something that had put her in imminent danger.

What if Cordelia was wrong?

The fact that the book had opened *itself* to this page, combined with the fact that Beatrice had no other earthly idea what to do—oh, for fuck's sake.

Using the same knife she'd cut herself with, she cracked through the wax on the seal. She unfolded the page.

It held nothing but a single sigil, drawn in red ink so dark, it verged on black. The parchment puckered around the ink, as if it were drawing the page into itself like a small black hole.

The image resembled an old-fashioned scale with one half missing. Two sharp slashes at the fulcrum were separated by a jagged, stabbed line. An arrow pointed down, diving into what looked like a teardrop, which bled its own tears.

Looking at it felt worse than almost drowning. Beatrice struggled to breathe, the air in her lungs almost as heavy as water.

There were no words on the page, nothing to help her parse what the sigil could do.

She shouldn't have known what it meant, what it stood for.

But she did.

She knew exactly what it meant, and she wished, instantly, that she didn't. The very image of it seared itself into her brain, and when she shut her eyes, it was all she could see.

You will die for love.

The words filtered into her brain as clearly as if a person in the room had said them out loud, and it was followed by a perfect, clear understanding of what the image meant. The knowledge flowed into her like oxygen.

As clearly as if she'd been reading magical symbology all her life, Beatrice understood the sigil was the curse of the dead twin. It was baby Louise's blood on the page. Velamen blood. When Xenia had stripped Anna and Louise of that half of their magic, when Louise hadn't survived, Xenia had locked that power on this page.

The inevitability of the curse crawled into her veins. It was hers now. Or did she belong to it? And was the curse somehow related to the way the Velamens would try to bring a Holland to the other side, to die to give them power?

She had no idea, and it didn't matter—it couldn't. She still didn't know where Minna was. And when it came to that girl—Beatrice *would* die for love if she had to.

She scrubbed her face, rubbing her eyes.

Who the hell did she think she was? How had she thought *she* could find Minna? Minna was loved by her mother and grandmother, two women who had true power. If they couldn't find her, with their advanced magic, what had Beatrice been thinking by trying to help?

She barely knew what love was. And she was pretty goddammed sure she wouldn't live long enough to figure it out.

I will never know enough.

Fine. True. Yes.

But the second unexpected thought came so swiftly and sweetly that it felt like a gift. *No matter what, I would never know enough, even if I lived forever.*

A floral scent wafted lightly through the open door.

Gardenia.

Beatrice lunged into the bedroom, where she'd left Naya's letter. Grabbing it from the bedside table, she raced back to the kitchen. Without looking again at the image in the grimoire, she slammed the book shut, dragging the notebook and pen toward herself.

One last try. *Naya, I need you.*

She took a breath. Auto-writing didn't bring miracles—she didn't have to fear it. She wasn't suicidal. Just desperate. Naya would help.

She held the letter in her hands as she imagined the nib of a fountain pen fitting itself into the padlock. Carefully, she recited the spell.

It came on fast this time—the urge to scratch the itch with the pen, the feeling of floating away from her body but not really being anywhere else while she was gone. Then came the pop of returning to her body, and she looked down to see what words she'd left for herself.

The scent of gardenia was almost overwhelming, and Beatrice had to blink hard through her tears to see the page.

> Button, you must trust yourself. You have everything you need, and you always have. Minna is with her ancestors, as am I, as you will be soon. Don't be afraid. Not now. Not ever. She needs help only you can give her. Go now.

She covered her mouth. Minna was with her ancestors?

Dead?

The thought was too big, larger than the universe, impossible to imagine.

But then, Minna wouldn't need help, so it had to mean something else—was she in the cemetery?

Cordelia and Astrid would have searched the cemetery, surely. They'd have searched the aboveground crypts, all the ones open enough that a girl could sneak into but—

Minna had said the old Holland crypt was locked.

Beatrice grabbed her cell phone and ran.

CHAPTER FORTY-NINE

The craft of magic is the marriage of energy and intention. When those two get hitched, it's a true love match, yes. But watch out for surprises. Love likes to keep a trick up her rather voluminous sleeve, just like that one you're *totally* pulling off right now.

—*Evie Oxby, in conversation with Lady Gaga*

Beatrice entered the cemetery on the street side, not through the gate in Cordelia's yard. She couldn't see her sister's house, and she was glad of it. She would send a text soon—she had it drafted in her mind, but she'd get closer to the crypt before she did.

She stumbled over grassy hummocks and went down two wrong lanes, mixing up the landmarks she hadn't managed yet to commit to memory. The Holland crypt was just to the north of Xenia Holland's grave, right? Under the tall stand of pines?

But there were a few tall stands of pines, and it took her ten minutes, maybe more, of scrabbling at vine-covered epitaphs on the aboveground tombs to find the right one.

The gate around the Holland crypt was rusted, so that she could tug at it until it screeched open far enough for her to slip through, but the small marble building was still closed, the stone door shut tight. From the seasons of leaves built up on the ground, it didn't look like anyone had entered for years. Maybe decades.

Naya, are you sure?

Putting her hands on the door, Beatrice leaned forward, trying to feel—what? Heat? Life? She placed her forehead against the marble.

But she felt nothing but her own despair.

The wind picked up, and the pines overhead moaned. A pair of rowdy crows squabbled on a branch above as two motorcycles roared past on the side road.

A scent of gardenia wafted past.

She froze.

Minna *was* here, somewhere. And if Minna wanted to hide from her mother and Astrid, she'd have to do it very well and very thoroughly.

Beatrice had no idea how to break through that kind of magical camouflage. This went so far past anything she'd learned in the last week. She needed help.

She fumbled for her phone and typed out a group message to Cordelia, Reno, and her father. I'm at the Holland crypt. I think she's here. Please come.

But when she hit Send, the message remained pending.

No bars of service.

Fuck, fuck, fuck. This stupid *town*.

The passing seconds beat in her chest like she'd choked down a clock.

Okay. She stared up into the sky—so blue, there wasn't even a cloud to hang her gaze on.

Help.

She was alone.

No one was coming to her rescue. And she didn't know how to do this the right way.

So that just left her way.

Whatever that looked like, it was going to have to be good enough, because it was all she had.

Think, Beatrix.

Beatrix? Where had that come from?

Trust.

Fine. She could be her mother's daughter, Beatrix, for a moment.

How, exactly, just a few days after she'd come to town, had she figured out how to imagine the pen going into the lock to make the auto-writing spell work?

The answer had simply come to her, without trying. The answer had just been there.

But how the hell was she supposed to try to *not* try? It was a riddle that would have been amusing to parse while sitting on a meditation cushion in a yoga studio, but she was here, facing a closed, silent marble tomb, which was real as fuck.

Was it real?

A chill ran through her.

That illusion of water, of drowning, had been so real—she'd *felt* it. She'd been soaked. And freezing. Choking on the water and struggling to breathe had been real. And at the same time, she'd been safe on board her dry houseboat.

This—this crypt could be under the veil of an illusion, too.

But crap, that would require a spell to reverse, right? And she didn't know that kind of spell…

Something like serenity lifted the weight at the top of her lungs. *I can write the spell.*

Beatrice took a deep breath and planted her feet firmly, hip distance apart. She sent her roots back into the earth and connected with that molten ore. Did it matter if the connection was real or not? She might be imagining all of it, but the cool stream of energy that flowed into her bones felt real enough.

Was she a good enough witch to pull this off?

Probably not.

But a novice witch was still better than no witch at all.

Again, she kept it as simple as possible. Placing her hands against the door of the crypt, she said calmly and clearly, "One, two, three, reveal Minna to me."

Then she fell forward through the marble as if it were only cool air and not stone.

There she was.

Minna sat inside with her back to Beatrice.

CHAPTER FIFTY

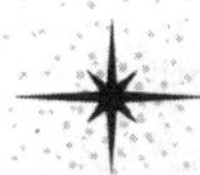

Fear is its own sort of magic and requires a set of tools that I'm only starting to learn how to use.
—*Evie Oxby, in conversation with Brené Brown*

Beatrice had never been in an aboveground crypt. The tomb had seen better days, and cracks ran through the marble. Part of Anna's final resting place seemed to have collapsed in on itself on one side, but it was bigger inside than Beatrice would have thought, maybe eight feet square. Three candles burned at the front of the space on a raised dais of stone. At one time, it must have been used as a small altar, and a vase still stood there, whatever flowers it might have held long turned to dust. The air smelled of mildew and cold dirt. Behind her was the door, transformed back to marble. To the left and right were seats chiseled into the stone. Above each seat were dark, carved plaques. *Anna Holland. Rosalind Holland.* So Anna was here with her daughter, Rosalind. Was Anna's lost twin, Louise, here, too? Or somewhere nearby?

After her cursory glance, Beatrice returned her gaze to her niece, sitting alone on the dusty floor, her father's tattoo gun pressed against her arm. Even though it wasn't plugged into power, the metallic buzz of it echoed through Beatrice's teeth.

"Minna."

The sound stopped, and the girl spun around. "What the fuck? How did you get in?"

Beatrice said honestly, "I'm not quite sure. I said some words, and they worked."

A breeze moved through the room, moving the dust into small eddies.

Oh, god. In a sealed tomb, the dust could only come from one thing.

Minna shook her head. "You can't be here."

On her arm, Beatrice could see the same *T* that the girl had been drawing on Taurus's grave. A small ooze of blood rose up along the lines. "What are you doing?"

Her niece's face looked carved of marble itself, her expression stubborn. "I'm going to assume you don't actually need me to answer that."

"Minna, your father—"

A flicker of fear raced across Minna's expression, and in it, Beatrice recognized the girl she loved. The old Minna was in there, the one who didn't have Taurus guiding her hand.

The fear switched off, Minna's features stilling. "He *loves* me. All he wants is to hug me one time. He said so."

"How? How do you know?"

"I hear him now." She looked down at her forearm. "I hear him more with every drop of ink. We just don't know the final lines I need to draw, to power this sigil to get to him. Or to get him here. I'm not—I'm still figuring that out."

"What is he saying to you?"

"*Nothing*, with you here. He's gone silent."

"He's a Velamen, Minna."

Minna laughed. "Nice try, but no. He's a Diaz."

"From a long line of Velamen blood." Beatrice raised her arms to either wall. "These are your ancestors on your mother's side. Your father's side, though, is trying to claim you for themselves."

Emotions flared across Minna's face, changing too rapidly for Beatrice to follow them. "Who told you that? My mother?"

"And your grandmother, yes. They're terrified he'll try to take you from them." Could he hear them now? A shiver raced down her spine. "Listen to your gut. You know I'm not lying to you."

Minna gripped the tattoo gun so hard, her knuckles went white. "He loves me for who I am."

"Your mother loves you for who you are. And you *lied* to me about that. She never rejected you."

She tossed her hair back from her face. "You believed me because you wanted to. You wanted to feel special, like I was choosing you over my mother."

Ridiculous.

But—the truth was ice against her skin. Beatrice *had* loved it when Minna had chosen her for a confidante. She had felt special.

Minna continued, "Just because your real life was stolen from you doesn't mean that mine should be, too."

"Hang on." Beatrice took a careful step toward her. "My life wasn't stolen. I wasn't raised by my mother, okay, but I was raised by a loving father who helped make me into who I am. My dad's full of flaws, yes, but he loves me, deeply. Taurus, though—he doesn't love you. He's only trying to steal your life. Your *power*, Minna. And not so he can be with you."

Minna's eyes burned dark. "Stop it."

"He's using you. He only wants your power, not you. When he takes it from you, it'll leave you dead, stripped of everything. You won't even have your soul left."

"You don't know that."

But Beatrice did. Somehow, somewhere deep inside her gut, she could feel what Cordelia had said was true, and Minna—if she let herself listen—might know it, too.

Minna, though, picked up the gun and went back to work. "I'm going to figure this out. Once I complete it, you'll see. You'll see he was right." She gritted her teeth and continued drawing the straight line into her skin.

A spell—Beatrice needed a spell—but what the hell kind of spell would banish a malevolent spirit trying to lure his own child to her annihilation?

She didn't know.

No fucking idea.

Naya.

Naya had gotten her this far.

Her brain stalled, unable to think up a rhyming spell, so Beatrice prayed, instead. *Naya, please help me get her out of here. Away from him. I can't lose this girl. Please don't let Taurus take this girl's soul.*

A low laugh bounced off the marble.

Minna's head whipped up, the gun buzzing still in her hand.

The scent of gardenia blew through, raising the dust again, followed by a fetid, sewer-like smell of flowers left to rot, maggot-filled meat abandoned in the sun, a smell that made Beatrice want to retch.

I'm so glad you're here, Button. The voice wasn't audible exactly—it was a rumble instead, one that she felt inside her chest rather than hearing with her ears.

But it was clear.

It was real.

And it was male.

CHAPTER FIFTY-ONE

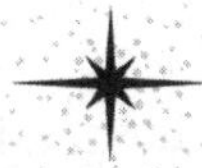

When you're looking for one ghost, but the wrong one bashes through? Run, honey. Just run.
—*Evie Oxby, guest appearance on* Ghost Hunters

The despair that filled Beatrice was icier than the frigid water illusion. The bleakness in her soul felt worse than the day of Naya's burial.

Naya wasn't with her. She hadn't written through Beatrice's hand, nor had she told Beatrice where Minna was.

Taurus had.

That laugh rose again, the one that made her skull ache. *For someone who wants to understand, you're very slow sometimes.*

"What do you want?" Beatrice tried to sound strong, but her voice wavered on the last word.

Give her the sigil.

Beatrice looked at Minna. "What's he talking about? I don't know his tattoo sigil, and I wouldn't give it to you if I did."

Instead of looking victorious, Minna looked scared. "I've been trying to get to Valeska to receive the rest of the sigil, but she won't come to me. He said only one person could help. I thought we would raise the answer by starting the tattoo." She looked down at her arm, the dark black ink mixing with the red of her blood. "But then you came. So I think...you might be the answer. The lost twin."

"I don't know shit."

"Did you open the sealed page?"

Beatrice sucked in a breath.

"You did. I *know* you did. What was it?"

The page of the other lost twin. The curse.

But she'd never, ever tell this girl. The sigil was how to die for love. Of course that's why Taurus wanted it—he wanted his child to die of love for him, to cross over to a place where he could take her power and leave her carcass to rot.

"You have to tell me." Minna held up her arm. "He was only able to give me this much."

Taurus did know part of the symbol—she could see that now. The *T* she'd seen on Minna's arm, the one she'd been drawing on his grave, wasn't for Taurus. It was part of the broken scale, but there were no slashes, no arrow, no bleeding teardrop. *Shit.* She shouldn't even think about the image, in case he could see inside her mind.

"Please tell me, Aunt Bea."

Tell her.

Minna's voice broke her heart, but Taurus's voice inside her chest almost stopped her breath completely. It hurt so much, she wondered if he was tying the ventricles of her heart into knots.

"It's a love sigil. It'll bring me and Dad together. You'll see. You have to tell me."

"Honey, that's *so* not what it is." She sucked in half a breath. "It's a Velamen curse so dangerous, it needed to be sealed away forever."

"You're so full of shit—he was right about all of you." Minna rubbed her hands together slowly, reminding Beatrice of when Astrid rolled the bloody threads into a ball in her palms. "I didn't want to do this, but he was right. I have to."

Minna began chanting the words of the auto-writing spell.

Fine, while she did that, maybe Beatrice could figure out how to get them both out of here—

But something was wrong. The spell was being said inside her own chest. Taurus was there, his voice reverberating against her lungs, mixing with Minna's higher voice.

Beatrice's own lips began to move. She pressed her fingers against her mouth, but she couldn't stop the spell from slipping out between her teeth. "*Bent canth ilno trill—*"

Minna was helping him take over her body.

Maybe that had been his plan all along. He obviously couldn't read her thoughts, or he'd already have seen the cursed sigil in her mind, so he needed her to write it down.

But she wouldn't. If she had to throw herself against the marble walls until she knocked herself out, she would, and no matter what, she wouldn't imagine—she would *not* imagine—no, she wouldn't—

Her hand cramped, and she looked down. Somehow, she was holding an old-fashioned fountain pen, dripping with dark red ink.

Minna kicked a notebook toward her, sliding it through the dust on the marble floor.

Fine. They wanted her to auto-write? She'd fake it, then.

She'd fake it so well that Taurus would believe it, and somehow she'd get Minna out of here if she had to grind through the stone walls with her teeth.

Dropping to sit cross-legged, she picked up the notebook. "I don't know why you want this, but okay."

She drew a square and then fit a slim oval into it. A peaked roof—the crypt, with Minna inside it. Maybe if she could draw a door crumbling to dust—

But the chant kept going, kept sounding inside her chest and, *no, please, no*, she wouldn't—she wouldn't

she wouldn't imagine the pen slipping into the lock she wouldn't—

no she couldn't she wouldn't—

A girl's laugh bounced off the walls, and Beatrice's eyes flew open.

She'd fucking done it, hadn't she?

Yes. She knew she had, could feel the spent, empty place in her core. Looking down, she saw the full sigil, captured on the page. She'd drawn the sigil of the lost twin, the one that held the long-ago-stripped-away Velamen power.

Her fingers flexed and clutched, but she couldn't hold on to the notebook—it was ripped out of her hands, flying across the small space into Minna's hands.

Now Taurus had what he needed. Now Minna would be able to complete the tattoo.

It wouldn't make any difference now if Beatrice tore the book away from her—Minna had seen it. That was all she needed.

The gun whined frantically. Minna glanced over her shoulder. "He'll get to hug me," she said almost apologetically. There she was again, the true Minna, the one Beatrice couldn't lose. "It's my first tattoo, Auntie Bea."

"Please. Don't do this."

Minna grimaced as she pushed the needle against her skin. "It kinda hurts more than I thought it would."

Of course it did. It was more than a tattoo—it was the curse that would bind Minna to him.

A rumble rose below the whine of the tattoo gun.

Taurus. Beatrice could feel him. The coldness. The sheer fury of him.

Minna blinked quickly, a tear streaking down her cheek. But she smiled. "He's getting stronger."

"I'm here." Taurus's voice wasn't just in their heads anymore—it was audible in the air now, a booming, hollow pulse.

"Daddy." Minna moved the gun faster. "I'm doing it."

"I'm so proud of you, my son."

No.

His words hit the air and bounced off the marble, echoing again and again, becoming crueler every time. *My son, son, son…*

Minna's hand stilled as her head dropped.

Beatrice could almost see the pain shoot through her body. "Honey, you can still stop. Don't complete it. Drop the tool."

Her niece's hand shook so badly that Beatrice could see the ink skip on her skin. Good. If the tattoo was broken, damaged somehow, would it not work?

That was it—she'd break the gun. Why hadn't she thought of that? It was probably strong, but so was she, and while Taurus was now a real voice, he didn't have a real body. She'd only be fighting Minna. And this was a fight she would need to win.

She leaped toward Minna. Or rather, she tried to.

Her legs, though, didn't move. Her body froze as solid as it had in the cemetery when Minna had run away. She could breathe, and she felt her heart pounding in her chest, so presumably blood was still circulating in her veins, but any movement that was usually under her conscious control was impossible. She couldn't even blink.

And everything hurt—each muscle in her body felt strained to the breaking point, as if the supernatural tension placed on them was what kept her from moving. The only part of her that didn't hurt was the spot on her wrist where Naya's new sigil was tattooed.

When Minna had put it on her—how could it have only been yesterday?—Beatrice had felt Naya inside her. No matter what illusions Taurus had created today, Naya *had* been with her yesterday. She had sent them the letters in the bottle as confirmation. Taurus couldn't have faked that.

Beatrice had to believe.

Minna was sobbing now, but her hand still moved the tattoo gun along her left forearm, faster and faster. It wouldn't be long now before the cursed sigil was complete. Then it would be inside Minna's body, just as Naya's tattoo was inside Beatrice's, flowing through her veins.

The image of the *S* on Reno's chest rose in Beatrice's mind. The dead body of Scarlett, her ash, was now part of Reno's living body because of the tattoo.

She tried to suck in a deeper breath. *Move.*

The dust in this tomb—it was the dust of their ancestors. Sure, probably some of it was made of dead spiders and crumbling marble, but a big part of it would undoubtedly be microscopic bits of Anna's and Rosalind's bodies floating out of the cracks of the crumbling tomb. Some of the particles were bound to be getting into the wound Minna was dragging into her skin. Would that help or hinder the power Taurus hoped to take?

Beatrice's heart rate was too fast now, so fast she saw silver flashes of stars at the edges of her vision, but it wasn't as if she could sit down and put her head between her knees.

The corrugated spite of Taurus's laugh ricocheted in her head.

No one else was coming to save Minna. Even if Beatrice's text went through, what would they do, hire a bulldozer to knock their way into the tomb? Surely Taurus would have strengthened the spell Beatrice had broken to get in.

It was up to her.

Evie's words came flooding back. *Sometimes we have to act before we think. Sometimes that means we get arrested for indecent exposure, but other times it means we're following Spirit. There are times when the only thing to do is to act before thinking a single damn thought.*

Act without thinking. Act without knowledge.

Act without even being able to move.

A sigil was simply a symbol imbued with energy.

She'd drawn one with bubbles, and it had worked.

So, then, she would draw a symbol with the only thing she had left.

Her mind.

Beatrice's eyes stayed open because she couldn't close them. But Minna faded from her sight as she went inward.

With every ounce of will she had left, Beatrice placed a whiteboard in her mind. She chose the one from her home office, the triple-size one that she used daily. In her mind, she erased the calendar and her to-do list. Then she focused on the new lines she drew with her mind.

She drew a capital *B* and made the top and bottom holes into a pair of handcuffs. *The simplest spells are the strongest.*

Carefully, she drew a horizontal line through the middle of the *B*. That was the fuse.

Her breathing continued, autonomous. She could neither take a deeper breath nor hold one. But she could *picture* blowing air out of her mouth, flammable air that took only one flick of an imagined yellow lighter to light the end of that fuse.

The line through the *B* wobbled as it burned.

And then the midsection blew, separating the *B*-shaped handcuffs.

Beatrice was free. She blinked as she fell sideways, catching herself painfully against the marble chair underneath Anna's name.

In front of her, Minna swam back into focus. She'd slumped, and sweat mixed with the tears rolling down her face. "I can't make it stop," she whispered in Beatrice's direction. "Tell Mom I'm sorry."

Beatrice leaped at Minna, but the tattoo gun made one last buzz, connecting the tip of the teardrop to the scale, before clattering to the floor.

Minna collapsed sideways.

Frantically, she grabbed Minna's shoulders. "No. *No.*"

But the sigil was complete. A cold wind kicked up the dust inside the tomb, and Minna's body slumped, as Beatrice heard her last breath leave her lungs.

Beatrice knew what to do.

Finally, she knew *exactly* what to do. She'd done so many CPR certification classes, just to be on the safe side, that she knew more about the recent Heart Association changes than some of the instructors did. She knew she should flip Minna from her side to her back and start compressions. With a huge amount of luck, that would get Minna's heart started, and it would have to, because it wasn't like she could call an ambulance, but maybe if she screamed so loud, the sound made it through the slab of marble…

But she didn't flip Minna in order to start compressions.

She didn't do the one thing she knew she should do.

Instead, she stood.

She threw back her head.

And then Beatrice roared, "Give her back, you fucking son of a *bitch*."

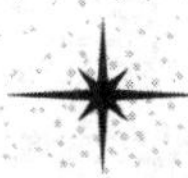

CHAPTER FIFTY-TWO

Sometimes the ones we hear from are the angry ones. Take care with them. For a soul to manage to stay angry once they understand the magnificent workings of the Universe, well. That's not fun for anyone.

—*Evie Oxby,* Palm Springs and Bat Wings, *Netflix*

The wind in the tomb increased, the dust thickening in the air. Beatrice could feel that Taurus was furious, and she didn't know why—hadn't he just gotten exactly what he wanted? His daughter?

No, he wanted the son he'd never had. He could get fucked and die, except that had already happened, and now what?

Now Beatrice knew nothing, except that she had to move, and move fast. Minna had—what—four minutes of not breathing before brain damage started to set in? Eight minutes and she'd be gone forever.

Beatrice had one motherfucking miracle left to spend.

What she didn't have was time to figure out the right way to do this.

There was only one way. Somehow, she'd *make* that way right.

She dropped to her knees, ignoring the howl of the wind that grew in her ears. It didn't matter if it was an illusion or real. She didn't care.

The fountain pen—there it was. It felt perfect in her hand. Red ink still dripped from it, but she honestly didn't need the ink.

She needed the dust.

Moving as fast as she could, she scraped her palm underneath the marble bench to her right until she had a handful of dust and dirt. *Grandmother Rosalind. Great-grandmother Anna. I need you now.* She plunged the pen's nib into the dust. *I am the lost twin. Baby Louise, wherever you are. Help me. All of you, please help me now.*

Then, Beatrice became the padlock.

She drove the nib into the flesh of her thigh, shoving the dust into her skin with it. She drew the cursed sigil into her own skin, claiming it. She wouldn't *let* Minna have it. It was hers. Beatrice was the one who'd unsealed the page—she owned it.

The lines Minna had drawn on her own skin were thin. Beatrice's lines, on the other hand, were thick and sure. Her blood didn't pool, it poured. It surged.

And she felt them—Anna and Rosalind Holland—she felt their power enter her with the ash of their long-crumbled bones. *Be brave, daughter.*

She pushed the pen harder with more assurance. It hurt like hellfire, but she'd endure it for eternity if it meant Minna would catch her breath again.

Then Louise was with her, too, a soft petal of touch on her cheek. *Move faster. Do it for your twin. For her daughter.*

Taurus's voice was deafening. "*Stop.*"

"Fuck!" She paused briefly to look up toward the ceiling, where the sound came from. "You!"

The broken scale was complete—now she needed the other

lines. She'd gone so deep, her flesh tearing, that it would be difficult for anyone to understand the sigil's lines because of the blood, but it didn't matter.

It was her sigil.

Hers.

Not Minna's.

She was taking it back.

Taurus was screaming then, threatening her, but somehow, as she pushed the metal nib through her skin, she was able to tune him out.

You will die for love.

Oh, shit—oh, shit! Through the pain, through the noise, through the fear that was so strong, she didn't how she'd live through it, Beatrice realized what the curse actually meant.

She'd gotten it wrong.

It wasn't *YOU WILL DIE for love.* She'd focused on the wrong thing, the death part.

It was *You will die FOR LOVE.* She'd almost missed the deeper meaning—the curse was about making a trade. Death, traded for love.

She could trade *her* life for Minna's.

This was how she would spend her seventh miracle.

Perhaps, if she'd puzzled over the sigil with Cordelia and Astrid for months, they would have figured out what it meant. They could have conjectured and wondered and studied for as long as it took.

But by acting, by just doing the thing, the answer had been revealed.

The pain was past anything she'd ever felt. Every muscle shook as she got ready to connect the very last line, and every fiber in her body shrieked with agony as the sigil took hold. Even feeling her ancestors moving through her blood didn't help. But it didn't matter.

It was all for Minna.

"Give her back to me, *now.*"

A growl echoed throughout the chamber, and she saw him then, a ragged black shape in the candlelight that widened and thinned as it breathed, its lungs sounding like flapping wings, its form composed of ropes of smoke. Taurus was gaining power, sucking it from Minna, leaching the last strength from her dying body.

Something smashed outside the tomb, as if someone was trying to break their way in.

There was no time to wait for a savior, though. Just this one final line to cut into her skin—

Taurus was on her then, wresting the pen out of her grasp, sending it flying through the air and smashing into the marble wall. The pen shattered into a million pieces.

No.

"You've lost." His forearm pressed against her shoulder—he felt both real and noncorporeal at the same time, there but hollow, as if he weren't completely assembled yet. His breath was guttural and foul. "Come with us. If you offer us your power willingly, it becomes stronger. That said, I'm happy to take it off you by force."

A weapon. She needed some kind of weapon.

The pen had shattered. That left only the tattoo gun.

It still lay next to Minna, both of them silent, both of them getting colder by the second.

Beatrice shoved against—no, *through* Taurus—and grabbed the tattoo gun. She felt the malignancy of him rushing toward her, around her, as if he were in front and behind her—the smoke of him was all around and there was no time.

A simple spell. She might have only half a second left. Less.

She closed her eyes and let it come: the whisper, in Naya's voice. Naya's real voice? Her only option was to trust that it was.

Make your mark, kill the dark.

She said Naya's words out loud as she shoved the gun into the darkness that was the sooty cloud of Taurus's malformed body. The tool buzzed to life, the energy roaring up her arm and into her chest. The scream that rose was such agony that she couldn't tell if it came from her or Taurus. Her ribs felt as if they were ripping apart, bone from sinew. Pain darkened her vision and she gave a tortured gasp. In her hand, the whirring gun felt slick, as if coated with blood.

As hard as she could, Beatrice drove the vibrating needle upward into the black energy of Taurus.

He shrieked, a torn and ragged sound that drained all hope from the world.

His shape contracted, shifting, breaking.

Then, Taurus simply shredded, drifting apart into thin black ribbons that curled into acrid smoke. The scream continued for another few seconds, but he was gone so fast, the room felt as if a vacuum seal had been broken.

Fuck.

Minna's face was whiter than the marble she lay on and exactly as still. No life moved in her. The trade for Minna's life hadn't yet been completed. The sigil Beatrice had cut on her thigh wasn't yet done. Minna still wasn't breathing—more than a minute had passed now, maybe ninety seconds.

There wasn't a single second to spare. Not a second to say good-bye to her sister, to let go of the people she loved.

Only Minna mattered.

The last miracle—it was time to spend it.

With the gun chattering in her fingers, Beatrice scored the last piece of the sigil into her skin, connecting the line of the teardrop to the scale.

CHAPTER FIFTY-THREE

Death is the biggest surprise of all.

—*Evie Oxby,* Come at Me, Boo

Everything stopped.

All sound—gone.

All pain—lifted.

Could she feel anything at all? Of any sort? Beatrice wasn't sure if she could. She wasn't in a body, or if she was, she wasn't sure she fit inside it.

She wasn't uncomfortable.

Neither was she comfortable.

She just...was.

The space around her wasn't light, and it wasn't dark. She couldn't see, but she couldn't not see, either.

She knew one thing, though. She didn't like it. Any rhapsodic glory that should have been on the other side seemed to be sorely missing. Maybe she'd taken some kind of wrong turn on her way here?

She was frightened, the kind of terror that might make her

limbs shake, but she didn't seem to *have* any body parts, exactly, so the emotion ran through her with no obvious way for it to exit.

What the hell was she supposed to do next?

Somewhere close to her non-body, a voice spoke. "Hey, you."

It was the sweetest sound Beatrice had ever heard. "Cordelia?"

"I'm right here, sister."

Cordelia's voice.

The voice of love.

"I can't see you."

"That's okay. I'm right here."

"I'm scared."

"I know you are. But you don't have to be."

"How do you know?"

"Because I know some stuff."

Her sister's voice was so close to her that Beatrice felt like she could lean on it. So she did. And to her surprise, the sound was solid and warm, and whatever kind of non-body Beatrice was in, she found that the soft support was exactly what she needed. "Keep talking to me?"

"You can't get this wrong. I'm here with you. I'm not going anywhere."

"What do I do next?"

"Well." A pause. "People do different things. What do you want to do?"

"I want Minna to be okay."

"Oh." Her sister's voice broke. "Minna's okay. I promise you."

"Really?"

"You saved her."

"I did?"

"She's breathing again. She's awake. She's going to be fine. And now you get to choose what to do." Her sister's voice was tight around her words.

Beatrice didn't have a choice. Not anymore. She didn't know much, but if Taurus came for her in here—wherever here was—she'd keep fighting. The Velamens couldn't have their girl.

But she was so tired.

"Beatrice?"

"How do I keep them from taking my power?"

"They can't take it. Taurus is gone."

"Dead?"

"More than dead. Totally gone."

"Really? You're not just telling me that?"

"I'm not going to waste the time we have right now lying to you. I promise."

"How much time do we have?"

"That depends on what you do next."

"Like, walk to the light, that kind of shit?" If Beatrice had known where her hands were, she would have slapped them over her mouth for swearing in this . . . whatever this place was, but she didn't, so she let it go.

"Do you see a light?"

"I don't think so."

But she was wrong—there was a sudden flash of light and a wallop of pain that filled the body she was used to being in. "Come on, Beatrice!" shouted a hoarse voice she couldn't quite place.

Someone screamed—was it her?—and then she was back in the quieter place again.

Deliberately, she took a beat to breathe.

Except . . . she wasn't exactly breathing. But she wasn't *not* breathing.

Cordelia was still with her here; she could feel it. "What was that? What just happened?"

Her sister's voice was tighter than it had been, but her words seemed unhurried. "It... it seems like you might be hanging out in an in-between place."

"What does that *mean*?"

"I think it means you have a choice."

Stay here.

Go back.

"But I used the last miracle to save Minna. That was the seventh."

Someone gave a kind laugh, but it didn't come from Cordelia.

It was Naya's laugh. Beatrice would know it anywhere, and this time it was unclouded by Taurus's energy. It was that happy chortle Naya made when Beatrice was *this* close to figuring something out for herself. The first time she balanced on her bike long enough to turn the pedals. When she'd swum a whole lap without the water wings. When she'd paid off the last scrap of her student debt.

But Naya didn't say anything. She was just here. Close by.

Loving her.

This might be a nice place to stay. If Naya was here, that was a plus-ten in the pro column, for sure.

What, then, did Naya think she was about to figure out?

Then it came to her. Using the sigil to save Minna hadn't been a miracle. It hadn't been an unearned gift. "That was magic?"

"Oh, sister," said Cordelia, with even more joy in her voice than Naya's laugh had held. "Exactly. That was just magic, not a miracle. You fought Taurus. You used the sigil in the trade to save Minna, but you defeated Taurus. You destroyed his soul completely, cutting off his connection with the other Velamens. You negated the need for the trade to be complete." There was a slight pause. "You negated the need for the trade to be final."

"Really?" A tendril of hope bloomed somewhere deep inside Beatrice's non-body.

"I think you might have one more miracle waiting for you. If you want it."

Oh.

Oh!

Minna's sweet face, and the rapturous look she got when she couldn't fit all her excitement into her skin, when it exploded out of her in bounces and exclamations and awkward, too-tight hugs.

Cordelia's hands with the yarn trailing through them, the way she held together her world and moonlighted by spending time here, wherever here was. Forty-five long years ago, she and Cordelia had lived someplace like this, swimming through a void side by side. They'd been together, and that had been enough. Beatrice had missed her every moment since then, but hadn't recognized it as loss until now.

Reno's eyes. The grief she bore like a war wound, the way she thought she shouldn't be trusted even though she was trust itself. Her stillness. The joy that shimmered just under her skin.

"I want..."

Knowledge. Understanding. Certainty.

But—she'd had plenty of that in her life.

And none of that knowledge or learning had ever given her any control over a single damn thing. Ever.

First, she spoke to Naya. "I'm sorry I wasn't there for you at the end."

You were there. Naya's words weren't audible, exactly, but they rang clear. *And it wasn't the end.*

"I love you."

I know.

Then, she spoke to her sister. It came out in a whisper, but it came out.

"I want to live without needing the knowing."

The pain came then.

CHAPTER FIFTY-FOUR

> I don't know what happens when you pass over. I only have some guesses. But I have to say, I think it might turn out to be a good time.
>
> —*Evie Oxby, in conversation with Michelle Obama*

It wasn't like in the movies, at least not as far as she could tell. Beatrice didn't wake up in the hospital with a small moan, only to spend long minutes figuring out where she was by puzzling over the beeps and IV lines.

No, she woke up hard and fast and *loud*.

And she woke up so panicked that it took two nurses and one grumpy-looking orderly to hold her in the bed that first time. She couldn't scream. Had they taken her voice completely? But she knew exactly where she was—a hospital. And she knew what she wanted—to get out of it as fast as possible.

Apparently after a major skin graft to her upper thigh, getting out quickly wasn't an option.

Every time she woke up punching things, they slipped another cocktail into her IV and she slept again. The sleep wasn't restful, though. Desperately, she wanted that deliciously lightweight nothing-feeling of the in-between place she'd shared with Cordelia. Instead, she got nightmares and hallucinations. Taurus loomed over her, the tattoo gun rattled, and Minna stopped breathing over and over again.

But in between punching sessions and nightmares, sometimes she had a few minutes of holding someone's hand.

Sometimes it was her father's hand. She'd never seen him cry, not even when Naya had died. Then, his eyes had just been red all the time with the heat of unshed tears. Now? He cried. Then he laughed. Then he cried again.

Once, it was Iris. "I'm so glad you're awake," she said. "Oh, babe, I'm so glad you're alive. Don't ever do that to us again, you hear me?"

Sometimes the person next to her when she woke up was Cordelia. Her sister.

Her sister.

Cordelia held her hand the way Beatrice would have held Cordelia's, had her twin been in the bed. She got confused occasionally, thinking Cordelia was in the bed and she, Beatrice, was sitting with her as she recuperated. They talked constantly, Beatrice nodding and murmuring, her voice becoming stronger as Cordelia spoke. At first, they talked about Taurus and saving Minna, turning it over again and again, making sure they hadn't missed a single detail. It turned out Beatrice still liked to understand things.

"But it was out of order," insisted Beatrice. "Seven miracles, and then I would die. That didn't happen. It was six miracles, then I died, then a miracle let me come back." What if it had all gone wrong because of the wrong order, and she was only a moment from losing everything again?

It was Evie Oxby, of all people, who cleared it up. She and

Cordelia were in the same Facebook group (Beatrice had boggled). *I didn't say seven miracles and* then *she'd die. I told her "You're going to experience seven miracles. And you will die." I honestly didn't think the order would matter that much.*

In the end, the order had been perfect.

Eventually, Beatrice and Cordelia talked about other things, from their favorite childhood foods (they'd both loved Top Ramen with the addition of frozen peas), to the make and color of their first cars (used purple Honda Civics). But even when they stopped talking, the conversation didn't cease. For Beatrice, just being next to Cordelia felt like a discussion. It was the conversation she had come back to keep having.

When she was strong enough to ask what had happened, Cordelia said, "Reno was the one who brought you back. I was busy being with you in the middle space, and Astrid was busy casting spell after spell of healing and protection on both you and Minna. But Reno started CPR instantly. She didn't let up until the paramedics got there. A firefighter had to physically tear her off of you so someone else could take over."

But Reno didn't visit. Beatrice never woke up to find that Reno was the one holding her hand.

Sometimes, though, even Astrid came. No hand-holding, of course. The first few times, they sat together in awkward silence until Astrid said briskly, "Well, I left a concoction for you on your tray. See if that male nurse will give it to you with your water—he's sensitive enough that he might be on our team. Or just tell him it's powdered electrolytes; I don't care."

The next time she visited, Astrid brought the grimoire with her. "Thought I might read you some spells. Tell you what I think of them. How to do them right." Relieved, Beatrice nodded, and as Astrid told her how to warm raindrops on a chilly day, she realized that maybe she was a *tiny* bit like her mother. Maybe.

One afternoon, as Beatrice came out of a nap, she opened her eyes to see Astrid staring at her, with tears running down her face.

Unable to stop herself, Beatrice held out her hand. “It’s okay,” she whispered.

Astrid grabbed her hand, holding it tightly. “I’m sorry.”

“I know. Thank you.”

“You don’t even know for what.” Astrid sniffed. “I could be sorry for giving you that rather crooked top lip.”

“I love my crooked top lip.” Beatrice was saying something else, of course.

And Astrid heard it. She nodded. “I’m glad.” She stood and gave her one swift kiss on the forehead. “I’m very, very glad.” The moment of vulnerability passed like a summer thunderstorm, and Astrid swept dramatically away, leaving the scent of cinnamon and cranberry in her wake.

Winnie came by and gave her a tarot reading. She said when the Death card came up that it only meant change, and Beatrice just laughed, choosing to believe her. What choice did she have? Fritz was with her, and the besotted looks they tossed each other were so wholesome, they helped Beatrice’s stitches itch less.

Keelia came by to give her the Book Concierge. She spent an hour getting Beatrice’s reading preferences, and then she brought book after book, laughing when Beatrice insisted that she hadn’t even gotten through the preface of the last one she’d left. “You won’t always sleep this much. Never too many books. Oh, I just thought of two more you need to read! I’ll bring those tomorrow.”

Often, Minna was there. When Beatrice awoke to her niece, Minna always gave a small, shrill scream before racing into the hallway to yell at any nurse who might be passing by, “*She’s awake!*” Then she’d scuttle back and refuse to let go of Beatrice’s hand while the staff did the things they had to do. Best was when Minna didn't ask her a single question, just rattled on about everything and nothing. Still finding it hard to talk in those first few days, Beatrice raised a hand, waggling her fingers in the air. Minna got it immediately. "You want your nails done? Oh, my god, yes. I'll do them today! The solar system! You want the solar system? I did that on Olive's nails yesterday and it looks amazing." Minna clutched Beatrice's hand in her own, crushing it with excitement, and Beatrice was instantly dragged back to sleep from the sheer exhaustion of the joy running through her body.

A few days later, when Minna was next to her, reading a fantasy novel in a library dust jacket, Beatrice spoke through chapped lips. "What if I called myself Beatrix?"

Minna dropped the book into her lap. "I love that name. But I thought you preferred Beatrice. Wait, why are you asking me?"

Beatrice's hospital gown felt tight around her neck. "Because it would be me going back to a birth name. Kind of the opposite of what you had to do to become who you really are."

"Would calling yourself Beatrix feel more authentic to who you are?"

Beatrice balances budgets, color-codes Post-its, and can't see what's in front of her.

Beatrix chants spells, communicates with the dead, and saves her loved ones from destruction.

"Maybe?"

"Then try it." Minna's expression fell. "Um, I've been meaning to say. I'm really sorry I lied to you. About all that stuff I did."

"It's okay. I get it."

"You do?" She blinked.

"I do."

A huge grin was Beatrix's reward. Minna said, "I could still call you Aunt Bea, but I could *also* call you Auntie Trix, and that would be even better."

Beatrix it was, then. She'd explain it to people later, when she was stronger again.

Reno would probably like it.

Not that she was worrying about what Reno thought of her name.

Not really.

Then, one morning, right when she was about to give up hope, Beatrix opened her eyes. She felt warmer and better than she had so far.

Reno was—finally—the one holding her hand.

"I've been looking for you," said Beatrix. She'd done more than that—she'd tried the Push-Me-Pull-You a few days before. It hadn't worked, maybe because Reno hadn't been there to physically pull? It had just left her exhausted.

"Here I am," said Reno.

"Where were you?"

"Close by. I told you. I'd been waiting."

Her heart rate sped up. Embarrassing, since they could both hear it beeping on the monitor behind them. "For me?"

Reno nodded. "And I almost lost you." She rubbed her chest. "Wasn't sure I could trust myself to handle that."

Beatrix squeezed her hand. "I trust you."

"I know."

"Don't let me go again, then."

With a duck of her head, Reno said, "I'm sorry I doubted you."

"Apology accepted. I'm sorry I kept things from you."

Reno's acceptance was in her kiss, which was soft and controlled, with the assurance of hard and wild to come. Beatrix, if asked, would have ranked it her best kiss ever, but she wasn't asked, so she just kept kissing Reno in relief and joy and the promise of something much, much deeper.

And of course, Minna tumbled into the room just as that promise started to heat up.

"Oh, no! Ew!"

Reno pulled her head away but stayed close to the bed, her fingers firmly entangled with Beatrix's. "You have the worst timing."

Minna stuck out her tongue. "And you have the *best* timing apparently. Aunt Bea, did you know the paramedics told Reno that her CPR was, like, perfect? I saw on TikTok that 'About Damn Time' by Lizzo is 109 beats per minute, which is perfect timing for compressions. Were you thinking of that?"

"I absolutely was not," said Reno. "But it's good to know."

"Auntie, did you know she gave you mouth-to-mouth, too? Shades of Sleeping Beauty, right? Although we might have to chat about enthusiastic consent again."

Reno dropped a slow wink toward Beatrix. "I will hereby respond only to Prince Charming from here on out."

Cordelia pushed her way past the hanging curtain into the room. "I fucking *hate* Disney." She smiled at Beatrix and dropped a bag on a chair. "You look bright today."

Astrid was right on her heels, apparently finishing up a complaint about the smell of bleach in the elevator. "I'll just take the stairs next time. And I'm going to write the board a letter."

"Have fun with that," said Cordelia. "Where's Dad?"

Something jolted inside Beatrix's chest. Cordelia was referring to Mitchell as Dad now? And Astrid...would know the answer to that question? They'd told Beatrix she'd been in the hospital about a week—how had that been enough time for all of these changes?

Holy hell, was Astrid actually blushing? "He went to get us bagels."

Cordelia humphed. "Went to get *her* a bagel, she means."

"Well." Astrid tried to plump the pillow that was still caught behind Beatrix's head. "He might be less of an idiot than I thought."

"Oh, my god," said Beatrix.

Astrid snapped, "At least swear to the goddess, can't you?"

Minna perched carefully at the foot of the bed on the side of Beatrix's good leg. "Your dad is really nice."

There was so much behind those words, an echo of her loss.

"I'm so sorry," said Beatrix. "I really am."

Minna straightened. "I know. But I never knew my father. He would have killed me and destroyed my soul."

So I did the same to him. The thought still frightened Beatrix though she regretted nothing. "Still. You deserved a better father."

Minna looked at her nails, now painted bright blue, as blue as the sky. Her expression shifted, sliding to something softer, sadder. "I...I got my power from my father, so I kind of want to know what I can do about that."

Cordelia had begun balling a skein of yarn, but her head shot up. "Ex*cuse* me?"

"You said." Minna looked past her mother, fixing her eyes on Astrid. "You said their power was patrilineal and passed down through the males in a family. So that might...that might be a good thing, right? Like, maybe I can learn to combine my powers with the ones you taught me?"

"Oh, screw *that*—" started Cordelia.

But Astrid held her hand. "Our power is matrilineal."

"I know, Gran—"

"I *said*, Minna, our power is matrilineal, and our power is passed from female to female." Her voice was fierce. "Your strength comes from all the women who came before you. The twin power your mother and aunt share is strong, but mark my words, you'll be the strongest woman of all of us. Never, *ever* doubt that, child."

A lump rose in Beatrix's throat.

Careful not to jostle Beatrix's legs, Minna stood and threw her arms around Astrid. "Love you, Gran."

Astrid gave her a swift peck on the cheek. "Obviously. Cordelia, did you bring that embroidered sigil you flubbed last night for me to fix?"

If one wasn't looking closely, as Beatrix was, one could easily miss the fact that Cordelia had tears in her eyes as she reached for her project bag. "Yeah, Mom. I did."

"Who sent those flowers?" Instantly recovered, Minna was bouncing around the room touching things, as usual. "They're *hyyooooge*."

"Grant and Dulcina."

Cordelia's eyebrows shot up. "Really."

"It's fine. I love orchids in a bouquet mix." On Naya's hot pepper scale, she'd felt the anger of a bell pepper dipped in mayonnaise when they'd been delivered.

Minna smelled the unscented orchid and wrinkled her nose. "They don't smell like anything, but they sure are gorgeous."

"Agreed. So. What's next, then?" Beatrix wasn't addressing anyone in particular. She just liked a plan. Reno's hand was still warm in Beatrix's, solid and real and perfect.

"Well." Astrid scowled at a tangle of embroidery floss. "You have a lot to learn."

"Thank goddess," said Beatrix Holland.

ACKNOWLEDGMENTS

As always, huge thanks go first to my agent, Susanna Einstein, who *really* understands twins (and me). And to Kirsiah Depp, thanks for your keen eye and your belief! My gratitude also to Theresa Stevens and Catriona Turner, for your gorgeous editorial brains. I couldn't have written this book without Monna McDiarmid's gentle encouragement—thank you, my sweet friend. Thanks to Dharma Kelleher for doing a great (and swift!) sensitivity read. To my sister Christy, thanks for being my psychic buddy. And to my sister Bethany, the nonbeliever, thanks for humoring us. To Lala, my true love, always. And to Sal, thanks for (literally) everything.

AUTHOR'S NOTE

I've always wanted to believe in magic.

Just as Beatrice did as a kid, I used to stand in the backyard on an old stump and close my eyes, just *waiting* to lift off. In my recurring dreams of flight, it was always so easy. I didn't flap like a graceless bird; instead, I floated upward smoothly, the way a soap bubble did, iridescent in the sun.

I spent a lot of time on that dang stump, waiting for the moment I became weightless. I planned to drift over the treetops, rising and falling as I desired, touching back down to earth with a graceful glide that would probably impress Mrs. Ross, my pretty second-grade teacher.

Reader, I never floated. No matter how hard I concentrated, gravity remained a thorny, unsolvable problem.

Most writers, of course, can't help inserting bits of themselves into the characters they write. Like Beatrice, I believed in magic when I was young before I stopped, becoming obsessed in the same way she is with safety and spreadsheets and planning.

Eventually, like her, I found my belief in wonder again through the power of love. (Yes, it's cheesy. But it's true.)

And please know that I didn't base Reno on my wife, Lala (though they both look fantastic in slouchy beanies and flannel). But the subconscious will have its way, and I had no idea Reno was a widow until she told me on the page.

Two years before I met Lala, her wife, Aura, died of swift-moving melanoma.

The story of how this young widow and I fell in love is—truly—magical.

We met in our early thirties. It was supposed to be a casual thing, but we were engaged after six months (cue U-Haul–spiced laughter). As I learned about Lala, I learned about Aura, and I couldn't get enough of the Aura stories. She had been one of those sparkly, larger-than-life people, a drop-dead gorgeous red-head smarter than anyone else in the room, bound for law school and stratospheric success. Everyone loved her.

Even though I'd never met her, *I* loved her. My favorite story about her was how, after she'd died, her actually evil stepmother had been playing Scrabble on the porch with Aura's best friend. A bee insistently dive-bombed the stepmother until she screamed her way inside, and the four tiles left behind on her rack spelled *AURA*.

I was bereft that I'd never gotten to meet her. Everyone said we would have loved each other, and I felt it, too. By then, I was deeply in love with Lala, but I frequently said, "I wish Aura had lived. I'd trade *us* for you to have her, for you to never have known this pain." I wasn't being noble—I was simply being in love. I would have done anything to take away Lala's pain, including giving up the greatest love I'd ever known.

One day, I went shopping. Now, I've never been a shopper. Malls horrify me, and I'd rather eat barbed wire than spend a morning trying on clothes. But that day was different. I *shopped.* The whole time, I was thinking of Aura, wondering what she would like, what she would have tried on, what a day of shopping and gossiping with her would have been like.

When Lala came to my place that night, she gasped.

I was wearing my new pink sweater and a short pink skirt. To complete the look, I even had sparkly pink mules that clacked when I walked. I didn't know how to read Lala's face, though. Did she like how I looked? Did she hate it? "What do you think?"

"You look great," she said. "You look hot. And so...pink. I've never seen you wear pink."

"I usually hate it." I didn't mean to say it, but I blurted out, "I think I went shopping with Aura. Did she like pink?"

Lala dropped into a chair, still staring. "It was her favorite color. She loved it with her red hair."

I hadn't known that.

She asked, "How was the shopping?"

"The most fun I've ever had in a mall."

Lala laughed. "Sounds about right."

A few months later, I awoke after having a beautiful dream in which I'd tried on a long evening gown covered in sparkly green seed beads. I'd tried it on to get Aura's opinion, but when I looked in the mirror, I hated how it hung on me. I insisted she try it on, and she was *radiant* in it, her hair glowing above the glittering seed beads, her face overjoyed. "It's yours. Keep it," I insisted. "This dress was made for you."

When I woke up, I desperately wanted to find my way back into the dream, which had been so warm and real. Lala's eyes opened, and I told her the dream.

Then I started to rise from bed and felt something on the sheet. I picked it up and stared.

One solitary, sparkling green seed bead.

Neither Lala nor I could ever figure out where it came from. It matched nothing we'd ever owned or worn or even seen. We kept it in a shallow dish next to the bed.

We started to plan our wedding, and oh, we were *broke*. We were pockets-empty, eating-beans broke. So we put a deposit on the cheapest hall in the hills of Oakland and decided the dinner would be a potluck. A friend was going to bake our cake, and another would play photographer.

Lala wanted only a wedding ring. I wanted an engagement ring, though, and in Berkeley, we finally found one that we could afford, an Edwardian filigreed band with five teeny diamond chips. The name of the store was, of course, Aura Jewelers. By then, it didn't even surprise me.

Just before we got married, my mother asked me what our wedding rings looked like.

"Eh," I said. "I'll just use my engagement ring." We hadn't bought a wedding ring for Lala yet, still searching under couch cushions for the money to buy one.

"Oh, no, really?"

"We can't afford anything else. A ring is a ring, though. Right?"

"Why don't I send the family rings to you? You can each choose one."

We're not the kind of family that has Important Family Rings, but Mom had a small collection of gold bands passed down from aunts and cousins long gone. Each was worn thin by time, and around each ring were pieces of tape that read things like *Cousin Lucy* and *Grandma Moore*.

Immediately, I fell in love with another filigreed ring. It was two toned, a delicate platinum band fitted over old yellow gold that peeked around the edges. *Grandma Wilson*, it read. Lala chose the one labeled *Grandma Ashcroft*, plain gold, thick and sturdy.

I called Mom back, confused about the women who'd previously owned these rings. "Help me out. Grandma Wilson was your mom, right? But the Ashcroft one—is Lala's ring *your* grandmother's ring?"

I could hear the smile in her voice. "You chose my mother's ring from her second marriage. Lala chose her first ring, the one my dad gave her."

We'd chosen the same woman's rings. And Lala had chosen her widow's band.

Aura would have approved, I thought.

When we wrote our wedding invite list, we put Aura's name at the top, the very first to be invited. At the wedding, all the chairs in the front row were filled by family members except for one reserved empty chair we kept for her. Aura's best friend Jodi was our officiant. (Adorably, Jodi had obtained a minister's license, even though our wedding wasn't legal in any way, and wouldn't be for years.)

I knew Aura was there, dancing with us, part of the enchantment of that perfect night.

In *Seven Miracles*, Beatrice's sister, Cordelia, says, "Magic is the intentional transformation of energy to affect an outcome. A miracle, on the other hand, is an unearned gift."

Now, many years later, I choose magic daily. I pull tarot cards and let them (or my subconscious, it doesn't really matter) guide me through the day. Yesterday I pulled the five of swords, or as I like to call it, the *Don't be a dick* card. Remembering its advice saved me from picking a fight with Lala over the mess I thought she was making in the kitchen as she cooked me dinner. The chicken she made was incredible, rich and buttery, and we spent the entire meal happily groaning about how good it was. I could practically feel the alternate evening's squabble in the room with us, hanging in the air. The way it could have gone. When

I next walked past the five of swords card sitting face up on the shelf, I gave it a little pat. *Thanks. I remembered.*

That, to me, is magic. I use energy to intentionally transform and affect outcomes.

Miracles, though, are simply gifts, and I'm rich with them.

Twenty miraculous years have passed since Lala and I fell in love. That we still not only love each other but also *like* each other—another miracle. Honestly, most days with her, the love comes easy. And on the hard days, in the same way Beatrice decided to believe in magic (no proof needed), Lala and I make the same decision, over and over, to believe in this love.

For a long time, Aura visited me in my dreams. Then she just kind of…faded. I like to think that she's the kind who would become very busy and popular over there, wherever *there* is. Evie Oxby or Cordelia might have more information on what that space is like—I certainly have no idea.

But I know this: Very occasionally, I still feel Aura nearby. She usually visits when I'm holding Lala as she sleeps.

I've got her, I say to Aura. *I'm still here, loving her as hard as I can for both of us.*

Good, I think she says. *That's the job I chose you for. Keep it up.*

I need no proof.

I have love, which is, after all, the strongest magic of all.

Visit **GCPClubCar.com** to sign up for the GCP Club Car newsletter, featuring exclusive promotions, info on other Club Car titles, and more.

READING GROUP GUIDE

Discussion Questions

1. By the end of the book, Beatrice changes her name to Beatrix. What do you think is the significance to her adopting her original name? How does this book explore the importance of self-identity?
2. Beatrix's family all commune with the dead in some way, helping to guide themselves and others through their grief. Which of the Holland family's gifts do you think would help you work through your grief? Why?
3. When Beatrix finds out her husband has been cheating on her, she decides to go on their planned trip alone. Do you think this was a wise idea and something you would do? Why or why not?
4. Minna is unabashedly herself, even when others, like Astrid, question her. What kind of courage do you think it takes for someone so young to assert her identity, especially to her own family?

5. Reno has secluded herself from the rest of the town in her grief and fear of her own actions if she lets herself get close to anyone. Why do you think Beatrix is able to help Reno open up about her past and accept new love and friendship?
6. Minna is so desperate to connect with her father and gain his approval, she's willing to put her life, and the lives of her loved ones, on the line. Why do you think this is so important to Minna? What do her actions prove about the importance of family and love?
7. Cordelia knew about Beatrix her whole life, but never tried to find her. Why do you think that is?
8. Astrid made a really difficult decision to separate Beatrix and Cordelia when they were babies. Now knowing why, would you have done the same thing? Or do you think Astrid should've kept her family together? Why or why not?

Author Q & A

Q. What inspired you to write this story? Were there any personal inspirations or did you imagine everything on your own?
A. When thinking about writing a book, I ask myself what *I* want to read next. I try to imagine what would make me happiest to find on a bookstore shelf, and then I ask why I want it. For this book, I wanted sisters finding each other (my sisters and I have lived an ocean apart for the last three years), and I wanted a nonbeliever learning to believe in magic (basically, me!), and I wanted a sweetly unexpected love story. Once I knew those things, I wrote the book that pleased me most. Every time I got stuck, I asked myself—or my tarot cards—what would be the most fun thing to write next. Then I just followed along and got to know Beatrix and Cordelia and Minna and Reno, and the little town of Skerry Cove, which I want to visit!

Q. This is a hard question, but if you had to pick one character you like the most, who would it be? Why?

A. Oh, that's easy! I *love* Minna. I think it's because I was such a shy, scared kid, always worried about getting something—anything—wrong. I hid myself behind the louder, cooler kids, trying to remain unnoticed. Minna knows herself, and even though she has the normal adolescent problems (and some magical ones, too!), she knows exactly what she believes. She's not scared to share herself as who she truly is. I look up to her, and I'm so grateful we got to hang out in the pages of this book. I miss her already.

Q. What about witches interested you to write a novel about them?

A. Just like Minna, witches know who they are and what they believe in. They aren't one thing, of course—there are many schools of magical practice and belief. But overall, the witches I've known are confident, smart, and loving. They're good at loving themselves, too. What could be better than that? I don't claim the title of witch, but I'm certainly witch-adjacent—witch-ish, if you like. Reno borrowed my words when she talked about Sal, the truck stop waitress of the universe. Sal knows my order and she has my back. I don't call that force God and I don't need to understand how or why it works, but I believe in it. And here I am, being as brave as a witch, sharing that with you, here.

Q. What is your writing process like? Do you plot out everything in advance? Or do you let the story flow as you go along?

A. I definitely let it flow. I usually know something about the situation the main character ends up in, but I never know what's going to happen next. At the beginning of this book, Minna's single parent was the man I thought Beatrice would fall in love with. Ha! That sure changed quickly. All I really knew was that Beatrice would be told about the seven miracles and that she'd find a twin sister she never knew about. Everything else that happened was a surprise.

Q. What's one piece of writing advice you would give to aspiring writers?

A. Don't wait until you feel like you're a good enough writer or until you have more time in your life to write. No writer feels prepared, and no writer has enough time. We just do some adequate work in the margins of our lives, and then we revise that work to be good later. We never get the *really* great ideas until we're actually doing the writing (the Muse rewards the worker, not the dreamer), so ignore your feelings about your skill level and just write! (You can sign up for my writer's email list here, if you'd like more tips! https://rachaelherron.com/write.)

Q. Why did you decide to have your witches all connected to the dead? What about the other side fascinates you?

A. I'm fascinated by the fact that *no one really knows* what's on the other side, and at the same time, we're all guaranteed to find out. Isn't that wild? It's a bit scary, yes, but also very beautiful to me. I've had the honor to be present when people have left this particular plane, and it's an inexplicable moment that leaves me both curious and humbled. Having my witches be tangled with the other side gives me some comfort. This is fiction, of course, and I do make all of this up, yes. But my imagination is fueled by inspiration, which is another power I don't understand. It doesn't come from me—it comes from something better than me. So I can choose to trust it. And I do.

Q. What's one thing about yourself that you want all of your readers to know about you?

A. Three years ago, my wife and I sold our house and most of what we owned, leaving all our family and friends, and moved around the world to New Zealand. Wellington, the windiest city in the world, is home now, and I've never been so happy about making such a terrifying decision. I'm currently sitting in a pool of early winter sunlight in my office, looking up the green hill behind our home. I swim in the harbor at least once a week (even now that it's down to 12°C/54°F), and I do my Kiwi part to keep our top spot as the country that eats the most ice cream per capita. It's a dream to be here permanently, and I'm so glad we took the leap!

Q. Your story does have a queer romance in it between Beatrix and Reno, but there isn't a strong focus on that. They just fall in love like any other romance might happen. Was that a deliberate choice on your part? Why or why not?

A. Totally deliberate. I'm *technically* bisexual, like Beatrix, but my queerness doesn't define who I am. While the love I have in my life is incredible and magical, it's also completely prosaic and normal. I fell in love with my wife because of her personality, not because of her gender identity. I do admit, however, that I feel grateful to have a female partner because who doesn't want a wife? They're so great!

ABOUT THE AUTHOR

Rachael Herron has published romance with Avon, upmarket women's fiction with Berkley, memoir with Chronicle, and most recently, thrillers, under the name R. H. Herron, with Dutton. She is a dynamic member of the writing community who teaches both fiction and memoir writing and hosts the popular podcast *Ink in Your Veins.* A dual US/NZ citizen, Rachael escaped to New Zealand with her wife during the pandemic; they now live in Wellington.